TEARS OF THE TYRANT

The Narvan · Book Five

Jean Davis

Tears of the Tyrant: Book Five of The Narvan

www.jeandavisauthor.com

ISBN-13:   978-1-962708-00-5 (print)
            978-1-962708-01-2 (ebook)

First Edition: October 2023

Published by StreamlineDesign LLC

Also by Jean Davis

The Last God
Sahmara
A Broken Race
Destiny Pills and Space Wizards
Dreams of Stars and Lies
Everyone Dies
Not Another Bard's Tale
Spindelkin
Frayed
19

The Narvan

One Shot at the Sphinx
Trust
The Minor Years
Chain of Gray
Bound in Blue
Seeker
Tears of the Tyrant

For Stella

*Thank you for inspiring the story you didn't even know
you were asking for.*

Anastassia

When your mate holds the power to kill with roughly twenty seconds of thought, people get twitchy if he falls into a sour funk. Despite the general continuing success of Vayen's mission to bring healing and unification to worlds and colonies surrounding the Narvan and beyond, his mood had gradually been growing darker. He'd been downright angry at everyone and everything for the past few months. I'd held out hope that he'd get over whatever was pissing him off, that maybe it was being away from his homeworld for too long. But a week-long visit with Neko, who'd taken over the Narvan Advisory position, and even some quiet time at our Artorian estate, away from the Iber's crew and demands of our mission hadn't helped. If anything, the one night he'd stayed up late talking and drinking with Neko had worsened his mood. I'd asked Neko for some insight, but he'd kept his mouth shut. That could mean only one thing, whatever Vayen was angry about, it had to do with me.

I'd spent six days away to give him some space. Maybe I'd been hovering, or nagging, or we'd just been spending too damned much time together. To feel useful, I checked in with several of the planetary advisors that we'd set up on our travels along the universal trade routes and did a few Seeker sessions with clients I'd reconnected with on Veria Minor. I'd planned to be gone longer, but Ikeri sent me a message, begging me to return. If our daughter couldn't calm the savage beast, trouble was only a breath away.

Trouble, in Vayen's case, could mean instantaneous death for thousands or himself. With Seeker Etara traveling with us, monitoring Vayen's quest to not go off the evil deep end, I couldn't chance him doing something that would drive her to flip his kill switch.

I'd never minded his darker side, with the exception of it being aimed at me on rare occasions. Honestly, I was drawn to it. We were alike in that, as with many other traits that would scare away any other sane person; our maladjusted moods and habits drew us together, made us perfect for one another even though we fought and often spent days not speaking. We understood each other. I loved him dearly and didn't want him to die. Ever.

I contacted Daniel, who took care of Jumping me whenever his father wasn't the one to do it, to bring me back to the Iber, the massive Jalvian cruiser that we'd commandeered when we'd set out to sow our vast advisory union.

Daniel arrived in our mostly unused house on Veria Minor where he'd spent the first few years of his life as a carefree child. He wasn't at all care-free now. His glower near rivaled his father's.

"What's got you in a mood? Trouble with the wives?"

A grin flashed over his face, proving my guess was far off the mark. "Meera and Arden are fine, Mom. Quite fine. They both had scans at the clinic yesterday. I got to see the babies."

Babies. I was going to be a fucking grandmother. Maybe that's what had Vayen in a mood. But he'd been pissy far longer than that. Daniel had only announced that both of his wives were pregnant a few weeks ago.

"That's wonderful." Barely nineteen and already married. Twice. Now with kids on the way. I shuddered. "So why the scrunchy face?"

Rather than take my offered hand and Jump me to the Iber, he took a seat, filling the chair that had been his father's. He nodded me toward the my-sized chair. Curious, I sat.

"He doesn't think it's wonderful. Any of it." Daniel ran his hands through his long, dark hair, pulling the thick mass behind his broad shoulders. The armor he wore looked just like his father's, well-used, comfortable, and hiding a small arsenal.

"What do you mean?" I tried not to slip into my Seeker tone, but I'd been doing it for days. It was a hard habit to break.

"What do you think I mean?" He glared at me. "I don't need a damned counseling session, Mother. He does."

"Your father?"

"Yes, the walking grenade that is my father. Is it too much to ask that he be happy for me? I've always done everything he's asked."

Whatever tension had been brewing between father and son since Daniel had taken on non-official command of the Iber when we'd set out nearly four years ago had remained strictly between them. The rift seemed to deepen with each passing year. Neither side was forthcoming. I'd chalked it up to two strong personalities in tight confines—if an entire cruiser could be considered tight.

The crew loved and respected Daniel, even beyond his fame as the son of the Advisors of All. He had a solid understanding of the ship's systems and everyone's position in it that impressed even me. Our son had put the years he and his father spent searching for Ikeri to good use. That a Jalvian crew would choose to follow an Artorian signified great strides toward the unity Vayen and I had sought to establish when we'd held the Narvan. One would have thought this would have greatly pleased his father, but the man who had been Daniel's partner in mischief earlier in his life was a far cry from the tight-lipped, time-bomb we lived with now.

"You have," I put on my best reassuring smile. "I'll talk to him."

"Mom, it isn't talking he wants." He let out a disgusted growl. "Ikeri said she'd talk to you about it."

Unease formed a cool puddle in my stomach. Did everyone know what had Vayen on edge but me? He'd been cordial enough toward me, considering his mood.

"Dammit, I shouldn't have said anything." He stood, offering me a sympathetic smile.

The chill in my gut amplified. I stood and held out my hand. This time, he took it without hesitation.

I sat in Ikeri's suite, watching my seventeen-year-old daughter making a quick braid of her light brown curls that hung halfway down her back. She'd taken to shaving one strip along the right side, just over her ear to show off the Seeker tattoos that covered her entire scalp, but she'd let the curls grow to please her father.

She'd asked for a simple room on the Iber, no bigger than the average crew quarters. The plants she'd collected, some flowering, others with bright-colored or lacey leaves, filled the open spaces. She loved her jungle. As much as I also liked plants, the room made me claustrophobic. And no matter how many times I saw her smiling and bustling around in it, the jungle reminded me of the flower-filled room on Brustus where she'd been entombed in a stasis chamber while we'd searched for her for years.

I cleared my throat for the second time. "Daniel said you had some insight into your father's mood?"

Since her return to us, Ikeri and Vayen had been inseparable, often working side by side on their healing expeditions. While Ikeri and I talked often, the relationship she had with her father was different. She kept him blanketed in a calm that augmented the peace of the bond he and I shared, and he didn't let a soul near her that she didn't authorize first. Most of the male members of the crew didn't dare look her way, let alone speak to her unless it was necessary.

Ikeri settled onto the other end of the couch, putting a comfortable distance between us. She tucked her legs under her and set one of the square sky-blue pillows on her lap, running her fingers over the seam.

"Get on with it before I imagine something far worse than whatever it is you have to say."

"I don't know about that." Ikeri sighed. "The darkness is eating at him, Mom. Badly. I'm doing all I can, and I know you are too."

The fear of losing Vayen had been building for years and now it threatened to overtake me. I couldn't lose him. Not after all we'd been through together. "So we get rid of Etara."

Ikeri frowned. "You know I don't like when you talk like that. But really, Mom, you don't think Etara hasn't considered that action and planned for it?"

It figured that the wily little Seeker who had spent years on this mission with us, who had been in Vayen's mind as much as I had, would have made contingency plans.

"All right, what do you suggest?"

"We alleviate the main factor that is detracting from him maintaining control over his abilities."

While I didn't like that our daughter had the capability to peruse our minds at will, I did appreciate that she had a logical solution to keep Vayen among the living.

"And this factor would be..."

"He's jealous."

"Of what? Who?" My mind sped through anyone I'd been spending too much time with. Our monthly dinners with Isnar on Karin were attended as a couple. Neko consulted with me on Narvan matters regularly, but that was business. For most anything else, either Vayen or Daniel accompanied me.

"Daniel," she said.

Though I was vastly relieved to learn I wasn't the problem, her answer didn't offer much insight. "Whatever for?"

Was this some vain mid-life crisis? Daniel was a handsome young man, just like his father had been at the same age. Vayen was still handsome in his own way, but his years in service to the now-decimated High Council had left him scarred, aching, and greyer than his years warranted. Daniel had attracted the daughter of the new Premier of Artor as a second wife, for goodness' sake. Behind Meera no less, who, though she was a lovely girl and an excellent body guard, was a social and political nobody. Artorians hadn't even condoned the Jalvian practice of multiple mates. Not until Daniel and Arden had ignited that movement.

Ikeri crushed the pillow to her chest. Her gaze dropped to her lap. "Dad wants a second wife."

"What the hell? Why?" I sprang from the couch, unable to sit still, I stood there stamping my feet for lack of anywhere to go. "Absolutely not!"

She flinched, curling in on the pillow.

"I'm sorry." I forced myself back onto the couch and fought to get my raging emotions under control. "I'm not angry with you. I just... I don't understand."

I thought Vayen and I were good, better than we'd ever been, actually, according to the memories he'd shared with me. But there were so many pieces of us together that I was still missing. Even now, years after the Arpex attack had stolen him from my mind, not a week went by that I wasn't asking Vayen to share some snippet to fill a gap in our past.

Had he been lying about his feelings toward me this whole time? Was he merely staying with me out of obligation? In the back of my mind, I began to question everything I thought I knew about him.

She peeked up from her pillow, her green eyes like mine, filled with sorrow. "I didn't understand either. Not for a long time. One of the last things I did before I..." She shook her head. "Before I went with Jey and Kess, was to yell at him for desiring someone else. I was so angry that he would do that to you."

He'd considered a second wife seven years ago? While my heart remembered how to beat at a normal pace, pieces fell into place. "When he'd freed the slaves from Tacesh. When he fell in with Saka and Buria and whoever the hell else?"

Ikeri nodded.

"Well, he's out of luck. Saka is happily contracted to that Jalvian officer. Markus told me the man was recently promoted. He keeps in touch with her even though she's been off our payroll since they adopted a baby."

I remembered how much Daniel had disrupted my life, how protecting him had driven me deeper and deeper into the mess that had led me to Vayen. Maybe that wasn't all so bad but still… "Babies disrupt everything. You should tell that to your brother."

"He's aware. Arden plans on watching both children so Meera can maintain her position."

"He's got it all worked out. Just like his father," I grumbled. That damned man always seemed to have a plan. "Last I knew, Buria was stationed on Brustus, overseeing Cragtek security for Gamnock. I'm sure she's found someone by now too. The pretty ones always do. We handed the contact information for the rest of that lot off to Neko, and it's been years. They're attached by now if they had any inclination to do so. Who the hell does he have his eye on?"

I began to run through the Jalvian females in the crew, considering and discarding them as quickly as their faces came to memory.

"Not all the pretty ones." Ikeri clutched her pillow again, putting me on alert for more bad news. "He still talks to Buria. She's been his agent within Cragtek since she went to work for Gamnock."

That they kept in touch, possibly beyond a business relationship, shouldn't have come as a surprise, but I'd been more focused on Saka who had been in our service where I could keep an eye on the two of them. He'd passed my test with her, but maybe that was because he had Buria off safely in the wings out of my sight. My mind spun, pouring over our schedules, searching for when he may have been sneaking off to visit her.

"It's not that. Not that I found, anyway."

This one time, Ikeri's ability to slip into my mind brought me a bit of solace instead of irritation. I let her continue without censure.

"They just talk. But she's available and he knows it."

I felt a snarl forming, and though I did my best to mask it, the tightness in my voice made my thoughts on the matter quite clear. "Buria. I liked her once."

Ikeri's tone matched mine. "You might consider liking her again."

Granted we were talking about managing Vayen's violent tendencies, but my daughter was condoning him having a second wife? I could only sit there gaping.

"He's talked to you about this?" I said at last.

"Not exactly. You know I don't go traipsing around in his mind regularly. Anymore," she clarified with a guilty look. "It's just that he's been so angry at everything, and everyone's been on edge, and you were gone, and I didn't know what else to do to help."

"Might as well spill it then. We can both be guilty."

Ikeri cracked a smile. She handed me a pillow that matched the one she held. "You're going to want this."

My daughter had been in my head enough to know me well, far beyond what a daughter should know about her mother. I took the offered pillow and clutched it much as she'd been doing with hers. My stomach lurched and she hadn't even said anything yet.

"Seven years ago, he was already in a bad political light with Artor and not in a position to change policies of that magnitude. You were jealous of his attraction to the women he'd freed. He might have pushed it with Artor anyway, but he put Buria aside for you."

"He mentioned wanting to venture into other beds. Once. We weren't getting along so well at the time."

She quirked a single brow. "Are you ever? Seems like you're both always bickering over something, even if it's quietly."

"That's just what we do. Trust me, we're fine. You and the entire crew would likely hear the fight if we weren't."

She sighed. "Why can't the two of you be like Daniel and his wives? It's clear to everyone that they all love each other. You never see or hear them arguing."

"That's how it should be, I suppose." I played with the seam on my pillow, finding it comforting. "We were both on our own as teen-agers and that made us overly independent. Neither of us had good examples of how a relationship should be. Well, he did early on, I suppose." I shook my head. "We have issues. Both of us. Baggage from past bad relationships. Betrayals. Bad habits." I shrugged. "Nei-ther of us are nice people on our own. You know that full well."

"I do," she said softly.

"You and Daniel haven't had the best childhood, but we've done what we could to make it better than what we had, to give you the best of who we are. I'm glad Daniel can be happy, that he's a generally well-adjusted being. I hope that one day, you'll be happy too."

Ikeri rose up on her knees and worked her way over to sit beside me. She rested her head on my shoulder. "I hope that for you too."

I kissed her forehead. "I was, until I got your message."

"Right." She sat up. "So here's what I found out."

TWO

Anastassia

Ikeri had talked to Isnar first, who had been like a father to her during the years we'd lived on Pentares, consulting with him on the Artorian bond.

Neko had given her the in-the-field view of the contro-versy surrounding the movement Daniel and Arden had ignited on the Artorian worlds. It seemed that adopting the Jalvian practice of multiple mates had created a stiff divide among Artorians but had put Artorians in a much more favorable light with Jalvians, who now saw them as less arrogant and more relatable.

Etara had offered advice on how to talk to me about it. I wasn't sure how much of what Ikeri was doing was her own and what was borrowed from Etara's wisdom. What I did know was that the little outcast Seeker had changed my mate in ways I still didn't fully under-stand. She could also kill him within the same twenty seconds he could take out anyone else. The two of them were tied together.

At least he wasn't looking to add her to our bed.

Ikeri had also cornered Daniel to ask him about the process and what it was like adding another person to the mix. He'd answered her questions tastefully but thoroughly. That had to have been uncom-fortable, but he'd admitted that he wanted to see us stay together and his father to stop giving him the cold shoulder.

"Did you talk to your father?" That seemed like an important part of the equation.

Ikeri grimaced. "No."

"So it's fine to talk to everyone else about your father, but not to him about the issue directly?"

"Do you want to talk to him about it directly?" she asked.

"Not until I figure some things out first."

She gave me a pointed look.

"Fair. Fine. I'll take it from here."

Take it from here, I scoffed internally. Was I really considering this? Did I have a choice?

"You're not going to yell at him, are you? He's near to cracking. I mean it, Mom. Don't set him off. Etara's been watching him closely. She can see it too."

"No. I won't yell at him. I promise." I handed her the second pillow.

She watched me with a calculating look.

"Or stab him, or kill him in his sleep." I leaned over to hug her. "I'll figure something out. If I have questions or need a pillow to strangle, I know where to go."

Ikeri smiled. "Good luck."

"Thanks." I left my daughter's jungle room and went straight to Etara's quarters.

Etara answered her door in seconds. She waved me in and went for the teapot she always seemed to have ready to go.

Despite having been outcast from Veria Prime by her fellow Seekers, Etara still wore her robes and kept her tattooed head bare. The petite Verian woman moved with a dignity and grace that marked her as a Seeker even more so than her appearance.

"I've been expecting you." She handed me a cup of tea and settled into the other chair at the two-person table.

Though she also had collected an array of greenery during our travels with which to decorate her otherwise austere quarters, it was of a more manageable quantity. I felt at home here, the smell of burnt candles, incense, and oils bringing me back to the Seeker shop I'd had on Veria Minor.

I nodded. Ikeri had probably sent Etara a message the moment I'd left her room—if a five-minute walk gave her time to expect me.

"In the interest of expediency, let's bypass standard session protocols," she said. "Your mate is in danger."

"From me and why I'm here or because of what you've seen in him?"

Etara smiled and shook her head. "Both."

While I was attempting to make light of the situation, Vayen was in more danger from Etara than from me. I might yell or throw things now and then, but I had no true intention of hurting him.

"You work closely with him and are in his mind in ways that I am not. Tell me what you've seen," I said.

Etara sipped her tea, watching me over the edge of her cup. "Over the past few years, anger, jealousy, and frustration have been steadily building. Dark thoughts. He hasn't stopped what we've set out to do; he still diagnoses and sets up his deals and offers assistance to colonies and worlds that need it, but he's struggling. Heavily. Darkness is consuming him."

The fact that Ikeri had warned me ahead of time didn't soften the blow. The same words in Etara's voice, words I couldn't discount, issuing a threat from outside my tiny circle of trust, were ominous. I savored the heat of my cup but had little desire to put anything into the raging squall of my stomach.

"He's starting to blatantly lash out at Daniel. It's only a matter of time before his ire spills over to Meera and Arden. With both of them pregnant, they don't need that stress. He can be harsh and unyielding. Merciless."

My mate, the death-bringer, as the Arpex had named him, could indeed flip into wrath-mode at a moment's notice. He'd wiped out the entire colony of Brustus with his mind-twisting ability and more since our mission had launched. I'd seen the bodies.

"I don't want to have to kill him, Ana." Etara wrung her hands. "I may be his conscience, but I'm also struggling with my own."

"You have condoned more violence than I'd expected you would," I said carefully, hoping that I was leading her to expound on how much more she'd allow rather than digging into an open wound for the expelled Seeker. It was Vayen's fault, our fault, I supposed, that she wasn't happily practicing her Seeker arts on Veria Prime among her own people.

"We're doing so much good. It balances out what I've allowed. Hasn't it?" she asked plaintively.

"Yes. Without a doubt. No one is questioning your judgment, Etara."

Though she held the key to Vayen's life, I had to remember she was a young woman far from home, far from the life she'd expected to have. As good and grand as this one was, it was not without its share of violence and death, whether we were looking for it or not.

She offered me a tremulous smile. "I know how much he means to you, to all of you, to this mission. He means a good deal to me too," she admitted.

That didn't surprise me, nor did it make me jealous. Whatever strange relationship Vayen and Etara had developed wasn't sexual. And frankly, the affection she held for him was keeping her from killing him.

"Please know that I do not take my responsibility lightly. I, like you, will do everything I can to help maintain a balance with his abilities," Etara said.

That precarious balance kept him from diving into the blackness that we all saw looming when he went death-bringer on anyone. Sometimes it took a merciless man to do what must be done, to harm some for the betterment of others, to protect our expedition in the face of hostile forces.

"What do you suggest we do to help him maintain his balance?"

She sighed. "Give him what he wants. I have no desire to flip his switch. Not unless I'm left with no choice. We're doing so much good on a scale I'd never dreamt possible. His resources, his connections, the funding, what we can offer these people, it wouldn't be possible without him."

"Half of those resources, connections, and funding are mine, you know."

She sipped her tea and set the cup back on the table, watching ripples move across the contents until they stilled. "I don't presume to minimalize your contributions to this mission. However, would you be on it, would you continue it, if he weren't at the center?"

What would I do without him? Though the threat that his death could come at any time had been a truth I'd lived with throughout the years we'd been together, I didn't often allow myself to think about that horrible outcome or anything afterward. Would I want to continue without him? He was a part of me, an integral part. I swallowed hard, feeling moisture welling in my eyes.

If I were to carry on without him, I'd fall back to something I knew, something safe, where I could break down in private, because I surely would if he were gone. If I had to watch Etara snuff the life out of my hulking, wrathful Artorian mate... I sniffed and wiped at my eyes. Swallowing down the grim thoughts, I focused on optimistically answering her question.

If Vayen was no longer beside me, I'd be at home, probably on Veria Minor, going about my own Seeker practice with Ikeri beside me where I could keep her safe. Barring that, I'd haunt the estate on Artor, assisting Neko as he needed. The Narvan was in good hands. I had no desire to take that away from Neko or to take up another advisory position of my own. What I would not do, under any circumstances or coercion from my grown children, was stay on the Iber where memories of Vayen were on everything I touched.

"You have a point," I conceded.

Etara nodded. "Ikeri is doing what she can for Vayen, but I also need your help to make sure the mission continues. To make sure your son, his wives, and their future children remain happy and whole. The advisory union you're building and shaping needs you and Vayen at its core."

"I understand, but there must be a way to alleviate his itch without allowing a second wife?"

Etara seemed to have learned Vayen's merciless stare. "You are used to difficult choices, sacrifices. Consider this one more."

My tea had lost its comforting warmth. "We've worked hard to get where we are as a joined couple, working through my memory loss and his alterations. Where we are now, it's exactly where I want to be. We're good together."

Etara nodded but her unyielding gaze didn't waver. "You know he leans on certain behaviors to maintain his balance."

Behaviors. What a Seeker word. It wasn't like I didn't realize that Vayen was prone to addictions. He'd shared memories of the tense time between us when the High Council had him hooked on what was likely a precursor to the drug the Masters used on Tacesh. His penchant for alcohol had never been a secret, and he'd never hidden his enjoyment of the rush of the jobs we used to do together. Sex seemed to work as a substitute for either of those. Even though we'd been together a long while, the attraction between us hadn't faded, and I'd held onto that as a source of pride. But was sex just another of his addictions, a coping mechanism that I didn't mind indulging?

Fuck. Were we good together? My thoughts flew, reexamining our relationship with my Seeker training at the forefront. Was *I* a coping mechanism? Just another addiction that was no longer enough to combat all the dark urges that built up in his mind?

I gulped my tea, hoping to wash the distasteful revelation away. Surely we were more than that.

Etara watched me as if she could see my thoughts arriving at what she already knew to be the truth. "I'm so sorry, Ana. He needs this if we are to have a hope of keeping him under control."

Her pity-filled eyes begged me to understand. Fucking hell.

"I don't want another woman in our damn bed. Meera might be

into Arden, but I'm not wired that way."

"I've studied this Jalvian practice. Nothing requires you to be *into* his second mate. In fact, if you were to agree to this, you'd be within your rights to seek a second mate for yourself."

Like that was some sort of golden lining to the situation. I wasn't like Vayen, I didn't have another prospective lover waiting in the wings, and I had no inclination to find one.

"Even Jalvian women don't often take that route."

Etara pursed her lips. "True, they are usually busy tending to children. Others turn to one another for additional companionship rather than expand the household to encompass yet another person."

"And you know this—"

"I've counseled plenty of the Jalvian crewmembers since taking up residence on the Iber. Jalvians are much less restrictive with their family dynamics." She straightened her cup on the table, stroking the handle with her slim fingers. "Your children are grown. There is plenty of room here." She waved her hand in the air to indicate the whole of the Iber.

"There are several prominent Jalvian families headed by women. Women who take multiple husbands. Many families of all social levels have equal partners, first mates, if you will, with seconds, and even thirds, all living under one roof or with separate living arrangements. There are options, Ana. Taking a second of your own would put you on equal standing with your mate. It would set a strong example for other women, for the movement for adopting such practices on Artor."

All the years working beside us, balancing policies and other-world politics had made our little Seeker just as adept at handling delicate situations as Vayen and I.

Staring into the cooling contents of the cup, everything she'd said, that Ikeri had said, played through my mind.

"I don't want anyone else." The words came out whiny, but I didn't care.

"Then think of it as: how do you keep the man you do want?"

Did I want a mate who only saw me as a crutch to lean on? That couldn't be all we were. My gut and my heart were adamant that we were more. We had to be.

"Sharing is not keeping," I snapped.

"Ana, I've watched you negotiate deals that I held out little hope of us benefitting from, but you always manage to make us come out on top. Go, talk to Buria, negotiate an arrangement that works for all of you."

The only thing that would work for all of us was to keep Vayen alive and spearheading our mission. "I don't like being forced into something, especially when it's something I don't want. At all."

Etara nodded. "I know. He knows it too. That's why he refuses to bring it up with you. He's talked to me and Neko."

"And what did you tell him?"

"The same thing I'm telling you, find a way to make it work. Coincidentally, Neko keeps trying to talk him out of it, telling him that a second mate is a terrible idea and that he shouldn't do that to you. He values Neko's counsel as much as mine."

"That explains his downward mood slide since they talked." I leaned back in my chair, massaging my temples out of habit even though I didn't have a headache yet. I surely would soon. "Why does he think he needs a second wife? He's been hung up on being a proper Artorian as long as I've known him, needing to be joined, to have children. He even went so far as to pay outrageous bribes to gain rights on Artor for me and the kids."

Etara poured herself another cup of tea. I shook my head to more.

"Vayen is far from a proper Artorian these days. Surely you understand that the Arpex alterations have changed him internally on many levels."

I stared at her blankly.

"Ana, much of the Artorian fiddling with natural genetics has been slowly unraveling in our death-bringer. He's not constrained in the ways he used to be."

Swallowing hard, I let that sink in. *Surely* I'd known.

No, I'd been too busy working beside my time-bomb of a mate. Too occupied with union deals and wrangling Vayen into Etara's grey zone to consider that my decision to keep him alive by fusing Arpex larvae to him would eventually tear him away from me anyway.

Etara smiled softly, reaching out with a consoling hand before quickly retracting it. She knew better than to pull Seeker procedures with me. I'd trained beside her teacher.

She cleared her throat. "Daniel sought to continue what you and Vayen set out to do, bringing Artor and Jal closer together by embracing one of Jal's primary customs."

"Yes, but Daniel hasn't bonded to either of his wives."

She shrugged. "The public doesn't know that. They will assume what they will."

The public was good at assuming. I sighed.

"Jalvians may not bond, but many have a person who is their focus, who grounds them, a mate or commanding officer. Some bypass a person, devoting everything to their job. I believe this is a lingering vestige of the natural bond. Artorians and Jalvians are one people, broken by differences, yet the same at the core. You are neither. They have drives, ambitions, and customs that are different than yours."

"I'm aware. I was involved with a Jalvian before Vayen."

"And would your Jalvian have wanted a second wife?"

"That Jalvian wouldn't have bothered to contract me in the first place. He wasn't into commitment. Neither was I."

Etara nodded. "But Vayen changed your mind on commitment."

"He dragged me into it kicking and screaming. But yes, after several years, he showed me that it wasn't as terrible as I'd thought."

She chuckled. "Maybe he could change your mind on this too."

I considered throwing my cup of cold tea in her face, getting up, storming out, and demanding a conversation with my explosive mate in our quarters to put an end to this once and for all. I got as far as wrapping a hand around the cup before what she'd said hit me.

"If his Artorian urges are unraveling as you called it, does that mean his bond is gone?"

"Gone, no. Weaker, yes."

"Will it vanish, do you think?"

Etara shook her head. "That urge is natural but is perhaps manifested differently than what his ancestors designed it to be with their modifications. I dug into it as much as I was able, but there isn't a lot of information available to outsiders."

This couldn't be true. It just couldn't. "Are you sure this isn't just some mid-life crisis whim? Some need to seek out a younger woman and procreate a few more times? What if he just thinks he wants Buria because he can't have her?"

Etara's hand started toward me again before she dropped it to the table. "I'm sorry, Ana, I've been in his mind. I've talked to him. Extensively. If it's any comfort, he can't procreate with Buria. She's barren."

"There are procedures to fix that. It worked with Meera."

"I'm sorry," she said again. "I have no good answers."

My fingers and toes felt distant. "Is our weaker bond enough to keep him from falling into darkness?"

"We wouldn't be having this conversation if it were."

The room suddenly seemed smaller, colder. "I see."

I stood and walked out before I did anything to make life more difficult for Etara than my mate already had.

With my vision swimming in tears, I made my way back to Ikeri's quarters. I couldn't go to my own. Vayen might be there, and I wasn't ready to face him yet. I used my override code and went in without invitation.

Ikeri looked up in surprise from her perch on the couch. I grabbed the pillow she'd given me earlier and screamed into it.

THREE

Anastassia

Gamnock provided me with Buria's location. Daniel Jumped me there.

When Neko had initiated the move of Cragtek out to Brustus, I hadn't known quite what to expect, but it had worked out wonderfully. The staff enjoyed having free reign of the whole colony without the oversight of the Jalvian government. They'd created a community here, cleaned up the mess left behind by my death-bringer mate, and within a year, profits had doubled. Now, four years later, they were about to triple.

There was more than enough room for everyone and their families, their extended relations, friends, and anyone else approved to join their ranks. The port city was again bustling with activity, looking like any other prosperous colony and not some seedy den of thieves as the original Cragtek had been when I'd taken it on with Gamnock's father. Neko had taken what Vayen had done with the operation and multiplied it. I was quite proud of him.

The massive estate where Ikeri had been confined, which had been ground zero for Vayen's extermination, had been razed. A memorial stood there now, listing the names of all who had once populated the city. I'd seen a still frame but had no desire to ever walk those grounds again.

Buria, as with all of the Cragtek staff, had taken over the homes of those who were no longer, shuffling and trading the belongings of the dead. She had claimed a sizeable apartment for herself on the edge of the port with a full clearplaz wall view of the activity. As Gamnock's security supervisor and Vayen's agent here, it was a fitting location.

We may have handed the Narvan to Neko, but there were some things Vayen hadn't let go of, like his stake in Cragtek. And Buria.

Daniel and I left the jump point after checking in with the guards posted there and headed to the address. I was too wrapped up in what I was about to do to chat with Daniel as we walked. The ride up the lift passed in silence. I was surprised she hadn't taken the top floor apartment, but from the semi-stalker level of research I'd done on her in the past day, I'd learned Buria didn't openly flaunt her position. However, she did subtly manage to keep her floor devoid of any other occupants. I reluctantly respected her for maintaining a quiet level of power.

Daniel grabbed my arm before I could step off the lift and start down the hallway. "Are you sure you want to do this?"

"No, definitely not, but according to everyone else, I have to anyway." I yanked my arm out of his grasp and started toward the room number Gamnock had given me.

"Do you want to contact me for a Jump later or should I stay here?" Daniel called after me.

"Staying might be wise. If you hear screaming, give me a few minutes to take care of the body."

"Mom."

"I'm kidding." I wasn't.

"If you lay a hand on her, Dad is going to be pissed."

"I won't." I'd learned plenty of ways to take care of someone without touching them when I'd done my time as one of Marin's assassins. The inner pockets of my armored coat were well stocked.

"Mom." Daniel caught up with me and stared me down with his father's eyes. "I'm serious."

I wanted to scream at him. This was his fault for breaking the ice on the whole multiple marriage issue. But my son was happy. And going to be a father. And he desperately wanted his father talking to him again. I sighed.

"I won't harm her. I'm just here to talk."

"I'll be right outside the door."

He waited against the wall, two strides away so he'd be out of sight when Buria answered. She took her time doing so.

When the door panel did finally retract into the wall, she stood inside, trepidation clear on her face. She also wore armor and had one hand on a weapon. Gamnock had warned her I'd be seeking her out.

"Advisor," she said tightly.

I matched her tone. "Buria."

So this was who he wanted to put in our bed. My replacement. We had a similar build, but she had a few inches on me. With her midnight skin and braided ropes of black hair, she appeared to be my younger, dark counterpart. My hand twitched.

I felt Daniel's warning glare without having to tear my attention from the woman inside.

"May I come in?"

Her gaze darted over me, noting the obvious weapon bumps and likely estimating how many others were hidden. Threat level assessed, she stepped aside and gestured for me to enter.

The apartment was spacious, one expansive room with a few doorways off to the far side. Done in neutral tones and minimal clutter, I couldn't find fault with her decorating taste.

"It would seem that we need to talk." I walked over to the windowed wall without further invitation and surveyed the view.

Shuttles lifted and landed, ferrying stock to and from ships in orbit. Sunlight glinted off the mover units scurrying around with crates and containers, shelving and retrieving items from the massive warehouses that lined the landing zone. Though we were close by, I couldn't hear any of the port noise, only the pounding of my pulse in my ears.

"Would you like to sit?" she asked, sounding more like she was asking if we were going to fight on our feet or spar verbally.

"That might be wise." I surveyed the options and chose an armless cream-colored chair in case I needed to move fast.

Buria perched on the edge of the deep brown two-person couch across from me. "What would you like to talk about?"

Though I'd seen her momentarily when Ikeri had been found here, we hadn't spoken in person or otherwise since I'd disarmed her and shoved her in a cell in Isnar's underground dungeon after Ikeri had been taken. Not like I was going to apologize for that. Vayen had set her free and she appeared to be doing just fine now.

"My mate is stomping around the known universe, pitching a fit because you're not in his bed."

"What?" she squeaked. "Why would I be? He told me years ago that wasn't going to happen, that he was choosing you and only you."

Her surprise seemed genuine.

"I know the two of you talk. Surely he's mentioned his desire for you to be his second wife?"

Her mouth dropped open and her eyes went wide. She sat there gaping for a suitable amount of seconds to assure me that my charming mate was just as open with her as he was with me. Despite wanting to hate her, I couldn't.

She shook her head, the host of tiny braids sliding over her shoulders. "We do talk. Often. I assumed you'd found out about that and were here to silence me."

"For talking to him? No. We have bigger issues to settle."

Buria held up her empty hands. "I don't know the first thing about this second wife business. He hasn't mentioned it. I swear."

"What do the two of you talk about? Often?"

"Business mostly. Sometimes he'll ask how my day was, or if I've put anything new in the apartment, what I'm having for dinner. He tells me about the worlds he's visiting, sometimes about the Iber's crew." She shrugged. "Just conversation. Nothing more."

Toss in asking after the kids, and it sounded no different than our conversations, like he was already as close to her as he was to me. Other than being in her bed. Even though he technically wasn't doing anything wrong, it felt like a betrayal of the relationship I thought only I had with him. Caught between bristling and hurt, I kept my lips tightly pressed together until I got myself under control.

"And these talks, are they by link or does he come here?" I peered around the room looking for one of his carved patterns. "Does he have a direct jump point?"

"Link. He's visited me on the job a couple of times but only when he's on Brustus for business. He's never been to this apartment."

I knew how my mate's tell-the-truth-by-omission routine worked and she had three floors under her control. "Does he have an apartment? Somewhere else that you two meet up?"

"No. We've never..."

"Never?"

She shook her head. "He only kissed me that one day on Tacesh when he was under the influence of the spray. We teased each other a little after that, but nothing came of it, just words. And nothing at all since he made it clear he could have no relationship with me other than business."

I sat back, hands sliding to my lap. It seemed no weapons were going to be used on this visit after all. "Did you want anything to come of it? I guess, more importantly, do you still?"

Buria's gaze dipped to the floor and she smiled for a second before quickly schooling her features back to neutral. Though her dark skin didn't show it, I'd have put credits on a bet that she was blushing.

"I'll take that as a yes." I considered Etara's advice on the matter, threw out most of it, and charged forward on my own. "I'm going to give the two of you eight days. You can both do whatever you want in the privacy of a suite on the Iber for this one week. I don't want to see it. Any time you are outside of the suite, it's hands-off. Is that clear?"

She nodded hesitantly. "You want me to have sex with your mate?"

"Don't make me say yes. It's not a matter of want. It needs to happen. He needs to get this out of his system." I explained why his life was at stake if he didn't get his abilities and mood under control.

Buria sat up straight and had the nerve to stare me down. "And what if he wants more after these eight days?"

I wanted to declare that he wouldn't. That his stupid longing for a second wife was just a whim, and that after sating his desire for Buria, he'd be back to himself, that we could go on as we always had. But would I forgive him for this? Could I overlook that he needed more than just me? Could I accept another woman in our relationship? A sharp pain in my gut said no.

As Etara had said, I'd made sacrifices before. I had a week to figure out if I could make another one. If not, could I walk away from him? My vision began to blur. Dammit, I wouldn't show weakness in front of this woman.

"We'll deal with whatever might come next once this week is over."

She nodded solemnly. "When?"

"When are you available?"

"Give me an hour to get my team in order here. I'll need a jump point."

Of course she'd drop everything to sleep with my mate for a week. Which was exactly what I was asking her to do. Logic, bitterness, and jealousy locked horns in my mind.

"I'll have Daniel relay a jump point." I stood, needing to get out, to not see her, to not imagine the two of them together doing the things Vayen and I did behind closed doors.

She stood and closed the distance between us in a heartbeat, wrapping her arms around me. "You are very brave. Sharing the man you love can't be easy."

I stood there woodenly, shocked by her compassion. "Be good to him," I whispered.

Buria nodded against my cheek. "I will help you save him."

Put that way, I had to admit that I did like her a little. I supposed that was a start.

I returned her embrace for an awkward moment and then removed myself to the hallway to send Daniel in to give her the jump point.

When Daniel returned and the door closed behind him, he looked me over. "Are you all right?"

"No."

He hugged me too, but it was less awkward, familiar. Safe. When he let me go, he asked, "Where to?"

Like hell was I letting Vayen have at Buria for a week without a word from me first. "Back to the Iber. I have arrangements to make."

"Not of the funeral variety, I hope?"

"Not at the moment." I managed a half-hearted smile to put him at ease.

"Good. I'd like to keep both of my parents among the living." He took my hand and slipped us both into the void.

FOUR

Anastassia

I'd called Vayen into our bedroom, the one place, no matter where we were living, that we could openly talk to one another in private. It didn't matter that we lived alone these days, both kids having their own suites on the ship and sans any guards. It was a habit we'd both stuck with.

Our bedroom also had the best soundproofing credits could buy, both for privacy and in case a screaming match did break out.

Standing there in our private space, feeling lifeless and empty, the deal with Buria tumbled out of my mouth in an ungraceful string of staccato sentences.

Vayen stared at me as if I'd grown a second head. "Are you serious?"

I nodded. "One week with Buria, no repercussions. Get her out of your system. And if that's not the case, if you're dead set on this second wife thing, we'll talk about it after."

He grabbed me and crushed me to his wide and solid chest until I couldn't breathe. Thank goodness he wasn't wearing his armor or half of my face would have been abraded. I tapped him on the shoulder until he loosened his grip.

Vayen looked down at me, searching my face, likely still verifying that I wasn't kidding. "I don't know what to say."

"Clearly. I had to find out what's been aggravating you from everyone else. They all seemed to know."

He bowed his head. "I couldn't ask you for this. I tried. A hundred times. Every angle I came up with sounded selfish and like I was moving on, or putting you aside, or... Geva, none of that is true. Please believe me, it's not."

He looked entirely earnest. I forced a nod.

The little part of me that had held out hope that he'd deny that he wanted another woman, that he'd declare I was all he needed, was crushed. Maybe it wasn't such a little part of me because I wanted nothing more than to crawl into bed and hide under the covers until the next week had passed.

"Stassia." The way he almost breathed my name sent a shiver through me. "I'm sorry. I've tried so hard to not need this."

He'd tried damned hard not to do a lot of things but here we were. Damned instincts and urges and whatever other fucking words Etara had tried to smooth this over with.

I wanted to say that I understood, that I didn't blame him, to ease his conscience in some way, but the lump in my throat didn't allow for any of that.

If it weren't for his slipping hold on his ability to stay in Etara's grey zone, there was no way in any of his fucking hells I'd be agreeing to this no matter how much he wanted or needed it. But need was the word he'd used, and maybe that was the honest truth. He was doing everything he could to stay in control just as much as I was. I cursed his Geva and every other deity I'd heard of over the years for putting me in this position.

The datapad in my pocket pinged twice, the signal from Daniel that Buria had arrived. He would be escorting her to the suite that I'd provided for her far from ours.

"She's here," I mumbled.

"I don't need to go running over there, for Geva's sake. I can stay here with you for a while."

What was the point? He was going to go over there and have sex with her. There was no denying the hot buzzy action going on in his head. It was loud and clear through our bonded connection, and I was no longer deluded enough to assume that pertained solely to me.

I wrapped my hand around his arm and led him out of the bedroom. We got as far as the suite door before he pulled me to a halt.

"You don't have to go with me."

The sympathy in his voice nearly made me cry, but I held my head high. "I do. If you're going to do this, we'll do it the proper way. Courting a second wife at least has a little more honor than a blatant affair."

He swallowed audibly and put his other hand over mine where it rested on his arm. "Thank you. I know this isn't easy."

"It isn't," I said as we left the safety of our suite to walk down the public corridors toward Buria's room. "You'll understand when I cut our connection down to minimal levels. I will not be a voyeur to whatever you two are doing."

He stiffened but nodded. He was as used to me in his head as I was him, but he'd know I was all right and vaguely where I was. That would have to do. If he wanted to talk to me, he could do it in person. Hell, not having him in my head was going to be hard for me too.

Though the Iber was a large ship with a sizeable crew, word of Buria's arrival had already started to spread thanks to Daniel. He'd suggested that the best course of action was to make the courtship public and had offered to set the facts out for the crew. At least that way we could tame the rumors to a more tolerable level.

The central jump point we all used wasn't private. If Vayen wanted Buria here, he was going to have to deal with the whispers and speculation. There weren't any blatant stares, but there were definitely more people in the corridors than normal operation warranted.

"I didn't need an audience," Vayen muttered under his breath.

I didn't need him to bed another woman. A host of other sharp retorts flooded my mind but I kept them to myself. Starting a fight on the way to visit his long-desired love was a sure way to drive him into her arms.

Maybe she'd be horrible in bed. But she'd had plenty of training in that department on Tacesh. Or somehow incompatible. But Isnar had been with her when she'd been employed by him.

Maybe Vayen would get bored and be back in my bed in a day or two. Holding onto that hope, I did my best to ignore the sympathetic glances from the Jalvian women we passed.

Conversations grew hushed as we progressed. No one spoke to us directly. Vayen walked stoically beside me, not saying a word. Rather than his recent aura of hostility, waves of trepidation and excitement rolled off of him. Sadly, I knew the trepidation was for me. His excitement was for Buria.

When we at last reached her door, he turned to face me. And then dropped down on his knees.

Everyone in sight turned heel and scattered. The corridor was suddenly empty.

He took my hands in his and held them so tightly it verged on painful. "Know that whatever happens between me and Buria, she will never have me as you do. I will never share a bond with her. Never share what we do mind to mind. Above all, no one kills me but you."

Despite my efforts to keep my emotions in check, tears rolled down my face. I leaned down to kiss his forehead. "I love you too."

With nothing more to be done, I lifted him to his feet and turned away, unable to watch him enter the room where Buria waited. I shuttered my end of our bonded connection, leaving nothing but the barest hint of him in my mind.

The walk back to our suite was too long. I had never wished so badly to be able to Jump on my own as I did just then. I would have liked to have gone anywhere else. Having to stay on the Iber, knowing what they were doing, seemed impossibly cruel. But if I left, if I portrayed any clear sign of resentment or anger, I'd be showing everyone that this wasn't consensual. If we were going to make this work, to have the respect of the crew and of the population of the Narvan on our visits home, it had to be.

"Mom?" Daniel fell into step next to me. "Where do you want to go?" he whispered.

The crew was back in the corridor. Everyone's faces were distorted, nightmare-warped, their eyes too large, staring. Their voices were sharply defined and grating, yet their words all jumbled together.

"I don't know. Where should I go?"

He knew how this worked, what was socially acceptable.

"You need to be seen. I'll stay with you. Come on." He took my hand and placed it on his arm, just like I'd done when walking with Vayen. A sob threatened to burst from my mouth. I choked it back.

My feet moved, keeping pace with Daniel's. I didn't pay attention to where we were going. There were too many people around, too many voices.

"I want to go home," I whispered.

"Not yet." He peered around. "Come on," he muttered.

And then Ikeri was on my other side. "Sorry, I was in a session with a client. Where are we taking her?"

"Let's get something to eat."

"I'm not hungry," I protested.

"Mom, you need to be seen. We'll both stay with you until you can go back to your room," said Ikeri.

We entered the dining hall to a sudden dip in the volume of conversation. A ranging look of warning from Daniel brought the pitch back up.

"Get her something," he urged Ikeri toward whatever the cooks had prepared. He settled into a table near the entrance, guiding me into the seat next to him.

Was this what it was like to be old? Having your children coddle you? I'd been noticing more grey hairs of late. Buria didn't have any.

"Mom, here, eat." Ikeri slid a plate of steaming food in front of me and sat with one of her own.

With Ikeri back on babysitting duty, Daniel went up to get something for himself. Several officers approached him, speaking quietly, one outright pointed in my direction.

He came back with a plate, looking grim.

"Trouble?" Ikeri asked, picking at a tangle of green noodles.

"Not exactly." He pinched the bridge of his nose. "They want to know if Mom is also in the market for a second."

Ikeri giggled, then looked at me and quickly sobered. "Are you?"

"No."

"Maybe you should pretend to be. That would get Dad out of that suite in a heartbeat," Daniel muttered.

I pushed a few things around on my plate and took a bite, not tasting anything. "I thought you were supporting your father's choice."

"I was, until I saw you."

"Don't hold this against him. We'll work it out." The last thing I needed was deepening tension between Vayen and Daniel.

He nodded but didn't look convinced. "I didn't consider the bond you share. Meera and I have never had that. Not to mention, she was the one who suggested Arden after we met her at a party at the Premier's estate. They had a mutual attraction from the start."

"Have you considered forming bonds with your wives?" Ikeri sat back from her plate and crossed her arms in front of her as if she had her Seeker robes on. Instead, she was dressed in simple oversized clothes that masked her figure, her default attire when she wasn't working.

Daniel erupted in an incredulous look and gestured at me. "Can you not see what a pain in the ass the damned bond is? Seriously, Ikeri, what the hells?"

"So you've never tried it," she said blandly.

"No, I haven't fucking tried it. Have you met our parents? Is that not enough of a cautionary tale about bonds with non-Artorian people? Not to mention, we're not exactly full-blooded either."

As I moved food around on my plate, I watched the two of them bicker, marveling at how calm they were despite their difference of opinion. Thank goodness they hadn't copied us in that regard.

"Arden is. I'm sure she'd love it," Ikeri said.

"And Meera isn't. As a Seeker, are you encouraging me to drive a wedge between my wives?"

"Of course not, I'm encouraging you to try with both of them."

Though he was keeping his tone level, I easily recognized the irritated body language that matched Vayen's. "Even if I were inclined, which I'm not, I wouldn't even know where to start. It's not like Dad has offered any advice on that topic. Or any other, for that matter."

"Have you asked him?"

"Fucking drop it, little sister," he said tightly.

While Ikeri got along splendidly with Vayen, Daniel and his father had been business-only for the last few years. She was ever trying to mend their obstinate and mysterious divide. Before the conversation grew more heated, I spoke up.

"Your father is just doing what comes naturally to him. The alterations have undone some of the engineered changes bred into all Artorians."

Daniel snorted. "Dad is anything but natural."

Ikeri glared at him.

"He's acting no different from most Jalvians of his age. And unlike an Artorian woman, I can turn my end of his bond off."

Ikeri gasped. "You didn't."

"Would it be better to witness everything he's doing right now?"

"Euw." She cringed.

"Exactly." I took another bite, chewing methodically.

"Isn't that going to set him off? I mean, I thought your bond to him was keeping him at least sort of level," Daniel said.

"I'm sure he's plenty distracted right now. She's probably—"

"Mom." Daniel shook his head. "Really."

Ikeri kicked me under the table.

The two of them traded inane conversation while I made a half-hearted effort to eat.

"How about we go check on the jump gate progression?" Daniel suggested once they'd finished eating.

The ship's operations had nothing to do with me unless something was going drastically wrong, but I dutifully followed him out of the dining hall where we said goodbye to Ikeri and then took our sweet-ass time wandering up to the bridge. By the time we arrived, I was pretty sure well over half of the crew had set eyes on me.

I stood off to one side, staring blindly at a navigation terminal and occasionally pulling out my datapad like I might have been doing something useful. In reality, I was checking the time and assuring myself it was passing. I'd set myself up for a full week of this?

Daniel checked in with the bridge staff, exchanging banter and making an occasional suggestion. They all knew what they were doing. Most of them had been with him since he and Vayen had set out to find Ikeri seven years ago.

They'd given him the rank of commander though he'd had no official training and wasn't a member of their service. My son, Commander Ta'set. I shook my head. Vayen had always wanted Daniel to go into the military and now he was, even if he wasn't doing so by the traditional route.

An hour later, Daniel nudged me. "It's been long enough. You can go hide out now," he said quietly.

Hide out? Was that what I was going to do all week?

Looking concerned, he put a hand on my shoulder. "Mom, do you need me to walk you back or can you make it on your own?"

"I'm fine. Go on." I nodded him back toward the crew who were doing their best not to look like they were watching us.

"As you say." He gave me one last look before returning to the crew.

As much as I appreciated Seekers, and being a pseudo-one myself, it grated on me when those words were aimed in my direction. Did others feel the same way? The Verians I treated seemed comforted by them. Maybe it was just all the rest of us.

I made my way back to my suite. Attempting to look like I was paying attention to the datapad in my hand allowed me to avoid making eye contact with anyone.

Knowing no one would be waiting for me, it shouldn't have bothered me that the lights were out, that there was no enticing aroma of something cooking in our little kitchen, or that the bed was cold and empty. I stood there in the middle of the common room, staring at the floor, imagining him on his knees, making a declaration far more eloquently than he'd ever done before. He'd botched every single ceremonial moment we'd ever had, yet managed to turn that one, which had no official protocol at all, into a beautiful moment.

With blurry eyes, I made my way over to the wine cooler and pulled out a bottle. Once the cork was out, I considered a glass, but there was no one to put a show on for. I sat down on the couch in the dark and drank until the ache in my heart grew distant and the urge to close my eyes saved me from opening a third bottle.

FIVE

Buria

How did one seduce a man who loved his mate? And was I supposed to? He was the one who wanted me, after all. Not that it wasn't mutual, but he'd been firm when he'd told me we would never be intimate. And now here we were.

Ana had given her permission, her blessing, asked for my help. It wasn't like I was doing anything wrong, but the pain in her eyes had been difficult to bear. I couldn't imagine what she must be feeling, knowing her mate was on his way to my suite. The room she'd provided for us. Daniel had told me so when he'd met me at the jump point and escorted me here, making a tasteful show of support for his father.

Ana had left an assortment of liqour bottles on the kitchen counter and also a vial of golden liquid that I'd heard many of the Cragtek employees boast about using. They called it bang. It lowered inhibitions and acted as a sexual stimulant. Vayen had told me that he'd had the spray from Tacesh altered, split into two drugs, reduced the effects to a more manageable and marketable level, and that he was making a good sum off his cut of the profits. Did Ana think he was going to want to use it with me? Was I supposed to use it with him? Did he use it with her?

I held the vial up to the light, observing the shimmering contents. It wasn't like I needed any help in that department. All I needed was to look at him. I put the vial back on the counter.

The kitchen was small, perfect for two, and well stocked. I supposed she didn't want me out and about too much. Or him either, until our week was up. Seeing him, knowing he was with me, would be difficult for her. Maybe she assumed we'd be too busy in bed to want to leave.

I groaned. Having to take another woman's wishes and feelings into consideration wasn't something I was used to dealing with. They hadn't trained us for that on Tacesh, only for pleasing those who owned us.

It wasn't like I'd been celibate during my years at Cragtek. I'd had my fair share of fun with willing partners, but none of them had wanted any sort of long-term commitment. Being surrounded by so many people, most of whom were joined, contracted, or together in the term of their kind, it was hard to be alone. Not that I missed being on Tacesh as a slave, but I'd never been lonely there. Even when I'd worked for Karin's Premier, there were three of us there to talk to one another. We shared the experience of leaving our past lives behind and found our places in the new opportunity we were sold into together.

On Brustus, working for Gamnock, I had my security team, but I was in charge. Those under me didn't want to relax with me after work. With every trade ship crew that Cragtek worked with, I watched for some sign of interest beyond a passing encounter, but nothing real came of any of it.

I had a good, respectable position at Cragtek. I'd earned my own place on my own merit. I was free. But by the gods, I craved something real, something lasting.

No one had captured my attention like the giant Artorian who'd bought me my first official drink in a club on Twelve. Who had hardly known me. But upon learning I'd been a slave, took it upon himself to not only free me but all the other women on Tacesh. Who could make me quiver with a smoldering look. Gods, I'd replayed the kiss we'd shared enough times that the memory should have been worn out, but it remained so vivid I could still feel his touch.

And he wanted me here. On his ship. In his bed. Maybe even as a second wife. I grinned.

Should I undress? Maybe wait on the bed? The couch?

If we were to be alone, there was no need for armor or weapons. I removed everything but my clothes and then took into account what I was wearing. When I'd told Ana I needed an hour, I'd only considered what tasks I needed to wrap up. Everything else had seemed inconsequential given the news that the Advisor wanted me. Now I was standing in a suite on a ship far from home in a pair of worn leggings and a wrinkled shirt. I couldn't even remember what underclothes I'd put on that morning. Did they match? Would he care? When did I last shower? Gods, I hadn't thought to bring toiletries.

Footsteps sounded outside the door. They lingered there. Had they posted a guard? Was I to be forcibly kept in my room? That wasn't part of the arrangement, and I certainly wasn't going to stand for it.

I pressed the door panel with a scathing retort on my tongue only to find the Advisor there, alone and looking wrecked.

"Would you like to come in?"

"Should I? Buria, what am I doing?"

"What you've been given permission to do." I stood aside.

Two crewmen walked toward us, watching him. He turned to glare at them. They hurried by.

He stepped in. The door closed behind him. "The entire fucking crew knows I'm here. Geva, what she must be going through with them all watching her too."

"She knew what she was getting into when she set this up," I said as gently as I could for not wanting to talk about Ana when I was supposed to be enjoying a week of guilt-free sex with her mate.

He nodded and dropped into a chair with his head in his hands. "She cut me off. Our bonded connection. It's so empty without her."

I hated saying the words, but seeing him like this made me question the validity of what Ana had said. "We don't have to do this. If you don't want to, I mean. You could simply say that you changed your mind."

"Back to being my moral bodyguard?" The Advisor's gaze slowly wandered over my body. "I want to be here. Very much so. It's just..." He shook his head. "I need a minute to think this through. You being here, her offer, it's all unexpected."

"It is for me too. You never said you wanted this. Me."

One eyebrow quirked as he gave me another once over. "I'm pretty sure it was implied when we tangled years ago."

Tangled. I chuckled. "Implied then, yes."

"Buria, I don't idly chat with all my contacts regularly, and I definitely don't kiss them and then dream about it for years afterward." He smiled weakly, eying the bottles on the counter behind me.

I grinned at the knowledge that he was as fixated with that kiss on Tacesh as I'd been. Then my hospitality training kicked in. "Would you like something to drink?"

"She supplied all that, didn't she?" His eyes roamed over the options.

I nodded, following his gaze to see that it had stopped on the vial beside the bottles. Then noticing that I'd caught him there, he settled on a green bottle and pointed to it.

Hunting down two glasses, I poured his choice and after sniffing the contents of three other bottles, found one that smelled fruity for myself. With drinks served, I sat in the chair beside him.

"I can't believe you're here," he said softly.

"Me either." I sipped my drink while he downed half of his in one gulp as he watched the door.

"Maybe you could tell me more about yourself while we wait? Not as my contact, not about Cragtek, or bodyguard business, moral or otherwise. I mean you."

"Sure, but um, what exactly are we waiting for?"

"Her to burst through that door and to tell me she changed her mind." From the unfamiliar hitch in his voice, I wasn't sure if he was hoping she would or wouldn't.

I spent the next twenty minutes rambling about what I remembered of my childhood, what I'd been having for dinner the past week, and the recent performance review I'd had with Gamnock in which he'd praised my skills on the job. Which I was just realizing was job-related when I noticed Vayen's attention was mostly locked on the door and his glass was empty. I got up and took the glass from him, gaining a half-hearted smile.

"Do you think she'll change her mind?" I asked.

He reached out and wrapped one arm around my hips, pulling me closer. "I hope not, but I owe her the chance to do so before I…"

The way Vayen was gazing hungrily at me made me hope we wouldn't be in limbo much longer. I wasn't exactly on board with Ana's getting-me-out-of-his-system part of her plan, but I did fully intend to enjoy the rest of my time with him, however long it lasted. And in order to do that, the man needed to relax.

I slid out of his hold and brought his glass over to the counter. Opening the vial of bang, I tipped a generous drop into it before filling it with his chosen liquor and then returned to my seat.

"Thanks." He stared into his drink, unmoving and silent for a long moment. Then he took a sip and seeming pleased with my choice, settled his gaze back on the door.

Amid my seemingly one-sided conversation about my friendship with Elonka, one of Gamnock's three wives, and how she was as excited about my possible opportunity of a Ta'set marriage contract as I was, I noticed Vayen's attention was wavering between me and the door. By the time he'd finished his second drink, the door seemed forgotten and his intent gaze was locked on me.

Vayen nodded toward the open bedroom. "I've never done this with anyone other than her," he said like he was starting to get on board with why he was here. Maybe the bang was kicking in.

I swallowed the rest of my drink, savoring the sweetness, and stood, holding out my hand. "Well, then, Advisor, let's go where you're most comfortable before we explore the other options this suite has to offer."

He smiled. "I have a name, Buria. You may use it when we're alone."

"Vayen, then."

He nodded, his pupils dilatating as the drug took effect.

"Would you, Vayen, like to join me in the bedroom?"

He set his empty glass on the floor and took my hand. "I most definitely would, but first, I plan on resuming where I left off on Tacesh. Unless you're going to stop me again?"

I snickered. "Unlikely."

He tugged me into his lap where he proceeded to kiss me until I felt like I was the one who'd been drugged. His hands found their way under my shirt and then that was gone. Determined to keep up, I removed his, taking my time to appreciate the scarred and sculpted body beneath. His skin felt different from anyone I'd touched before, tougher, less supple. He left my lips to work his way down my throat. Pulling him closer, I discovered a dip in the back of his neck where he must have had a significant injury. I'd just gotten my fingers into his thick hair when he freed my breasts and proceeded to devour them.

The next thing I knew, he'd stood with me in his arms and we were halfway to the bedroom. No one had ever done that before; I wasn't the slight sort of woman that invited that sort of behavior. Then again, he was larger than most men I'd been with, both in broad frame and muscle mass. He maneuvered us through the doorway with a grunt as his shoulder hit the wall.

The moment my backside hit the bed, he shed his pants and boots. I'd barely had time to do the same before he was on top of me eager and ready. He pulled back for a moment, watching me. I nodded. And then he was in and any hint of gentleness left him. He set a pounding pace that sent me over the edge in no time flat.

I shifted position, seeking to give him more access which turned out to be an utterly gratifying move on my part as his pace continued without flagging.

It occurred to me as the second high faded that he was used to a telepathic component during sex, like the Premier of Karin had used when I'd first been in his service. I hadn't liked that, not one bit, but if that was what Vayen needed... I was just about to offer when he snapped into a manic pace and then cried out. His forehead dropped onto mine as he caught his breath.

I wrapped my legs around him, keeping him close as I kissed him.

He chuckled. "Not too awful then?"

"Definitely not."

"Good." He dropped down to lie beside me. "Give me about twenty minutes and then you can begin to show me what else this suite has to offer."

I turned to face him. "Really? You can go again that quickly?"

"You drugged me. So yes," he accused without any malice.

"You saw that? And you still drank it anyway?"

He draped a heavy arm over me and closed his eyes. "I trust you."

I snuggled against his vast warm body and grinned. A woman could certainly get used to this.

SIX

Daniel

The pin on my sleeve pinged. "Commander, we could use your assistance in the gym. Please?"

What the hells did they need me for in the gym? I finished the last two bites of my dinner. Having missed a meal with my wives the night before to keep my mother company, I'd elected to cook them something special in our suite. They were both chatting happily, devouring the seared prantha and crisp greens with the vigor of pregnant women.

"Trouble?" asked Arden.

"Sounds like it. Probably a fight." Jalvians tended to get hot-headed, especially the younger ones. My father's mission of unity and healing hadn't offered much in the way of release for their aggression.

"I shouldn't be long." I kissed them both, slipped my armored coat on just in case, and headed for the gym.

A dense crowd had gathered around the floor mats. I shouldered my way through, coming to a dead stop just as my mother delivered a punch that knocked a towering Jalvian onto his ass.

"Any other offers?" she asked, breathing hard.

Four other men stood on the far side of the impromptu ring. One had a cut lip. Another, a bloody nose. One held his ribs while another coddled an arm. All had swollen faces. They cheered with the crowd.

Damn. This was the woman who had fought beside my father before becoming my mother. I had to admit, I was impressed. He'd alluded to the fact that she could best him, but having seen him in action and never her, I'd not believed it. I'd thought she'd left those days behind in favor of threats backed up by him.

Though she did spend plenty of time in the gym, I'd assumed it was just to keep in shape. Apparently, she was.

Frad, my trusted informant on all crew relations, made his way to my side. "I would have contacted you sooner, but she was watching me, and I didn't want to end up like them." He nodded to my mother's victims. "Marks got a hard hit in that distracted her long enough for me to ping you."

"And she's still on her feet after five of them?"

"Six. The first one is in the infirmary."

On one hand, my mother was offering the outlet many of them needed. But six of them? I had to believe they were going easy on her because of who she was and their intention. Besides, she was my mother, dammit, and older than everyone she'd fought. However, I couldn't ignore the fact that her face was swollen too. Her stance and breathing indicated she'd taken on other injuries. She winced as she lifted an arm to push stray hairs out of her eyes. Maybe they weren't holding back very much. Either way, she wasn't going to remain standing much longer in her condition.

I stepped into the ring. "All right. Enough of that for tonight. Go." I shooed them all off. "And you, go get checked out," I said to the five men who had contended with my mother.

Once they were gone, I turned to her. "How are you feeling?"

"Tired." The light that had been in her moments ago had vanished. With her audience gone, she suddenly appeared about to keel over.

"How hard did Marks hit you?" I reached for her.

She waved me away. "I'm fine."

"He didn't look fine. And you'll have a black eye tomorrow." I sighed. "Which one did that?"

"The first one. I didn't catch his name."

"Good Geva, Mom, did you have to put him in the infirmary?"

She took a step and winced, felt her side, and winced again. "He broke a damned rib and gave me a black eye, so yeah, I did."

"And you fought five more after that?"

She glared at me. "I may have popped a stim before I got here."

I shook my head, chuckling. "Mom, that's hardly fair."

She shrugged and then grimaced.

I pinged Frad. "Get security on whoever she put in the infirmary."

"What for?" she asked, slowly making her way off the mat.

"In case Dad feels like caring that someone hit you."

"I'm sure he's too busy screwing Buria to care at the moment. Jump me to the tank and I'll take care of any evidence."

In light of her crass comment, I was half inclined to refuse and make her suffer the same as the men she'd fought, but in the interest of possibly saving a life, and because I needed her with the landing party tomorrow, I gave in and Jumped her to the buried ship on Frique where her regen tank resided.

"Could you please not fight anyone else? I need the crew in working condition."

"I'll send you a message when I'm done here," she said flatly as she started removing her shirt.

Not wanting to see her undress, I Jumped directly back to my suite, surprising Arden. She gasped and put a hand to her chest. "I wasn't expecting you to come in that way."

"Thank my mother. Sorry to startle you."

Meera groaned. "What did she do? Is your father going to go on a rampage?"

Sadly, my mother was probably right on that point. "Hopefully he's too busy to notice that she was fighting prospective seconds."

Arden gaped. "You said she didn't want a second."

"She doesn't. She was proving her point. If we're lucky, they'll take the hint and leave her alone now."

Meera snickered. "Don't bet on it. They've got six more days of semi-freedom before your father is back beside her. She might not have his mind-twisting ability, but she's a powerful woman in her own right. Becoming her second would be an enviable position for any of them. It's well known that she has no aversion to Jalvians."

It was. There had been whispers about her past with Kess since she'd walked onto the Iber four years ago. But no one had dared do anything about it while my father was present. I considered going to pound on Buria's door to fill him in on how his mate was dealing with his selfish desire. Geva, I could just imagine the fight between my parents that would ignite.

I stayed in my seat and prayed he'd see reason by the end of the week.

❧

Begrudgingly opening my eyes, I wished for a few more hours of sleep, but we had a scheduled stop at a new-to-us world in a couple of hours. Since my father was busy, that meant my mother was taking over negotiation duty. Please, Geva, I prayed, let her be her normal self today.

Enjoying the warmth of Meera on my left and Arden on my right, I used my link to check messages and was overjoyed to not have any emergencies to attend to. I carefully extracted myself from the tangle of languid limbs and got dressed.

Feeling good about the morning, I left my wives to their peaceful slumber and headed to the dining hall to find something to eat. Riotous laughter drew my attention to two long tables packed with men. And my mother.

I swore.

At least no one was bleeding. Yet.

My approach was marked by the quieting of conversation and laughter turning hollow and dying off. I rested a hand on her shoulder. "Good morning, Mother."

She gave me an annoyed side-eye. "Did you need something?"

I needed her to be the mother I knew before my father fucked everything up by wanting a second wife. Given that we had an audience, I pasted on a pleasant smile. "Will you be going with the landing party today?"

She nodded. "Will you?"

Like I'd leave her unsupervised. "Yes."

"Good. I'll see you in the shuttle bay in a few hours," she said pleasantly enough, but the kindly-fuck-off undertone was perfectly clear.

I left her to the growing host of suitors and headed straight for Ikeri's suite.

She answered, yawning as she waved me inside. "What did Mom do now?"

I sat at her table and filled her in while she made tea.

"Is she changing her mind, do you think?" Ikeri asked.

"At this point. I have no idea. Sad mom, I understand given the circumstances. Short-tempered, distracted mom is normal. Brawling mom surrounded by other men?" I shook my head. "Seems like inviting disaster."

"Agreed. We need to snap her out of whatever coping mechanism this is." She tapped her chin. "She would never dare do any of that if dad was present."

I sipped my tea. "Or would she to spite him?"

"Damn, you're right. We may need a distraction. Markus?

SEVEN

Daniel

The Ocelon people were short and thick, and from the moment we approached the table for our meeting, stern and sour. I set the translator unit on the table and tested it to make sure it was working. Over the years, we'd gathered quite a collection of languages to add to the Artorian University's database. While many of the Iber's crew had link implants and could utilize the translation function seamlessly, the populations we dealt with on our mission did not have that luxury. Thankfully most were able to provide language files that we could upload to our equipment, though some took more work to integrate than others. The Ocelon file had been troublesome. I hoped that didn't lead to translation errors that might turn them against us over a simple misspoken word. I preferred to leave as little as possible to chance.

My mother let me, Etara, and the representatives from the agricultural and technology teams take our seats before launching into the opening speech I'd heard countless times over the four years we'd been doing this.

Whereas my father laid down the offer of assistance, guidance, and unification in a commanding tone, my mother had a more subtle approach. She wasn't exactly smiling, but she did employ a friendly manner, gesture openly, and made eye contact with each person at the table throughout her pitch.

Though their faces didn't appear at all enthusiastic, body language seemed to shift in our favor. I allowed myself a sliver of optimism.

Scans had revealed large deposits of sought-after elements on their world. Whether they knew it or not, the Ocelon people had much to offer us. My father had made it clear he wanted access to those deposits. I had no doubt that he already had buyers lined up somewhere in his intricate web of deals.

If my father hadn't been an ass of the highest degree, I might have asked him to explain how his business methods worked rather than trying to figure it out from observation. But he was, and he didn't tolerate questions from me. Thankfully, my mother did. However, she wasn't in on his entire web either. The majority of his dealings were by link and she had no access to those. My father had been deep in his implant since we'd left our quiet lives on Veria Minor, ever only half-present if even that.

My mother turned over the pitch session to the agricultural team-leader and finally sat beside me.

"Not very receptive, are they?" she muttered in my head.

This wasn't the first world we'd encountered that didn't welcome us with open arms, but she was in a mood. That she hadn't been on board with my father's wish for a second wife, but was begrudgingly giving him a chance was a testament to how much she did love him. That she was here working rather than holed up in her suite either sulking or plotting ways to kill him was the best I could hope for.

"Give the opening session a chance, Mom. One of us will bring them around. We almost always do."

"Maybe, but my gut says no."

"Already? We just got here and Dad is prepared to stay as long as it takes."

At the mention of my father, I felt her mood darken. I backed out of her mind before I made it worse.

Once the Artorian woman from the tech division finished outlining what she could offer the Ocelon, it was my turn. Early on, my father had been the one to pitch the protection and safety benefits of being in our union. Then, back when we were still on speaking terms, he stated that it would be better for me to take that role since I was acting as commander of the Iber. What he really meant was that he wanted to portray himself as Advisor of All with the rest of us clearly as subordinates. As much as I'd wanted to point out his manipulation, having a voice in the negotiations rather than acting as his bodyguard had outweighed my annoyance. I could still clearly see his smile upon my acceptance—not that he was proud of me advancing in responsibility, but that he'd succeeded in getting what he wanted.

My father always got what he wanted.

I glanced at my mother, stern and exuding her usual confidence as though she was ready to conquer anything at any time. I'd seen behind that mask when Buria had arrived. My father couldn't be conquered, not even by her.

When I turned the pitch over to Etara and her healing arts, I settled back in beside my mother and joined her shitty mood.

After the group pitch was complete, my mother opened negotiations, going through the steps as I'd seen her do many times before, but her heart wasn't in it today. I spotted several occasions where she let subtle opportunities slip that she would have normally jumped on. My mother could manipulate masterfully, but at least she drew the line at family.

As she had predicted, the Ocelon we spoke with did not seem particularly interested despite what we could offer them. They specifically did not like the Iber in their orbit.

"You threaten us," one of the leader's councilors stated.

"We offer no immediate threat. The Iber is merely our transportation." I explained.

"We scanned your weapons. We've heard of your death-bringer."

"Sometimes word travels too fast," my mother grumbled.

I leaned closer to the translator. "We do not use that term, and his abilities are only used for defense. He is the Advisor, and he leads the union. He is also part of our healing team."

"We are not worthy of meeting your leader?" asked the Ocelon leader, his disapproval clear.

"He is occupied."

"I am also an Advisor," my mother stated. Again. She'd introduced herself as such, and as a joint head of our union when we'd begun.

The leader looked unimpressed. "We have not heard of you. You will bring us the Advisor when we next meet or we are finished here."

"He is occupied," I repeated.

The leader raised a thick, hairless brow ridge. "If he wants a deal, he will come."

I knew my mother's body language well enough to know she was ready to blow any shred of diplomatic stoicism she had left. I reached under the table to put my hand on her arm, keeping her seated.

"I'll see what I can do," I offered.

The leader sneered at me. Sneered. At me. When I was trying to give him what he was asking for? I considered letting my mother have at him but then reminded myself that my father really wanted this deal to go through.

"I believe we're done here," my mother declared, forcibly removing my hand from her arm and pushing her chair back.

"Don't blow this," I cautioned.

She glared at me. *"I was doing this before you were born. Perhaps you should go see what you can do to drag your father off of Buria for his precious fucking deal."*

"Sure." I already had one parent who barely spoke to me. I wasn't about to intentionally piss off the other one.

As annoyed as she was, I knew it wasn't at me, but it surely didn't help that I closely resembled the target of her ire. And I didn't especially appreciate being his substitute when it was my mother he was hurting. She might be making a show of this proposed courtship being consensual to prevent political disaster back in the Narvan, but what my father was doing was nothing like when Meera and I had courted Arden.

As I made for the door, I considered Jumping directly to the Iber to pound down Buria's door and drag my father out to beat the shit out of him.

Etara must have picked up on my mood because she cornered me while my mother and the tech head were caught up in an after-session conversation with one of the Ocelon.

"This is between your parents. You need to let them find their balance."

"I can't stand here and watch while he tears her apart. She's my mother, for Geva's sake."

Etara smiled, the same sympathetic one she used for when people were dying, when the medical team shook their heads and all she could offer was comfort at the end. I'd seen it enough times to know what it looked like. Her hands were tied with my father's demand too.

I wanted to shove her away, to yell at her for not having the spine to threaten my father enough that he'd abandon this foolish whim. But I'd spent too much time on Veria Prime training with the Seekers. Violence to one of her kind was anathema. As angry as I was, with her and with my father, I would never lay a hand on Etara.

"You're a good and kind man, Daniel. Your father is not. Don't take his path."

"I hadn't planned on it, but can't you see—"

She held up her tiny hand, the flared sleeve of her Seeker robe falling back to expose her thin, pale arm. "I see. I do. But they must find their balance. I've done what I can to guide them."

"You could have done more," I snapped, heading for the door

before I let anger get the best of me.

Ocelon's air was heavy with humidity. Swirling clouds filled the murky grey-green sky. We'd been warned a storm was brewing, but our pilot was capable of handling it.

Each step toward the waiting lander seemed to put me off balance. I'd been to plenty of worlds, but this one had the highest gravity I'd encountered. The stout Ocelon were built for it but the ground pulled at my bones, making each step an effort, like walking through sand after having run for miles. I couldn't imagine how my mother and Etara were dealing with the gravity with their lighter frames.

While I waited for the rest of the landing party, I took in the city around us. The structures were thick and solid, like the people who lived here. Nothing rose over ten levels high. Most of the buildings were long and low, the average at three floors, with most being multi-family homes with businesses on the ground floor. Ocelon seemed to be a prosperous world compared to most we'd been to. They had their own space port, manufactured their own ships, and established trade with several of the nearby worlds. Though they did not have jump gates or any similar technology, their weapons systems were comparable to ours.

There had to be something we could offer them that would catch their interest, that would entice them to take my father's deal. I ran through the other options the Iber's crew offered, forming a list of artists and engineers that might appeal to these prickly people.

When my mother emerged with Etara, engaged in a heated conversation, I hurried over to intervene. Angering the holder of my father's death key was a very bad idea, especially when Etara was in the middle of my parents' current turmoil.

"Etara, why don't you join the others in the lander? Mother, you're coming with me." Even knowing she was in a volatile mood, and that she didn't like me issuing orders, it was the best I could do to avoid disaster. I clamped my hand on her shoulder and Jumped her back to the Iber.

The look she shot me when we arrived at the public jump point made me let go and keep my distance as she stormed away. Not wishing to take out my shitty mood on my family, I decided to spend the rest of the day hunting down anyone who might be of interest to the obstinate Ocelon people so that we could get their union induction completed and my father could make his damned trade deal. Not that he would thank me for it.

EIGHT

Anastassia

Vayen had been with Buria for four days without showing his face. My fight stunt with the Jalvian suitors hadn't brought him out. He hadn't consulted me on how the meeting with the Ocelon had gone. He hadn't bothered to stop at our suite to get anything, at least not when I'd been there, and I was there quite a lot. I'd purposely not left any clothes in Buria's suite for him. So either he wasn't wearing anything or she had a high tolerance for his slovenly habits.

I finished off another glass of wine and pondered my conquered bottles. Maybe it was time to switch to something stronger. Wine didn't dull the ache that I hated to say was in my heart because that sounded trite, but damn, it really was.

If he hadn't grown bored of her and she hadn't managed to annoy him by now, I had to prepare for the worst. I rummaged through the bottles that I considered his for something tolerable but stronger.

He deserved to be happy, to do what came naturally to him. He did. But I hated it. Maybe his bond had worn off on me. Knowing he was with someone else, knowing I could be with someone else, that it was acceptable and even expected of me—the idea felt very wrong.

Wrong or not, I'd be damned if I was going to be seen as weak and inferior. We were doing this advisor thing together. If he decided to formalize his dalliance with Buria, I'd have to pick a second too. Waiting to find one until he declared his intentions would put me in a petty light, like I was retaliating. I wasn't, by any means. I was merely trying to set a good example like Etara had heavily suggested.

That's what I kept repeating as I poured a half glass of whatever I'd tasted that hadn't been abhorrent. It had a greenish cast in the glass, almost opalescent.

"Stop stalling," I grumbled to myself.

Settling into the chair by the terminal in our suite, I placed a call request to Neko. As expected, being as far as we were from home, the connection took close to an hour. I'd finished that glass and was well into another by the time Hedvika's face lit the vid.

She smiled, her round cheeks dimpling. "Hello, Ana. Are you well?"

"Well enough, I suppose. Is your mate around? I was hoping to pick his mind on something."

"He's in a meeting with the Jalvian Prime at the moment. I can have him back here in about twenty minutes if you'd like to wait?"

It amused me that Neko had converted his mate into his personal assistant the moment we'd dropped the Narvan in his lap. Hedvika hadn't flinched, instead rising to the occasion with the efficiency that had been brutally drilled into her on Tacesh.

"I'd appreciate that. I don't suppose you have twenty minutes to keep me company while we wait? I'd rather not lose the connection."

"Only if you'll tell me how the children are doing. I miss them."

The kids were a safe topic. I indulged her with the news that Daniel was expecting, Ikeri's latest healing endeavors, and I relayed the last update we'd had from Markus, who was doing an internship under General Tellison.

"Neko will undoubtedly tell you, so I'll save us all some time; there's been some political fall-out with the advent of the Artorian Premier condoning the practice of multiple mates. There is a large segment of those supporting the Jalivan practice that are demand-ing policy change. They are mostly from younger Artorians who want all new births to be done clean, with the genetic alterations stripped away. They're also loudly speaking out against the government polic-ing which bloodlines can procreate. They're angry that they're tied to bonding only fellow Artorians if they want to enjoy a full bond. If the Advisor of All can bond with a non-Artorian—"

"Our bond is useless. Clearly," I grumbled.

Hedvika offered me an apologetic smile. "Neko has been unwill-ing to divulge any clarification on the bond Vayen shares with you. He feels it would weaken Vayen's image as Advisor of All."

"Fucking public image," I grumbled.

"This sub movement wants to be the last fettered generation born. They want freedom for their future children. If they are suc-cessful, they could have real bonds with anyone of their choosing.

That would be wonderful, wouldn't it?" she asked wistfully.

Even Hedvika didn't see my bond with Vayen as real. I sent another wave of liquor down my throat to drown my sorrows.

When I didn't answer, she continued, "Both sides are getting quite heated. That's what Neko is discussing with the Jalvian Prime today—suggestions on how to bring about a better understanding of the alterations done to Artorians in the past. He's got the University working on it as well."

"That sounds messy." And also like it wasn't exactly my problem anymore. What Vayen was doing was only going to make this more heated. I sighed. "I'll see what I can do to help."

"Thank you, Ana."

She brought up a few smaller issues that I offered advice on while she took notes to relay to Neko. I'd finished the second glass and was definitely feeling it by the time Neko graced us with his presence.

"Ana." He grinned, his face replacing Hedvika's as he took over the seat in front of the terminal. "You look well."

"It's an illusion." I held up the bottle as I poured another few sips into the glass.

Neko scowled. "It's got to be bad if you're hitting his stash. What did he do now?"

"He's with Buria." The situation spilled off of my thick tongue, and by the time I'd run out of words, I was sobbing.

Neko had been beside me at several of the worst times in my life. He'd held me up and kept me going when I didn't think I could go on. He was also the only person other than Vayen and Isnar whom I didn't have to hide my emotions from. I trusted Neko to keep his mouth shut about what passed between us.

He let out a string of what I guessed to be expletives by the vehemence with which they were delivered before switching back to Trade. "Gods be damned, I told him not to do this. I begged him. Ana, I'm sorry."

I felt a little better knowing he was on my side. Not that it mattered. My side was all about sacrifice going forward, according to Etara.

"What can I do?" he asked.

"I need to find a second for myself."

He shook his head. "You know what that would do to Vayen."

"The same thing he's doing to me." I held up a hand. "Minus the wrathful death-bringer, but that's not why I'm looking. Etara is pushing me to provide a strong example of how this multiple marriage mess should work. Hedvika told me what you're facing in the Narvan. Let me help you. Daniel has Artorians covered, give me a Jalvian. Who can I choose as a second that will send a unifying message to the Narvan?"

"A political union? You'd let him indulge but go for the show for yourself?"

"I have no urge to indulge with anyone else." I was starting to slur my words and that just added to my annoyance over having to pick a second at all.

"How many of those have you had?" He nodded toward the glass in my hand.

"Probably too many."

He nodded. "Put the glass down, Ana. Don't be him."

"I'm not." I didn't think I could ever be, no matter who I picked for a second.

"If you promise to not take another sip of whatever that is, or anything else," he added, staring me down, "I'll pull up some suitable options. I'm assuming you've already explored what the current crew roster has to offer?"

I pushed the glass aside. It tipped off the edge of the table. The meager contents soaked into the carpet. It wasn't the first stain I'd left in the past few days.

"I wasn't impressed with the crew."

When Vayen and I had returned to the Narvan and announced our mission to the Primes and Premiers, they'd jumped at the chance to place their promising favorites in our service on the Iber. There were plenty of brilliant scientists, healers of all sorts, and some of Jal's brightest military stars aboard. The moment they'd got wind that Vayen was pursuing a second marriage contract, proposals to be my second husband came pouring in. Though I had half-heartedly entertained their offers, none of them had met my standards. Maybe those were too high, considering who I based those standards on. There was only one of him.

While Neko's attention was wrapped up in his suitor search, I considered my future. If, in four days, Vayen showed up with one of those charming grins that had nothing to do with me, could I face him and keep my thoughts to myself? I would have to open up our bonded connection again. He'd know exactly how not on board with his second wife plan I really was and that would only create a bigger problem between us. I'd given him Buria, it wasn't like I could take that back now. His request had been granted. The damage was done.

I pondered my collection of empty bottles. Drinking wasn't cutting it, and that was a coping mechanism he knew too well. Could I convincingly fake my acceptance? Fuck no. Snide comments were already bubbling up just thinking about having to see the two of them together.

The vial of bang that I'd left for Buria and Vayen in the hopes of speeding along the fulfillment of his lust gave me an idea. It was because of him that shit was in circulation. I couldn't exactly find too much fault with that considering the profits from the two halves of the drug he'd brought home from Tacesh were bringing in. I'd seen Vayen on a different version of it before. This one was much safer or I wouldn't have offered it to them. Maybe the other half was my answer.

"Do you think I could get a case of boost or whatever they're calling it now? I'd like to set up a few dealers while we're out here."

He glanced up from his datapad. "Sure. When do you need it?"

"We're in negotiations onworld for the next couple of days. Do you happen to have a linked courier handy?"

"I'll set up a drop. I'm assuming you'd like to be notified upon arrival? I don't know as Etara would consider distributing recreational drugs for profit in her approved grey territory."

"Yes, please."

He grinned, shaking his head. "You two never cease to amuse me." Then he sobered. "I'm sending over my top seven now."

My terminal pinged a few minutes later as the files transferred. I skimmed the still frames first. If I was going to be looking at a Jalvian face up close and personal, it had at least better be a non-repulsive one.

An array of big-boned, bulky, blonde-haired men with piercing blue eyes paraded across the vid. The third one was thin, almost slight, and the youngest of the bunch. Only four years older than Daniel. Definitely not. I deleted him without looking at his file further. The sixth one looked interesting, like he'd been around action from the jagged scar under his left eye, and unlike the stern flat line of the first five, his lips had an enticing hint of an amused smile.

The last one made me do a double take.

From the threads of silver in his sandy hair and narrow hazel eyes, he appeared just far enough out of the norm for a Jalvian that

I was intrigued. I skimmed his file. Two years younger than me and only three inches taller. He didn't appear small or thin, but his recorded weight suggested a lighter build than average. He'd done a fifteen-year stint with the military and had listed residence years on Jal, Rok, Syless, and Moriek.

"What's the deal with this Tabor Desu?"

Neko laughed.

"What?"

"I had a feeling he would be the one."

"That's a bit presumptuous." But he was probably right, given the other options. Neko knew me well. "Really, though, why him?"

"Older brother of the Prime of Rok and his main competitor for the position. Tabor's grandmother wasn't Jalvian and he had the misfortune of manifesting the impure genes. He's had a rough go of getting where he should be in life."

"I've never heard of him."

"His brother keeps it that way. Between us, Tabor has a better handle on Rok's economics and the way we like to do things. He's launched successful businesses on each world he's had to move to in order to evade his brother's heavy hand of quit-outshining-me. I've dealt with him many times over the years."

Even when Neko had worked for us, he'd had a wealth of his own contacts and connections. I was not at all surprised that he had a solid hold on the Narvan and its undercurrents despite advising the whole system on his own.

"What's his current harem look like?"

"Doesn't have one. As in, he's never been contracted."

"Why not?"

A man his age, and Jalvian, no matter how impure, would have had an urge to settle down and start a dynasty by now. They weren't that different than Artorians.

Neko winked. "You'd have to ask him."

"If he's agreeable, are you prepared for the fallout with the current Prime of Rok?"

"If Tabor is agreeable, you'll have to ask what he expects out of the deal and get back to me. I don't know as I'm prepared to toss Rok into a civil war."

I shrugged. "There are more direct ways to take care of a body you no longer have a use for."

"Ana, aren't you supposed to be following Etara's code of ethics?"

he asked, chuckling.

"Those are for Vayen. She doesn't have anything on me."

"Duly noted." He shook his head. "How about I contact Tabor, and if he's open to meeting with you, have him Jump the case of boost?"

"He's linked?" Very few Jalvians were. Now I was even more intrigued.

Neko grinned. "I told you, I knew he'd be the one."

"Let's see if he wants to 'be the one' before you pat yourself on the back."

"I'll send a message as soon as I have an answer." Neko signed off, looking quite pleased with himself.

With nothing to do but wait on that front, I took a shower to sober up and spent the next hour collecting empty wine bottles and glasses, straightening the pillows, folding the blanket that I'd been using when sleeping on the couch, and adding the wine and now liquor stains, to the cleaning bot's list of tasks. By the time I'd wrapped that up, I allowed myself a glance at the terminal to find that I had a message from Neko. Tabor was coming to the Iber and he'd arrive in half an hour.

Fuck. Was I ready to talk to an actual prospective second? Not just entertain the off-the-cuff offers of enthusiastic dreamers in the crew, but a true political joining?

No, I definitely wasn't ready. I'd never expected to have to be ready. Fucking Artorians and their natural fucking urges.

I went into the bathroom and stared hard at the mirror. A miserable, tired, and half-drunk woman ten years over her prime stared back at me. Who was going to want to join with a fifty-five-year-old human, no matter what her position was in the grand scheme of things. No wonder Vayen was off screwing Buria senseless.

Without a second thought, I was back in the kitchen, pouring myself a drink of the green liquor. If Tabor was at all warned about who he was meeting, the poor man would be doing the same.

Fucking Vayen. I hurled the bottle at the wall and sipped from the glass. The bottle shattered. Swirls of opalescent green liquid dripped down to the carpet.

It occurred to me, as I slammed the empty glass onto the countertop, that the public jump point was a fifteen-minute walk from my suite. If I didn't hurry, I was going to be late.

Wearing nothing remotely impressive to denote my rank or figure or any other damned thing, I hurried out of the suite in a baggy grey shirt, black pants, and my well-worn boots. Tabor was going to get a no-frills introduction to my proposal, assuming he didn't take one look at me and vanish into the void.

That would be the smartest move.

I made it to the jump point with three minutes to spare, but the Jalvian that stepped out of the void was not the one I expected.

"Markus?"

Every time I saw him, I swore he grew another inch. At thirteen, he was all arms and legs. He looked healthy and happy. The navigation internship General Tellison had offered him seemed to be working out well.

Markus stepped away from the jump point and nodded to his escort who Jumped a moment later. "Hello, Mom." He hugged me. "Surprise."

"I didn't know you had a leave scheduled."

"Hence the surprise." He laughed. "I heard there was a family emergency?"

"Is there?"

His eyebrows rose and he smirked. "Your breath smells like Dad's, so I'm going with yes."

Ikeri's arrival cut off my reply. She greeted Markus and gave me an innocent smile. My damned kids were plotting against me. This could mean nothing good.

Tabor arrived, an unmarked cargo container in his hands. "Anastassia Ta'set?"

I nodded.

"Tabor Desu. I'm honored to be in consideration for your second."

Both kids gaped.

"Excuse us. We have business." I gestured for Tabor to follow me and hoped I'd thrown a wrench into whatever my children had been plotting. Served them right. Young people should be concerned with their own damned drama and keep their noses out of mine.

NINE

Daniel

*"**W**e need to talk now."* Ikeri's strong voice overruled the crew evaluations I'd been working on through my link while sitting on the bridge of the Iber as the crew worked around me.

"Where?"

"My room. Markus is here."

There was nothing really to do while we were sitting in orbit around Ocelon unless they decided to forcibly reject our offer. I'd already gone back to the surface with my contingent of artists and engineers, which had garnered slightly more interest than our previous offers, but the Ocelon leader still demanded to meet with the Advisor himself. That was going to have to wait until I had the opportunity to speak directly to my father. I wasn't going to chance alienating myself further by introducing that delicate situation to his heavily distracted ass by link. He hadn't been seen in person in four days.

I let the attending officer know I was leaving and went to find my siblings.

The moment I walked through Ikeri's door, Markus wrapped me in a long-armed hug. He was already almost as tall as me. Ikeri, waif-thin and barely up to my shoulder, smiled beside us.

"It's been too long since we were all together," she announced, inserting herself into our brotherly hug. With an arm around each of us, she steered us toward her couch.

"So, with our three brains now in one room, how are we going to keep Mom and Dad together?" I asked.

Markus cocked his head. "They are still together. Aren't they?"

Ikeri rolled her eyes, reminding me this wasn't Seeker Ikeri talking, but my sister. "Yes."

"Legally," I clarified. "But Mom isn't Jalvian or Artorian. She may have gone along with Dad's customs up to this point, but she's drawing the line on this one."

Markus glanced at Ikeri. "You didn't tell him?"

"I've been with you. When would I have told him?" she asked.

He playfully poked her forehead. "Anytime? Mind speech?"

She smirked and knocked his finger aside, looking at me. "Mom moved the line. She's meeting with a prospective second right now."

"She's what?"

Ikeri nodded. "Someone new. He Jumped so he's linked. Maybe Jalvian?"

"She must be serious about it if she's bringing someone in, don't you think?" asked Markus. "He looked pretty Jalvian to me, not pure though."

"I'm glad," said Ikeri. "Dad will be pleased that she's going along with this. He really wants the second joining to work out."

Was Ikeri delusional? "No, Dad wants a second wife. He most certainly will not want Mom to have a second. He's got his bond with her. It's not like he can override that."

Markus scowled. "But that's how second marriages are supposed to work. Both sides agree to have or allow a second partner."

Ikeri nodded.

"That might be true, but when was the last time Mom and Dad did anything how they were supposed to?"

Not to mention, my mother had made it pretty clear she didn't want a second. From what I could tell, she'd just been screwing with the crewmen, not seriously entertaining any of their offers. Maybe she'd been hoping that by doing so, she'd get my father's attention. It hadn't worked.

But now it sounded like she had a serious prospect. Maybe that would be enough to wake Dad's single-minded ass up and get him back to Mom's side. He'd had a few days with Buria. He should consider himself lucky he'd been given that much, considering how testy he'd been with everyone lately.

Markus was the safest distraction. My father was always happy to see him and catch up on what my little brother was doing.

"Hey Markus, how about we go have a talk with Dad? I'm sure he'd be happy to know you're onboard." I suggested.

Ikeri gave me a narrow-eyed stare. "You better not be starting any trouble. Let this play out. If Mom is serious about taking a second too, let her. It will be best for both of them. Hells, maybe she'll actually be happy with this one."

Mom did deserve to be with someone who made her happy, I couldn't argue with that. But my gut told me that person was my father, not some stranger.

"No trouble," I said to Ikeri. "I do need to talk to him though. He's been hiding in that suite for days. We have the Ocelon to deal with and he's not even bothered to check in with me on the progress. That's highly unlike him."

"Maybe he's enjoying a few days off. When was the last time he took a vacation? Other than being unconscious, I mean," Ikeri said.

She had a point, but far more than briefing him on the situation with the Ocelon, I needed to know where he stood with my mother. If there was anything I could do to make him see reason, I would, whether that meant he never spoke to me again or not. He had to realize by now that Mom wasn't like Meera or Arden, and his bond would surely have something to say when he realized my mother was within her rights to take a second mate also. Hopefully, that alone would snap him back to reality.

"We won't stay long," I said to Ikeri while herding Markus toward the door. "I'll let you know how it goes."

Markus gave me the side-eye as we walked toward the suite where I'd deposited Buria. "What are you really planning to do?"

"Exactly what I said."

"Uh huh." He shook his head.

When we arrived at Buria's door, I decided it was best to give my father a little warning rather than just request entry on the panel.

"Do you have a minute? Markus is here for a surprise visit."

"Give me five."

There was a good amount of noise erupting from just inside the suite that left nothing to the imagination as to what he was using those five minutes for. Markus went red from head to toe beside me.

"I'm guessing he doesn't realize how loud they are. Mom had soundproofing installed in their bedroom when they took up residence on the Iber. I monitor all customization of the ship," I said, trying to distract Markus.

"They're not in the bedroom." He cringed as the wall in front of us emitted a particularly loud thud. "Maybe we should come back later." He retreated to the opposite wall and appeared ready to bolt.

I tried to remember what it was like when I was his age, how seeing my parents kiss had made me uncomfortable. Then again, they rarely just kissed, it was usually more of an all-in sort of thing. Markus would have a much clearer appreciation for what was happening on the other side of the wall if he ever got his head out of his studies long enough to be attracted to someone. However, it was my father in there making all that racket, and I had to admit, that made me cringe too.

Just as I was about to agree with Markus on the bolting plan, the door opened. Thank Geva he'd put on a pair of pants but his lack of a shirt left the red marks on his neck in plain view. And were those teeth marks on his shoulder? He must have noticed our discomfort because he yelled for Buria to bring him a shirt.

He turned to take the shirt from Buria's hand, who wore nothing but a barely fastened shirt of her own. She smiled at both of us and then quickly retreated into the bedroom and closed the door.

Markus went from flushed to mortified.

It wasn't as though we hadn't seen our father naked before. He'd been in the tank plenty of times. Hells, we'd both helped him get in there or to his bed afterward, but the scratch marks on his back were not caused by weapons, not to mention the other evidence of his recent activities.

Behind him on the counter in the little kitchen, I spotted an array of his usual staples, many of which were half empty. It was the vial sitting next to them that grabbed my attention. From the color, I guessed it to be what people were calling bang. That explained what he'd been doing in there for days.

A giggle came from the bedroom that was definitely not from Buria. That was confirmed a second later when Buria shushed whoever it was.

"She better not be one of the crew."

He shrugged. "Friend of Buria's, and no, not from the crew."

With that, he ignored me and started to chat with Markus as if nothing unusual was going on. Markus stammered a few short answers, mostly glancing at me as if to confirm the dots he'd just connected. I nodded. No reason to keep him in the dark.

I wondered if Ikeri knew about this additional development and if she'd still be so supportive.

Since shortly after adding Arden to my joining with Meera, I'd been ignored and snapped at by my father far more than before. Having him go so far as to copy my joining arrangements in spite of my mother made me nearly as uncomfortable as Markus.

"I suppose I should thank you," he said.

Silence stretched on for a few seconds before I realized he was talking to me.

"For what?"

"Paving the way." He tipped his chin over his shoulder toward the bedroom. "Your mother would never have agreed to this a few years ago."

She wasn't agreeing to it now either. If he'd get his head clear of bang and Buria, he'd realize that. But Mom had brought Buria here and made an arrangement of some sort. Not knowing the details, I couldn't openly disagree. I settled for a shrug to maintain my precarious neutrality, at least for the moment.

"Did you want to join Mom for the meeting with the Ocelon?" I asked, choosing my words carefully. "They're being decidedly difficult and they've demanded to speak to you directly. Having you there would encourage them to be more agreeable."

"I'm sure she has it under control."

"Mom is meeting with a prospective second," Markus blurted.

The sound of two women talking in the bedroom drifted toward us. Another giggle.

Dad started to look annoyed. "Is she now? She's been doing that for the past few days if rumors are to be believed."

"This one isn't from the crew," I clarified, hoping to snap him out of his fascination with all things Buria. "He Jumped here. At her invitation."

"When did he arrive? When are they meeting?" he demanded, fastening his very wrinkled shirt.

"He arrived when I did," said Markus. "They walked off together."

"Buria, Jump Sefani home. We're going for a walk." He glanced around. "Where the fuck are my boots?" Once he'd located them, he set them back down and shook his head. "I need some clean clothes first."

He gave Markus a quick hug and nodded my way. "I'll talk to you both later."

Having been dismissed, Markus and I backed away.

"That wasn't how I'd planned to tell him," I muttered to Markus as we walked back toward Ikeri's suite.

"Sorry. That was just...not what I expected. Did Mom agree to Buria's friend too?" His forehead and lips took on a frustrated twist.

"Do you think he'll go back to Mom now?"

Oh, he'd go to her. No doubt about that. It was what would happen when he got there that spurred me to consult the Iber's network and locate my mother.

"Thank Geva, she's in the dining hall." I let out a deep exhale. "He won't do anything rash in public."

TEN

Anastassia

Tabor and I had walked halfway back to my suite when I realized I didn't know where I wanted to talk to him. It needed to be somewhere public. Bringing him to the suite I shared with Vayen was out of the question. Especially because he was linked. Neko might know Tabor, but I didn't.

"If you'll give me the container, I'll take care of that and meet you... Are you hungry or thirsty?" I asked.

"Let's start with hungry and go from there."

I gave him directions to the dining hall and hurried the heavy container to the suite. Opening the lid, I was pleased to find minimal amounts of packing and copious amounts of product. After hiding a handful of the tiny vials in one of my drawers in the closet, I adjusted the rest of the contents to mask their absence and closed the lid. If I didn't need any of them in a few days, I could put them back. If I did, hell, I could skim a few more off the top. If Vayen went through with this, I had no idea if I could ever look him in the eye again and not scream resentment back at him without some sort of buffer.

Tabor, dressed tastefully in what had to be tailored pants from the way they fit him perfectly, and a bright blue shirt that was probably meant to offset the lack of blue in his eyes, sat at a table for two in the middle of the dining hall. His hands were clasped together on the table before him. He wore his hair loose and cut just above his shoulders, combed back from his face. The sandy locks had a soft wave to them that I found appealing. He looked like he was waiting for a job interview. I supposed he was.

He smiled upon spotting me and stood as I approached the table. On cue, murmurs sprang up around us. I resisted the urge to shut them up with a glare. To be seen was why we were here, and likely, why he'd chosen a table at the center of the half-full hall.

"Should we at least make a show of getting something to eat so they can talk about us while we have our backs turned?" he suggested.

Maybe it was the drink I'd slammed before he'd arrived or nerves, but I couldn't help but laugh. "Yes, I suppose we should."

He walked beside me to peruse the kitchen's offerings and slid a few items onto his plate, filled a cup with water, and waited for me. We returned to our table, the whispers following us as we walked. I caught a few words: "She's serious … explosive … Advisor … get ugly". If those were in the context that was running through my head, they were all entirely accurate observations.

Tabor picked at his food, watching me. He didn't appear nervous but perhaps wary. I shoved around the three forkfuls of noodles I'd put in the center of my plate and tried to think of what I wanted to say.

"You're disappointed," he said.

I glanced up, startled. "What? No. Not at all. Why would you think that?"

He shrugged. "Usual reaction."

This was business, I repeated to myself. Just a prospective transaction for both of us. No need to get personal. At least, not up front.

"Neko said you've worked with him before?"

"I've moved some product for him from time to time," he said levelly.

Neko had said that Tabor knew how we did things. "To mutual benefit or because you owed him?"

"We have a business relationship."

That was promising. "You've spent a lot of time on multiple worlds."

"So have you. Far outside the Narvan even."

Either Neko had briefed him or he'd done some digging on his own. "What do you expect to gain from me?"

He chewed slowly and set his fork down. Then he took a sip of water and also set the cup down before meeting my gaze. "A position that my brother can't touch or rip away from me. Preferably something meaningful and at a post somewhere not too desolate if you don't want me around in person."

I gave up pretending to care about the food. "Why wouldn't I want you around?"

Tabor licked his lips and took another sip of water. "Neko

mentioned that you were looking for more of a political arrangement, not emotional.”

From his use of Neko's name rather than his title, I gathered they'd known each other a while, and maybe they were closer than an occasional business relationship.

“Yes, but appearances would need to be kept.” I gave him a good long look. Trying him on, imagining him near me if not intimately, at least in a convincing manner for the sake of political appearance “You haven't ever explored a marriage contract? I'd think with your family name and brother's position...”

“You didn't look at my medical history. He didn't warn you. Fucking Neko.” Tabor started to get up.

“Sit,” I hissed. “They're watching.” Once he did, I cracked a smile. “You have no idea how many times Vayen and I have uttered those same words. Now, what should Neko have warned me about?”

“No one wants to marry the impotent brother,” he grumbled.

“I might. No medical fixes? Therapy? Pills?”

He gave me a flat stare. “You don't think I haven't explored all that? My brother made sure he was the lead in the family. He was quite thorough in his methods without outright killing me.”

“You're still here, and to be honest, that makes you perfect.”

My assessment didn't seem to offer him any ease. He kept up with the stare.

“Neko said you were looking to pull in Jalvian support. Wouldn't a couple of children do that for you? I can't even offer that by artificial means.”

“I have a Jalvian kid. And at my age? Another one? Hell no.”

“Is this about retaliation then? I hear your mate can kill with a thought. Am I to be fodder for your jealousy?”

“If he lays a hand on you, I'll put him on the floor myself.” I shook my head. “I didn't want to be sitting here, looking for a second. And to be honest, I hope I'm not. I hope he comes home in four days and tells me that he's got that itch out of his system and that we can go back to how we were. But if he doesn't, I will not stand for any less than what he has.”

Tabor nodded slowly. “May I ask why you want to promote this movement for Artorians to join outside their kind? Adopting the Jalvian way seems rife with issues, given the drives bred into them.”

That he was questioning my motives and thinking of the bigger repercussions solidified my conclusion that I'd picked the right man.

I was used to bouncing ideas off of Vayen. If Tabor had a good enough grasp of how we ran things and the bigger picture within the known universe, we might be able to have similar conversations. He could assist me rather than just serve as a political pawn.

"Many of the younger Artorians want change, to expand beyond the confines of their race, and for their children to be born without genetic manipulations. Some still obsess about pure bloodlines, but since the war with Jal ended, others have come to see that other races enjoy blended families. They want that too. I can tell you from experience, that the current modified bond isn't very fulfilling for either side when it is activated with a non-Artorian.

Tabor's curious gaze held mine with unwavering interest. So were many of the occupants of the dining hall. I did my best to block out their avid attention and focused on the man before me.

"Even more, thanks to the truce with the Fragians, the Narvan has settled into peace. The need to keep the population contained to a limited number of worlds is no longer there. Keeping Artorians with Artorians and limiting their offspring were the main goals of the genetic manipulations."

"You're advocating the return to their natural state?"

I nodded. "Our continued work to unite the Jalvian and Artorian people back to their combined roots have gained enough traction that I feel at least allowing, if not outright promoting, aspects of unified culture is the next important step."

"But what about the vast majority of already bonded couples? I don't see them jumping on a second joining."

"We don't expect everyone to jump at the chance. Change is often slow. At this point, acceptance is the goal. We're hoping to assist the faction that is moving for a reversal of the alterations—not for those already born, but for future generations to be in their natural state. Those alterations were part of what fractured the Narvan's people."

Tabor grinned. "Acceptance."

I nodded.

"I'd very much like to be a part of that."

Good as that was to hear, we had further negotiations to cover. "I'll ask again, what do you want? What are your feelings regarding your brother? Do you want Rok?"

His mouth gaped. "Are you saying what I think you're saying?"

"That depends on how well you think you know me."

He picked up his fork and pondered his plate for a moment before taking a bite. He chewed thoroughly and swallowed. "With the current political situation in the Narvan, this does not feel like the ideal time to take you up on the offer to dispose of my brother so that I can take over as Rok's Prime. Even in the future, that might be a little too transparent in terms of favoritism."

Neko had nailed this one. I'd have to pat him on the back myself the next time I saw him.

"What about being used as a dangled replacement in return for your brother's utter cooperation?"

His eyes lit up. "Would it be too much to ask to be the one to deliver those threats?"

I grinned. "Not at all."

He took a bite and savored it. The enjoyment, which likely had little to do with the food, was plain to see on his face. As far as Jalvian faces went, I liked his. It didn't remind me of Jey or Kess or anyone else from my past who had betrayed me.

"And what would I offer you?" he asked. "I don't hold any enticing position other than a high-ranking dignitary due to my family name."

"Brother of a Prime is acceptable. Honestly, if you could just be a man I can tolerate being around on a regular basis, I'll take it."

He had an ease about him that relaxed me. And from his accent, though he spoke clear enough Trade, it was obvious he spent most of his time speaking refined Jalvian. I could listen to him talk for hours as long as he didn't slip into his native language. I'd never learned much Jalvian, instead, relying on my link to translate.

"Perhaps you'd settle for seeing if we can be friends?" I offered.

The wariness vanished and a true smile shone through as Tabor nodded. "With possible benefits, if they should arise. Not necessarily in the bedroom. Though, if you are interested, I am well-versed in other methods of pleasing women." He winked.

I laughed. "Agreed. I'll contact you once my situation is clear."

The murmurs in the dining hall came to a dead stop. Several chairs scraped over the floor.

Tabor went stiff.

"Fuck. He's here, isn't he?" I asked.

Apparently meeting with someone outside of the crew had drawn Vayen out.

Tabor nodded the tiniest fraction. "What do we do?"

"Don't show him that you're afraid."

"Bit late for that."

Familiar boots approached behind me. I didn't turn around but he came up alongside our table and stopped to take us in with Buria right beside him, I wanted to strangle him. Or her. Mostly her. She looked so fucking happy.

He'd stopped at our suite because he wore clean clothes. Which meant he'd seen the smashed bottle. Or maybe he'd been in such a rush to get back to Buria that he hadn't noticed. Thank goodness I'd picked up the rest of my mess before he'd seen how well I was truly handling this arrangement.

"Anastassia," he said, the menace clear in his voice. "Who is this?"

Tabor gave me a look that begged my leave to Jump right then and there. I shook my head. If he was going to be in my life, he was going to have to earn Vayen's respect.

"This is—"

Tabor stood and performed a charming half bow as if he had resolved himself to die in that second with what dignity he could muster. "Tabor Desu, Advisor. Your mate's prospective second."

I knew the look that flashed across Vayen's face. I shot to my feet. "Don't you dare." I jabbed my finger into his chest, regardless of any audience foolish enough to have remained in the dining hall. "You will swallow that tirade right back down and allow me what I'm due or you can reconsider what you want when your week is up. Your choice, but Tabor will remain untouched by all your means. Got it?"

Vayen glared at my finger, and at me, and then at Tabor before turning on his heel and leaving. Buria ran to catch up to him.

I watched them go, feeling the ache in my heart grow impossibly greater. A hand on my own registered. Tabor placed it on his arm and walked us out of the dining hall at a reasonable pace.

"I have no idea where I'm going, but you looked like you needed to get out of there."

"Thank you," I whispered, my voice having lost all volume.

"No, thank you. You were magnificent. I think it's safe to say I owe you my life after that. Geva, the rumors are all true. The fucking Advisor of All was going to flay me alive. He was in my head. I could feel him. The sheer malice, holy hells! I thought that was it. One half-assed meal with you and I was dead. Very disappointing." He paused and let out a long exhale. "I'm rambling. I'm sorry."

I squeezed his arm as I walked blindly beside the man Vayen would surely hate forever no matter what happened going forward. "As am I."

ELEVEN

Buria

"Vayen, wait. Please." I ran to catch up to him as he barreled down the corridor, knocking aside anyone too slow to get out of his path.

He turned around to look at me, anger and hurt warring on his face. I belatedly realized I'd used his name in public. He'd only granted permission to do that in private, but after spending four glorious days wrapped in his lavish attention, I'd grown comfortable. I'd been lulled into a sensual stupor where his long-time mate and partner didn't exist. In that suite, he'd been mine, wholly and completely. He hadn't left, hadn't even been distracted by his link. He'd given me his sole attention and focus. It had been everything I'd dreamed about in the years since the day we'd kissed on Tacesh. The moment he'd seen her, the dream shattered.

He slowed, his rage visually dissipating.

Relieved he didn't appear mad about my slip, I caught up to him.

"I need to be alone for a while. Go back to your room."

I'd plainly seen what he was about to do to the man Ana had been talking to. And she'd only been talking. In public. Etara was onboard and if Vayen went erratically violent, she'd have no choice but to kill him. I wasn't about to let that happen on my watch. Ana was trusting me to help keep him in a semi-level-headed state.

If Markus and Daniel hadn't shown up to inform him that their mother was meeting with a potential second mate, we could have enjoyed the rest of our week in peace. He'd showed no signs of flagging interest, and had been eager to try everything I suggested.

Though he'd been dosing himself with bang, I hoped it was to dull the guilt and not anything to do with me. He was enthusiastic and whispered the sweetest and most wicked things in my ear. But at some point soon, I wanted to know if that was how he truly felt or if it was only a byproduct of the drug.

I'd been thinking a good deal about my future and how it might be on the Iber, in that room with him. Now that I was having to chase him down and keep him from doing something we'd all regret, I could see why Ana had enlisted my help. He could turn fierce and violent in a heartbeat.

"Are you sure being alone is wise?"

"Probably not," he admitted, staring down the corridor to the distant dining hall where I could make out Ana leaving on the arm of the man she'd been talking to.

"How about we go for a walk?" Calmly. At my pace. Where I could hopefully further dial him down and undo some of the whispers that were likely already racing around the ship after his jealous display in the dining hall.

He dropped into step beside me but remained silent. If I'd learned anything about him in the time we'd known each other, it was that he didn't talk much. He let me talk plenty and asked questions, but unless asked something directly, he kept his thoughts to himself.

That wasn't going to work if we were going to move forward, and I very much wanted to. I liked the idea of my future being here with him, even if it meant sharing his attention and affection.

"If Ana was agreeable to us being together, why are you opposed to her also finding someone else?"

His gait grew stiff and I could feel the tension exploding in him again. Maybe I should have left the attempt at trying to help to the Seekers.

"She's mine," he said sullenly.

"And you're hers, but here you are. With me."

He bowed his head and his pace began to lag. "I shouldn't be."

"Do you regret the days we've had together?"

"No," he said without hesitation.

Did I want to hear the answer? Going back to Brustus after immersing myself in a taste of what life beside Vayen could be like was a dismal thought. I imagined telling Elonka that I'd walked away from the opportunity to join with Vayen. That wasn't a conversation I wanted to have.

"Do you want me to leave?" I asked hesitantly.

He grabbed my hand and pulled me against him. "No. Buria, please, don't ever leave."

With no care for the fact we were in a public corridor, I melted into his arms, reveling in his embrace, knowing we were being seen and that he was doing it anyway.

When he let go, I stayed right beside him, keeping to our slow pace as we walked. Once our week was over, even if it ended well, I wouldn't have this freedom with him again. Ana would always have public priority. I would need to maintain a tasteful distance, a degree of separation in deference to her. She'd gifted us this time and had asked that I give very little in return. One of those things was to keep my hands off him in public. But I couldn't. Not for these few days. I'd have to attempt to make up for my lapse in decorum.

I glanced at the silent, sullen man next to me. "I would prefer to never leave, but that's not up to me. Nor is it solely up to you."

He nodded the slightest bit. "Did she really approach you about this? About coming here? About being with me? On her own?"

I pictured Ana's face when she'd shown up at my apartment. I'd seen versions of it on too many women on Tacesh: resolved to her fate. But that wasn't what he was asking, nor what he wanted to hear. "She was alone, yes. She was civil and asked very little of me, considering."

He let out a loud groan. "I don't know if I can do that."

If he truly wanted me to stay, he would have to.

"Perhaps you should talk to her. Before what happened back there becomes an insurmountable obstacle."

"She's with him, that Jalvian," he snarled.

"It wouldn't hurt to apologize to him too," I suggested carefully, knowing I was treading dangerously close to telling him what to do. One did not tell the Advisor what he should or shouldn't do. Karin's Premier had made that quite clear when I'd worked for him. "You wouldn't want Ana threatening me in any way."

"I didn't threaten him."

Was he seriously pretending no one had seen the obvious? "You were going to kill him."

Vayen looked like he was going to punch something. I quickly put the distance I should have been keeping between us.

"I need a drink," he decreed as we reached the door to the suite Ana had provided for me.

"That's probably not the best course of action if you're going to talk to Ana."

He hit the panel with far more force than necessary and shouldered his way inside the moment the door opened. He headed straight for the bottles she'd left for him.

When I reached the little kitchen, he had a clear bottle of something green and almost opalescent in his hands. He stared at it but made no move to open it.

"What is that?" I hazarded to ask, hoping to get him talking about a neutral topic.

"There's a smashed bottle of this on the wall in our suite right now," he said quietly. "She's been drinking. A lot. Her wine rack is empty and she doesn't drink this. Ever."

He'd stayed away from her until he'd Jumped back to their suite to change after his sons had shown up. I'd been too excited about being seen in public with him to anticipate that his true intention had been to head right for Ana to see if what the boys had said was true.

"It sounds like she misses you."

Vayen set the bottle down and sagged into a chair at the table. "It sounds like she's not all right, Buria." He dropped his head into his hands. "I keep pushing her into things she doesn't want. None of this is her way, not just her people, I mean her. She never wanted me to bond with her, to join with me, to have kids. And Geva knows she doesn't want me to be with you."

I sat across from him. "But she's done all those things. She must love you very much. The Ana I've dealt with, the one the Premier warned us about, the one I saw in the dining hall today, doesn't give in to anyone."

"She doesn't," he whispered.

"She does for you." I reached for his hand. "Maybe in return..."

He glared at me. "You don't understand. The bond I have with her, I can't stand to see her with anyone else, to even think that she might indulge herself with someone else like we are. To consider any of it, makes me want to—"

"Kill someone?"

He nodded.

"What if you didn't know? I mean, you'd know, but not have it made obvious. What if however often you are with me, she gets time with him? I could distract you."

"I want to be with you far more than I want her to be with him."

I had to know where the situation stood. "But you do also still want to be with her?"

His gaze snapped to me with an intensity that made me wonder if

I'd accidentally just told him to fuck off. I made a note to never question his commitment to Ana again.

"Of course you do," I said as though it had never been a legitimate question. "Perhaps, it would be wise for us to give up this one night to make peace with Ana."

"She's probably spending it with whatever his name was," he growled.

"I bet that if you showed up to talk to her, she'd kick him out in a heartbeat."

He had a mesmerizing way of staring into me, but I didn't get the sensation that he was in my head, not like when the Premier had penetrated our minds.

"I wouldn't kick you out. Why would I expect her to?"

It might not be in a matter of seconds, but I had a feeling that if Ana arrived at our door and asked anything of him, he'd do it. I pondered my answer for a moment, glad he was receptive, that he was talking at all given how angry he'd been, but desperately not wanting to ask the wrong questions and set him off all over again.

"Do you know him? The Jalvian she was with? Has she ever mentioned him?"

"No."

"Does she often keep secrets from you? Would she have been interested in him and hidden it?"

"Not anymore. She's never given me any reason to think she's been interested in anyone else."

"Then maybe she's not."

He gave me a doubtful look. "She sure acted like she was."

"You were going to kill him. Maybe she didn't want his death on your hands with Etara around."

That made him pause. "I forgot about Etara."

A wave of satisfaction rushed over me. He'd been too wrapped up in us to remember the keeper of his death key was onboard.

He glanced at the bottle of green liquor and turned back to me. "You'll be here when I get back? Whenever that might be?"

"I promise."

He stood and then leaned over to plant a kiss on my cheek before walking out the door. I prayed Ana was in a forgiving mood because I wanted him back as soon as possible. This was my time and she'd better not keep him all night.

TWELVE

Anastassia

Tabor led the way, meandering through the public corridors. He allowed me emotional space, silently walking beside me at a leisurely pace as if nothing had happened. I appreciated that greatly.

My mind was spinning, but every line of thought brought me back up against a wall. I could turn off Vayen's bond on my end but he couldn't. I knew he'd have issues with me taking a second but I'd never entertained the thought of actually doing so until now. Toying with the crew had been in the hopes of getting his attention, maybe getting even a little.

Now, after meeting Tabor, I found it irritating that I might have to sacrifice my chance of any degree of happiness with him for the sake of keeping Vayen in Etara's good graces. I hadn't realized how lightly I'd been tiptoeing around my explosive mate until experiencing easy comradery with Tabor.

My prospective second had motivations that were understandable, relatable, and familiar. He had an easy-going personality, and he made me laugh even at a time such as this. Tabor didn't remind me of anyone else. He wasn't threatening, yet he seemed willing to hold his own if pushed to it. I could see myself maybe not loving him, but liking him if given enough time.

If Vayen wanted Buria, I wanted this one consolation, someone I could talk to, a neutral party I could vent with once we'd established trust between us. Someone who made me laugh when I felt like crying.

I glanced at Tabor beside me.

But nothing was about me anymore. My options were to give Vayen his way or watch him die when rage took over.

I wasn't willing to watch him die. It all came down to whether

I'd pushed him enough to allow me to be equal in this version of our relationship. Was there enough of him still lurking behind his Arpex-hardened skin to love me the way he'd proclaimed outside of Buria's door?

"I was thinking," Tabor said, pausing our walk by one of the view ports to take in the stars surrounding the Iber, "that I might stay here for a few days. Maybe get to know you a little more and get a feel for what you do here?"

"You'd want to with Mr. Kill-with-a-thought lurking nearby?"

Tabor shrugged. "I trust that you'll protect me. I mean, at least let me have a real dinner with you before you let him snuff me out?"

I could definitely grow to like him.

"I can assign you a room, but this wasn't exactly a planned trip for you. Don't you have business to return to?"

He tapped his temple. "Not your typical Jalvian, remember? I can work from here just fine. Besides, I'm sure you don't want me lurking over your shoulder every moment. You've got four days, right? Promise me one dinner and know that I'm available for you anytime if you want company beyond that."

I changed my estimate of how long it would take to grow to like him from weeks to days.

"I'd like that." I pulled out my datapad and made the arrangements. I started toward the room I'd assigned to him. It wasn't all that far from mine. "I'm returning to the surface tomorrow for further negotiations. Would you like to join me?"

"Is the populace peaceful?"

"They're undecided. Hence the negotiations."

"Would I be a problem? I'd rather not be the one responsible for injury to you or cause a social disaster because I stopped to pick the wrong flower."

"One thing. Never give me flowers." Vayen had done that the whole time Ikeri had been missing. Back when I thought I was enough, that we were fine, that our future was just the two of us.

"That's your one thing?" He chuckled. "I won't even ask. Done. No flowers for you."

"Thank you. As for accompanying me, I don't think the situation is quite as tenuous as that."

"Then I would enjoy watching you work. Let me know if there's anything I can do to assist you."

Not days. Hours. Damn. I'd hated plenty of people in less than two hours, but it was rare that I liked anyone that quickly.

"I'll do that. Here we are." I stopped in front of his door. "You can use your link to find a full map of the Iber if you'd like to explore. I've given you clearance to all public areas."

He put his hand on the access panel but pulled it back before the door opened. "Are you going to be all right? You're welcome to come in, you know, to the room you've given me on your ship." He laughed to himself. "What I mean is, if you'd rather not be alone, I'm perfectly fine with existing silently, or not, in the same room with you for as long as you'd like to stay. No touching unless invited to do so, I promise."

"That's very kind of you, and while I do appreciate all of your offer and may take you up on it another time, I sadly do have work to attend to, children to chastise, and a call I need to make." I took a step back to put distance between us in case he got any ideas. "It was very nice meeting you, Tabor. I'll have an aide find you when we're ready tomorrow."

"Thank you, Anastassia. I look forward to tomorrow." He offered me a charming smile, half-bow combo and entered his room.

Feeling considerably lighter, I contemplated returning all the boost to the container. Tabor might well be uplifting enough to keep my true feelings on Vayen being with Buria in check. I headed back to my suite, considering how much I wanted to inflate Neko's ego when I called to tell him that he was right.

The light was on when I entered. I reached for a weapon seconds before I spotted Vayen bent over, picking glass off the floor.

"What the hell are you doing here", "The bot can get it", and "You came back already?" all exited my mouth at the same time.

He dropped the glass in his hand and spun around. "What?"

"Nothing. I...didn't expect to see you back so soon, but I'm glad you're here."

"Are you?"

Ignoring his snarky reply, I wrapped my arms around him. If he was home, he wasn't with Buria. Did she not like angry Vayen? Maybe she'd stormed off. I didn't care. I stood there, with my ear pressed against his chest, breathing easier to the sound of his heart-beat. Without a second thought, I opened my end of our bonded connection, pouring my relief into him. He was home. I could let his four days with Buria go and we'd be fine.

"Stassia," he breathed my name.

I melted every damned time he did that. Forgetting all that had happened outside our door, I held him. Everything inside me fell back into the places where it should be, as if the universe had suddenly been set back to rights.

He rested his forehead onto mine. "I should take a shower," he said after a moment.

"I'll be right here." I let go of him and sat on the stool by the kitchen counter.

While he washed Buria off him, I pondered what I wanted to do. Part of me wanted to reclaim what she'd taken, but on the other hand, was I ready to forgive him quite that easily? My heart said yes, but my mind was not on board, especially now that the initial relief of having him back with me had worn off. Getting angry would only chase him right out the door. I needed some answers before I decided whether I wanted him to stay or not.

While I could still hear the water running, I ducked into the closet and applied one tasteless drop of boost to my tongue. As I returned to my seat to wait, I wondered if it would work, and would it be enough?

When he emerged from the shower and slinked into the kitchen wearing only a towel, his hair still dripping wet, the evidence of what he'd been doing with Buria was starkly obvious. No matter how restored to right the universe might be, I couldn't ignore that.

"You're into being bitten now?"

Panic flashed over his normally schooled face. "Oh fuck. I'm sorry. I should have..."

He was here and with me. I took a deep breath. "I'll let it go this one time. But if you choose to visit Buria again this week, yes, you should erase all of that before showing up here. How is she able to do that with your altered skin?"

His gaze dropped to the floor. "Bang allows me to feel more and with enough slow pressure..." he said quietly.

I watched his pupils when he hesitantly glanced up at me. It didn't appear he was on anything now. Ironically, I was.

If he'd used bang, maybe he'd burned through his lust for Buria. Or maybe he was using it to ease his conscience. Assuming he had a conscience left that needed easing.

I didn't want to consider what else he might be doing. Vayen had only ever been with me physically. Buria had a whole different skillset when it came to sex. Clearly, she was willing to employ everything she had to offer, and he was eating it up.

Vayen used his link to lower the lights, masking what his flesh couldn't hide.

He was here with me, I repeated to myself again. Forgiveness would come in time. I hoped. A fuzzy feeling softened my ire and relaxed my muscles. The boost appeared to be working.

If there was to be any accord between us, any hope for future forgiveness, I was going to have to swallow my true feelings on the matter and go along with the offer I'd presented. Not only to keep him near me but to see if I truly wanted to still be with him, if I could put my hurt feelings aside. I could, I chanted internally as I reached out and pulled Vayen closer.

"Damn, I've missed you," he said before kissing me senseless while doing wonderful things in my head.

I'd barely started returning the favor when I realized he was already close. I pulled away. Forgiveness wasn't even in the room yet.

"Four days? I think you owe me before I'm ready to grant you release."

He nodded, his mind and body buzzing with anticipation.

Boost tingled in my veins, tempering my biting comments into the domineering demands he liked. If he was going to screw around with a trained sex slave, I might as well benefit from it.

"Show me what you've learned."

He paused to look at me as if asking if I was really going there. Damned right, I was.

"Well?"

The next thing I knew, I was up against the wall beside the sticky green residue writhing with pleasure, followed by a couple of minutes sitting at the perfect height on the counter and then bent over the back of the couch until I saw stars. I gave him his due and we stood together, heaving until we caught our breath.

Boost may not have been the sexual intoxicant bang was rumored to be, but the stimulant it offered made everything more enjoyable, softened the edges. I didn't know whether to be thankful that Vayen didn't notice I was on anything or annoyed. Being angry seemed like too much work. I let it go.

Just when I was ready to straighten up and decide whether I wanted to talk to him or enjoy his warmth next to me as I slept, he leaned over and whispered, "We're not finished."

He picked me up and deposited me on our bed where he went to work with his tongue, fingers, and mind until I shuddered and begged for him to give me a minute to breathe.

None of this was new exactly, but there was certainly an element of renewed vigor that I could appreciate in my distant state. As far as experiments went, this one was flawed due to the drug, but it had kept my temper in check. As long as I had boost, I felt mostly confident that I could eventually forgive him.

If he never went back to her, that would be much easier. I put on an alluring smile. "Would you like—"

He caught my hand as I reached for him and kissed it. "I'm good."

"That you are." Boost may have had a lot to do with my assessment, but in the interest of keeping our relationship going, I stood by my statement.

He chuckled, dropping onto the bed. Once the mattress had absorbed his lumberous fall, I curled up next to him. The bed felt perfect with his weight on it beside me. The room was just the correct temperature with his body heat. He draped his arm over me and pulled me closer. I closed my eyes, feeling secure that I'd done the right thing by letting him have his few indulgent days. I had my mate beside me again.

When I woke three hours later, Vayen wasn't in bed and the effects of the drug were gone, leaving me irritable and wanting to punch Buria in the face even though she was doing exactly what I'd given her permission to do.

I sat up, slipped off the mattress, and grabbed the first item of clothing my hand located. Pulling on one of Vayen's shirts that was on the floor, my sleep-fogged brain started to clear. There was no light or sound in the bathroom. I crept out of the bedroom, heart pounding. If he'd stopped by only to have sex and then had run back to Buria, I was going to scream.

I found Vayen sitting at the table in the dark, his head in his hands. He looked up, startled as my arrival triggered the lights to flicker on in their dim nighttime setting. I wanted to be relieved that he was there, still in our suite, but the mournful look on his face led me to drop into the chair across from him. The room took on an eerie distant feel. I shivered.

"I was supposed to come here to talk to you," he said after a while.

I thought about what he'd said on his knees outside Buria's suite. He might have come to talk, but his one-track mind had gotten distracted by what she couldn't give him.

I was nothing more than a pit stop.

Anger boiled up but then fizzled for lack of energy. An emptiness swelled inside me, making my mouth dry and leeching all heat from my body. Though there was plenty of boost in the closet drawer, this wasn't a conversation that I could distantly fake my way through.

"I was supposed to apologize for wanting to kill...what's his name?"

"Tabor Desu."

He'd flipped into kill mode without even listening. Tabor could have died and been nothing more than a blip in Vayen's extensive body count.

I thought of the kind man I'd come to like in a single meeting and recovered enough energy to snap, "He could have been anyone discussing business for any reason, and your first reaction when seeing me after four days was to kill whomever was talking to me?"

Vayen's gaze dropped to his hands on the table. "Daniel and Markus told me who he was. What he was."

That was their plan? Poke the bonded death-bringer? My children were idiots just like their father. Their very jealous father.

"He has a name. Use it."

"Stassia, don't do this."

"It was never my intention to hurt you by finding someone for myself. You started this second mate business. If you want to follow through with it, you're going to have to accept the whole deal and set a good example for your people. Daniel has already ignited a movement that's in danger of escalating beyond a heated debate. If we're going to join it, we're going to show them how it's properly done for both partners."

"Why a Jalvian?" he asked in a tone that made me wonder if he'd ever truly gotten over his disdain for the other half of his long-separated race.

"Bringing your people together? Have you forgotten about that?"

"No," he grumbled. "But why that one?"

I was pretty sure Tabor would have mentioned crossing Vayen before, but we had only just met. "Do you two have a history I'm not aware of?"

"No." Vayen glared at me. "Do you?"

"No. He's the brother of Rok's Prime. Neko suggested him. We just met for the first time today. Feel free to peruse my memories if you don't believe me."

Openly abashed, he glanced away.

I crossed my arms over my chest, wishing I'd taken the time to get fully dressed before we'd launched into this dismal conversation. The room seemed to be getting colder by the second.

He'd used *supposed to* twice, indicating Buria had enough sway over him to tell him what to do or at least heavily suggest a correct course of action. I distantly appreciated her thoughtfulness as though I were an outside observer watching our joining fall apart.

I blurted, "Do you even need the rest of the week or have you made up your mind already?"

"I've asked Buria to stay."

And that was that. In those five words, the future I'd imagined for us evaporated.

"I see," I forced out before my throat closed off.

"You can have the four days with…Tabor," he forced the name out like it was the hardest thing he'd ever done. "While I finish out my week with Buria. We can arrange a schedule after we make things official. I suppose, if we're setting an example, that should include a ceremony of some sort."

The way he was with ceremonies? That was sure to cause more of a disaster than Neko needed to deal with. "Let's just file the proper documentation and leave it at that."

"Stassia, I'm sorry," he said earnestly. "I meant every word I said before. I do love you. I'd rip out my heart and give it to you if that would make you believe me."

"It's not that I don't believe you."

It was that neither of us were who we used to be. Through the memories he'd shared with me and the ones we'd made since the Arpex had eaten my own, it was clear I'd let him sway me all along this journey we'd been sharing together. I didn't regret being with him or our children, but I couldn't foresee a time when I would look back at this moment and be all right with it. It felt like the end.

Our bonded connection was wide open and I didn't hide any-thing, hoping to give him pause, to make him stay, to declare he'd send Buria home after the week was done. If he would, I'd send Tabor packing without hesitation.

"Stassia, I've tried ignoring this. I truly have. It's not something I can just turn off."

He sounded as miserable as I felt. Buria was a distraction he desperately needed to keep himself under control according to Etara. And he'd been struggling with his urges long before I'd set up the trial week with Buria. Fucking hell, he'd been pining for her for years.

If I adamantly refused him adding a second mate to our joining, he'd resent the hell out of me. Angry Vayen wouldn't last long, no matter how reluctant Etara might be to cull my mate. I couldn't put our children or the crew through his tirades until her tolerance came to an end and she was forced to end his life. My choices were to allow this or lose him forever.

"You have Tabor. Go distract yourself with him. I'm willing to give you what you want."

No, he wasn't. What I wanted was him alone. Us alone. That he was willing to allow me to be with someone else despite our bond was a testament to how badly he wanted Buria. Of how much I fell short. Of how I was no longer enough and hadn't been for years.

I tried to swallow but my throat had gone dry. I stared at my trembling hands on my lap, unable to look at him.

Though Vayen was willing to give me Tabor, I'd been very wrong. One consolation wasn't enough. There was no balance maintained. A man I'd just met for one who'd been beside me half of my life? One I might like for one I loved dearly, who knew all of me?

This wasn't sharing. This was being cut off, replaced, and shoved aside. I'd thought we were fine. Better than fine. Good. And all that time he'd been wanting someone else and had almost gone off the dark deep end rather than talk to me about it?

That someone I loved so much could deceive me for so long cut deeply. So deeply that my heart had taken on an erratic beat and my breath came in shallow little gasps. I couldn't remember having a full-fledged breakdown since Chesser had died in my arms.

Fighting to regain control, I forced myself to look at him, hoping to see that he understood what he was doing to me, praying to anyone who might be listening that he'd change his mind. But he was staring at the door. Like he couldn't get away from me fast enough.

"This will all work out. Just give it time, you'll see," he said with conviction as he stood.

He fucking stood. He was going to leave me and go back to her, knowing full well how upset I was, feeling it through our bonded connection. He was able to disregard it all. He was willing to.

I stared at the man I thought I'd known inside and out, who had shared memories of how much he'd loved me countless times.

His second bond wasn't like the surefire connection that had tied us together before. As Etara had said, he'd changed. Not that either bond had ever been what it should be, but I'd thought it was enough. It wasn't.

When he leaned over to kiss me, I let him, returning nothing, numb. If anyone's heart was getting ripped out, it was mine.

"I'll see you in four days, Stassia. I'll make them up to you. I promise."

There was nothing he could do to make up for choosing someone else. Someone in addition to me. For allowing me to think we had a future together and then tearing it away.

I was no longer his peace, and contrary to what he'd said, he wasn't willing to put his desires aside to be the mate I wanted. Unable to move, I watched him leave.

I could have shut down my end of the bonded connection again, but I clung to it, not wanting to let him go. I waited for a hint of love from him, some acknowledgment that I was still there, that he could feel what I was feeling, but all I got from him was a little uncertainty. He had to have muffled his end as much as he was able. Yet, I didn't get the sense that he didn't care or that he was oblivious.

It occurred to me that his stubborn ass didn't *want* to feel what I was feeling. He truly believed what he'd said, that we'd be fine, that we just needed time to adjust.

Time wasn't going to make a damned bit of difference.

After closing off my end of the worthless bonded connection, I went into the closet to open the drawer where I'd hidden the vials Tabor had delivered. Boost promised a flow of endorphins that would mask the devastation. But I had no reason to mask anything. Vayen wasn't here and he didn't care what my feelings were. The foundation that I'd built my memories on, of us, who we were to each other, shattered.

I didn't have to wait for Etara to flip his switch. I'd already lost him. He just wasn't ready to admit it yet.

He had her now, the woman he'd been talking to for years, yearning for, who would indulge him in whatever the fuck he wanted. Who, after four days in his bed, could tell him what he was supposed to do and he'd run off and do it. Fuck. Give Buria a week or two to get under his skin and all of his hells would freeze over before he'd bother with me again, no matter how much boost I poured down my throat to pretend I could accept this.

He didn't care if I could. I no longer mattered.

I yanked off his shirt and threw it on the floor, stepping on it as I pulled on a comfortable shirt and pants of my own.

I left the closet, curled up in the middle of the cold bed, and let the breakdown shatter me. Hours passed as hollowness swallowed me whole. Even with all the blankets, I couldn't stop shaking, couldn't get warm.

A sense of desolation permeated every breath, seeping into every pore until every thought was darkness. The one certainty in my life was gone. I'd been through heartache before, been betrayed more times than I wanted to count, but this, was this what it felt like when a bond broke? I couldn't imagine a more intensely devastating pain.

The conversation I'd had with Etara played back in my head. Would I be here on the Iber if it wasn't for him?

The end goal of this mission had been to set up the advisory union so we could step back and finally enjoy one another, knowing we'd done all we could for everyone else. The future was supposed to be our time.

The promise of our time wasn't enough for him, not even now with everything else we were doing. His version of our time included other people. That wasn't us, not what I'd spent all these years working toward, not the reward for everything we'd gone through together.

This was his mission, one I'd embarked on for him. He had everything he wanted. I'd wanted one thing and now that was gone.

We no longer had a future. Why was I even here?

My stomach twisted and clenched. Bile rose in my throat. I ran to the bathroom and emptied my stomach into the toilet. If only I could expel my heart too.

Sitting on the floor next to the toilet, all the moisture left in my body poured out of my eyes. I reached up to the counter with a trembling hand to locate a towel. Burying my face in it until it was difficult to breathe, I pondered whether that was worth the effort either.

If he could disregard me and the bond we shared, I no longer held much say in keeping him alive. That was in Etara's hands. And Buria's. He'd shown me just how much he cared about her.

Maybe there was another choice in this shitty situation, one where I didn't have to stick around to become fully obsolete. One where he could move ahead with a clearer conscience, where he wouldn't have to hold himself back from what he truly wanted any longer. A choice that allowed for the mission Etara felt was benefitting so many worlds to continue to move forward.

One more sacrifice, but on my terms.

I slowly got to my knees, dropping the towel on the floor. Using the counter, I pulled myself up. My feet shuffled on the carpet, each step a trial to pass before taking another one. I had no idea how long it took me to get back to the side of the bed. Once there, I tumbled to the floor on lifeless legs, pulling open the drawers that lined the bed frame. My bleary eyes viewed my exposed arsenal.

The kids didn't need me. Daniel and Ikeri had lives of their own. Markus had always been far more Vayen's child than mine. Did I want them doting on me, watching my every move, analyzing every look to see if I was all right? Hell no.

I wasn't all right and I never would be again.

The mission didn't need me. Daniel had a firm grasp of what we'd set out to do and assisted both of us regularly. Ikeri, Etara, and the host of other specialists we'd gathered, required nothing from me to go about their work. This was Vayen's redemption tour, not mine.

Neko and Isnar had lives of their own, jobs they excelled at. Both of them regularly asked for advice, but more often than not, it seemed like they just wanted to check in with me, not that they needed my input.

For a moment, I considered opening my bonded connection again, to let Vayen know what I was thinking, what I intended to do. Would he show up in an instant to stop me? Would he brush this off as a bout of melancholy I'd get over in time?

I ran my hands over the host of weaponry, seeking out what felt right.

Did I want him to show up to stop me? Would the further confirmation that he could ignore my feelings make the hurt any greater?

No on both counts.

Who would find me? What did I want them to see, the last image to remember me by?

It would likely be one of the kids or Vayen himself. No need for a tragic image, nothing to clean up. Something that looked natural. I picked up my little black case and opened it to expose the assortment of vials and tiny bottles.

I pulled out a dropper-topped brown bottle and held it up to the light. Something that would end the pain in my heart that had now permeated every cell in my body. A pain the tank couldn't erase. But this could.

Three drops would do it and there was plenty there.

Detached, I watched my fingers draw fluid into the dropper and unscrew the top. I put the case away and closed the drawers. Sitting there, clutching the bottle, I tipped my head back on the bed we'd shared, smelling him on the sheet dangling next to me. Time seemed to slow as I thought back on the years we'd had together, the ones I remembered and those flavored by memories that he'd given me.

My hand shook as I drew the dropper from the bottle.

The clear fluid had a bluish tint. It would be tasteless. One drop would slow my heart, make me sleepy, weak. Two would put me out in seconds, a sleep I may or may not wake up from. Three would fully stop my heart in less than a minute, relax me to death. Not a terrible way to go. No mess. No fuss. Quick and easy.

I lifted the dropper and opened my mouth. Squeezing out a single drop, I watched it fall toward me in slow motion. A tear of mercy.

Would he cry for me? Would he mourn?

My conviction faltered before the drop hit my tongue. What if my death was the thing that sent him into full wrath mode when what little bond we did have shattered on his end? How many casualties would that cause?

This might be a no-mess solution for me, but broken-bonded Vayen would mean chaos for everyone else.

The drop landed.

I frantically wiped my tongue.

Fuck. I should get to the tank, flush the effects from my system, but who could I contact to help me? Was I prepared to tell Daniel what I'd almost done? Vayen? Neko or Isnar? Of the linked options that had tank access, every answer was hell no.

Getting to my feet, I stumbled out of the bedroom. In the back of my mind, I knew I shouldn't be alone, not with even a single drop in my system. I wasn't exactly young and with all the heavy drinking I'd been doing, my body wasn't in ideal condition.

I could get to the infirmary and have someone monitor me there. But they'd ask why, and what I was on, and they'd be concerned. They wouldn't chance pissing Vayen off should something happen to me. They'd notify him immediately. Dammit.

Leaving the suite, I made every effort to keep my steps sure, to keep my eyes open and my words clear when I greeted crewmembers as I passed them. My feet brought me to the door I'd left hours before, full of intentions to be busy, productive, to try to move forward. Vayen had derailed all of that. I put my hand on the access panel, sending a chime I could barely hear from outside to alert Tabor that someone was at his door.

I held onto the wall, feeling my heart slow, my body growing lethargic. My eyes yearned to close.

The door opened after a few moments. Tabor blinked in the bright light of the corridor. "Anastassia?" he said sleepily.

"May I come in?" My words slurred together.

"Of course." He stood aside.

My rubbery feet tripped over one another three steps in. The door closed. Tabor reached out to steady me, one hand on my arm, the other around my waist. I supposed keeping me from falling on my face was a valid invitation to touch me.

"Need to sit," I mumbled, my head swimming.

My hands went numb. The unmarked, generic bottle fell from my fingers to roll on the floor in front of me.

"What did you do?" The nighttime lighting in his room might have masked his face, but fear was plenty clear in this voice. "Anastassia, talk to me. What is that?"

He guided me to the couch and then let go to retrieve the bottle and turn the lights on to full brightness.

He was back beside me an instant later, one hand on my forehead, the other rubbing my hand. "Good Geva, you're too cold. Anastassia, what did you do? Do I need to get you to someone? Shall I take you to the infirmary? Where's your mate?"

"He's going through with it." My voice was only a whisper. "He was there waiting to tell me when I went back to my room. I didn't think he really would. I didn't want to think he would."

"That doesn't answer any of my questions." He shook me gently. "What's in the damned bottle?"

"Didn't want to leave a mess. Supposed to be easier." I waved a numb hand at the bottle. "Changed my mind. Second too late. Need to sleep. If my heart stops, you can find him." I gave up trying to keep my eyes open.

THIRTEEN

Anastassia

When I woke, I found myself on Tabor's couch, my head on his chest where he'd fallen asleep propping me up, one arm over my shoulder. In the quiet of the dark room, I listened to his soft breathing and the heartbeat next to my ear.

It wasn't the one I knew.

The realization that I needed to use the bathroom goaded me to pry myself off Tabor's warmth. After washing my face and putting my hazy memories in enough order to recall what had brought me here, I made my way back to him and dropped into the chair across from the couch. He was awake and watching me.

The bottle sat on the narrow table between us.

"Thank you," I said, nodding at the couch. "I didn't know where else to go."

He nodded. "So, the second joining is happening?"

"Yes." The floor seemed to drop away from the chair where I sat. The ice-filled, detached feeling from the night before again took hold.

"Are you hungry?"

The thought of food made the knots in my stomach twist even tighter. "No."

He frowned and gave me a hard look. "Am I correct in understanding that you nearly ended your life last night?"

I stared at the bottle. "I can't do this."

"You'd rather be dead than spend a couple of days a week with me?"

He'd be spending those couple days with her. Hell, I was going to have to negotiate how much time I would get to spend with my mate. I both didn't want to spend any time with Vayen at all ever again and also every moment I could get. Damn him.

"I never wanted a second, to share him, to have the future I'd dreamed of ripped away. He knew damned well how much he hurt me last night, and he just walked out the door. My mate left me," I said, knowing full well that I was on the edge of breaking down all over again in front of a man I barely knew. "This has nothing to do with you."

His jaw went tight. "You offered me the one thing in the universe that I've wanted since I was twelve, and now you're telling me that you dying and taking that away doesn't involve me?"

"If you so dearly desire to be a political pawn, I can set that up with Neko. It doesn't require me being around."

He shot to his feet, looking as angry as any full-blooded Jalvian I'd ever seen. "I don't want a fucking consolation prize, Anastassia, and I wasn't talking about the bonus of harassing my brother. Neko can't set me up with another woman like you. There's only one."

"You barely know me."

"Perhaps not, but I have studied you extensively."

"I hate to poke holes in your story, but I wasn't the big catch of an Advisor when you were twelve. There were no Advisors in the Narvan then. It was all threats and war and no me in sight."

His gaze narrowed, but otherwise, his composed demeanor returned. "I'm well aware. Artor and Jal were at odds before I was born, but in my grandmother's time, they were more tolerant. I was twelve when my brother maimed me for having a degree of Artorian blood in my veins. Since that day, I've wanted to live in a time where I could be accepted, where I could be part of a movement of tolerance instead of the byproduct of a period that no longer existed. And then this outsider woman shows up, knowing all the right people, ending the war, and bringing about the time I'd been dreaming of. Your history is vague in many places, Anastassia, but you're a fascinating woman. I would love to get to know you better, to work beside you, to help in any way I can."

"You're part Artorian."

"That's the one thing you heard?" he snarled.

I rubbed my hands over my face and took a deep shuddering breath, exhaling slowly. "I heard all of it. Sit."

Rather than return to his seat, he settled onto the table directly in front of me, his legs bracketing mine for lack of room. "I never thought I'd get to meet you. I mean, I hoped I would at some point when I was serving in the military. You were known to pop up now and then, but the closest I got was a stern glare from Advisor Te once on an exploration mission outside of the Narvan.

"I wasn't even in the Narvan then. I was off raising babies elsewhere."

He shrugged. "When Neko contacted me, when he said you wanted to meet me, I dropped everything."

Just like Buria had. I rubbed my hands over my face, wishing for... I didn't even know what. My imagination couldn't come up with even a semi-acceptable alternative to any of this.

"I'm sure you're regretting that now, seeing what a mess I really am." Feeling lightheaded, I held onto the chair, assuring myself that this unbelievably shitty reality was indeed real.

His hand hovered over mine, not quite touching. He seemed to realize what he was doing and pulled back. "Your situation is messy, I will grant you that. Your mate is a terrifying man." He shook his head. "You are not a mess. You're not wired like he is. That's no fault of yours. Pardon me saying so, but he's a fool for not seeing what he's doing to you."

"Oh, he sees. He's just totally enraptured by the option now available to him. One that's new and far more distracting from everything in his head than me. Last night, he told me that I just needed to give it time and everything would work out."

Tabor glanced at the bottle next to him. "Taking yourself out of the equation was your version of everything working out?"

I nodded. "I was supposed to take three drops, but it occurred to me during the first one that he'd gone off the rails when our bond broke before. If he did that again, as he is now, he might well take the entire Iber with him."

"So you're stuck. Damned if you stay and damned if you leave."

"Yes."

"All right then." He stood and pocketed the bottle.

"I have plenty of other options," I said, pointing at his pocket. "Drawers full of them."

"Noted." He watched me a moment, a calculating tilt to his head. "As much as I'd love to go down to the surface and watch you bend this world to your will, you're not up for it today." He held up a hand. "No arguing. You're not, and you shouldn't be alone, so you're going to stay here."

I sank deeper into the chair, my limbs heavy. "That's exactly what he told me to do, distract myself with you for four days. Like that will make me forget he's off screwing someone else. I don't want a fucking trade-off."

"How gracious of him."

Tabor sounded as annoyed with Vayen as I was. That made me feel a fraction better.

"I don't know as I'm all that distracting, but I'll give it a shot. In the meantime, who can bring you what you need to stay here for a few days?"

"I can walk down the damned corridor and get what I need."

"No," he said firmly. "You nearly killed yourself in that suite last night. No going there alone to examine your other options. He wants you to embrace the new arrangement, to accept the concession he's made." He rolled his eyes. "An absolute fool. Let me tell you, if I were bonded to you there's no way in all nine hells I'd even look at anyone else."

"He didn't used to." Tabor was part Artorian. "Please tell me that you can't bond to me."

"I don't think so. The Jalvian blood overruled the genetic manipulations full Artorians carry. I'm stuck with what comes naturally to our people. However, there is one thing I could do, if you'd allow it?"

If he wanted me to join him in bed for a demonstration of his woman-pleasing skills as a method of distraction, I was far from in the mood.

A giddy grin broke out on his face, making his eyes twinkle. "You do have a degree of mind speech, right?"

"Not as much as I used to, but yes."

He sat back down, and this time he did grab my hand. Having passed out on his chest the night before, I didn't begrudge him a little physical contact.

"I've never done this with anyone before. Hells, I've never told anyone I could before. My family thinks I'm enough of a freak already. "Could I talk to you mind to mind? Like full Artorians do?"

No wonder he was so comfortable with using his link.

"I suppose we'll be spending a considerable amount of time together. It wouldn't hurt to try."

His grin melted into a lip twist of concentration.

I didn't feel anything to accept or deny. If he'd never done this before, maybe he didn't know how to establish initial contact.

"Let me try."

I reached out to his mind, seeking out any part of it I could sync with. His mind wasn't quite like other Artorians, a slightly different flavor, similar but different. Maybe this was how they used to be before the Jalvian half stamped out any inclination toward mind speech and Artorians went full in.

Thanks to my Seeker training, I recognized the wall he'd constructed for what it was, a thick protective barrier that kept everyone out and himself securely locked inside. By the time I'd made it through his defenses and made contact, I had a headache.

"You've never done this before?" I asked.

His jaw dropped. "Is that what it sounds like? Of course it is, you're talking to me. How do I..." His brow furrowed.

"Like this?" he asked hesitantly.

I nodded.

"I can talk to you like this anytime now that we've done it? Now that we have a connection?"

"Yes."

"Can this be our secret? If I'm to spend time here, I'd like the crew to accept me as a fellow Jalvian, not look at me like I'm an aberration."

"Of course."

His grin returned and then he realized he was holding my hand and let go. "I'm sorry. I got caught up there for a moment." He cleared his throat. "While I'm at it..." Tabor shifted forward off the table to land on his knees in front of me.

Fuck. Not another man on his knees. The last one had ripped my heart out.

"Don't do that."

He remained as he was. "Anastassia, if you'll have me, I vow to never set you aside for another woman. Or man. Or anyone. Ever. I will share you with no one but your mate. I will not bond with you or ask you to bear children. I will do my best to make you happy in whatever manner you're comfortable with in whatever time you choose to spend with me. Do you accept my offer?"

"I've heard a version of those vows before and look where I am."

He dug into his pocket and handed me the bottle. "If I break my word, you stop my heart."

"You're willing to openly put your life in my hands?"

"I am," he said without hesitation.

I looked upon the face that wasn't exactly Jalvian but not Artorian either and recognized the thing that had been missing from Vayen's for a long time. Devotion.

Leaning my forehead against Tabor's, I sighed. "I accept your offer."

He placed the bottle in my hand, wrapping my fingers around it. "Your hands are so cold."

The chill was everywhere and my body had no desire to move. I wanted only to turn the lights off and sit in silence for the rest of eternity. If Tabor wanted to sit there with me and maybe hold my hand, I'd let him.

The warmth from his hand on the bottle quickly dissipated. "Handing this back to me probably isn't the best idea."

Tabor knelt there, eye to eye with me, his face close to mine. His voice was soft in my head. *"You're not going to use it on yourself again. Or anything else. We need you, Anastassia."*

I wasn't sold on anyone else needing me, but Tabor seemed sincere. Maybe one person was enough. *"All right."*

He nodded and got to his feet. "We'll need a ceremony, the four of us, I mean."

"No, no. No ceremonies."

"Anastassia, we have to. It's historic moments like this that will continue to repair the wounds that tore my people apart."

"I'm not your people."

He shrugged. "Neither is Buria, but if a Jalvian and an Artorian can share a mutual joining, that's huge. You can see that, can't you?"

"Meaning we have to publicly focus on you being Jalvian and not mention any aspects of your mixed blood beyond what is on public record."

"Exactly. You'll keep my secret?" he asked.

"If you'll keep mine." I opened my hand to reveal the bottle.

"Agreed."

The thought of being in public, in front of people formally, and having to pretend I was happy that Vayen was joining with Buria made me want to throw up again. "I'm not feeling up to a ceremony."

"I'll be right there with you. You can lean on me as much as you need to. And don't worry about the planning. I'll take it up with Buria. It will give us a chance to know one another. You and your mate have other priorities. No one will think anything of it."

I wanted to ask him if he was sure, maybe give him a little grief for being so eager to jump into the chaos of my life, but it was more effort than my deeply wounded heart could muster. I nodded.

"Now then, back to you getting clothing and whatever else you need while we're sequestered here, getting to know one another."

"I'll send Ikeri a message. I reached for my datapad, only to realize I didn't have it with me. "I'll have to use the suite terminal."

"And who will continue negotiations in your stead?"

I wanted to do those on my own, it was one of the few things I enjoyed these days, but Tabor was right, my mind wasn't clear enough to focus on anything outside of the Iber, or even outside his suite for that matter. The Ocelon wanted Vayen, but in his current level of distraction, that would be disastrous. "Daniel. I'll contact him too."

"No. I will. I'd like to meet your son face to face. On my terms."

I wanted to be present for that meeting to see Daniel's reaction and to make sure my son's temper didn't get the best of him. He was like his father in many ways, though he thankfully lacked Vayen's Arpex-altered abilities. He was, however, fully capable of picking up on my mental state, and unlike Vayen, he wouldn't ignore it. Coming to my defense with Vayen would only drive Daniel and his father further apart. I'd have to trust Tabor to hold his own.

"All right."

"Thank you, Anastassia. I trust you'll be safe here for a short while by yourself? I won't be gone long. Perhaps you could speak to your daughter to keep yourself occupied?"

Oh hell, I'd walked into another hovering man. Or maybe he was just trying to take care of the woman who'd shown up at his door with poison on her tongue the night before.

"I can do that."

"Good." He studied me for a moment. "Thank you for coming to me last night, for trusting me. Even if you think you didn't have any other options. You did."

"They were all shitty."

He chuckled. "Thank you for considering me the least shitty of them then."

A smile snuck onto my face. Damn him. I wasn't in the mood to smile.

He grinned, and though he sounded like he had a plan and was ready to embark on it, he stayed planted there.

"What do you want?" I finally asked.

Tabor shook his head as if rousing from a daydream. "Not the right time. Never mind. I'll be back soon." He backed away, still watching me, and then hurried for the door.

I sat, pondering what had just happened. Paranoia urged me to consider that he had other motives, that he was acting suspiciously. I gave in for a few minutes, my mind spinning with what Tabor might be up to, posing theories and discarding them. Logic finally spoke loud enough to stop the flurry in my head. I knew that look, that hesitation.

He'd wanted to kiss me.

He had just proposed a marriage offer and I'd accepted. No matter that it had been a long-time dream of his. For me, it was only a last-minute-thrown-together attempt at doing something politically positive while suffering Vayen's desires. A kiss would have been an appropriate response. He could have asked or just gone for it like he had with holding my hand, but he hadn't.

If I had to have another man in my life, I was glad it was this one. Whether he would want to stick around after regularly dealing with Vayen face-to-face remained to be seen.

In the quiet of the otherwise empty suite that wasn't mine, I closed my eyes and considered how I might diffuse Vayen's bond enough to not send him into a wrath frenzy when it broke. If Tabor did leave, removing myself would again become my only option.

FOURTEEN

Buria

The door chimed. After the last time that happened, the sound made me wince. We were alone and happened to be eating. At least we were both fully clothed.

Vayen sighed. "I might as well answer that."

He strode over to the door and palmed the panel. I caught sight of the man Ana had been sitting with the night before. She was not with him now. In an effort to keep Vayen under control as much as I was able, I hurried over to his side.

"Advisor."

"Tabor, is it?"

He nodded. "I've come to inform you that Anastassia has accepted my marriage offer. She has told me that you intend to take Buria as your second wife."

"I do," Vayen said.

He did? Officially? Is that what he'd discussed with Ana? Vayen had returned quiet and subdued in the early morning hours and remained so. He hadn't yet made any official gestures in my direction.

My heart began to race. Was this real? I couldn't wait for Tabor to leave. Vayen could make his marriage offer and I could then run to the terminal and share the news with Elonka and my other Cragtek friends. They weren't going to believe this.

"It would be best to hold a ceremony to reap the most political benefit from this joining," Tabor said.

The man at our door was far more composed than he had been in the dining hall. I supposed meeting Vayen for the first time and being caught in his rage probably played greatly into his earlier demeanor.

"Anastassia doesn't want a ceremony," Vayen said firmly.

"True, but she does understand the opportunity that is open to us and agrees we should take advantage of it. I'm sure you have plenty to deal with. Buria and I will take care of the arrangements and submit them to you for your approval."

"And Anastassia's," he said.

"She will do what is required but wants no other part in it."

Vayen nodded stiffly.

Tabor kept his gaze level and tone neutral, but he had an air of someone who was used to being in charge and getting what he wanted. He turned to me. "If you have a few minutes, I would like to go over some preliminary arrangements with you so that we can get announcements out promptly."

"We were just finishing our meal." What was I supposed to say?

"You could join us," Vayen said, managing to make it sound like a threat rather than an invitation.

Tabor remained perfectly composed. "I will. Thank you." He stared Vayen down, waiting for either of us to move aside.

In the interest of maintaining peace, I retreated to the table. The two of them followed, keeping pace with one another until they sat simultaneously. They settled into their chairs in similar positions, both with their hands on the table in front of them.

If it weren't for the overwhelming tension in the room, I would have laughed. Whoever this Tabor was, he had a whole lot of nerve. It probably helped, knowing he had Ana's backing and now that his offer had been accepted, Vayen couldn't lay a hand on him without losing Ana's approval of me.

While Vayen had invited Tabor to join us, he made no effort to offer him a plate or anything to drink. My training screamed at me to make up for this lapse in hospitality but the strain between the two of them sealed my mouth shut.

"When are you thinking?" Tabor asked me.

I looked to Vayen, hoping my helplessness in this situation was loud and clear. Protecting people, supervising security at Cragtek, or entertaining Vayen in the bedroom, I could handle. Planning a political landmark wedding? No way.

Vayen came to my rescue. "Sooner rather than later. Two weeks? That should allow travel time for any dignitaries who wish to attend."

Tabor nodded. "All Narvan Primes and Premiers for sure. Advisors you've appointed that deal with the Narvan. Important contacts? Any new advisors you wish to impress?"

"I'll get you a list." Vayen may have visually been keeping himself in check, but knowing him, I could sense his bristling.

Tabor nodded. "And location? The Iber will not do. Not enough space and too many security risks with an influx of important guests. Somewhere in the Narvan would be ideal."

Annoyance flashed across Vayen's face and then settled in. "You think I don't know that?"

Unruffled, Tabor maintained his level gaze. "I was merely stating the facts. Do you have a location in mind?"

"I own several suitable properties," Vayen growled.

"As do I. Let's start with which world then? Jalvian or Artorian?"

I had no idea where Ana had pulled this man from, but if her plan was to give Vayen some competition, her message was loud and clear. There might be no one like Vayen, but he wasn't the only powerful man to be had.

"Would you prefer Rok?" Vayen asked. "Perhaps at your family estate where you can rub this joining in your brother's face?"

I gave him a warning glance. He ignored me. Protecting other people, I amended. I was good at that. Vayen was his own creature, a volatile and powerful one that only allowed reining in when he felt like it.

"Is that what she promised you? That you'd get your brother's position?" Vayen slammed a fist on the table, making the plates bounce and clatter. "Set it all up with fucking Neko, no doubt."

Looking at me, Tabor said, "I'm the heir to one of the five most prominent Jalvian families, yet the Narvan's Advisor at the time," he nodded toward Vayen, "selected my younger brother as Rok's Prime."

"He was—"

Tabor cut Vayen off with a wave of his hand. "The status associated with being your mate's second compensates for your oversight."

From the tightness in Vayen's jaw, I imagined I could hear his teeth grinding together.

Tabor sat back. "Neko did connect us, but Anastassia made no promises. At this time, I have no desire to hold my brother's position unless it becomes necessary. I have my own ventures."

"I'm sure having a powerful wife will help those ventures succeed."

"Anastassia has shown no interest in my business. Nor have I proposed any such thing."

"Then why the fuck are you here?" Vayen snarled.

"Because your actions made my presence necessary. Thank you for that, by the way. I've admired Anastassia since she showed up in the Narvan but I never had the opportunity to meet her until now." Tabor stood. "I would suggest Jal over Rok or Artor if you wish to have the most impact. Buria and I can connect on that later once you've decided. I'll let you get back to your meal."

Tabor took one step toward the door and then turned back around. "Would you mind establishing a link contact? In case I need to reach you regarding Anastassia for any reason, and for planning purposes, of course."

The change in his voice was subtle, not exactly submissive, but there was an undercurrent there I couldn't quite put my finger on. Was Tabor worried about Ana? Surely, Vayen could sense any issues with her through their bonded connection. That was one of the few things I would never have with him and it grated on me, knowing she had a part of him I'd never see or feel.

As if Tabor's suggestion had soaked up the rivalry crackling between them, Vayen nodded amicably. "Yes, that would be wise."

They were quiet for a moment before Tabor looked at me. "Would you mind, also? In case he's busy."

I looked to Vayen. He nodded. I established a link connection with Tabor.

A moment later, he left.

Vayen stared at the remains of the meal he'd made with a scowl carved deeply on his face. "Fucking fuck."

"That went better than the dining hall," I said in the hopes of lightening his mood.

He glared at me and stood, heading for one of the comfortable chairs. "I'm going to get some work done." Vayen closed his eyes, shutting me out.

This was the Vayen that Karin's Premier had warned me about. After seeing only the softer side of him for years, I'd begun to think all the talk of his dark and shitty moods were an exaggeration. Once we were joined and the excitement of having me passed, would he be like this more often than not? Did I want to be joined to this side of him?

It wasn't like he'd proposed yet. I hadn't agreed to anything more than a week of fun. He'd asked me to never leave, but that was simply a request. A request by a powerful man who was used to getting what he wanted, just like Tabor. But I wasn't a slave anymore. He didn't own me, not that he ever had, although he had given me my freedom.

I had the freedom to walk away.

Contemplating my options, I pondered the large man in the chair.

With his head leaned back and his eyes closed, he could have been napping but the activity beneath his eyelids said otherwise.

He'd been enthusiastic about trying everything I'd suggested. He'd been utterly attentive and said the nicest things. And the way he looked at me, my heart raced just thinking about it.

He could also go wrathful death-bringer at any moment. Subtly managing him was going to be a full-time task.

Was I the right person for that? I didn't have Ana's sway or history with him. I certainly didn't have the power or experience Ana, Vayen, or even Tabor had. I was an utter nobody in comparison.

I cleared the remains of our meal and cleaned up the kitchen. The bot could have done the work, but I needed something to keep my hands busy while I attempted to process my options.

By the time I'd put everything back in order, I'd decided to Jump back to my apartment on Brustus. A few hours away from Vayen might make the correct course of action easier to see. Besides, in my eagerness to get here, I hadn't packed for a week-long stay. Even if I did return for only four more days, fresh clothes would be welcome. I turned to the chair to let Vayen know I was leaving only to find myself face to face with him.

His scowl was gone. He pressed a hand to my cheek. "What's going on in there?"

Had his mood flipped so quickly because I was there? Or was this just the beginning of him falling back into his regular ways—when he wasn't basking in the flames of a new relationship?

"I'm going to Jump back to Brustus for a bit. I need some fresh clothes. And time to think," I managed to sneak in quickly before I lost my nerve.

"Buria. Don't go." He grasped my hand and pulled me against him. "I'm trying to do this better. Better than I did with Anastassia. I screwed up so much with her. We both did. It was never like this, just easy, relaxed. Fun," he nearly purred the last word.

With my forehead on his shoulder, and his arms around me, it was hard to think clearly. I wanted to stay, but was that best for either of us?

I could walk away, return full custody to Ana and pray that they fixed their relationship. But there were so many possible benefits if I could make this work.

Taking a deep breath, I kissed his cheek and stepped back. "I'll be back soon. Perhaps you could assist Daniel with Ocelon while I'm not eating up your time. It seemed like he wanted your help."

"Wait." He slipped a hand into his pants pocket and came out with a tiny box.

My heart pounded.

"I wasn't expecting Tabor and his announcement. It wasn't that I didn't intend to ask you to join with me. I just hadn't gotten to it yet." He studied me in that penetrating way he had. "Knowing that, do you still want to leave?"

Yes. No. That he could scramble my thoughts so easily confirmed that I did need some time away.

"I'll be back in a few hours. We can do this when you're ready. No need to rush."

"That's exactly what we're doing isn't it?" He dropped the box back into his pocket and shook his head. "Dammit, why did I tell him two weeks?"

"You could contact him and change it," I suggested.

"No. He's right. We do need to make a strong statement with this joining. It's better to jump on that now if the arguments are growing heated on Artor and beyond. We could ease a lot of political tension with a simple ceremony."

"Nothing about this is simple."

Vayen frowned. "I know. I'm sorry." He stepped back. "We'll talk when you return?"

I nodded and then Jumped to Brustus before I foolishly said yes to everything he had to offer.

Alone in my apartment, I spent an hour pacing, weighing my options but finding no answers. I sat at my terminal and called Elonka.

She answered in seconds, grinning. "Tell me everything."

"You know I can't." Feigning a confidentiality conflict seemed the safest measure. I didn't want to give Vayen a reason not to trust me.

"At least tell me if it's good. Is he good? Are you happy? Did you get an offer?"

"Very. Mostly. Mostly. Not yet."

Elonka's bright smile faded. She glanced behind her before turning back to the vid. "I'm alone. Why only mostly?"

"'It's complicated' doesn't even begin to cover it." I sighed. "I'm in way over my head. But by all the gods, Elonka, would I be an idiot to pass up this opportunity?"

I told her about his pending offer and then vaguely sketched out his volatile moods, the bond problem, and the fact that Ana had also found a second.

"Buria, you may have known him for years, but you've only been close to him for a few days. Relationships take time. They don't usually just click magically into place. I mean, I want you to be happy, but any length of marriage contract with the Advisor of All will benefit you all of your days. Not that I'm advocating using him for personal gain, but you do need to watch out for yourself. If you can find happiness in that along the way, consider it a bonus."

My mouth dropped open. "Where is this coming from? You and Gamnock are so happy. I don't think I've ever heard you say a bad word about him."

She shook her head, chuckling. "Things between us weren't always winks and smiles. My family wanted an in with Cragtek and I was it. I wasn't sure Gamnock and I would renew our initial marriage contract, but as it turned out, I enjoyed getting into the business and settled into being an integral part of it beside him. Finding my place with his first wife and children was a challenge, but we worked through that too."

"And when he signed a contract with Tamika?"

Elonka shrugged. "I wasn't happy about him wanting a third wife, but he suggested I find a second husband and everything fell into place after that. Not that I renewed with Huel, you never met him for that reason," she said in response to my questioning face. "But he was a fun distraction for a couple of years."

While that had all seemed to work out splendidly for Elonka, I didn't see myself being any more at peace with Vayen wanting a third wife than Ana was with him wanting me. And myself finding a second? Good gods, finding an accord with my first was going to be a task in itself. Hopefully an enjoyable one, if what Elonka said was true.

"You've just got jitters," Elonka said. "Give it time and you'll be just as happy as I am."

That was the goal. She and Gamnock always looked so content with one another, sharing private jokes and touches. That was what love looked like. That's what I wanted with Vayen, even if it could only be in my suite on the Iber.

I just needed to give it time.

FIFTEEN

Daniel

"**W**ho the hells is interrupting my breakfast?" I yelled at the door in response to the chime. The crew knew better than to come to my suite with requests. That's what the damned pins were for. I checked mine to confirm that I hadn't missed something while getting dressed.

"Maybe you should just answer the door," suggested Arden with a sweet smile to let me know she was teasing rather than nagging.

"I'll get it," Meera offered. "Food isn't sitting well today anyway."

She did look a little pale. I watched her carefully as she headed to the door, checking to make sure she was all right. Mother had warned me that carrying a hybrid baby could be difficult for my wives. I'd have to spend more time with them to make sure they were taking care of themselves and to verify they weren't just telling me what I wanted to hear.

I returned to my meal, keeping half my attention on Meera across the room. She kept one hand at her side where she always kept a weapon and stood blocking the doorway as it opened. I could hear her talking to someone but not what they were saying.

"Daniel?" she called over her shoulder, her tone uncertain and not taking her eyes off the visitor I couldn't see in the corridor.

I gave Arden a warning look, to which she got up without question, went to our bedroom, and closed the door. I didn't expect an attack on our ship, but I wasn't taking any chances.

Meera didn't move when I approached. We'd yet to agree on when she'd be surrendering her bodyguard duty in favor of being my pregnant wife whom I would do anything to protect. I slipped my arm around her waist, enjoying the feeling of the bulge there, and gently moved her aside. She took the hint and gave me a little space, but stood only a few strides away just in case.

"Commander Ta'set," said a solemn stranger.

In a heartbeat, I knew who he had to be, the questionably Jalvian suitor Markus had tactlessly divulged to my father.

"I'm Tabor Desu, and I'm sorry to interrupt your meal, but I've come to inform you that your mother is not herself today. It would be best for your mission if you were to step in for her on the negotiations."

"She's been leading that."

He didn't blink. "And now you will. Your father is...busy."

I'd seen more evidence of that than I wanted to yesterday. "Why didn't she inform me herself?"

His neutral demeanor devolved into a deep scowl. "You and your brother caused quite a scene yesterday, as I'm sure you're aware. Not only did it nearly cause me to lose my life, which I don't appreciate, but it also caused your mother a great deal of distress. I appreciate that even less."

It seemed my mother had a new bodyguard. "That wasn't our intention. But again, why did she send you? Is she all right?"

"No." His voice slipped into a cold and deadly tone that rivaled my father's. "She is not. Perhaps your father has also been too busy to inform you that he's decided to move forward with taking a second mate. Officially. Last night."

"Oh shit." I reached for the wall beside me to keep my balance as the one certainty I'd known all my life slipped through my fingers. No matter what, through all the years of being apart from one another when he'd been imprisoned, the tense years searching for Ikeri, the fights they'd had, I'd known they would still be together. He'd sworn he would never leave her. And technically, he wasn't. But certainly, in her mind, he was.

"Indeed." He held out his hand. "Your mother didn't send me. I wanted to meet you myself. We will soon be family. She accepted my marriage contract offer this morning."

Did she accept because she was pissed at my father? Because she wasn't taking this well? Because this man had something on her? I didn't know him, where he'd come from, who he was, or what the fuck he might be capable of.

Ignoring his hand and Meera's barely audible growling of my name, I took a step out into the corridor and let the door close behind me. "Where is she?"

"My suite. I assure you she's..." His assertive manner dissipated into the level of concern I would have expected from my father, not a stranger. "Not well. I promise I'll take care of her, but she's not in a good place right now. She doesn't want to see anyone."

"But she's making major decisions? I don't think so."

"Vid call if you want to, but don't push her. She's fragile."

I laughed. "I don't doubt that she's either livid or sad, but my mother hasn't been fragile a day in my life."

"She is today. Thank your father for that." He turned on his heel and left.

I watched Tabor Desu walk away, trying to imagine my mother walking beside him. Trying to imagine her beside anyone but my father.

He looked like he could handle himself, shorter than me by a couple of inches, not young, and not particularly handsome in terms of a typical Jalvian. His skin had a ruddier tone, like he regularly worked under the sun. No high-standing Jalvian would stand for resembling any shade of Artorian coloring. Yet, from the fact that he had no qualms about placing blame on my father and considering his clothing and manner of speaking, he had to be from a prominent Jalvian family.

She'd found him damned quickly for declaring she wanted no part in a second mate only days ago. She'd had help. I was sure of it.

I darted back inside, shook Meera off, and sat in the nearest chair. "I'll explain in a minute. Tell Arden she can come out."

Meera nodded and left my side so I could sink into my link.

"Neko, what the fuck did you do?"

His unaffected answer sounded like he'd adopted it from my father. *"Could you be more specific?"*

"Tabor Desu. My mother. Ring any bells?"

"That's between me and your mother. Your father made his fuck-ing foolish choice."

I'd never heard Neko voice disapproval in regard to my father before. It took me aback. *"Is Tabor safe? Vetted? Where the hells did he come from?"*

"Of course he is and he's based on Rok. Beyond that, it's not your business. Let your mother find a little happiness. She deserves it." He cut contact.

I trusted Neko. He'd been around since I was five and had stood stalwartly beside my parents through all the nine hells that had been my life thus far. If he backed Tabor, I'd have to take his word for it.

But Geva, my mother with anyone else, that she would be with anyone else, it went against everything I'd ever known. I had to be sure.

Using my link, I found Tabor's suite information and noted that my mother had assigned it to him last night. She'd known him for one night and had accepted his proposal? That didn't seem possible. At least my father had known Buria for years before he dove off the deep end of tanking his joining.

I went to my seldom-used terminal and called Tabor's suite. My mother answered within seconds.

"Expecting me?" I asked and then instantly regretted my snide tone. She looked terrible, dark circles under her eyes, her hair hanging loose in her face, and her eyes empty.

"I just finished talking to your sister."

She sounded way worse than the day Buria had arrived. I'd never seen my mother so off-kilter, so far from her usual take-charge attitude. Hells, she'd been in better shape after brawling with six Jalvians.

"Mom, is there anything I can do?"

"Take over on Ocelon. I'll send you my notes and proposal."

"I meant with you and Dad."

"No. That's over." The raw despair in her voice made my heart ache.

I'd seen her desperate for my father to wake, for him to heal, watching him in the tank, on a bed at home, at the University. She'd waited for years for him to find Ikeri. She'd taken the Narvan on again for him even though it had nearly killed her. I'd witnessed plenty of their fights, but they'd always made up.

"Mom. It's not. He's still here. He's still coming home to you just like always."

I glanced over to my silent, waiting wives, listening anxiously, holding each other's hands. My mother would never have that sort of companionship with Buria. She'd had my father to herself for longer than I'd been alive and she wanted to keep it that way.

"Not like always." Her voice broke on the last word and it brought tears to my eyes.

I hated to admit it, but Tabor had been right. Fragile was now a word associated with my mother.

I'd watched my father strike down the original population of Brustus where we'd found Ikeri and make a show of smiting crowds of others since, but I'd never held that against him. Watching him kill didn't bother me, but watching him crush my mother infuriated me beyond reason.

"I'll talk to him. I'll make him do the right thing."

"There is no right thing." She shook her head. "Let him be, Daniel. He's already decided. We talked. He knows how I feel. And he decided."

He couldn't have done that. There had to be some sort of mistake, a misunderstanding. My father wasn't a monster. Well, not when it came to family.

"Has the tea helped Meera and Arden?" she asked as if we hadn't just been discussing her and my father.

My mother had never been an emotional woman. Not in the way most were. She showed anger. Beyond that, she wore a carefully maintained mask of control. She'd bared enough. She was covering now. I let her. It hurt too much to see the truth.

"Yes, Mom. Thank you. I met Tabor. He seems nice."

"I'm glad you think so."

"He's got a good threatening tone. Might give Dad a little competition in that arena."

A faint smile drifted over her face but quickly faded. "Take care of Arden and Meera."

"I will." Something in her voice sent chills through me. "Mom?"

She watched me from behind her tenuous façade.

"You'll be here to help deliver the babies, right?" I glanced over at Meera and Arden, both watching me with wide eyes. I wasn't alone in feeling what I had.

"I'll make sure the doctors here can assist Meera and Arden in case I'm tied up when the time comes, but yes, I'll do my best to be there."

That was not the committed answer that would have erased the unease in my stomach.

"I love you, Mom."

"I know."

Her mask slipped again for a moment, revealing the mother I'd known on Veria Minor when I'd been little: softer, kinder, who read me stories and snuggled with me on the couch. She wasn't the advisor of anything. She was just my mother. And she loved me. There was no doubt about that. Then or just now.

She ended the call.

Tabor had warned me. I prayed he knew how to take care of her as he'd promised. My father sure as hells didn't.

I barely got to my feet before Meera and Arden wrapped their arms around me.

"You should go talk to her in person. She isn't well," said Meera.

Arden shook her head. "No, you should talk to your father. He needs to fix this."

My pin indicated a new message. From my father. A ship-wide announcement, copied to all of the Narvan news outlets. A formal ceremony and celebration would take place in sixteen days to formalize the Advisors each adding a second mate to their joining.

I sank back into the chair. "It's too late."

SIXTEEN

Anastassia

Ikeri stood in the doorway of Tabor's suite, a bag filled with everything I'd asked for in her hands. She looked me over.

After the call with her and then Daniel, I was in no mood to talk further.

"Thank you." I took the bag and reached for the panel to close the door.

"Mom, are you sure about this? You barely know this man."

"I know enough."

"Dad issued an announcement. It's everywhere. A joining ceremony in two weeks? What's the rush?"

"There isn't one. I didn't pick the date. Go on. I'll be fine."

I shooed her away and shut the door before her questions led me to snap at her. She meant well, but this change between me and Vayen was going to take some time for adjustment. For all of us. Ikeri had Etara to lean on. I couldn't be her mother right now, not after what I'd almost done the night before, and knowing it was still my backup plan if I could iron out a few details.

Carrying the bag into the bathroom, I took a quick shower and changed into clean clothes. I stepped back into the suite that wasn't mine. A soul-crushing wave of desolation swept over me. I dropped back into the chair I'd previously occupied and let the bag fall at my feet.

Would this be my new home? How many nights a week would I sleep here? How long would Tabor remain supportive before he started to expect reciprocation?

It had been so long. How did one begin a relationship?

I'd never been good at that even when I was in the mood for it. My usual method was to get them into bed and, depending on how that went, latch on from there to see where they could take me. But I had no desire to share a bed with anyone, not even Vayen after he'd had the nerve to walk away the day before. And really, I didn't have anywhere else to go. I'd accomplished everything I'd set out to do.

Except retire happily with the man I loved.

Maybe I could just stay in the chair until everyone moved on enough to let me go. After all, I had nowhere I had to be for two weeks. Vayen owed me. He could deal with Ocelon and our meddling kids.

Tabor walked in, disrupting the quiet with a giddy laugh. "Oh Anastassia, you should have seen it." He sat across from me but sprang back to his feet five seconds later, nearly dancing in place and wildly gesticulating. "I used everything I knew, all my tactics for dealing with my self-righteous brother and my disdainful family. I faced the Advisor of All and lived to tell about it." He grinned. "He wasn't happy. Not one bit, but he didn't do anything about it other than grouse a little. I have the Advisor of All as a link contact. Can you believe it?" He laughed again.

Caught up in his glee, I found myself smiling. "He established contact with you?"

"I suggested it. With Buria too. They both agreed. I didn't crack, not even a little. Holy Geva, I can't believe I did that." He danced his way over in front of me. "Can I please hug you? I really want to hug you right now."

What harm would that do? It wasn't as intimate as the kiss he hadn't pushed for, and he was so happy I could feel joy emanating from him. Maybe some of that would rub off on me. I nodded and stood only to be immediately wrapped in his arms.

Tabor held me to his chest but not too tightly. His shoulders were lower than I was used to and not as thick with muscle. His warm cheek rested against mine. I hesitantly raised my arms to wrap them around his thinner-than-I was-used-to waist. What surprised me was that none of that felt horribly wrong, just different. Maybe because it *was* different. I wasn't trying to replace Vayen like I had by finding Raphael on Pentares, the human equivalent of the man I'd desperately missed. Tabor's body didn't match any man I'd been with before. A clean slate.

"Geva, I can't believe I'm here. With you. If you had asked me a week ago what I'd be doing right now, all of this would have been such a far-fetched dream that I wouldn't have even considered it a viable wish."

"I'm sure the joy of it all will wear off soon enough," I said against his shoulder.

"Maybe, but Anastassia, you gave me my balls back. I haven't had a solid leg to stand on since I was twelve. No true respectable position other than the ones I made for myself—roles that fell through my fingers whenever my brother or my family flexed their muscle. I was born and trained to be a dignitary, to be the head of my family in whatever capacity we could climb to. All of that was ripped away from me. They can't take anything from me now. I have it all back and more."

He squeezed me. I felt his smile against my cheek.

"I know this isn't what you want. That I'm not what you want, but Geva, woman, thank you for allowing me to be here. You have no idea how much I needed this; this dream I never dared to have."

He sounded so sincere, his gratitude so heartfelt, and what little Seeker sense I had left told me he was being honest. Honest men were hard to come by. Grateful and sincere honest men, even more so.

I picked up my head to land a quick kiss on his cheek. "You're welcome."

Tabor went still.

He stepped back after a moment but kept his hands on my shoulders. "I'm going to kidnap you for a night. If you're agreeable?"

"That's not how kidnapping works. At least it never was when I went about it."

"It sounds like you have stories to tell." He snickered. "What I mean to say is, I'd like to take you to my estate on Rok for dinner. If we're to be contracted, you'll have a place there, even if it's only used on occasion."

"You're going to make me meet your family, aren't you."

Tabor grinned. "Yes, but not tonight. I may have lied a little when I spoke with Vayen. Fuck, I'm on a first name basis with the Advisor of All."

I rolled my eyes. "You'll get over that pretty quickly too. He's not that scary once you get to know him."

"Easy for you to say. But really, I did tell him that I had no intention of rubbing my marriage with you in my family's face. To be honest, I plan on rubbing that in their faces until they bleed."

Laughter burst out of my mouth. I felt a little lighter.

"Also, being honest, I may have rubbed our marriage in Vayen's face too since he was the one to appoint my brother instead of me."

"Good for you." I let him have a moment before getting serious. "To be clear, you got away with it today, but he's also going to get used to you being around, and I can't promise he'll handle it well. He's bonded to me. That's going to cause problems where you and I are concerned. I wouldn't make a habit of antagonizing him." I held up a hand to halt his defense. "I'm not saying you can't stand up for yourself. Please do. But be smart about it and choose your battles wisely."

"Noted."

"So this trip to your estate. Did you clear that with him?" I asked.

Tabor cocked his head. "Why would I? You can go wherever you want. Can't you?"

"Not exactly." I returned to the chair. "I don't have a link. You know that, right?"

"You have to," he sputtered. "All you did—"

"I used to have one, but for medical reasons, I no longer do. Which means I'm dependent on Vayen or Daniel to bring me anywhere. They get antsy if I'm away from the Iber without them."

"But you can talk to them. In your mind, can't you? Like we did?"

"That doesn't help if I'm unconscious."

"They're worried about you being hurt." His voice softened. "I wouldn't allow you to be harmed in any way. I have security. I can Jump you just as well as they can."

"You'll have to earn their trust with that."

"All right, but I really would like to bring you to my home."

"I'll handle the clearance. Mostly because I'd like to get off this damned ship for any reason other than work for once."

Tabor settled onto the table in front of me, gripping the edge and looking anxious.

I opened my bonded connection with Vayen just enough to talk to him. *"I'm leaving the Iber with Tabor. We'll be at his estate on Rok. I'm assuming you already know where that is, what security he has in place, and probably how many pairs of shoes he owns."*

"It's adequate," Vayen said sullenly. *"Be safe."*

"You too."

Touched that he'd dredged up our old parting words, I spared a wave of warmth for him even as annoyed with him as I was. I might not be in favor of this whole second joining mess, but I knew me being with Tabor was hell on Vayen too.

"All set."

Tabor stood and took my hands to pull me to my feet. He looked me over, not letting go. "I don't do a lot of double Jumps."

"You'll have to get used to it and do it enough that it becomes second nature if you want to win Vayen and Daniel over."

"If it means I get to practice with you enough that it becomes second nature, I'm in." He winked.

The damned man had a way of making me feel better. Where Vayen had a searing smile and his moments with dark humor and giggle-worthy innuendo, Tabor was simply happy and uplifting, with a twinkle in his eye and an easy smile. I wondered how different he would have been if he'd become the Prime of Rok, bearing all the responsibilities and obligations that came with the position.

"Have you considered that everything that happened to you before we met was for a reason? That your Geva was shaping you for this, right now?" The words slipped out before I gave thought to keeping them to myself.

His hands grew warm and a tremble passed through them into me. "If you're right, I would endure it all again a hundred times over."

He spoke with conviction, without hesitation, passionately, and from the heart. Neko had cleared him. Vayen had no doubt probed Tabor in his subtle way if he was begrudgingly fine with me being alone outside the Iber with him. I wasn't worried that Tabor had a hidden agenda, or that he planned to work against me or my family. I didn't have to subconsciously manage him in case he might blow up at any moment. He wasn't under my command. For once in my life, I felt like I could relax around someone.

"Take me to your estate. I can't do what comes next here."

Tabor licked his lips and nodded slowly.

Two minutes later we stood in an unfamiliar room in a bright and airy house. He stayed right where he was, holding my hands, and watching me. The tremble in his hands intensified.

"I'll get faster. I promise. Anastassia, what comes next?"

I may have been trembling a little myself. "We do what you didn't ask for this morning. Just that, nothing more."

Unblinking, he nodded. "Are you sure? This hasn't been an easy day for you and yesterday..."

"Then take my mind off it."

He leaned in slowly as if savoring the moment rather than leaping at the opportunity, a restraint I found endearing.

His lips brushed over mine, feather-light, testing their reception. As long as he stayed within the bounds I'd issued, I had no fight to give. The kiss was for him, what he yearned for. Not me.

Tabor kept to his slow pace, in no hurry at all. Other than dropping my hands to pull me closer, he didn't wander further beyond kiss territory. He nipped at my bottom lip and then his tongue began to explore. I returned what he gave, all the while waiting for it to feel natural, that on some level, I wanted this. Maybe that would come in time. I hoped it would. The man deserved full reciprocation.

He pulled back, his forehead resting against mine. "Before I get carried away, I want to show you something."

"After which, you'll get carried away?"

He laughed, taking a step back. "Only when you're ready. It's too soon. I know that. But thank you for allowing me a taste."

His manners and consideration soothed my nerves. I'd never met a man like him before. He combined Marin's smooth tongue, Vayen's air of authority, and Kess's wit in one genuine package.

Tabor gestured to the house around us. "This is the one estate my brother cannot touch. It's mine by right as the eldest son. I keep everything I love here, the things I would be devastated to lose."

Would I be one of those things? I considered asking him to repeat what he'd said so I could better analyze the undercurrents of what he wasn't saying, but also because I wanted to keep hearing his voice.

Tabor gestured for me to explore the room. He stayed where he was while I wandered. For a jump point, it was far more open and distinctively decorated than I would have ever gone with, but I got the feeling he was the only one who Jumped here. If this was where he kept his treasures, he'd use other locations for business and whatever pleasure he could find.

The rose-colored room was spacious, easily the size of the entire suite I'd given him on the Iber. High windows with long diaphanous white curtains let in the natural-looking light. The Artorian-manufactured dome high overhead provided faux sunlight and protected residents from an otherwise toxic planet. Others like it covered all the cities on Rok.

The room was filled with a scattering of expensive-looking furniture and a host of sculptures of all sizes. Paintings filled the walls. The high windows allowed illumination, but protected the art from direct light.

"Do you collect, or is this the family horde?" I asked, examining a small detailed portrait of a young, blue-eyed girl with a crooked smile who seemed to stare just over my shoulder.

"Collect. It's one of my many endeavors."

I looked up to catch his gaze that was locked on me. "Do you deal as well then?"

"And procure. I have people to assist with that." He winked.

"Art thief? I fear I've fallen in with a criminal."

Tabor grinned. "Among other things. I did mention that Neko and I had a working relationship."

"You did."

"The Premier of Karin is one of my best customers. I believe Neko mentioned you were friends?"

Damn, Isnar knew him too? I let myself relax a little more.

"Come on," he waved me over to a set of double doors. "I think you'll like this."

The door opened to a long hallway lined with thick clearplaz from floor to ceiling. I stopped one step in and gasped. An expansive and intricately planted garden filled my view to either side. Beyond, were fields of yellow flowers as far as I could see.

"What is all that?" I asked, pointing at the fields.

"Stareopantika."

I shook my head. "Never heard of it."

"It's used for medicinal purposes." Tabor came to stand beside me. "As it turns out, the dry seed pods are the primary ingredient in bang and one of the supporting elements in boost. Your mate has made me a very wealthy man."

"You were already growing it?"

"Not as much, but yes. Medicinal." He shrugged, pointing at the fields. "Out there, I grow what pays. Up here, I grow what I like."

I turned to face him, making sure he wasn't joking. "You garden?"

"Is that so hard to believe?"

"No, it's just that there's a shortage of gardening, drug-growing, art-dealing, dignitaries."

"We're an exclusive club." Tabor smiled as he pushed one of the windows, revealing that it was actually a door identical to all the other panels. I wouldn't have spotted it.

An amazing scent washed over me. "What is that?"

"The stareopantika. We can't stay out too long without breathers or you'll end up high as all hells. The pollen is quite potent as well but the processing costs are higher. It's more profitable to sell the pods."

I took one more deep breath and then dropped to my knees to dig a hand into the rich soil. "It's been years since I've had the luxury of time to play in the dirt." I let the soil fall through my fingers, enjoying the feathery feel, and the comforting familiarity of the action.

"I expected your estate to be in a city, close to the capitol, to your family, to business," I said.

Tabor tapped his temple. "Business is anywhere I am. I avoid my family as much as possible, and like I want to be anywhere near my brother?" He reached out to stroke a white-barked branch of a nearby tree. "This is the family country estate. Mine by rights. None of them would have set foot in it anyway. Too far from society and none of them are linked. They need to be where business is.

"In the past, it was only visited sporadically as a vacation destination or to hide whoever was misbehaving until whatever trouble they'd caused blew over. Family funds pay for the upkeep and fields. We used to have staff here growing food to sell to the populace. Now my family enjoys a percentage of the sales of my crops and they don't ask questions as long as I keep the credits flowing and stay out here."

I rubbed my dirt-covered hands together, brushing off the worst of it. His gallery held works of art but the garden was truly a masterpiece. "You must have a staff taking care of the upkeep. Every plant and planting looks flawless."

"Thank you. I do most of it myself, but yes, I have help. I got little over-ambitious with the size when I expanded the original beds."

He pulled me to my feet and held my dirty hand without a second thought. We walked together, slowly, side by side with the alluring scent of stareopantika swirling around us. Paths lined by a host of plants, most of which I'd never seen before, kept my mind occupied. They brought me back to simpler times on Veria Minor when I'd collected plants for my Seeker shop and my early years covered in dirt while my father and brother studied farming techniques on various worlds.

Thick bushes, manicured into fanciful shapes, hid the views throughout, making each turn in the path a mystery waiting to be solved. Gravel crunched underfoot. Bugs buzzed around my head and birds chirped in the trees.

"It's hard to believe this is all under a dome. The sky looks so natural. And all of this," I waved my hand at everything around us, "It feels like I'm on Artor, like this was always here, not all shipped in."

"Rok was originally settled by Artorians and this is one of their domes. They do have a gift for colonization, for bending the most hostile environments to their will or finding ways to work around them, like here or Syless."

"They do."

Even though the air was filtered here, just like it was on the Iber, all the plants, the open soil, and the heat of the simulated sun above, offered an authentic feel. It was like standing in the deep forest of Frique but without being near the house that held too many memories to offer me any measure of calm.

We passed the next line of shrubbery to discover a walled pond easily four of me across with a fanciful fountain in the middle. Water sprayed in arches, nearly reaching the knee-high edges that were lined with tiny tiles in shades of blue, green, and gold. Movement under the water caught my eye. I wandered closer with Tabor unresisting beside me.

A school of colorful fish flitted about, darting in and out of the floating water plants bearing bright pink flowers that bobbed on the surface. The edge of the wall offered a wide enough lip to sit on. I settled there, dunking my hand in the cool water and watching the fish. Tabor sat beside me, smiling softly.

"Neko may have mentioned that you liked plants."

"I could stay here forever, away from all of it."

I sat listening to the water hitting the surface of the pond, the birds, the insects, and under everything, the faint hum of the irrigation, temperature controls, circulation and filtration systems that were another specialization of Artor.

"If it were up to me, I would love for you to do just that. I could use the help," he said with a playful smile.

It wasn't up to him. My heart sank as reality rushed back in. Vayen and I were going to have to sit down at that damned kitchen table and haggle for time. Time, I realized, I did want to spend with Tabor, even if it was only to sink my hands in soil, and leave everything else behind for a while. Time I wouldn't have to see Vayen smiling at Buria like he used to smile at me. Time I would have to pretend in public that I was agreeable to it all, that we were all happy.

We had an image to uphold, an example to set. And a civil unrest in the Narvan that we could quell if I could fake my way through every day of the rest of my life.

"Anastassia," Tabor said softly, squeezing my hand. "Let all of that go. It will be waiting when you return. Here, you can simply be."

I took a deep breath, wondering how many of those I'd need, how long I needed to be outside for the high-as-all-hells to kick in because that sounded very good at the moment.

"I'm sorry, I'm not good company today."

He wrapped his arm around me. "I don't mind."

"I'm not good company most days. You should have fair warning. Unless Neko already filled you in on that too."

Tabor chuckled. "He may have mentioned that. He said he was ninety percent sure you'd pick me and wanted to make sure I didn't cause more heartache than you already had going on."

"Ninety percent, huh?" I shook my head. "I need to talk to Neko. Do you have a terminal I could use?"

"As a matter of fact, I had my staff set one up for you in the room that will be yours here. I had a feeling you'd want to stay in touch with your kids and contacts even when you were supposed to be relaxing and away."

His preparedness made me smile. "Neko did brief you quite well."

"All the connections are secure, but I won't be offended if you wish to verify that yourself. My security team excels at staying out of sight. I prefer my illusion of solitude." He lightly knocked his shoulder into me. "That I hope will not always be quite so solitary."

"Arrangements will be made." Though I tried not to think further about having to make them.

We stood and started back down the path, slowly winding back toward the two-story house that looked like it belonged in the garden, all curved lines and natural surfaces, or at least masterfully manufactured to appear that way.

My thoughts drifted back to beginning a relationship and how I'd done it before. How this time needed to be different. I wasn't that woman anymore.

"If I snap... Who am I kidding, when I snap at you and you feel it's unwarranted, you have my permission to Jump me here and drop me in the garden. No warning needed. No explanation required."

Tabor laughed. "Deal. As long as you'll wear a breather mask if you're going to be fuming for a while. I don't need you pissed off *and* high."

I laughed. Damn, he could make me do that so easily.

"Come, your room awaits." Seeing the excitement gleaming in his eyes, I put my life on the Iber on temporary hold. Feeling a true smile forming, I eagerly set off to see what other surprises Tabor had in store.

SEVENTEEN

Buria

Vayen poked at his lunch with his fork but hadn't eaten a bite despite usually being ravenous. "What do you think they're doing?"

"Do yourself a favor and don't think about it. You're supposed to be enjoying your time with me, remember?"

He smiled weakly. "Sorry. It's just...the bond."

The thing I'd never have with him. How could I forget?

"I know she's not here, aboard the Iber. That she's elsewhere. With him."

"You can talk to her anytime, can't you?"

He shrugged half-heartedly. "She leaves me alone when I'm with you. I'm trying to give her the same consideration."

"That sounds like progress in the right direction."

He set his fork down and pressed his fingers into his temples. "I don't know how she does it. It's fucking distracting as all hells."

"What exactly?"

He was supposed to be distracting himself with me, not wrapped up in having Ana gone for the day or a few days or whatever she was doing. It didn't matter. She wasn't underfoot and this was my time.

A scowl settled onto his face, creasing his forehead and hardening his eyes. "You wouldn't understand."

"I understand that she asked me to be here. That you wanted me to be here. That she, despite the bond between the two of you, was able to allow us four uninterrupted days and would have allowed four more had your sons not shown up to set you off. So why can't you do the same for her?"

"She can turn the bond off. Meaning she doesn't talk to me. She can't feel me. She's gone."

"And you can't."

He shook his head. "Artorians are wired differently. The bond may have been something else at one time, but it was modified genetically a long time ago, ingrained in us now, in our social structure. Anastassia, not being Artorian, doesn't follow any of the known rules. I never should have bonded to her, to anyone who wasn't Artorian."

"But you did."

He let out a rueful laugh. "Yes. Twice. It turns out we can bond outside our people, despite what the Artorian government would like anyone to believe. Not that I'd recommend it. I mean, it's been rather half-assed for both of us, far less than half for her. She's never gotten a damned thing out of it beyond me aggravating her with this kind of shit." He waved his hands absently at his head before raking them through his long hair.

"Our connection isn't what it used to be, not as intense. At least on my end. It never was for her. The bond, when she's nearby, helps keep me...under control."

I clasped my hands together on the table to keep my sudden burst of panic contained. Did I need to get Daniel or Etara to contain him? "Are you feeling out of control now?"

Vayen eyed my hands, slipping one of his over mine and squeezing. "I'm fine. Well, not fine, but no, not rushing off on a killing spree."

"If you want this to work, you and me, I mean, you're going to have to find a way to contain your bond."

"Contain it?" His voice rose and his hand vacated mine. "The bond is a part of me, Buria. It's a lifetime commitment."

"She found room in that commitment to ask me to be here."

He pounded a fist on the table, making his plate bounce and noodles spill onto the surface. "You don't have to keep pointing that out. I know."

My heartbeat stuttered. If this was control, how bad did he get when he lost it?

Moments passed in uneasy silence. I forced myself to take a bite and then another while his fist slowly relaxed. He finally took a deep breath and let it out loudly.

"What I'm saying is, I'm not like her. I told her she could have that fucking Jalvian, but I don't know if I can go through with it."

I tried to keep my voice level and calm just like the Masters taught me. "Go through with what exactly? If she doesn't get what she wants, do you really think she'll allow me to stay?"

Vayen's eyes narrowed and his voice grew lower and yet louder. "Allow? She'll find a way to allow it. Dammit, she wouldn't do that to me."

Either he didn't know Ana half as well as he thought or he was being entirely delusional about the situation. "The crew respects Ana. If you backed out of your arrangement with her, they'd have questions. And your announcement has already been released to the Narvan's media outlets. Changing your stance now would cause far more problems than Neko was dealing with before."

"Oh, now you're an expert on the political situation?"

"I didn't say that."

I hadn't realized I'd backed my way into our first argument but here we were. The only redeeming point so far was that he didn't have a drink in his hand. However, he'd had several before we'd sat down to eat. He'd been drinking since she'd left.

Vayen raked his loose hair over his shoulders, tipped his head back, and exhaled loudly. Again. He took several bites before speaking in a much more neutral tone. "I'm going with Daniel to Ocelon to see if I can prod this arrangement along. Would you like to join me?"

"I would, on one condition." My heart was pounding again and by the surprised look on his face, I wondered if he could hear it. But I wasn't a slave anymore. I had my own life and a job, one he'd mostly handed to me, but they were mine and I could go back to them. "Can you keep yourself under better control than you have since you walked in? If you're going to be yelling and fist-thumping the whole time, I'm not interested."

He stood slowly and took care of our plates before turning to face me. "Right. I'm sorry. While I can't promise there won't be yelling or fists involved, they won't be aimed at you."

"All right then." Hopefully, this excursion from my suite would be more pleasant than the last one.

He'd told me of his meetings on various worlds over the years, now I would finally be standing beside him, visiting somewhere other than Brustus for once. Somewhere new, as the prospective second wife of the Advisor of All. A shiver passed over me and I couldn't help but smile.

❧

Vayen provided a jump point to the building where the Iber's crew had been meeting with the Ocelon people. When I stepped out of the void seconds behind him, Daniel and Seeker Etara were already there with someone else.

Etara looked me over, neither smiling nor scowling, but yet not exactly neutral either. At the same time, Daniel avoided looking my way at all and barely glanced at his father as he introduced the Advisor of All to the Ocelon leader, a short, thick, bald-headed person that I got the feeling was male, but displayed no openly confirming factors. He had no hair at all. A deeply furrowed forehead intersected defined ridges over his nose that stretched outward where eyebrows would typically be.

"We've been waiting for you," the male said, his voice low and rumbling through the translator unit in Daniel's hand.

Vayen did not introduce me but launched into a fast-paced conversation that didn't seem to be very sociable even though this was his first contact with these people. Maybe there was some truth to what Karin's Premier had remarked years before when I'd been in his service: The Advisor doesn't do friendly.

I stood on the edge of the conversation, having no part in it and not following much beyond Vayen making it clear that he wanted to make a trade deal over several mineable materials.

The Ocelon leader shook his head and crossed his arms over his wide chest. "Show me."

"Show you what?" Vayen asked, making no effort to cover his annoyance over the sudden halt to their conversation.

"That you aren't a weapon. That you heal."

Vayen looked to Etara. She shrugged.

"I don't heal, but I can tell you what is wrong."

The man huffed. "What good is that? Doctors know what is wrong." He stuck his thumb out toward Etara. "She said you offer healing."

Daniel spoke up, "We have very good doctors and resources you may not have here, though you are more advanced than many of the worlds we encounter."

"You heal or no deal."

Vayen took a menacing step toward the Ocelon representative. "The only way I can heal you is to tear you apart first. Would you like that?"

Then Vayen's menacing glare snapped to Daniel, who glared right back. I assumed the two of them were bickering telepathically. Etara watched them both, her hands clasped tightly in front of her. In the hopes of defusing my half-intoxicated, hair-trigger, intended husband, I hurried to Vayen's side. After all, we had an agreement about yelling and fists.

"Perhaps you could bring him to the Iber and give him a tour of the medical department? Show him what you have to offer?" I suggested.

"We don't typically allow—" Daniel started to say.

"Who is this one?" asked the Ocelon leader, looking me up and down. "What does she do for you?"

Vayen turned his dark glare on me as though daring me to answer the question. He might not be yelling, but he didn't appear happy about what he clearly saw as me intruding.

I might hold an important position for Gamnock that allowed me to be comfortable and respected on Brustus, but it was quickly becoming obvious that I held no level of esteem here. Not with Daniel or Etara, and outside my suite, apparently not with Vayen either. I swallowed hard, unsure of how to proceed on any front.

Etara stepped forward, clearing her throat loudly. "Buria is observing. She is considering joining our crew."

Considering. I snorted inwardly. What had seemed like an offer that needed little consideration was quickly becoming one I was having serious reservations about.

I supposed Etara's answer was true and far more diplomatic than attempting to explain the second wife situation or what exactly I'd spent the last few days doing with the Advisor of All. That's who he was here, not Vayen, the man I'd been sequestered with.

The Ocelon male snorted. "You would join them? Why?"

Inadvertently getting myself stuck in the middle of delicate political situations seemed to be a gift I hadn't known I possessed. Or a curse. Probably that.

Even Daniel, a kinder copy of his father, watched me warily now.

"They offer many opportunities I wouldn't have on the world where I live," I said carefully, praying I wasn't making anything worse.

"Do you live on a poor world? You have a hard life?"

"No." Knowing nothing about these people or what I was supposed to say, I left it at that.

"No?" He laughed. "What will this one do on your crew that she speaks so few words? Perhaps she has other uses that do not require talking? Is that what you offer me now?" He bared his teeth at Vayen.

Daniel darted in front of the Ocelon leader, blocking him from

Vayen's wrath-filled glower. He gestured the male to the outer door. "Definitely not. Why don't we take a walk and you can better explain who or what you need healed?"

The male pushed Daniel aside. "Little clone, I told you we would only deal with the Advisor. Now he is here. We will talk. Not the rest of you."

"If you will speak to the Adviser, I must stay," declared Etara. "And he must stay with me." She nodded toward Daniel.

"Go. You've done enough here," Vayen grumbled through my link.

"I didn't mean to do anything."

He just shook his head, disappointment and dismissal clear enough that I didn't attempt to argue. While he did keep his word about not yelling, this wasn't an improvement.

I Jumped back to the Iber, but as I made my way to my suite, the angrier I got. He hadn't introduced me, hadn't spoken up to give me a role. Hell, he hadn't briefed me at all. He'd invited me to go with him and then left me to fend for myself in territory where I had zero experience? How was that fucking fair?

If he had so little regard for me, what was I doing here at all? At least I was respected on Brustus. Why was I even bothering to go back to my suite? My steps ground to a halt.

A sudden wash of cold liquid flooded down my back along with an impact that made me take a lurching step forward. I turned to find a mortified woman with an empty cup in her hand and three datapads scattered on the floor at our feet.

"I'm so sorry. I—"

I forced a smile. "It's fine. I was just leaving anyway."

Dripping wet, I Jumped to my apartment on Brustus to give serious reconsideration to accepting Vayen's proposal that he'd yet to even make. To make things more annoying, I couldn't chance calling Elonka to vent. In my anger, I'd surely slip in details that should remain private and if that got back to Vayen, not only would there never be a proposal, but I'd be justifiably on the wrong side of his volatile temper. Whether we went forward with this relationship or not, that was a place I never wanted to be.

Vayen's voice hit my link hours later, *"Where are you?"*

"Home. Where I'll be staying." For lack of being able to storm out

of the room, I cut contact. It would make him angry but I didn't care. He'd made me angry too.

It was twenty minutes later that he knocked at my door, the exact amount of time it took to get to my apartment from the public Cragtek jump point. If I let him in, he'd no doubt have a jump point in my apartment before he left whether I wanted him to or not.

Standing with my back against the door, I let him knock.

"Buria."

"What."

"Can we not do this in the hallway?"

"There's no one else on this floor. You can say whatever you're going to say out there."

Where I didn't have to look at him. Where he couldn't look at me in the way he did.

"Buria," he said with more pleading this time.

Did he not even know why I was angry? Because if he did, he should have been apologizing already. "You could have done about twenty things differently today to prevent me from looking like an idiot. Instead, the only thing you did was get angry."

"I'm not used to having to cover—"

I slammed my palm onto the panel, opening the door. "Cover for me? That better not be what you were about to say. You invited me to come with you, no warnings, no information, no preparation whatsoever, and instead of stepping up to introduce me, defend me, or set anything straight at all, you just let me flounder."

Since he wasn't apologizing yet, or alternately, storming off, I took a chance. Thrusting my hands onto my hips, I walked right up to him. "I've never done any of that before. If that's the kind of wife you want or need, you already have her. So why don't you just go back to your ship where I won't embarrass you ever again."

"It's not that you…" He closed his eyes and shook his head. "I'm sorry. I didn't consider that you'd never been involved with one of our negotiations. I'm just used to—"

"Anastassia being there and knowing what to say and do? In case you hadn't noticed, I'm not her."

One of those toe-curling smiles crept over his lips. "I've definitely noticed." He closed the few inches of distance between us, his hands closing over mine as he pulled my hips against him. "Perhaps we could continue this inside?"

"You've barely apologized."

"Buria?"

I glared at him, waiting.

"I'm sorry. Really. It's been a rough day but I shouldn't have taken my shitty mood out on you."

I nodded. "And?"

"And I'd really like you to invite me inside so I can make it up to you."

Looking into his eyes in close quarters was likely a mistake, smoldering as they were, but I had to know if he was here for me or if all we had between us was his voracious appetite for alcohol and bang.

His eyes were clear and not dilated and his breath was liquor-free.

I twisted out of his grasp and stood aside, allowing him to enter my apartment. "I'm still mad at you."

He grinned. "Good. Stay that way for a while and don't let me off easy."

My pulse quickened. I'd spent days showing him what I liked. This was the first time he'd been open with me about what he enjoyed: dominant women—at least when he was in the mood for it. His relationship with Ana, their strong personalities frequently butting heads, suddenly made much more sense.

If he was willing to hand over the dominant role, at least when we were alone, I might be able to reign him in enough to make this work after all.

Working under Gamnock, I'd seen plenty of people like him and Elonka, people with strong personalities, have successful relationships. Cragtek tended to draw that sort in. Vayen's sort. I'd just never been inclined to be in one of those relationships before. In fact, I wasn't sure that I wanted to be in one of them now. But the way he was looking at me and the promise of having control over the Advisor of All even if only for a little while, did have an allure I found incredibly tempting.

It wouldn't hurt to try.

EIGHTEEN

Anastassia

When we came inside from the garden, I realized I was lightheaded. The room full of art was in sharp focus, the colors too bright, too real. The air crackled like I could hear every filter, scrubber, and pipe working. The sensory overload raked across my raw nerves, threatening to send me into another tear-filled breakdown.

I pressed my eyes shut and drove my fingernails into my palms to try to keep my emotions in check. "I think I stayed out there too long."

"Sorry, I assumed you had some tolerance. None of that case of boost was for you?"

The sound of his voice calmed me enough that I dared open my eyes to look at him. The hyper-focus of the pollen brought out the shadows and highlights on his facial bone structure, the golden flecks in his eyes, and the glittering silver in his wavy hair that promised a silken soft texture if only I slipped my hands into it.

I cleared my throat. "It was, but I don't know if I need it now that I've met you." I clamped my hand over my mouth. Fucking stareopantika-inhibition-freeing-pollen.

"I see." Tabor's lips twitched but he held his smile back. "How about I show you to your room where you can make that vid call and maybe take a nap until the effects wear off. Unless you'd rather talk for a bit while it's easier?"

"A nap sounds wonderful."

"I had a feeling you'd say that." He shook his head, chuckling under his breath.

We walked through his gallery and passed through a set of double doors at the far end. They opened into a sitting room that led to a dining room and then a kitchen. Beyond the kitchen was a stairway. The curved staircase opened into a spacious landing that appeared to be outfitted as a library. A hallway led to the left and right. Plenty of doorways led me to believe the house could comfortably hold the majority of his family, should they be inclined to visit.

Tabor brought me down the left hallway to the second doorway from the end. He palmed the panel. The door slid open silently.

I wasn't sure what to expect the room to look like considering Tabor and I had just met and he hadn't had time to prepare other than what his staff had managed at the last minute. He didn't really know me other than Neko's briefing and whatever rumors he'd heard or research he may have done. I did my best to quell the majority of public details regarding my private life.

The room was done in beige and orange, and far too feminine for my taste in terms of décor, too frilly and fluffy.

"You hate it." It was the first time I'd heard his confidence falter, as though he feared I might storm off at any second. "I'm sorry, I didn't have time to change anything. I wasn't expecting a house guest until I got the idea and—"

"There's a bed, and given the quality of everything else I've glimpsed in this house, it's going to be high-end and extremely comfortable. I'll take it."

"When you're feeling up to it, tell me what you'd like and I'll have it redone for you. Anything you want."

What I wanted was my bed on the Iber with a big Artorian in it and no one else. My vision blurred.

"Thank you. I'll try that nap now."

"Yes, of course. I'll be downstairs if you need me." He took a step away but then spun back around. "I shouldn't have kept you outside that long. I'm sorry. The breather masks are in a box just outside the clearplaz door. Assuming you want to go back out there at some point. I'm truly sorry. I wasn't trying to get you high so you'd spill everything. I promise."

It occurred to me that this was all new for him too, the idea of actually having a wife, of it being me, and all the limitations and baggage that entailed. As excited as Tabor had been after talking to Vayen this morning, after "regaining his balls", as he put it, it had to be frightening to think I could storm off and take that all away again.

"Tabor?"

He studied me with a darting gaze, licking his lips, and shifting his weight from foot to foot.

I channeled the loose-tongued effects toward keeping my private turmoil to myself while putting him at ease. "You're not the problem. My life is a fucking mess right now. I know you're trying to help. The room is fine. I'm sorry to interrupt your plans for the day."

He nodded and backed away before turning to hurry down the hall and to the stairs.

Wondering if he was rushing off to confer with Neko on how to handle me, I decided to cut him off. I sought out the terminal in the corner and sank into one of the fancy chairs that molded to my body size and shape. It was heavenly. Why had I never purchased one for myself?

I sent a call request to Neko and sat back, reveling in the cloud-like chair.

"Anastassia?" Neko's voice jolted me back to full awareness.

The pollen made the sound of Neko's voice too sharp, too loud. I adjusted the volume.

"Sorry, I'm visiting Rok. I'm not used to the connection going through so quickly."

"Rok is it?" Neko grinned. "You wouldn't be at a certain Jalvian's estate, would you?"

I didn't have to watch myself with Neko. Allowing myself to relax, I let the stareopantika take the edge off the ragged wounds in my heart.

"I might be." The triumph in his gaze was impossible to not meet with a grin. "You briefed him well. Either he's playing me masterfully, or you found exactly what I needed."

"I've known Tabor for years, Ana. I'm going with the latter."

"All right then. I owe you a freighter full of credits, a lifetime of favors, or a hug."

"Given the circumstances surrounding the need for the gratitude, I'll settle for the last one." His merriment dialed down. "How are you? Really?"

"I'm still alive."

"Keep it that way," he said with utter seriousness.

I nodded, unwilling to let my loose tongue divulge more details on that topic. Neko might be safe, but that didn't mean he wouldn't run to Vayen if he got wind that my life was in danger. Especially if that danger was from me.

The pollen's effects buffeted gently against the pain inside, easing, comforting, and washing the sting away. While that was a relief, I knew it was temporary.

"Vayen's announcement has lit off a reform movement far larger than the slow-build Daniel started. It's offered a new level of credence, a legitimacy to it all." Neko shook his head. "I hope he knows what he's doing with this ceremony. If it goes poorly, if there's any doubt that it's not fully consensual, the opposition is going to have a heyday. I'm already working on supplying extra security for the usual riot locations just in case."

"Good idea. Tabor is helping to plan the ceremony, or spearheading the planning, it seems to me, if that makes you feel any better or worse about it."

"Better. Delicate politics are his arena. Trust him."

"I am." Though how Tabor would pan out remained to be seen.

"I hate to ask, but how did Vayen take you and Tabor?"

"I wasn't there, but we're all still speaking so I guess well enough?"

Neko's eyes went wide. "He met Vayen alone? To discuss his joining with you? That could have gone poorly in seconds."

"He's still alive too, so it didn't."

"You'll keep him that way? Help him?"

I nodded. So, they were more than just business contacts. "How long have you known Tabor?"

"Longer than I've known you. We met through Cragtek and we've been friends since. I tried to put in a word for him when Vayen chose Rok's new Prime but I was overruled."

"Thank you, Neko."

He nodded. "Take care of yourself, Ana. I'm here if you need me."

"I know."

He smiled and then ended the call.

Feeling a little more at peace about going forward with Tabor, I left the terminal and approached the bed that would be mine in Tabor's house.

I'd never had a bedroom in another man's house before. They'd always come to mine. This man had a life of his own, his own staff, security, credits, and status. He needed me and yet, he didn't. He'd gotten by just fine before me, but my presence at his side, being there and visible, would greatly improve his status and help Neko. Anything we were to each other beyond that was up to me. Up to what I would allow.

I pulled back the fluffy layers of ivory and peach, the silken fabric sliding between my fingers. The dirt on my hands glared at me against the pristine cleanliness of the bed. I unlaced and kicked off my boots and then went to one of two narrow doorways inside the room. The first opened to a spacious but empty closet, the other to a bathroom that matched the bedroom. Cream tiles lined the floor with a smattering of orange tiles that formed scattered flowers. Thick towels sat in stacks on the counter. A deep tub, a plaz-walled shower, a sink, and a toilet. All the usual amenities, but fancier than what I was used to.

Our estate on Artor that had belonged to the previous Premier had the foundation of being like this. It had been cleared out before Vayen had purchased it, and I'd never put in the effort to return it to opulence. Material luxury had seemed frivolous, but I was going to be the wife of a dignitary. Frivolous or not, luxury would now be part of my life.

I stared into the framed oval mirror on the wall over the sink and wondered what my life would have been like if I'd gone down this path earlier. With the right leverage, I could have attached myself to a wealthy man, maybe even a Prime or Premier. I could have given up my Kryon position and the dirty work of the High Council, put my weapons down, pulled infant Daniel out of stasis, and lived in a house like this one, full of security, enjoying someone else's credits. I'd still have my link, though probably little need for it, and fewer scars and aches. Far less baggage. Especially under my eyes. How was it possible to have enough excess skin for wrinkles, yet appear gaunt, and also have dark puffy bags under my eyes? It was not an attractive combination.

After washing my hands and face and drying them on the thickest, softest towel I'd ever used, I shed my outer clothes and slipped into the bed. The pillow smelled like sunshine. The silken sheets slid over my skin. After two tries, I got the right Jalvian vocal command to turn out the lights. The heavy drapes were already pulled. I'd check the view later. For now, I closed my eyes and imagined living here, enjoying this bed on a regular basis, and sleeping alone without the hope of Vayen's familiar warmth and weight joining me.

Placing my trust in a security staff I hadn't seen and a man I'd met only a day ago, I tried to sleep.

The room was too silent, the bed not my own. Maybe it was the pollen making me more paranoid than usual. Chancing that I'd catch something I wanted no part of, I cracked open my bonded connection with Vayen just enough that I got a sense of him, safe and familiar.

He must have been on alert for me because he was in my head in an instant.

"Stassia, are you all right?"

"I'm inadvertently a little high, but yes. Trying to sleep it off."

"Tell me about it later? I see why you ran off with Tabor. These Ocelon are a pain in the ass."

For a second, we were back to normal. It felt so good, tears welled in my eyes. Then I remembered why I was on Rok instead of in our bedroom with him.

"Go easy on the wrath. You can win them over."

"I will."

I got the sensation that his attention had darted elsewhere. With my mind still linked with his, I closed my eyes.

When I opened them again, four hours had passed and my head felt much clearer. I dressed and went into the bathroom to straighten the mess that my hair had become during my apparent tossing and turning, likely thanks to the pollen. I took out the remains of the braid and tamed the chaos with the brush waiting on the countertop.

What the hell, I wasn't going anywhere other than downstairs. Maybe being out of work mode would help me relax here. I left my hair loose and went to find Tabor.

A man stood in the kitchen, juggling two pans and a tray of golden-brown knots. Mouth-watering scents wafted my way, making me realize how hungry I was. When he turned around, I snapped out of my fixation on the food. He wasn't Tabor.

"Sir," he called out. "She's awake."

Tabor rushed into the room wearing the distracted look of someone deep in a network. "This is Mycel, my cook. Did you sleep well?"

I nodded to Mycel before turning back to Tabor. "Well enough, I suppose."

Tabor motioned for me to follow him into the next room.

"About five minutes, sir," said Mycel.

"Very good. Thank you." Tabor turned to me. "I was just about to come up and wake you."

He took a seat on one side of the long rectangular dining table and indicated for me to sit directly across from him. At least we weren't to be at opposite ends of the table. A bouquet of blue and white flowers sat in the middle between two actual place settings, the kind with multiple utensils and various glasses. The only one that was filled contained water. That was just as well. I'd had more than enough alcohol lately.

"What's all this?" I waved my hand over the table.

"Multitasking." Tabor smiled, his eyes doing that merry twinkle thing again. "You have to be hungry by now. I was hoping to entice you to visit as often as you like by having Mycel impress you with his culinary skills."

Too used to Vayen's truth-by-omission routine, I stared him down. "That's one thing."

"I'm also planning the menu for the signing ceremony. Having tasted the food on the Iber, none of you are qualified to impress the level of guests who will be attending."

Enjoying the mouth-watering scents coming from the kitchen, I smiled. "Fair. Food beyond sustenance has never been a priority for us. Both Vayen and Daniel have a fair amount of skill in the kitchen, but the crew doesn't get to benefit from those."

"I'm glad you don't suffer the lack of taste in the dining hall on a permanent basis."

He took my positive mention of Vayen in stride. I added graciousness to his growing list of attributes.

I picked up three differently sized forks. "You're intending to make this a whole ordeal, aren't you?"

"Your guests will be expecting a magnificent spectacle. They're going to get it."

Mycel came in and set a small plate before both of us. My stomach rumbled.

Tabor picked up a fork and took a bite. Chewing, he looked pleased. He nodded to Mycel. The cook gave a little bow and left. I tried a bite. Lost in the stunning flavor for a moment, I simply enjoyed the food.

"Do you like it?" Tabor asked.

"Very much. Definitely far beyond what I'm used to, even at home." I shoved another bite into my mouth and then considered that I should probably work on my table manners given my immediate company and who we would be dining with in a couple of weeks.

"And who is paying for this spectacle?" I asked after the four bites on the little plate had been eagerly consumed.

Tabor tapped his chin. "This is one of those choose your battles moments, isn't it?"

"Why do you say that?"

"Because Vayen should. He's the one initiating this mess, as you call it. The cause for the need of the spectacle." Tabor shook his head.

"But being joined, that would mean you also would be paying for half of it, and to be honest, I don't think I can stomach that given how much pain you're in."

"There's no need to get all chivalrous on my account. I agree. He should pay."

"As the man who will be your husband, at least for whatever length of contract you allow me, I'll get chivalrous if I damned well want to."

I watched him for a long moment, not sure if he was joking or utterly serious. Still not sure, I smiled. No one had been chivalrous on my account in a long while. "What do you propose?"

"I'll pay half."

"Not meaning to offend, but I don't know your financial situation. Is that feasible for you?"

"I'll make it work. Threats, favors, I have a host of both I can call in as needed."

"I appreciate that." I did, equally that he spoke a familiar language of business and also that he was willing to spend his leverage on my account.

Mycel appeared with another set of plates. We spent the next hour gorging on his culinary creations until I couldn't take another bite.

"I can safely say, my taste buds have never been so happy."

Tabor laughed. "I'm glad to hear a least a little of you is happy." He wiggled his eyebrows. "Just wait until tomorrow, when we sample desserts."

"Promise me we won't do this regularly because my metabolism isn't what it used to be. I don't want to buy a whole new wardrobe."

"Speaking of that. I was thinking about what you should wear for the ceremony."

"Oh no. I agreed to be there, not to play dress up. I'm sure I have something suitable in my closet. I'm assuming this will be a no armor event?"

A deadpan stare answered my question. "This is a political statement, Anastassia. You'll need to look the part. I'll pass my recommendation on to Buria for the two of them, but you're far more my concern."

"Excuse me?" I'd give him something to be concerned about. Except I didn't have any weapons on me and I was a guest in his house. I settled for a glare and gripped the dainty dinner knife for good measure.

"Buria is an unknown. No one is expecting anything of her. Vayen has his own image to maintain and no one is going to dare openly judge him one way or the other. You, on the other hand, are a prominent public figure and you're marrying into a prestigious Jalvian family. We need to make sure you and I look credible as a couple. This cannot appear to be a business arrangement. We're supposed to be setting an example."

"All right. What do you consider credible?" I set the knife down.

"First of all, no weapons at the ceremony." He glanced from the knife to my hand and shook his head. "We'll have plenty of security on site. With that many important people in one place, we can't afford for anything to go wrong."

"Can we agree on no visible weapons? Vayen will certainly want his own protection too."

Tabor didn't look happy about it, but he nodded. "Secondly, I know we just met, and I don't expect you to mean any of it, but in public, we need to appear involved with one another."

"Romantically, you mean."

His tone was suddenly strained. "Yes."

If I could fake being all right with Vayen sleeping with Buria, I could put on a show of falling for a man I could easily tolerate. "All right. I can do that."

"Can you do it with Vayen present?"

Damn, I hadn't thought that far. Could I keep our bond muffled while in the same room? It was one thing when we were apart, but the pressure of having him there would make cutting our connection off difficult. And likely make him more irritable than if he were in my head while watching me put on a show with Tabor.

"Can you sell it enough that he doesn't know you're not sincere in your feelings for me? We need his reactions to be genuine to prove to other Artorians that a bonded couple can do this."

"He'd be much more apt to put on a positive performance if he knew we weren't seriously involved."

Tabor caught me in a hard stare. "Do you want him to know our agreement is merely out of convenience rather than driven by feelings as his relationship with Buria is? Do you want him to think you have anything less than what he's demanding?"

"I'm thinking this push to fool Vayen is more about you getting even with him than whatever my feelings are on the matter." I slid my chair back and stood. "As per our arrangement, I'll be in the garden."

Tabor found me sitting beside the pond an hour later. The transparent breather mask covered my nose and mouth. He didn't wear one. I imagined his tolerance must be quite high or perhaps he didn't expect to be outside very long.

Settling onto the wall beside me, he rubbed his fingers over the tiny shimmering tiles. He spoke quietly, reluctantly. "Be honest with Vayen if you wish. As long as we all play our parts convincingly. That's what's important." He held his hand out to me. "Will you come back inside?"

"Not yet, but I will walk with you. I need the exercise after that extravagant meal."

Tabor nodded and stood, still holding out his hand. I took it and let him help me to my feet. My stomach hurt, likely from stuffing myself. But my legs were also stiff and so was my back and neck.

"Would you mind if I stretched a bit first? I've missed my usual workouts for the past few days and my body is apparently on strike."

"Of course." He let go and settled back onto the pond ledge.

I stepped into a patch of neatly shorn grass just off the gravel path and dropped into the first pose of the Seeker forms, holding it for a minute before moving to the next.

"Where did you learn those? Do you mind if I try?" Tabor asked as I moved into the third form.

My hold on the pose faltered. I quickly put the foot that had been up in the air back on the ground to keep my balance. In all the years I remembered, Vayen had watched me do the forms, but never once had he made any effort to learn them or join me.

"Sure." I guided Tabor into the second and then third forms while telling him about my years of Seeker training and practice.

"I had no idea. I mean, I knew your daughter was a Seeker, but not you. Why do you hide it?" He studied me as I moved to the fourth form and copied it.

"Left arm higher." I nodded as he made the adjustment. "I don't hide it. It's just not important here, with what we're doing, or anywhere in the Narvan. Ikeri and Vayen's gifts far outshine anything I can do. I was never very good at it, the full practice, but I bumbled along in a fairly satisfying manner for the years we lived on Veria Minor."

"Do you still practice?"

"Occasionally." We moved to the fifth form, placing both hands on the ground with one leg up in the air. I peered past my stationary leg to get an upside-down view of Tabor following me with applaudable precision. "Good. The damage that necessitated the removal of my link ended much of what I used to be able to do in terms of being a Seeker, but as a blunt old Verian woman once told me, I still have hands. Most of what I do these days uses those and the forms help keep me limber and in shape for doing what I can. I travel to Verian Minor now and then and still see some of my clients."

"That's amazing." He mimicked the sixth form.

"Is it?" I checked his stance and found nothing to correct.

"You are, yes." He smiled. "It would seem we've both lost an integral part of ourselves. Though, I think you've done a better job at moving forward despite it."

"I may be able to help you with that," I blurted. I couldn't even blame the pollen for my slip. It was all him being nice, and joining me in the forms, the food, being so honest. The way he looked at me. The way he'd slipped neatly into my life, filling a void I hadn't known existed until Vayen had exposed it.

Neko trusted Tabor. Isnar did business with him. Vayen had even accepted him, albeit begrudgingly. I didn't have to hide anything from him. He wasn't out to take anything from me. We were just two people who were going to be spending at least a couple of nights a week together for the foreseeable future.

And I liked him. Dammit.

His hold on the precarious form wavered. He caught his balance and stood straight, watching me, lips parted, breathing fast.

I let the form go. "You have mind speech. Surely you're aware of how Artorians join minds for sexual gratification?"

"I've heard about it, but I never..." he said, desperation all over his face. "I never dared tell anyone I had mind speech before. What Artorian woman would want to pleasure a Jalvian in that way?"

"It doesn't have to be an Artorian woman. I'm quite familiar with the practice."

"You could? You would?" He looked ready to burst on the spot.

I held up a hand. "Let's try a little first and see if it's an option before you get too excited. You're not typical to either end of the race. I don't want to get your hopes up."

"Too late." He grinned. "Try. A little. A lot. Please, woman, whatever you're willing to do."

"Sit."

He dropped onto the grass like the most eager acolyte I'd ever seen. I sat in front of him, my back to his chest, and pulled his hands into my lap, entwining our fingers so I could feel if what I was about to do was working. I wasn't ready to look at him, to acknowledge who I was with, to have that personal connection. This was a form of therapy, an exercise to find relief for a man who had a long-suffering condition.

I closed my eyes and devoted everything I had to making my weak presence known in Tabor's mind. Once, I would have done this with no effort at all, but my telepathic abilities and their strength weren't what they used to be.

His mind was unlike the one I was used to slipping into, the pathways in slightly different places. When I finally located his pleasure center, I ran a cautious caress along it. Tabor gasped, his breath warm against my ear.

Normally I would have been touching him and he would be touching me, we would be sharing those sensations, our thoughts, what we wanted, what we needed with one another. It had been a long time since I'd played at mind sex without any physical aspect, and he had no experience in his own pleasure to play off of in terms of imagery. I wasn't ready to share any imagery of my own, and while I could have pulled up some general sexual mental footage, I guessed he'd had plenty of experience with pornography, though to what end, I had to wonder.

With a shake of my head, I realized I was overthinking this test. If he'd never done this before, it wouldn't take much to learn if we could get the job done.

My mental caress repeated, more intent this time, imaginary fingers stroking, exploring. His hands tightened around mine, confirming that my efforts were working. The test was a success.

I could stop.

"Anastassia," he pleaded in my ear with a hoarse whisper.

It wouldn't hurt to see if he felt the level of gratification on his end was worthwhile.

My imaginary fingers worked his pleasure center, rubbing, stroking, and placing pressure on just the right places—I gathered from the panting in my ear and the low moan that followed when I eased up for a second.

Without any imagery, the process felt wrong, clinical rather than passionate. While it might be an experiment on my end, this was his first time. He deserved more than a quick poke in the brain. We'd kissed before, I could live with sharing that again.

Blanketing his mind with images and sensations, our lips, tongues exploring, his hands on my back and mine on his, I increased the pressure, stroking faster. A ragged moan a few moments later along with the burst of light and a momentary mind-numbing hum confirmed the success of my efforts.

Just as I was pulling out of his mind, Tabor ripped the breather mask from my face and kissed me hard and long, his arms locking me to him. Despite my efforts to keep this experimental, I found myself enjoying his touch.

When he finally broke off the kiss, he lingered, his lips only inches away. His face was flushed and his gaze seemed to drink me in. "My dearest and only, I am never going to let you go."

NINETEEN

Anastassia

I wanted to point out that Tabor would have to let me go, that we couldn't sit in the grass forever, especially now that I wasn't wearing a breather mask, but I let him have a moment to catch his breath.

"Can we do the walk later? I think I did too much breathing in," he said.

"Maybe you should have worn a mask too." I got to my feet while he did the same.

"I'm usually fine for an hour or so. But I didn't anticipate...that." He wrapped one arm around me as we headed back to the house. "Please let me know if there's anything I can do to entice you to do it again. Anytime. And I mean anything."

I laughed. "Be careful what you offer me. And really, it can be much better than that. More involved."

"I don't remember hearing evil temptress in Neko's briefing."

I laughed harder. "We do have a signing night coming up in a couple of weeks. As I recall, it is customary to exchange sexual gratification on such an occasion." And by then, I hoped I would be more ready to make good on that offer.

Tabor opened the door to the house. He held it for me while I put the mask away. "Please don't make me wait two weeks. Not after that. I've waited fifty-three years," he said plaintively.

"We'll see."

"I mean it. Anything." Then, as if sensing he was testing my patience, he backed off. "I need to work for a few hours. Will you join me for dinner later?"

I nodded and headed for the stairs. He watched me go, the sensation of his gaze only fading once I reached the library landing.

It seemed that even when I did try to do this relationship differently, better, my pattern was set in stone. Sex reeled them in every time. The question was, what did I want from Tabor in return?

Dinner was quiet, passing in an awkward exchange of getting to know one another with amicable silences in between. The food was again fantastic, and Mycel flushed when I complimented him on the meal. My dinner companion, however, seemed out of sorts.

Once the plates had been cleared, and a drink had been offered, which I declined but Tabor did not, Mycel excused himself to clean the kitchen and retire for the evening.

Tabor sat, idly wiping condensation from his glass, taking distracted sips and avoiding my gaze. Without my datapad and with no link of my own, just sitting there seemed like wasting time. Either we were going to talk or I was going to my room.

"What is it then?"

Tabor's gaze snapped up to my face. His mouth opened once, then closed, grimacing instead.

"It can't be that bad."

"My family is denying my request."

"Request for what? They can't deny our marriage contract. I can overrule them," I assured him.

"No. My request for my grandmother's dress, the one she wore for her signing ceremony. She intended to have every heir's first wife wear it."

"Did your brother's wife wear it?" If she did, maybe that would void the legitimacy of the outdated heirloom.

Tabor snorted. "She wouldn't be caught dead in someone else's clothes. Her words. So no, Enud couldn't talk her into it."

Well, damn. Maybe there was another angle to use to get out of this. "If your family doesn't see you as the heir, they're not releasing the dress then?"

"Only as a technicality. Not in practice. And yes, they're refusing to hand it over."

I shrugged, relieved. "I'll wear something else."

"You're supposed to wear the dress. It's a statement," he all but snarled. "My grandmother made that very clear to me when I was the heir. Before." He gestured at his lap. "She was the only one who stuck up for me afterward, but my parents didn't heed her advice other than to grant me the house."

Having never met my grandparents, I couldn't exactly relate, but I had plenty of experience with dysfunctional families. If Tabor's grandmother had a hand in molding the kind man before me, I owed her a favor. And besides, I considered as I glanced at the armband that signified my joining to Vayen, at least I would only have to wear whatever monstrosity of a dress this was for one day.

"I guess that means we need to go meet your family so I can demand the dress be turned over to us."

A slow smile eased the tension on his face. "I'm going to love having you around."

"Probably not."

"I meant what I said earlier, dearest and only. Besides, you're welcome to make it up to me if you're feeling snappish at any time."

He was already throwing endearments my way? I shook my head. Like many other things he was enamored with at the moment, he'd get over me soon enough.

"When would you like to put on this show of force?"

All eager kid again, he asked, "Can we surprise them? Can we do it now?"

I made a show of checking my invisible datapad. "It appears I do have an opening in my schedule."

He grinned.

"Is there anything I need to know going in?" I asked.

"Don't worry about protocol or manners, this isn't the ceremony. They already hate me. You can't make anything worse. Just be you."

"Got it." I beckoned him over to my side of the table and held out my hand.

Tabor dashed to my side and pulled us both into the void fifteen seconds faster than the first time. He'd have to keep working on it or Vayen and Daniel would pitch a fit.

We stepped out of the void into a black room. A flood of trepidation surged through me. I didn't know this place, barely knew this man, couldn't leave on my own, and I couldn't see a damned thing. A second before I contacted Vayen, Tabor squeezed my hand.

"Don't worry. It's safe," he said, swinging a door open in front of us. I blinked in the bright light to find that we stood in a small shed that was empty but for a painted pattern on the floor.

"They won't allow you to Jump into the house?"

"Nope. I have mentioned that they don't like me, haven't I?"

"You have."

I wished I had my armor and a host of weaponry to back me up, but those were all safely aboard the Iber in the room Tabor decreed I shouldn't go into alone. At any other point in my life, declarations of that sort would have driven me into instant rebellion, but he was right. The suite I shared with Vayen was a gaping wound I wasn't ready to face.

The reality of what I'd thought was my future, my relationship with my long-time mate had been a daydream. A lie. A lie Vayen had been perpetuating for years. And I'd blindly let him.

If I walked back into that room alone with the truth rushing around me, it was very likely I'd again find myself pondering the contents of my arsenal. I might like Tabor, but the devastation of my true situation lurked too close to the surface to ignore if I ventured into familiar territory.

Tabor's pace slowed. He turned to give me a concerned once-over. "Are you sure you want to do this? I can try them again tomorrow or maybe you could just send them a threatening message instead?"

"I'll be fine," I said, forcing certainty into those words...just like Vayen had when he'd walked out of our suite. A deep breath later, I crammed my emotions back down where they belonged and focused on the task at hand.

Walking up to the Desu family home beside Tabor without armor and weapons reminded me of my early days of feeling out my place on Artor beside Chesser. Long before I'd fallen in with Kryon and the High Council, before I'd even owned armor, back when my life was simple.

The Desu home rivaled the lofty mansion I'd owned on Merchess, fronted by plenty of ornamentation to flaunt their wealth and status. Precise plantings with manicured shrubbery lined the immediate foundation and walkway up to the seven wide steps that led to the front door. Three spotless, high-end land transports were parked in the drive, each with a charging port.

Tabor palmed the panel at the front door and then entered his name on the keypad next to it. Then we waited. Seemingly not bothered by being locked out of his family home, Tabor peered at the landscaping with half-hearted interest until the door opened seven minutes later.

"What do you want?" asked an arrogant woman who had Tabor's eyes but otherwise appeared fully Jalvian.

Tabor turned to me. "This is my sister, Renia. Sorry about her manners. They leave much to be desired." He turned back to his sister. "Renia, perhaps you'd like to invite Advisor Ta'set into the house and then ask our parents to join us in the sitting room."

Renia looked me over as if trying to reconcile my current casual appearance with my usual public image. "Advisor Ta'set? *The* Advisor?"

"One of, yes. Are we having this meeting on the porch or inside?" I asked.

"Come in," she said hastily, moving aside to allow us entry.

"You were serious?" hissed Renia as she walked beside Tabor ahead of me. "You're entering into a contract with the Advisor Ta'set?"

"I am," Tabor said proudly.

"How much of the family fortune did you blow on this endeavor? What did it buy you? A week-long contract? A month at most? You have nothing to offer her, you idiot!"

I gently brushed Tabor aside before slamming his immaculately dressed sister against the wall and shoving my arm against her graceful throat just above her thick gold chain bearing a polished semi-transparent blue gemstone the size of an eyeball. "Enough."

Startled, Renia gasped but otherwise went still.

"The Advisor would be pleased to never hear you speak again. Do as you were asked and then join us." I let her go.

Renia dashed away. Her delicate high-heeled shoes tapped a frantic rhythm that slowly faded into the depths of the house.

"Sorry, she was getting on my nerves talking to you like that."

Tabor laced his fingers into mine. "Have I told you that I love you? I do."

I snorted. "You love what I can do for you. You're welcome."

His fingers lost their rigidity and his steps slowed. Not seeing any immediate reason for his hesitancy, I towed him along.

The straight hallway opened into a grand, round room with glossy stone floors in swirls of browns and ivory. Light shown from above through the small plaz squares that comprised the arched ceiling. There was a fucking fountain in the middle of the room that was the size of an average suite on the Iber.

"Tabor, who have you brought for us to meet?" asked a Jalvian woman easily thirty years older than me. Her coiffed hair had gone white, and even the artfully applied plaster of cosmetics couldn't mask her age. Not that I looked much better.

Behind the woman I assumed was Tabor's mother, entered a broad-shouldered but slender man with thinning blonde hair and piercing blue eyes. Two younger, near-identical men followed him with Renia behind, all rushing forward to gather around the matron.

They looked to me, ignoring Tabor completely. He dropped my hand and stepped back. The man I knew to be Rok's Prime was not present, yet Tabor seemed to be visibly shrinking. The excitement he'd exhibited before we'd left and even after I'd sent his sister scurrying was gone.

"What are you doing?"

"Just get the dress." Even his voice was limp and lifeless.

I missed his exuberance, the hint of fun we were going to have here terrorizing his family. He'd been onboard up until...

Dammit, I'd never been good at saying the right thing, always managing to inadvertently crush men who loved me. Chesser and I had constantly verbally stomped on one another. Marin, well, talking had never been the focus of our relationship, but I'd managed to tick him off the few times we'd tried. Kess had taken his fair share of my vocal misfires and Vayen had suffered my snide comments in numbers beyond counting. Now I was stepping on Tabor.

"I heard you. I'm sorry I made light of your feelings for me."

He stepped closer, arm brushing against mine but he didn't say anything.

"How about we do a warm-up for the marriage ceremony? You can tell me if I'm convincing enough."

"Sure, all right," he said without the enthusiasm I'd hoped for.

"This is your family. Stand up to them and know I have your back."

Tabor glanced at me. *"Do you?"*

"I do." I looped my arm in his, resting my hand just above his wrist.

Standing even with me and seeming to reinflate, Tabor launched into introductions, as if Renia hadn't already told everyone who had walked into their house beside her disregarded brother.

"And you're signing a marriage contract. With my son?" asked his incredulous father.

"Is that so surprising?"

"For how long?" asked his mother. Her haughty tone indicated she was just waiting for the punch line to what certainly must be a terrible joke.

I placed my other hand over Tabor's, pulling him closer. "Indefinitely."

"She'll cancel it the next day when she finds out," snarked one of his younger brothers.

The other laughed.

Drawing myself up to my full height, and mimicking the imposing stare down one's nose that Jalvian's were so fond of, I said, "She knows and she doesn't care. She will not cancel the contract."

The two younger brothers quieted, watching us warily.

"He'll never be Prime. Enud would be a much better match. I'm sure he'd be happy to take a second wife such as yourself," offered Tabor's father.

"Second wife?" I scoffed. "I am second to no one. And don't be so sure about Enud remaining Prime. It's Tabor's rightful position, and I know exactly who kept him from it."

His father's chest puffed up and his chin rose in a clear challenge. "Your mate did. He chose the right Desu to lead Rok."

In my anger, I let go of Tabor and got in his father's face, jabbing a finger into his lackluster chest. "Because you, Tabor's own family exiled him to keep him out of sight, persecuted him across worlds, kept him from the life that was rightfully his all because of the cruel act of one of his brothers. A brother who stood to gain by the grievous injury he caused. And you backed that son instead? What kind of people are you?"

His mother rolled her eyes. "Is that the sob story he told you? Poor Tabor," she mocked.

Could a mother be so cruel if what Tabor had told me was the truth? Had he lied? I glanced over my shoulder. His gaze didn't waver. He showed no sign of worry that he'd been caught. Instead, he came to stand next to me, glaring at his mother.

"It's the truth. One you refuse to believe. You always favored Enud. Did you give him the idea?"

She sniffed, refusing to look at him even though he was right in front of her. "You weren't seriously injured. Quit blaming everyone else for your failings."

"Not seriously injured? he snapped

I'm going to have a raging headache, but I need to know. So do you."

"Anastassia?"

"Keep her talking about the attack."

While the two of them verbally sparred and his father joined in to defend both Enud and his wife, I probed Tabor's mother. Without full use of my telepathy, I couldn't go too deep or stay in her head very long. What I did see took me aback.

"You heartless bitch." I slapped her so hard that she stumbled backward and fell to the floor on her knees, clutching her face. "How could you do that to your own son?"

Tabor's father took a step back. Renia ran to her mother's side, helping her to her feet. The brothers, still locked in their uncertainty, stayed as they were.

"You could do that to a twelve-year-old boy?" My voice trembled, but I didn't care. Let them think it was out of rage. I'd done some pretty horrible things in my life, but I couldn't imagine being so callous as to instruct one of my children to maim the other. There were no motives that made that all right. Not even with my ambiguous conscience.

Tabor's mother shook off Renia's grasp and faced me. "You don't know what you're talking about. He's blinded you with his sad story. Woe is Tabor, the overlooked son."

If I'd had a gun, things would have gone very poorly for Tabor's mother, but I didn't. However, I knew someone who did, who had a stake in this, and who had learned justice from the death-bringer himself.

"Tabor, please summon Neko here immediately. Tell him I'm asking for him. Flash him a jump point. Do you know how to do that?"

He nodded, looking stunned.

"My son won't let you harm me. He's the Prime of Rok!" Tabor's mother screamed at me.

"I saw the truth in your mind." I shook my head. "Your favorite son won't be Prime for much longer."

"You only sleep with an Artorian, you're not one of them," she sneered.

"No, I'm a whole different problem for you. I happen to like your son, the good one. Quite a lot, actually. And now I find out that you maimed him. So be very thankful that I don't have a gun in my hand right now."

"Would you like one?" Neko's familiar voice greeted me.

"It's probably better that you take control of this situation. Vayen's wrath may be wearing off on me."

"Could you clarify the situation?" he asked cautiously.

"Tabor's mother was the one to orchestrate the success of Rok's current prime. She instructed him to mutilate her eldest, not-Jalvian-enough son. I probed her. It's all there. You'll want an unbiased Artorian interrogator to confirm, as this is a high-profile case."

"And you'll want Enud Desu removed from office?"

"Definitely. And publicly charged."

"Tabor is to take his place?"

I looked to Tabor. A subtle head shake confirmed the answer I'd already guessed.

"I have more important plans for him. Shop around for a suitable fit." I eyed Tabor's siblings. "It would seem the Desu line isn't suited for Prime for a generation or two."

"You can't do this," scoffed Renia, clutching her mother's arm.

"She just did," said Neko, wrenching Tabor's mother from Renia's grasp. "I suggest the rest of you be on your best behavior. Tabor is a good friend of mine, and I'll be watching all of you closely."

His father shook his head, glancing from his wife to Tabor and to me and then Neko. Finally, he addressed Tabor. "You have connections with the Narvan's Advisor too? Why haven't you ever said anything? You could have been using this to our family's advantage."

Tabor scoffed. "You had no interest in using me for anything. Why the hells would I help you? Any of you?"

Seeing him standing up for himself filled me with warmth.

"I'm going to go find a suitable place to hold your mother. Please keep your soon-to-be-wife from killing anyone."

Tabor nodded to Neko. Neko vanished with Tabor's mother in hand.

"Are we even inviting them to the marriage ceremony? Can we trust them in a room filled with the most important people in the Narvan and beyond?" I asked Tabor.

He looked like he was going to say no, right down to the shake of his head and scowl on his face, but then he seemed to rethink his answer. "Yes, they should be there so they can tell their grandchildren how one of their line married into the Ta'set family even though he wasn't whole or perfect."

"He is," I assured his father and siblings. "You were all just too blind to see it."

The look of sheer adoration Tabor gave me about melted me on the spot. I walked over to stand beside him. Through the pounding in my head from the probe, a sudden rough nudge registered. Just as I was about to question Tabor, wondering if he was fumbling an effort to speak telepathically, the nudge smoothed out to a soft warmth accompanied by a distant musical hum. The warmth wrapped around me, through me, soothing my headache and my host of usual aches like the most effective calming balm. I sighed deeply with the relief from it all.

A familiar sensation of closeness, of not being alone in my head, settled over me. Like a bond. Every ounce of my attention flew at Tabor, seeking answers, but he was distracted with his father.

"Before we go, I need one thing from you," Tabor declared.

"Get the dress," his father called to Renia.

"But mother said—"

"Now."

"I'll get it," offered one of the younger brothers. He darted off the way they'd all come.

Despite wanting answers, questioning what had just happened between us in front of his family would destroy everything he'd just gained. While Tabor fidgeted in his aggravation, I took the long and awkward minutes to poke internally at the new sensations swirling in my head. Pleasant and peaceful sensations, that despite the tense situation, offered the allure of curling up inside and basking in them for a good long while.

His bother returned with a thick bag draped over his arm. He handed it to Tabor. "I'm sorry. We didn't know."

Tabor nodded, taking the bag. He placed a hand on my arm and then we were back at his house in his gallery full of questionably acquired art.

TWENTY

Anastassia

Tabor reverently draped the bag containing his grandmother's dress over the nearest piece of furniture, and then, with his arms free, pulled me into a fierce hug. His entire body shook. Tears registered against my cheek. I held him there in the gallery, surrounded by all the things he couldn't bear to lose.

After a few moments, he took a shuddering breath and wiped his face. "Sorry about that. I don't normally—"

I kissed him. Actually kissed him. Because I wanted to, because I didn't want the warmth and hum to end, because I wanted him to feel it too.

He pulled back, resting his forehead against mine. "You were right. I do love what you can do for me. I only wish I had something to offer you in return. Other than being a man you can tolerate and a placeholder for political reasons."

"Did you do something? Before we left just a few minutes ago? With me? Something you've maybe never done before?"

He lifted his head to meet my gaze. "I... I wished I could show you how I feel, that you could see that I meant what I said. Like talking in your mind, but with feelings? Did I do something wrong?"

"No, not wrong exactly."

If I could allow Vayen's natural urge to find another woman, I could indulge Tabor's long-awaited urge to bond. Especially if this was what it was like, calming, musical, and warm. With anyone else, I would have been raging and cursing every deity I could think of, but here with Tabor, I only smiled.

"I know it's too soon, that we just met, that I'm not the one you want, but Anastassia, I can't help it. It just feels right. You and I."

Tabor took a deep breath. His gaze dropped to the floor. "Your performance was quite convincing. You'll do just fine at the ceremony.

"It wasn't."

"Oh, it was. Even I believed it for a moment there."

I brought my hands up from his waist to his shoulders, pulling him closer against me. "It wasn't a performance."

His gaze danced over me until he slowly smiled. "So you do like me."

I nodded. "I'm not ready to commit to more than that just yet, but yes. And whatever you did back there, you got your wish. I can feel what you feel."

"Seriously? You can?"

"Yes." I led him out of the too busy room. The pain in my head was starting to overtake the balming hum and warmth. "You managed to initiate a bond with me."

Tabor winced. "I'm so sorry. I didn't realize that's what I was doing. I've never even considered that I could." He sighed. "I pledged that I wouldn't, and here I go breaking vows already. Do you have the poison on you? We might as well get this over with. At least I'll die happy."

Though he appeared utterly serious, and I did recall his declaration over the poison he'd returned to me, I couldn't stop the laugh that burst from my mouth.

"That won't be necessary." Making use of our new connection, I made sure he understood I was sincere despite my laughter. "I think this is what the bond is supposed to be. Vayen's was never complete with me because I'm not Artorian and then the damage to my abilities made it even less, but I got a glimpse of it a few times. Maybe this is what it was naturally, before all the intense spliced-in enhancements?"

Tabor watched me intently, as if waiting for me to explode or change my mind about the poison.

I settled onto one of his very comfortable couches. On any other day, I would have said falling out of one bonded relationship right into another was a curse, but having lost everything I'd come to depend on, an unfamiliar acquiescence delivered the ease I desperately needed.

"Vayen didn't mean to bond with me either. Seems to be my fate, I guess." I tugged Tabor down beside me and rested my aching head against the back of the couch. "His bond is very one-sided in his favor as far as feeling anything like this, and we lost his original one thanks to me and an Arpex. He formed a second bond with me, but it's weaker, less compelling. Everything that happened to him after he was fused with the Arpex has been unraveling the genetic alterations that make Artorians what they are today. Vayen has changed but I didn't want to see it." I sighed, mourning the satisfying life I'd thought we'd had while Vayen had secretly been miserable.

The calming warmth intensified, embracing me as Tabor's excitement danced around us with light tinkling notes.

If I could feel what Tabor was feeling so clearly, what he was doing used a different part of the brain, a part that wasn't damaged. A part that was compatible. That was something Vayen and I hadn't ever had.

"This is different. I...like it."

He gifted me with another heart-melting smile before putting his hand to my forehead. "How bad is it? Should you take something?"

"A long nap after a strong drink usually works as well as anything else."

The concern on his face was also in my mind. "Are you sure? Should I contact Vayen?"

"It's just a headache. I'll be fine. I get them a lot, especially when I overtax my limited abilities."

"Not a fan of having anyone take care of you, are you? Soldiering through everything you and Geva throw your way?" He slowly, almost absently, ran his fingers along my hairline, pulling the loose strands away from my face.

I managed an assenting mumble while concentrating my attention on his relaxing touch and the soft musical hum and tingle flowing between us. One thing he'd said I couldn't disagree with, no matter how much logic said it was stupid and that wasn't possible in the short span we'd known each other: He and I, this, it did feel right. From the moment I'd seen his still frame in Neko's files, I'd felt something, a connection.

"If you're going to rest, would you like a different room? There are plenty to choose from while we redecorate yours."

"Leave it. It's fine."

The very fact that the room wasn't me at all helped set this place apart from my life with Vayen on the Iber. It was the room of a dignitary's wife. That's what I would be here, not Advisor Ta'set.

"Let's get you that drink then. I could use one myself." He stood.

I closed my eyes, listening to his footsteps and the distant clink of glasses and bottles. Of all the times I'd had to reinvent myself after loss and heartache, this one felt easiest. Maybe because Vayen was still there and my life as Advisor beside him wasn't entirely gone. Maybe because I wasn't alone in having to find my way in this new role.

The thought of having to go back to the Iber in a few days and having to see Vayen made me feel sick. He'd have been with Buria while I was here. I'd have to face him, knowing that this was going to be our life going forward, sharing him. He was going to see that I was happy with Tabor and that would throw even his weakly bonded-ass into a tizzy. None of that felt like something to look forward to.

Tabor returned with two glasses, pressed one into my hand, and then sat beside me. I took a sip of liquor strong enough to warm my tongue on initial contact. Vayen would have liked it.

I didn't want to think about him, not with Tabor's calming bliss floating around me. Yet, I couldn't help but wonder if Vayen would break his pledge too. He'd never been typical in Artorian terms, and with all his alterations, who was to say that he couldn't form some degree of bond with Buria? Whether he meant to or not.

I took a long pull from the glass, closed my eyes and returned my head to the back of the couch. Did I want him to bond to her? If he did, I could bow out, maybe stay here, maybe not have to look him in the eye and pretend I was happy to share.

But I did want to see Vayen. We had too much history for me to ignore him. He held memories of so much of our lives together that I'd yet to recover, so many pieces of myself that were linked to him.

This arrangement we'd have to make, choosing days to be together, felt far too much like when he'd been searching for Ikeri, only coming home three nights a week. Neither of us had been happy then and I couldn't see us being any happier with the arrangement now.

Despite liking Tabor and enjoying the peace he wrapped around me, he wasn't Vayen, and this wasn't the life I'd envisioned being my future.

But did Tabor need to be like him? Would this life be so bad?

"You can talk to me, you know," Tabor said softly.

"I don't know where to start. There's a lot on my mind." I reached out blindly, found his leg, and patted it. "And you're not exactly impartial."

"That doesn't mean I can't listen."

Vayen and I talked through plans of attack, negotiations, deals, offers, but rarely about feelings. Neither of us were good at it. Or maybe we didn't because it was uncomfortable, exposing a weakness. Tabor was different. Maybe here, in the safety of his house, I could be different too. Hell, it was worth a try.

"When Vayen bonded to me, his version, without my consent, without my full knowledge of what the hell it even was, I flew into a rage. Having anyone tied to me for life was the last thing I wanted. It was a weakness that could be used against me, against us. He'd been very adamant about not wanting to bond to me either."

I turned to Tabor. "Is it a sign that I'm slipping, that I'm amenable to the same thing now?"

"But you said it's not the same. And you're not the same woman now that you were then. That's not slipping, Anastassia. We all change." His hand settled over mine on his thigh. "Until today, I would have never confronted my parents or considered opening myself to anyone like I did with you. It's frightening as all hells knowing that you could walk away from me just as quickly as you arrived in my life."

"You're stuck with me, I'm afraid. For better or worse." I squeezed his hand and took another sip from the glass before finding his shoulder made a more comfortable resting place for my head, putting pressure on the right spot to alleviate the worst of the ache.

"I don't mind one bit. Worse or better." He rested his cheek against my head.

"Have you ever wondered if your life could have been entirely different? I was here on Rok early on when I came to the Narvan, working with Cragtek and then taking it over. Before I was tied to being an Advisor, when I was exploring my career options. What if we had met then?"

"You would have met a bitter young man who hated everyone, who didn't bother to talk to women because he couldn't see past what had been taken from him. I was too busy drowning my sorrows and wallowing in my exile here in this house to consider what other opportunities were out there, like my later affiliation with Cragtek, farming, and art. Geva knew we weren't ready for each other until now."

"I suppose you're right. I had far too much ambition then to have considered this an option."

"This, being me. And being less ambitious now, you'll settle?" he said with clearly forced neutrality.

I sighed. "This is why I don't talk about feelings or what's on my mind. There's no filter."

"All right. Maybe I need to take your unfiltered conversation less personally."

"Yes, but also no." I sat up so I could look him in the eye. "What I mean to say is, I wouldn't have appreciated this," I gestured to his house, "or what you have to offer then. I was too busy looking for the next thing to conquer, to be a bigger threat than the people who were threatening me."

"Woman, we've quite established that I'm severely lacking in the 'what Tabor has to offer' category."

I swallowed the rest of my medicinal liquor, bolstering my resolve to venture further into feelings territory. "Maybe you're looking at the wrong things." I again held up my invisible datapad, a testament to how much I missed having mine, but he'd found it amusing before, so I ran with it, pointing to an imaginary screen.

"It's all clear on my list." I made is if to show him.

He smirked. "I'm sorry, I can't translate that. You'll have to read it to me."

I ran my finger down the imaginary list. "You make me laugh. You kept my secret when I asked you to even though we'd only met hours before. You're not wrapped up in your link nearly every moment when we're in the same room. You maintain a gorgeous garden. You respect my ever-shifting boundaries. You're a normal person, in as far as someone I choose to associate closely with can be."

He laughed. "Far less exciting than you're used to, you mean."

"Maybe I've had my fill of exciting. There tend to be consequences that rip my life apart every time the excitement implodes."

"I shall endeavor to bore you to avoid further heartbreak," he teased.

"Just be you. That is what you have to offer."

"I can do that." He smiled and took the empty glass from me. "Now go rest. If you need anything, I'll be up working for a while."

He'd likely be using that time to ask Neko about the inquisitor's report, assuming Neko had found someone to do that already, or grilling his family to see if they had known the truth.

"Just promise me that you'll do your business from here? I'd feel much better knowing you're close by." I couldn't lean on Vayen every time I wanted to sleep. I'd have to get used to doing that in an unfamiliar place on my own. Telling myself that Tabor was on guard duty might help.

He nodded. "Link or vid calls only."

"Thank you." I headed for the stairs.

The liquor lent a pleasing distance to the throbbing in my head, but Tabor's calm faded the further from him that I got. By the time I'd used the bathroom and slipped out of my clothes and into the bed, the throbbing had taken on a deeper level of discomfort.

I'd pushed the probe hard the instant I'd seen that Tabor's accusation had merit. Disbelief had driven me to dive even deeper to verify the truth.

A stim would have helped as would a dip in the tank, but I didn't have access to either of those while in Tabor's care. Working at the terminal to distract myself from the pain, served for a short while.

Though I'd pulled up what information on Artorian bonds I could find before accepting Vayen's second one, I reviewed it again now. None of it mentioned music or tingling, only a peaceful sensation and the exchange of feelings that I was generally familiar with from Vayen's bond. After initiation, the connection took a few weeks to fully solidify. For the most part, the public information was clinical, focusing on the beneficial aspects of providing openness and forming tight monogamous family units that best benefited Artorian society and the authorized children that would form future generations.

Maybe Vayen had never felt this level of connection with me and not even because we were different races, but because the altered bond had cut out some benefits to more tightly focus on other aspects. If he had, if we shared something like this, would he be anything like he was now?

Realizing none of this was helping the relentless throbbing in my head, I closed my searches and curled up in bed with the lights out.

It took me over an hour of attempting to will the pain away before I caved and reached out to Tabor, hoping he'd bring his balming bond back in my proximity.

"When you're done, can you come here?"

Footsteps rushed up the stairs and down the hall. A knock sounded on my door seconds later.

"Come in."

He did, not bothering with the lights, but rushing over to the bed. "Do you need to go back to the Iber? Good Geva, woman, I can feel that now that I'm in here. How are you conscious?"

"You can?" A thrill ran through me. This different sort of connection we now shared worked both ways! I wasn't limited. Not broken. "You can feel what I'm feeling?"

"Yes, crazy woman who is both overjoyed and in immense pain, I can."

His hand went to my forehead. Even in the light from the hallway, I could see the concern on his face as well as feel it. "Do you have something that can help? Do you need Vayen? You'd tell me if you did, right? I don't need him pissed at me because you're hurting. Surely, he can feel your pain too."

"He can't. I have our bonded connection muffled. And even when it isn't, my part in the connection is minimal. His bond is different."

Tabor's calm permeated the intense throbbing, bringing back the relief I needed. "That's much better. Could you stay here? Would you, I mean?"

"Would I?" He shook his head, grinning. "Woman, I've been trying to get into your bed since we met."

TWENTY-ONE

Anastassia

I spent the next three days doing nothing more than sleeping, eating Mycel's fabulous creations, and working alongside Tabor in his garden. I couldn't remember a time when I'd felt so rested. At least once every few hours I'd get twitchy, wondering if I should check in with Daniel or Vayen or check reports on the terminal Tabor had provided for me, but then Tabor would say something funny, or his calm would soothe the itch to touch the chaos that was the other half of my life.

I had two halves now. No longer whole.

"Are you going to show me this fabled dress before I have to go? It will need to be fitted, I'm sure," I said, taking my time at the kitchen sink, washing the dirt off my hands, knowing it was the last time for this visit.

His eyes were twinkling merrily again, as they often did when I asked anything about the ceremony that he assured me he had under control. "It will be perfect. Don't worry about the dress, and I'll take care of you. I promise. We should test out your dancing skills though."

"Definitely not."

Tabor handed me a towel. "Do you think our other couple will be willing to lead that portion of the festivities?"

"I've never seen Vayen dance but Buria might. Her training may have included some version of dancing. You two can have at it."

"I'll consider that a backup plan. Come on, indulge me, here where no one is watching."

Like hell was I going to dance. Anywhere. "What about your ever-present invisible security staff? I'm sure you have in-home vid monitoring. Mycel could walk in."

He went distant for a moment. "We have twenty minutes. No

monitoring and Mycel has been told to take a break."

Damn. That hadn't worked how I'd intended. I set the towel on the counter. "What if I agreed to indulge you another way in return for never bringing up dancing again?"

He grinned. "Enticing, but I've kind of resolved myself to your proposed mutual exchange after the ceremony."

"Kind of?" That left me an opening to work with. I slithered into his mind and lightly stroked the spot that had lit his fire last time.

"You're evil," he said, not putting up much resistance.

The musical hum surrounding me took on a different pitch, one that made my heart beat faster. The air seemed to vibrate, the calm quickening like a charge building around us. Caught up in the change, I let go of his mind and gave my sole attention to the unfamiliar electrifying sensations.

"What is that?" I stared at the air, as though there should be some visible evidence of what I was sensing.

"I was hoping you could tell me." Rather than waiting for an answer, he kissed me.

I didn't have any answers. All my mind wanted to do was shut up and enjoy whatever it was. We made out for what I'd hoped was all of his allotted twenty minutes until I was seriously considering inviting him upstairs to get a head start on the mutual sharing he'd been willing to hold off on.

Then Tabor broke off and stepped back, keeping my hands in his. "Now that you're suitably relaxed, give me the five minutes of privacy we have left to see what I have to work with."

That he'd managed to turn my manipulative effort back on me amused rather than infuriated me. "Fine. Five minutes."

He was right, I was relaxed. If he wanted to twirl me around while no one was watching, I'd allow it.

Tabor placed one of my hands on his shoulder while keeping the other in his grasp. Soft music suddenly flooded the room.

I'd mirrored enough footwork in my life to follow along without stumbling too badly. When one song ended and another began, he changed the steps. I groaned.

"How many songs are we required to dance to?"

"At least two. Then we can mingle. We will need to talk to everyone, at least a few words. No offense, but I don't trust our other couple to put on the proper face needed for this sort of event. We will need to make sure to convey the appropriate sentiments. Anyone Vayen and

Buria also speak with will be a bonus."

"Assuming they don't say something wildly inappropriate or Vayen doesn't flip into wrath mode."

Tabor grimaced. "We can only hope." He cut the music with his link. "You'll do. We'll practice a couple of times between now and then."

"I'll do?" Given that I'd managed to make it through the five minutes without stepping on his toes, albeit only barely, I couldn't manage a fully offended tone.

"You're going to be fabulous." He kissed my cheek.

I mock sniffed. "Going to be?"

"Indeed." He grinned before turning away to take his time hanging up the towel I'd used. His humor vanished. "I suppose I should return you to the Iber. You're already packed, I'm sure."

As much as I wasn't looking forward to it, I couldn't avoid the inevitable any longer. Our four days were up. "Actually, I'm unpacked. I hope you don't mind. I thought I'd leave a few things here?"

Tabor nodded, his back still turned. "You'll let me know what arrangement you both come to? When I can see you again?"

Though the calm around us remained, the hum was barely discernable. The air felt heavy.

"I will."

He held out his hand. I took it. A moment later, another few seconds faster, we were at the jump point on the Iber. He let go. I turned to tell him that I'd miss him, to thank him for the time we'd shared, but he was already gone. Our pocket of calm dissipated, leaving me in the cold filtered air of the Iber with activity bustling around me. The smiling faces of the jump gate guards greeted me but I had no smile to return. I merely nodded before heading to the suite I shared with Vayen.

By the time I arrived at the door, my stomach was in full churn. All hint of my peaceful time away had leeched from my body, leaving my muscles stiff and every ache amplified. I went inside to find the lights out and no sign anyone had been there since I'd last been home.

The air was too thick. I couldn't catch my breath. The reality of what had last transpired there closed in, both Vayen walking out and what I'd done after. I rushed into the bathroom, sure I was going to throw up, but stood there gripping the counter, avoiding the mirror in front of me until the nausea passed. After splashing cold water on my face with trembling hands, I retreated to the bedroom.

The drawers under the bed called for my attention. With unsteady steps, I backed away toward the closet.

The clothes I'd worn at Tabor's weren't any different from what I wore on the Iber, but it felt like I needed to fully leave any hint of him behind. I couldn't face Vayen wearing the shirt Tabor had his hands on, like Vayen might smell him. I changed and went back into the bathroom to braid my hair, erasing the fact that I'd left down for the past few days. I scrubbed my face and cleaned my teeth. Having suitably wiped all sense of Tabor from my person, I went to the couch, opened my bonded connection with Vayen, and sat back to wait.

Minutes crawled wherein I simultaneously wished Vayen would hurry so I wouldn't be alone there another moment and dreaded seeing him, knowing there was a distance between us that I could no longer ignore. Vividly remembering how he'd walked out. How despite professing to love me, he wanted someone else bad enough that he was willing to disregard whatever remained of our bond. I clutched a pillow as I suffered alternating chills and sweats.

Vayen arrived over an hour later, freshly showered. I didn't want to dwell on whether it was from a tank visit to erase all evidence of whatever he and Buria had been doing from his body, or simply a shower. After setting my strangled pillow aside to appear more natural, I quickly regretted having nothing to keep my trembling hands busy.

"You're back," he said after an awkward silence.

I'd hoped to feel some relief, maybe to be happy to see him, but instead I felt empty. "So are you."

"Stassia."

When I didn't respond or even look up at him, he sat beside me but wisely kept his hands to himself.

"Did your visit not go well?" he asked cautiously.

"It was fine."

"Have you changed your mind about him? About wanting a second?"

Hope slipped over our connection that wasn't in his innocently posed question. How dare he hope any such fucking thing.

"I haven't changed my mind," I snapped.

"Stassia, I thought you'd be happy. We're both getting what we want."

I had been happy at Tabor's estate. Away from all this, from the truth of my life, my mate, and the political situation he'd dragged me into. Did that make what I'd felt in my time away a lie? I didn't want it to be.

Could I find a way to make both of my halves happy? It occurred to me that I did have a solution for that in a drawer in the closet.

"I'll be right back." I nodded toward the bedroom.

He watched me go with a confused twist of his face.

Making quick work of my clandestine task, I closed the bedroom door, darted into the closet, and slipped a hand into the drawer to pull out one of the vials of boost. I placed a generous drop on my tongue, trying not to think about the last drop that had landed there, but I failed. I bit my lip and dug my fingernails into the palms of my hands until I managed to shove the desolation down far enough that I could consider facing Vayen again.

After I placed the vial back in the drawer, I grabbed a long, light jacket from my side of the closet and put it on. When I returned to the main room, I found Vayen mid-pour from a thick brown bottle.

With considerable effort, I managed a quiet but steady voice. "I got used to the warmer air in Tabor's garden, I guess."

"Did you spend a lot of time there?" he asked hesitantly.

"I did." I watched him put the bottle away, wondering if a drink along with the dose of boost was a good idea. Anything to help me get through this was better than the alternative.

His gaze followed mine to the glass in his hand. "You want one? I restocked for you."

I noticed that my recently depleted wine rack was again full. He could be thoughtful about that but willfully oblivious to my feelings? I gritted my teeth and begged the boost to kick in. "Sure."

He poured me a glass and handed it over. I must have been doing a fairly good job of masking my mood because he smiled and gestured me toward the table. Like I wanted to sit at the fucking table where he'd dropped the bomb that he was keeping Buria.

"How about the couch?" I went there and sat, silently willing him to follow.

He sat next to me, his shoulder against mine, balancing his glass on one knee. He pondered the contents and licked his lips but didn't drink. I did.

"How's Tabor coming along with the planning?" he asked.

"He says he has it under control and will get with Buria shortly."

"Buria has no idea what to do about the ceremony." He rubbed his forehead. "Politics," he sighed, "are not her strong point."

"She better figure it out. You'll have to coach her."

I had a pretty clear idea of what her strong point was for him.

"I was going to have her handle security."

"As long as you're comfortable with her setup."

He wouldn't be comfortable with anything less than complete and redundant coverage of not only our lives but also the host of high-ranking guests.

He nodded. Finally taking a sip.

"If you're keeping Buria out of the planning, you'll have to consult with Tabor. He mentioned having suggestions for your attire."

The room took on a soft glow. My muscles loosened. I rolled my head across my shoulders. My neck emitted a satisfying crack. Thank all that was holy, a pleasant distance formed between me and reality.

"You could just tell me what he has planned," Vayen suggested.

"I don't know. Don't care. I'll be there. That's it." I shrugged. The wine tasted better than it had in a while, like it was a better vintage. Or maybe it was because I wasn't attempting to drown in it. Perhaps boost made everything a little better.

Vayen set his still mostly full glass on the floor and turned to face me. Oh hell, he had that earnest-going-to-make-a-dramatic-pledge look about him again.

I'd missed that face, not the earnest one, but his, familiar, safe. And handsome, I had to admit. It was probably the boost admitting it, but I smiled anyway. This stuff was good. No wonder people ate it up on the streets.

"I missed you," I said, hoping to derail whatever he'd been about to say. Whatever it was, he'd think he meant it, but it wouldn't matter. I had to give in to him anyway. At least this way it hurt less. And I had missed him. It hadn't been easy to not talk to him for days, even though he'd wounded me so deeply.

"Did you?"

Ah, there was the jealousy I'd been anticipating. I knew how to derail that too. I slammed the rest of my wine and dropped the empty glass on the carpet, hoping the alcohol would mask the effects of boost in my system if he got the urge to question or look.

"I did."

I reached for the thick shoulders I knew so well and straddled his lap. His heated buzz was in my head in an instant. No more good-intentioned promises or other pesky words that might hurt or annoy me, just lips, tongues, and large, rough hands slipping around my waist and up my back under all three layers of my clothing as if they presented no obstacle at all.

In a matter of moments, he was in my head doing wonderful things with an expert touch built on years of experience. He knew exactly how hard to push and where and when to back off until I was squirming for more. To keep him busy and distracted enough to drag this delicious act out as long as possible, I tortured him in return until he was gasping and frantically unfastening his pants.

A ping rang out from the pin on his collar. He undid two clasps and yanked the shirt over his head, flinging it across the room.

If it was something important, Daniel would let him know. I made quick work of removing my clothes.

A distant second ping sounded on the far side of the room. Vayen let out an annoyed groan and then picked me up and ran into the bedroom where he closed the door behind us.

"The fucking Ocelon can wait ten minutes."

Apparently, Daniel had been in contact since Vayen seemed to know what the notifications were about. Yet, he wasn't racing off to deal with it.

Any other day I would have quipped about the time constraint or thrown the fact that he'd been happy enough to race back to Buria last time in his face, but boost made me shrug it off in favor of enjoying the sensations around me.

Nine hard, fast, and rough minutes later, he sat on the edge of the bed catching his breath while I watched sparkles dance in the air. Why the hell hadn't I tried this stuff before? It was fabulous.

"Are you coming to the surface with us?" he asked, pulling his hair back and starting for the closet.

"I'm sure you and Daniel don't need me. Go ahead."

"Is it too much to hope that you'll be waiting right here when I get back?"

It would have been nice if he'd at least pretended that my presence in negotiations might have been needed or even wanted. But no, stroking the right places in his mind, doing the one thing that Buria couldn't was all he required from me anymore.

"I might." I gave him what I hoped was an enticing smile and not a boost-induced, over-the-top, giddy grin.

He smiled, the kind full of promises of more sparkles in my near future. "I'll be back as soon as I can."

I watched him dress, slip into his armored coat full of weapons, and leave. Knowing how the Ocelon dragged out their meetings, I figured I had time to get dressed and get some long-overdue work done from my beloved datapad before he returned.

I'd just settled on the couch to read the notes Daniel had left for me on the Ocelon negotiations when Ikeri showed up at my door.

"I heard you were back," she said, looking like she wasn't planning on leaving even if she had to stand in the hallway to hear about my stay with Tabor.

So much for getting any work done, not that I was needed in that arena, but my pride needed to pretend that I was.

"Come in then." I stepped aside and resumed my position on the couch. Setting the datapad aside, I asked, "Are you here as my daughter or a Seeker?"

"Both." She sat at the other end of the couch and tucked her legs underneath her. "So, what's he like?"

"That sounds like a daughter question. I'll give you that one."

"Mom, you're smiling." She grinned.

"Am I?" Was it the boost or thinking of Tabor? It seemed wrong to smile about him here, in the home I shared with Vayen.

"It's all right to like him. I'm glad you do."

Where should I begin? How much was I allowed to like Tabor in the presence of my daughter? "He's not your father."

"It would be weird if he was. Like you're trying to replace him or something." She held up a hand. "I know you're not. That you didn't even want this. We all just want you to be happy."

"I think Tabor could do that."

"If you give him the chance," she said in a Seeker tone.

I'd already given him the chance and he had, but it felt wrong to admit that to Ikeri. Everything with Tabor was moving way too damned fast, faster than I'd ever allowed before.

Her eyes grew wide.

"You better not be skimming my memories. We have an agreement on that, remember?"

Her face flushed. "We do. Sorry. It's just..."

Even with boost attempting to aim me toward everything-is-great mode, anger boiled to the surface. "No excuses. If I can't trust you, leave."

Ikeri sobered immediately, hands in her lap, head bowed. "I was worried about you. We all were. I'm glad we didn't have cause to be."

"How much did you see?"

She peeked up at me through her long curls, a hesitant smile on her lips. "You were dancing. I didn't know... I've never seen..."

"For the signing ceremony. He was showing me how."

"Are you going to dance with Dad?"

A burble of laughter burst from my lips. "What do you think? Shall I have Tabor teach him too?"

She remained serious. "You could teach him."

"We don't have time for that. I don't even know what I'm doing. Besides, I'm sure he'd much rather dance with Buria if it came to that. We've gone twenty-some years without dancing together, at least that I know of. If the urge was there, we'd have done it by now."

She drew a breath and got one syllable out before I cut her off.

"If 'as you say' is the next thing out of your mouth, you better head for the door."

Ikeri sat quietly for a moment. "Will you tell me where you went?"

"His house on Rok. An estate far outside the cities. He has a beautiful garden and fields of flowers and medicinal plants. You would love it."

"You love it," she said, sounding relieved rather than accusatory.

"I do." That was a safe admission. "He has a fabulous cook. I don't think I can face the food in the dining hall after eating his creations."

"Better than Daniel?"

"Far beyond."

"Good thing you won't live there full-time. You'd get fat."

I laughed. "That's what I told Tabor."

"I'm glad you liked it there, but we missed you."

"You'll be missing me at least a couple of days a week. I have no intention of staying here to watch your father and Buria enjoying their time together."

"Would it be so bad to see him happy too?"

"I thought he was happy with me." I snipped. "Besides, I highly doubt he'll want to see me with Tabor. He'd be a wrath monster in no time flat."

"He was kind of a wrath monster when you were gone," she said..

"He'd only be worse with Tabor shoved in his face."

"He got into a fight with Buria. She left."

My heart raced. I nearly leapt off the couch to jump up for joy. "She did? We can call this all off?"

Ikeri shook her head. "He got her to come back."

I settled back into my corner and ran my hands over my datapad, finding solace in the familiar smooth surface. "Of course he did."

"Tell me about the gardens," she prompted.

I knew what she was doing, but I let her steer us back to a more comfortable topic. After a few more mostly thwarted attempts to get me to divulge feelings about Tabor, she hugged me and took her leave.

Almost finished with Daniel's reports and feeling my dose of boost waning, I was considering another trip to the closet when Vayen returned. From the look on his face, I ventured, "That didn't go well?"

"No, and now you're dressed and working." He let out a frustrated grumble.

I had a feeling wife number two would have been obediently waiting naked in bed. Obedient and I were rarely on speaking terms. "How about we go for a walk and we'll see if we can figure out a way to seal this Ocelon deal before I go have a talk with Etara about letting you go death-bringer on the whole lot of them."

Vayen paused his march toward his liquor horde. "A walk wasn't what I had in mind, but why the hells not."

I ducked back into the closet for my armor and a quick dose of boost. Feeling more myself with the familiar weight on my shoulders, I followed him out the door.

We'd walked in silence side by side for a good fifteen minutes, him doing who-knew-what in his head and me enjoying the return of the soft boost glow. All I could sense was frustration through our connection. I hoped the peace he got from being near me was helping him to some degree.

To break the silence, I started to ask him if he ever heard any musical sounds from his bond, but clamped my mouth shut. Curiosity on that subject would get Tabor killed for sure and that would piss Neko off. And, I considered further, Tabor's death would piss me off far more than it would Neko.

The thought of losing Tabor made me extremely anxious even with boost in my system. I took a couple of calming breaths. I'd call him later to make sure he was all right, maybe under the guise of seeing how the case against his mother and brother was going.

I realized I'd stopped in the middle of the corridor. Vayen stood beside me, his concern clear.

Quickly pasting a smile on my face, I chuckled. "Sorry, lost in thought there for a minute. What is our illusive quarry demanding?"

"That we give up this quest to unite independent worlds by any means. They don't want to be part of it."

"So we leave them be and move on like we've done with the handful of others who have declined our offer."

"They've been in contact with some of those worlds. I get the impression that the Ocelon are trying to unify them against us."

"For what purpose?"

It wasn't until he sat down that I realized we'd ended up at the dining hall. I'd been so wrapped up in walking beside him and lost in my thoughts while waiting to hear his, that I'd been on autopilot. Maybe that was the boost too; just going with the flow, not worrying about the crew watching us, which they were, I noticed, now that I was paying attention.

Vayen wore a strained attempt at a smile. "Figured we might as well put everyone at ease while we were out walking."

"I heard things were a little tense while I was gone?"

His gaze dropped to the empty table. "A little. Are you hungry?"

The thought of eating bland dining hall fare didn't appeal to me after experiencing Mycel's gastric delights. My stomach was still uneasy after indulging in those for days. "Not really, but go ahead."

I had no idea what kind of schedule he'd been on before my arrival, but he scrambled out of the chair and charged the buffet. He returned in short order with a heavily laden tray and proceeded to set a chilled cup of water and a small plate containing a petite assortment of my usual choices in front of me. The rest he dove into himself.

The few bites I tried weren't awful so much as lifeless. It was sustenance, fuel. Not meant to be enjoyed or savored.

He spent the next ten minutes methodically shoveling half the contents of his heaping plate into his mouth and then sat back with a sigh. "I don't know their purpose yet. It feels like a them versus us thing. I don't like it."

"Agreed."

"Buria thinks we should back off but keep them under observation. What do you think?"

Mention of Buria made me bristle but boost smoothed over my irritation. I hadn't been in contact for days. He'd needed someone to bounce ideas off of and Buria had been there for that. "I suppose observation rather than annihilation is more in keeping with Etara's rules, and I'd prefer you remain among the living."

"That's what she said. The part about Etara's rules," he clarified.

I had agreed to bring Buria into this twisted arrangement for just that reason: to help keep him alive. She was doing what I'd asked. But still. I breathed deeply and let the boost flow through me.

"I agree with Buria."

He set the loaded fork that had been on the way to his mouth back on the plate and cleared his throat. "She also suggested that we invite a small Ocelon delegation to the ceremony. To have them meet some of the other members of our union. Maybe they can better convey our unified intent."

Having been out of the negotiations and ready to cut our losses on the Ocelon front in favor of finding some resolution with my personal life, I shrugged. "If you think it might help."

"The worst they can do is say no, right?"

I could hear Buria saying exactly that. He was repeating her fucking words to me. I pushed my barely touched plate away and took a drink of water.

"That might be an invitation better delivered by you personally," I suggested. "You'll need to let Tabor know how many more people that will add."

"Three?"

I held up my hands. "Like I said. Not involved with the planning. You made a link contact with him. Use it."

He eyed the remains of his meal and scowled. Boost was keeping me on a more tolerant path, but if he fell into a mood, it would take a lot more than one drop to maintain my façade. I'd planned to talk to Tabor anyway; this would give me a valid reason.

"Fine. I suppose I could do a vid call with Tabor later and let him know."

I could just send him a message, but I really did want to see him, to know he was all right after his abrupt exit. That was much easier done with a visual than with words on my datapad or our newly forged mind speech connection that he was awkward at using.

Vayen seemed about to point out my unnecessary need for a vid call, but after a tense moment of studying me, nodded. "Find out what he wants with the ceremony attire while you're at it."

So much for making the two of them communicate. But it gave me more excuses to talk to Tabor.

"Speaking of seconds, I'm assuming you have given thought to the timeshare arrangement you'd prefer?" I asked.

"That might better be discussed in private," he said carefully.

In case I blew up. Did that mean he was going to ask for more than I'd expected or that he simply knew it was a touchy subject?

I pointed to his plate. "Finish that then. I'd like to get this out of the way so we can either both get some work done in silence or return to what we were doing before the Ocelon interrupted us."

"Can that conversation wait a few days? I'm kind of enjoying being on speaking terms with you." He made an effort to phrase it as a joke, but we both knew it wasn't.

"Then you should make a proposal I'll easily agree with," I said as lightheartedly as I could manage.

"Is there one?" he said not quite under his breath as he pushed his plate to the middle of the table and stood.

I eyed the half of a meal he was leaving behind. Best not to enter a battle on a full stomach.

We walked back at a leisurely pace. Daniel met us halfway.

He nodded to me but addressed Vayen, "Did you ask her about Ocelon?"

"She agreed."

Way to talk about me like I wasn't even there. I did my best not to glare at both of them for reaffirming the feeling that I wasn't truly needed. As they talked, I imagined them going about their day as if I wasn't there at all. I could almost feel a bubble of distance forming between me and them. Or maybe it had already been there and I was just now acknowledging it.

"All right then. I'll let the crew know that we'll be moving on. Let me know when you'd like to go to the surface to relay our departure to them," Daniel said.

"I can go alone."

"Definitely not." Daniel launched into a persuasive argument which his father countered.

I stood there, laughing internally, watching older Vayen debate with his younger self. Maybe it wasn't all internal. They both stopped and turned to me.

"Something funny?" Daniel asked.

"Yes, but I agree. You should go together and keep it friendly. No burning bridges or entire populations. And don't forget the invitation," I said to Vayen.

Daniel grinned victoriously. He gave me a quick hug and whispered, "I'm glad you're back," in my ear before seeming to sense that Vayen and I had other business to attend to. Or maybe Vayen told him to leave; that wouldn't have surprised me given his brusque manner with our son.

Vayen let me enter our suite first. He took in the glasses by the couch where we'd left them earlier and strode over to finish what was left in his. He picked up mine and set them on the counter. I expected him to refill his, down it, and maybe pour another before broaching his proposal, but he stood there, staring at the two empty glasses.

"You're much better at this than I am," he said quietly.

"What is this?"

"Us, dealing with us." He shook his head. "How did you do it? Going to Buria, bringing her here? Accepting this arrangement?"

Like he'd left me any choice? I'd accepted that I'd do anything to keep him alive. That was it, not a second wife, not fucking Buria.

Despite the boost, my throat had gone thick and my voice tight. "Because you can't reciprocate"?

He swallowed loudly. "Stassia, it hurts."

"You think it doesn't hurt me?" Alarms went off in my head. Every intent I'd had to go with the flow, to get along, to give him what he wanted, could fuck the fuck off. "You think it didn't hurt like all your hells when you ignored how I felt and went to Buria anyway? I didn't want..."

He wrapped his thick arms around me and crushed me to his chest. "I'm sorry. I shouldn't have done that. I shouldn't have agreed to any of this. It was just so damned..."

"Tempting?"

"Yes." He made that single word sound like admitting utter defeat. "I'm sorry that I need this. If it's any comfort, it's helping with the urges."

It. Not her. Though I wanted to correct his error in an effort to offer Buria some dignity in this matter, he was right. That knowledge *was* a comfort. Sleeping with Buria was a therapy, a diversion. I'd done the right thing. She wasn't replacing me.

Listening to his heartbeat, feeling his warm breath on my cheek, his hands on my back, my anger melted away. He was alive and with me. That was what mattered most.

Vayen drew a shuddering breath and released his hold on me. "Within the bounds of knowing this second marriage is going forward and at least one night a week is required to make this a legitimate arrangement," he took my hands in his. "I will submit to whatever sentencing you graciously grant."

I stood there, looking at my pale hands engulfed in his, large and brown, one thicker and far more powerful than the other. Hands I loved quite dearly for returning a slight degree of choice to me. Him purposefully calling it a sentence.

I took a moment to ponder my options, as narrow as they were. "When we set out on this mission, it was to begin to step back, to lay a foundation so we could, at some point, retire to some degree. Together. You and me. That is what I wanted, what I thought we were working toward. But it's not what you wanted."

He stared at his big black boots, worn to a matte finish, making my not-so-small feet appear petite beside them. "It's more than that and not that I didn't want—"

"You put this in my hands, so here's what I want." I glared at him and drew a deep breath, thanking everything holy that I had boost in my system so I could approach this somewhat levelly and not ruin what he'd offered by launching into a full tirade.

"We've been at this mission for four years. We have a solid foundation. The crew knows the operation. Daniel has it mostly in hand. We're going to start stepping back. You and me, one full day and night, you're mine. No work. Either of us. We can stay on the Iber or go wherever you want to take us, but that will be our time."

He nodded slowly, clearly waiting for the axe to fall.

"For the sake of appearances, Buria can work beside you for one day and night here. You get her elsewhere for an uninterrupted day and night after. I'll work with Tabor here and cover for you while you're gone and leave with him while she's working with you here. Fair enough?"

"No." He gripped my hand. "I fucked this up. I owe you more than that. "Two no work days for us."

Not that I wasn't pleased but... "You seriously think we can afford three days off of work?"

"Like you said, we're supposed to be stepping back. Not to say emergencies won't happen, but you get two. If I have to work through my Buria day, so be it."

"I'm kind of loving you right now," I admitted.

"Only kind of?"

"Don't push your luck."

He grinned.

TWENTY-TWO

Buria

Vayen marched into our suite looking victorious. My heart leapt into my throat. I jumped off the couch, eagerly awaiting good news. When he wasn't immediately forthcoming with an announcement, I sat back down.

"Well?"

"She said two days. One working and one off."

While I did enjoy the sight of him smiling, two days out of eight didn't exactly fill me with glee.

"Two."

"Yeah. I assumed she'd grant the bare minimum. She really is open to this."

While I'd held out hope that having secured a second of her own, Ana might be willing to divide her interest, it seemed far more likely that she'd picked Tabor solely to goad Vayen. She'd probably thought declaring she wanted two days with Tabor would make Vayen choose only one with me so she had to do the same. If that had been her game, she'd lost.

Not that I felt like I'd won. Elonka and Gamnock's other two wives shared equal time. In fact, they all lived together, so there wasn't even a hard time divide. I'd hoped for a similar arrangement so Ana and I could work together to keep Vayen in control of his abilities.

"The deal is that you live full-time on Brustus and only stay here the two days we have together," he said carefully. "Tabor does the same."

So much for working together with Ana directly. "I see. Do you think Ana might be persuaded to alter the agreement to a more favorable schedule once we settle into this?"

He licked his lips and studied his hands on his lap for a moment before again meeting my gaze. "This is a good compromise, Buria. It's not that I wouldn't want more, but there are factors you need to understand. The bond I share with Anastassia helps me keep this," he tapped his temple, "under control. By which I mean me, not even the Arpex part of me. As Etara has told me several times, I let the darkness in, basked in it, and now it's no surprise that it's hard to keep in check. The Arpex alteration added to it, exponentially. Ikeri and Etara have been helping to dull the urges. Drinking helps more, but I can't be drunk all day every day. You help too."

Enjoying the rare moment of unfiltered Vayen, I tried to process all he was saying, comparing it to what Ana had said and the private conversation I'd had with Etara on how to best deal with him. I quickly concluded that there was a lot he wasn't saying.

"How do I help? Wouldn't being with me longer help more?"

"When I'm with you, I'm not having dark thoughts. They are decidedly on another topic altogether," he said, smirking.

I had a feeling the consistently higher doses of bang had more to do with that than me. But he was openly admitting his struggle. He was actually talking. There was hope we had more than just attraction between us. I hoped so. I wanted that very much.

"So be with me more."

"Buria, I don't think I can. This new schedule only allows me four solid days of work. I'm used to eight."

"You have seven, unless I'm missing something?"

"I'm taking two off with Anastassia, away from here." He leaned forward, his dark gaze doing that thing that made me turn to liquid. "Work has always come first for me and Anastassia. I'm doing my best to not do that to you. You will be here when I'm working one day, beside me, I mean, but I'd like to keep my schedule light so we can enjoy what time we have. There are tasks I must devote my attention to, but you'll know when I'm doing them rather than me being half-wrapped up in my link all day."

I appreciated that he was making an effort to correct his previous errors. "I could distract you from work, if you'd prefer."

He chuckled. "You do that without trying."

As much as I wanted to continue with the derailment of this conversation, I needed to know what I was dealing with. "And you'll be all right with Ana having the same arrangement with Tabor?"

The smoldering gaze was gone in an instant and his face went dark and snarly. "No, I'm not all right with it. She'll be with him, elsewhere, where I can't know she's safe. She'll shut me off, like she does when I'm with you. Knowing she's not here, knowing I have to trust him to watch over her, that feels impossible."

He'd been her bodyguard a lot longer than her mate. Even though I didn't want to focus on how tightly the two of them were intertwined, I could appreciate his devotion to the job. "So tell her that she has to stay on the Iber."

"That's not the agreement."

"Then make it the agreement."

The second those words came out of my mouth I knew that I'd overstepped.

The darkness surged in him, and for a split second, I couldn't stop myself from backing away. Even without feeling him in my head, the sudden aura of malice that emanated from him was tangible. I immediately understood the terror that had been in Tabor's eyes when we'd initially met.

Vayen sprang from his chair and spun away to face the door. I wondered if he was going to storm out and whether I wanted him to given the terrifying charge in the air. "The agreement stands as is."

I forced a noise that I hoped sounded like agreement out of my frozen-in-fear body.

He kept his back to me while minutes ticked by in silence. The charge slowly diminished and my heart resumed its normal pace. When he finally turned to face me, all hint of the darkness was back under wraps.

Ana and Etara weren't exaggerating one bit. He was very close to getting his switch flipped.

He went into the kitchen and poured a glass full of amber liquid from one of the bottles. After drinking half of it in one gulp, he topped off the glass, and then settled back into the chair across from me.

Did he do this to Ana? If she was willing to invite me into his life, I had a feeling that he did. Only desperation would have driven her to this step in his preservation.

Was it foolish to keep him among us, among the living, knowing what he could do and how quickly he could do it? Having spent time with him, seeing how he could be when he wasn't on edge, I didn't want that outcome any more than Ana did.

He sipped his drink and then spoke as if nothing had just happened. "While I have a few minutes, I thought we might discuss term expectations for our marriage contract?"

"Elonka said two years was a typical length before a renewal?"

Vayen nodded. "I was thinking we should do five. It would set a good example since we're doing this publicly."

Did I want to be tied to him for five years if the fixation on Ana remained at the forefront of nearly every conversation we had? What if his moods didn't even out? Or if they got worse? Elonka made relationships sound easy once the groundwork was set, but she hadn't renewed with her second husband so maybe she didn't have all the answers. Not to mention, she didn't know a fraction of what the Advisor of All was dealing with behind his public image. Allowing us time to hopefully find a pleasurable accord before diving into a long commitment seemed a better choice.

"Perhaps embracing the Jalvian custom of two years would be more politically useful rather than trying to show that you are better than them?"

He smiled. "Good point. You'll get the hang of our business in no time."

Part of me basked in his praise, the rest noted that he made no attempt to negotiate for a longer contract and that he was satisfied with two days a week. While he had what might be legitimate reasons, it sure seemed like he wasn't fighting very hard for me. Like I was a short reward he got for getting through the week with Ana. And one of my days wouldn't truly be mine, not only would he be working, he'd be wrestling with the fact that she was away.

I sat up straight and put on my best alluring smile. Elonka said that she'd enjoyed immersing herself in Gamnock's business. With a little effort and patience, I'd find a way to work myself into into Vayen's too.

I'd let Vayen know I was aboard the Iber an hour ago. It was morning here but the middle of the night on Brustus. I'd adjusted my work schedule with Gamnock to allow me time to sleep before my arrival and for the time difference on my return before my next shift. Due to Iber time, I wanted to think Vayen was still asleep, that he just hadn't seen my message yet, but I'd been around him enough to know how little he slept. It was more likely he was having a fit over Ana leaving to spend her allotted time away with Tabor.

Vayen and Ana had just had two full days together for goodness' sake. Wasn't that enough to get her out of his system? It was my turn and I had limited time.

When he did arrive, it was unannounced and he did indeed appear ready to rip something apart. Anticipating that, I handed him the drink I had poured for him half an hour ago and almost started drinking out of frustration.

My thoughtfulness earned me a smile. Once the contents had been speedily sent down his throat, the tension on his face eased. He took my hand and reached into a pocket with his other one. When he pulled it out, he kept it closed.

"I was hoping to do another thing better with you, but to be honest, it feels like I waited too long, and well, ceremonial moments aren't my specialty. When I—" He cut himself off with the shake of his head.

I hoped he was realizing how much he brought Ana into our time and was making an effort to do better with that. I would let a lot of other things go if he could make that one improvement.

"Anyway..." He opened his hand to reveal a ring with a faceted square red stone that caught the light from seemingly every angle. "I thought we should make our impending contract official. If you're still agreeable?"

Good gods, the gem was almost as wide as my finger. "I am."

He grinned as he slipped the ring onto my finger. "I was hoping you would say that."

I laughed, holding up my hand to admire the etched golden band and the sparkling stone set in it. It looked fantastic on my hand. No one was going to miss that announcement of my marital status. I couldn't wait to show it to Elonka.

"I hope you don't have to run off already?" I asked, throwing my arms around him.

"I've got about an hour." He kissed me and then guided us toward the couch where he sat beside me, his hand on mine. "After lunch I'd like to take you to the regen tank, show you how to use it, and create a profile for you. I hope you'll never need it," he shrugged, "but being around me, you probably will."

He'd divulged the secret of his family's regen tank when I'd last been on the Iber. The promise of visiting one of his private places, somewhere only trusted members of his very small circle held access, felt like definite progress toward taking a meaningful place by his side.

"I look forward to it."

He smiled, his rough fingers absently rubbing slow circles over my knuckles. "How was your week?"

"Mostly the usual. The damned kids are at it again. Graffiti this time, thankfully, not sabotaging any shipments."

"If Gamnock would just agree to me exterminating the vermin, it would make your job much easier."

"Vayen, they're just kids."

More specifically, they were the children of the people he'd killed when he'd found Ikeri on Brustus four years ago. They held no favor for the Ta'set name. While most of them had been relocated off-world in our initial sweep, a determined pack of feral and elusive teens remained. They were an annoyance, but hearing him use words like *exterminate* took me aback. "You know Etara would never allow that."

He shook his head. "You said they were advancing to explosives? If you end up wounded because of them, I don't care what Etara has to say about it, I will wipe them out."

On one hand, I was touched that he'd risk Etara's vengeance on my account, but on the other, he was talking about killing children. Granted, they were unruly, hateful, and resourceful children who had managed to publicly distribute a brutal account of their side of the Brustus tragedy. Several news outlets had picked up their story and had been running updates as new transmissions leaked out. Though I had a team on it, we'd yet to discover how the signals were getting out or where the pack was holing up.

"I don't care what they say about me, but they're smearing Ikeri. That, I won't stand for."

His daughter was the root cause of the whole tragedy, having broken the minds of the original Brustus occupants with her mis-guided healing efforts. As much as I didn't like the sentiments the children were hurling about, there was truth in them. Vayen and Neko might have a hold on most of the Narvan's media outlets, but neither could censor them all.

Vayen pressed his palms to his temples. "She's just getting her life back together, trusting people again, trusting herself. If their broad-cast becomes anything more than sparsely-aired rumors she'll hear about it, and that would crush her. She was just a kid at the time."

So were they, I wanted to point out. Orphans because he mur-dered their families. He'd spun it as a mercy killing, but I had serious doubts about that, as did many others. However, the documented good he was doing elsewhere outweighed the speculation.

He did have a point about the disruption to Cragtek business.

"We'll work harder on tracking them down. You're right, now that they've advanced to broadcasts and sabotage, they are more than just an inconvenience."

"Thank you." He patted my leg and then launched into sharing updates on his mission progress.

Once we'd covered the usual topics, I figured I might as well get Ana out of the way so we could maybe have a few fun minutes before he had to work. She was a large part of his daily life after all, and I was attempting to be nice about it.

"What did you do with your two days off with Ana?"

"She wanted to go to our house on Veria Minor. Where we lived when we were happy together, away from everything. We had a normal life there when the kids were little."

I'd expected a short answer, something about a location and that whatever happened between him and Ana was none of my business or, more likely, him ignoring my question entirely and just grousing about her being gone with Tabor for the day. Instead, it appeared he wanted to talk. In the hopes that we were making continued progress in our relationship, I put on the feigned interest face that the Masters of Tacesh had beaten into us and set out to do my best for the man who owned my heart while he talked about his first wife.

"Why did you leave Veria Minor?"

He stared off for a moment and I'd thought I'd lost his attention, but then he answered quietly. "I wasn't given a choice initially. Later on, I could have gone back. We could have reestablished ourselves there or elsewhere, attempted to resume what we'd had." Vayen shook his head. "I let ambition take over and chose the Narvan instead."

"I'm sure your people are better for it. Ambition isn't a bad thing."

"Isn't it?" His gaze drilled into me. "She's different. Since this." Vayen gestured to our suite. "Like something between us is missing. Or maybe there's more, like he's there too now, even when he's not around.

That was no surprise. Ana had to feel the same way about Vayen and me.

Silence fell between us. I was about to change the subject when he spoke again.

"She didn't want to talk, not like avoiding me, but everything was surface level. On one hand, we were on friendly terms in close confines without the distraction of work, but on the other, it was almost unnerving. She wasn't her usual contentious self about anything."

"Unnerving because the two of you didn't argue?"

"Is that strange?" He chuckled. "I'm probably overthinking it. I should be grateful, I suppose."

I nodded. That was always the safest response. The Tacesh masters had beaten that into us too.

"I met with Rosh and Atalina, friends from when we lived there. Well, they worked for me. Rosh still does. Atalina retired a few years ago. Friends in as far as I have any, I guess." He shrugged. "I touched base with the investments we have on Minor."

"I thought you weren't working while you were there."

He offered me a pained smile. "I don't know how to do that. Anastassia can go outside and play with plants for hours. She does her stretching poses. She likes to go for walks or sit together and watch the local vids, commenting about reports that don't matter to us because we don't live there."

"It sounds like you need to find a hobby."

He stared blankly at me.

"Something you enjoy other than work."

"I enjoy work. I don't have time for meaningless shit."

We seemed to be venturing into prickly territory. I attempted a course correction. "How were your friends? Did you visit them together or by yourself?"

"Anastassia suggested we have them over for dinner."

I barely contained the laughter that statement elicited. Imagining the two of them in plain clothes, attempting to entertain guests like common people, holding average conversations, was one of the most amusing situations I'd considered in a long while.

He cracked a smile. "I know. I thought it was an absurd idea too, but it turned out to be nice. It gave the two of us something to talk about. Something other than work, I mean. And it was good to see them. It's not often that I get to reconnect with contacts in person after moving on."

"It sounds like you had a pleasant time together then," I said, hoping to wrap up talking about Ana so we could get back to enjoying ourselves, even if he was technically working all day.

"I suppose so. I don't know what I expected, but it wasn't that. She used to be the one who didn't know how to do mundane things and be normal. Somewhere over the years, she picked it up and I lost it."

My imagination ran with what he may have expected and almost all of it annoyed me. He'd spent his time with her. Now it was my two days. Two damned days, that's all she'd given me even after asking for my help.

Vayen scowled. "Do you think he knows how to do anything other than work? I've looked at his accounts. He's got his hands in a good number of businesses, both legal and otherwise. Not that I suppose I should have expected anything else, being Neko's recommendation."

"Maybe we could focus on us here instead of whatever Ana and Tabor are doing there?"

"Easier said than done," he smiled weakly. "She didn't want this, right? Maybe she's spending her day in his garden like she said she did last time. I saw feed of his estate. He does have impressive lands that would appeal to her."

"Yes," I said with all the tolerance and confidence I could muster.

"Right then." He stood and drew a deep breath. "I should get this day started. Would you like to come with me or stay here? I can join you for lunch later and probably do some work here via link after we visit the regen tank if you'd like."

Without any specifics on what his work might entail, I had no desire to repeat my performance on Ocelon and also, I wanted to call Elonka to show off my ring. "I'll stay here and see you when you get hungry. I can get some work done while I wait."

He nodded but his impenetrable expression had returned so I couldn't tell if he was relieved or disappointed. After a quick, unsatisfying kiss, he left.

I only hoped that after a few weeks, knowing Ana was with Tabor for her day, this would become more routine and we could all settle in and enjoy the time we had together.

Daniel

My father had wisely elected to bring Buria along only after we'd already signed the Andioneti people into our union. The trade station, a central point from which four colonies had settled on two nearby worlds served as our meeting point. The space station, having been converted from the original colonization ship was run down and cobbled together, but served its purpose well enough.

"Maybe Buria could go with you," my father suggested. "She could maybe look over their security and weapons and offer some suggestions?"

That was an awful lot of maybe from a man usually full of absolutes. Buria definitely had him off-kilter. Or perhaps it was the mess she'd made of our already messy situation with the Ocelon that spurred him to be cautious about leaving her unattended.

"Sure."

Etara approached us, her hands tucked into the sleeves of her robe. She spared a benign nod for Buria before speaking to my father. "Are you ready? They've brought the affected onboard and have them in isolation so that we can evaluate and treat them. Ikeri is already there with three of the medical team."

"Yes, I think so." He took a step toward Buria and raised an arm as though he was about to hug her, but then met my gaze and backed away. "We'll see you both later."

"That was awkward," I muttered under my breath.

"I think you make him nervous," Buria said, walking beside me as we headed deeper into the station where the central security hub was.

"Me? Make him nervous?" I laughed. "No, he knows I'm not at all pleased with how he's treated my mother. No offense. I know you didn't have any part in bringing on this nightmare."

"A nightmare? Is that how you see me?"

"No, not you. What he's doing? Yes."

From the hurt look on Buria's face, I gathered I wasn't doing a very good job of explaining myself. Or maybe there was no good way to do that.

When we arrived at the hub, the security team was lined up and waiting. The tall, thin men and women wore red uniforms with a white stripe on each shoulder that ran down to their waist. The harsh ship lighting cast shadows over their bare heads from the nodules scattered across their scalps. Their arms hung backward at an odd angle but swung gracefully like weeds in water as they walked. One thing I never tired of on our mission was seeing all the different races. Though many of them were built differently from us, we had the same basic needs as far as health, secure homes, and reliable means of providing food.

I set up a translator unit and introductions followed. From there, we were given a quick tour of all their equipment and brief explanations of their procedures by various members of the team and their leader, a tall, willowy female.

Buria, to my surprise, stepped right in to make suggestions. What she lacked in dealing with politicians, she made up for in security knowledge. I stood back and let her take the lead, only joining in a few times to make further suggestions. The staff was appreciative of our advice, taking notes and even making tweaks under our observation.

By the end of our session with the team, Buria appeared quite animated. It was a relief to see her succeed at something that would be useful to us, something my father would be pleased about. Not much pleased him these days.

This transition into life at my father's side, even part-time, couldn't be easy for her either.

"I think that went well," she said quietly as we left the hub and explored our way back to the jump point where we were all to meet up within the hour.

"It did. Thank you for your help."

Buria smiled. "Thank you for allowing me to go with you. I'd like to do this again if I could be helpful?"

"If you'll be here every week, I'm sure opportunities will align."

She nodded, appearing more at ease than I'd seen her since she'd first come to the Iber.

Someone called out behind us. I turned to see one of the security team techs hurrying toward us and reactivated the translator.

"I was hoping to catch you. Do you have a moment? I'd like your opinions on the inner station emergency airlock system."

"A member of our engineering team meet with you tomorrow," I offered.

"I was hoping to see if you felt our current pattern was suitable for not only maintaining air pressure in case of station damage but also to contain threats."

"We could take a look," Buria suggested.

I shrugged. The medical team wasn't yet at the meeting point so we had time. "Sure, lead the way."

"You must be excited about the upcoming ceremony," the tech said over his shoulder to Buria as we followed him around a corner and down another corridor.

"Yes," she said, glancing at the ring on her finger. "More so, I'm looking forward to the days after the ceremony when we can have some quiet time. All the preparations are time-consuming and stressful.

"I hear it will be quite a momentous occasion," he said. "This way." He ducked down a narrow sideshoot that opened into an octagonal room with a console in the middle and operations panels lining the walls.

"The Advisor is your father?" he asked me. "Will you be involved with the ceremony as well?"

"Yes, as a witness." I glanced over the console, trying to decipher the text on the controls.

He smiled apologetically and politely gestured for me to move aside as he dove into an explanation of their current procedure. The tech illustrated their last drill on the display. Buria seemed to have a better grasp of the console controls than I did. She made a few minor tweaks while I watched over her shoulder, attempting to put pieces of their written language together with the purpose of the controls.

The tech nodded. "This is why I wanted your advice. Very helpful, thank you. If you don't mind, I'll make the program adjustments right now and then we can run it again to make sure I got everything."

I checked the time through my link. *"How are you coming along?"* I asked my father. *"We're doing one last consult and we'll be ready."*

"Ten minutes," he said curtly and cut contact.

Buria and the tech conferred further while he switched a few more settings. The whole process was taking too damned long. We'd already offered plenty of assistance, and I didn't want to keep my perpetually irate father waiting.

"We should be heading back," I announced.

"Almost ready." The tech opened another panel on the wall opposite from us and switched several connections manually. Rather than watching what he was doing, he kept casting furtive glances at me and Buria.

My gut went on alert. The one thing Neko, my father, and Uncle Isnar all agreed on, and had drilled into me since I'd picked up my first weapon, was to trust those feelings. Even though I knew I was courting my father's temper by contacting him again, I wasn't about to endure his wrath if something happened to Buria under my watch.

I took one step back and glanced around the corner of the alcove.

"Do you need something?" the security tech asked.

"No. Buria seems to have this in hand."

He nodded. "She's been very helpful. You both have been."

The hallway was empty. Nothing seemed out of place.

I braced myself for a biting remark and reached out to my father over our natural connection. *"Everything all right in there?"*

"Yes, we're almost done. Why?" he asked.

"Something doesn't feel—"

A heavy blast hit my armor, knocking me to my knees. The ringing in my ears played havoc with the echoes of the blast reverberating through my head. I blinked hard, trying to clear my wavering vision.

The side of the console where we'd been working had blown open. Buria lay on the floor. Her armor had protected the majority of her body, but she'd taken the brunt of the blast. Shrapnel had penetrated her face and neck. Blood pooled around her head.

"Buria!"

Her eyes were open, but she didn't respond. My father's ring sparkled on her burnt hand.

Something hard hit the back of my head. Blackness threatened to rush in. Willing it away, I reached out blindly and connected with a warm body.

Something sharp sank into my shoulder. Blood splattered onto the floor. Gasping at the sudden burst of pain, I realized my armor had been compromised. This needed to end quickly. Adrenaline was only going to help me for so long.

I hauled the thin and flailing form down to the ground by sheer force, taking blows to my back and shoulders all the while.

My vision cleared enough to recognize the tech and a length of metal plating in his hand.

"We will not be slaves to Tyrant Ta'set!" he screamed at me, swinging the panel again. The edge connected with my face. I lost my grip on him.

Blood gushed from the cut that ran from my left eye down to the right side of my jaw. I reached out wordlessly to my father, wishing I had a clear jump point, but my vision was far too fucked up for that. Instead, I showed him our location on the station map we'd been working on in the security hub.

My father's fury flooded my mind, making it hard to think or even breathe. I blinked again and shook my head, fighting to clear the thundering echoes and ringing on top of my father's rage.

The tech stood over Buria, the sharp-edged panel in hand. With no further thought, I reached into my coat and pulled out an energy pistol. The tech swung the panel toward Buria's neck in a slicing motion. I fired. The charge blew a hole in his side that dropped him and the panel to the floor just behind Buria.

I shoved the pistol back into its holster and crawled closer. Buria's pulse was relatively strong but she'd lost a lot of blood. Knowing she'd be in the tank as soon as my father arrived, I decided to save him some time and started pulling shrapnel from her wounds.

He skidded into the alcove just as I was pulling the last jagged metal shard from her cheek. I left the ones in her neck in case she started bleeding more heavily from their removal.

My father was on his knees and in my face a second later. "Is he dead? Was he alone?"

"Here, attacking us? Yes. But he said, 'We will not be slaves to the Tyrant', so no, I don't think he was alone."

"You should have left him alive for questioning," he yelled.

"That was the plan until he tried to slice Buria's throat."

I wiped at the blood running down my face. Most of it seemed to be gushing from my nose. It hurt like all hells.

He gave the dead tech a hard kick in the head. "I wish you'd use projectiles. We might have been able to save him and question him later."

I preferred the same pistols the Iber's security team used. They held a long charge and were easier to maintain than the weapons my parents favored. They also didn't leave any sort of possibly traceable ammunition.

He finally seemed to notice Buria and the blood puddle around her head. An electrifying charge of malevolence filled the air, making my skin prickle. The urge to cower in the corner was near overwhelming. Having encountered the charge numerous times, I knew what was about to happen.

Now that the immediate threat was neutralized, I reached out to my sister and gave her the same map I'd given my father. If ever I'd wished she or Etara were linked, it was now. *"Dad's about to go off. I need you and Etara here. Fast."*

Though it was only a few minutes later when Ikeri ran into the alcove with Etara right behind her, I knew Andioneti bodies were dropping lifelessly all over the station.

Seconds later, my father was on his knees, clutching his head.

"You've got this?" I asked Ikeri.

She turned toward me and gasped. "Go, for the love of Geva, get to the tank."

"It's not that bad."

Her wide eyes said I was wrong. "Buria needs the tank first. He'd want her in far more than me."

Ikeri scowled, glaring at our father who was still suffering Etara's censure. "We need two tanks."

While that would be wonderful, we only had one. No matter how hard I looked everywhere we traveled, I'd yet to find another. Consulting with the University on replicating the tech would expose our secret, and if they were successful, make tanks public. We did not need our enemies healing as quickly as we did.

"Let Dad know where Buria is when he's coherent."

Ikeri nodded.

I'd never Jumped Buria before so it took me a minute to not only get my own bearings, considering the noise still thundering in my head, but also to lock in on her. When we arrived on the floor of the tank room, I discovered my shoulder bore a deep cut that screamed in protest when I attempted to pick Buria up to place her on the platform. The gurney method took longer but got her where I needed her.

If I thought watching my father decline to hug her in front of me was awkward, undressing my father's unconscious, soon-to-be second wife was a thousand times more so. Though it had not occurred to me to check before I'd gotten that far, I assumed my father would have a profile for her already in the system. I was right. Helpful as that was in this case, the fact that it did exist irked me. She wasn't even technically part of our family yet, and he'd already granted her access to our private sanctuary.

With Buria safely in the tank, I checked the listed profiles. Tabor did not have access. At least my mother was following the unspoken rules more judiciously.

After a brief contact with Meera to let her know I was safe aboard the ship, I leaned back in the chair and closed my eyes. The ringing had died down, but all I could hear was my father ranting about the tech I'd killed. Questions rolled off his tongue, but not one was about me. The only consolation was that none of them had been about Buria either.

A hand on my shoulder woke me. My face was tight, like I was wearing a mask. My head, back, and shoulder hurt like all hells. I moan escaped my lips before I could clamp it down. Ikeri's face hovered over me.

"Where's Dad?" I asked, moving my mouth as little as possible.

"He should be awake in an hour or so. Etara had to knock him out to get him to stop. Come on, I got Buria out. It's your turn." She tugged at my coat and then stopped abruptly. "You're going to need new armor."

I winced my way out of my coat to find that the explosion had torn one side of my armor completely open, the same side where the tech had sliced my shoulder with the metal panel. The odds that the armored weave would self-heal from that much damage were slim.

"Dammit, I like this armor."

Ikeri shook her head. "I like you alive. Get a new coat."

Nodding, I worked my way out of my arsenal and my shirt. Ikeri grimaced. I peered at my shoulder and followed the darkening bruise all the way down to my hip.

"If you'd been facing that terminal, you'd have been in the same shape as Buria. Thank Geva for that and good armor," Ikeri said.

"Indeed."

While I gingerly walked over to the tank, Ikeri sat in the chair and busied herself with loading my profile. I took that as my cue to remove my pants and get on the platform.

"I'm going to guess Dad will decree that you and Buria shouldn't be alone off world. And if he doesn't, I will."

"How many Andioneti did he take out?"

"Initial reports estimate a third of the station's crew."

"For the actions of one person."

"He's slipping, Daniel. Losing control. You did the right thing. Contacting me, getting Etara there to contain him. The body count would have been much higher."

I may have saved lives, but I wasn't feeling very good about it. No doubt the Andioneti would run from the union as fast as they could, and now word of my father's vengeance would spread further. How were we supposed to unify worlds when he tore them apart?

"Dad will be better after the marriage ceremony, once he and Mom get their routines established. You'll see," she said as the platform started its descent into the warm gel.

She sounded so hopeful. I wanted to believe her but my gut said otherwise.

When I woke on the ship after my time in the tank, I turned to find not Ikeri or my father sitting beside me, but Buria. She'd showered and changed.

"Your first time in the tank? Other than creating your profile, I mean?"

She nodded. "A truly miraculous thing, that tank."

"It is." I shoved my crusty hair behind my shoulders, wishing she would leave so I could take my turn in the shower.

"Your father wanted to talk to you, but I wanted to speak to you first. I let him know you were awake," she said somberly, staring at the red faceted stone on her finger. "Thank you for being on better alert than I was and for getting help. We could easily have both died in that room."

"You're welcome. I'm sorry I didn't catch on a few moments earlier so I could have prevented my father from taking out most of the station's occupants."

Buria reached over to rest her hand on mine where I gripped a handful of sheet over my chest. She smiled as she leaned closer and whispered, "No matter what he says, know that you did all you could. You are not your father, and to be clear, that's a compliment."

"Thanks?"

She chuckled as she headed for the door. "He'll be in shortly."

He arrived before I got further than both feet on the floor. My father didn't sit and he didn't smile. He stood at the end of the bed with his arms crossed over his chest. The only bright side was that he wasn't glaring at me. Yet.

"I don't want you and Buria alone with anyone again. You make too much of an enticing target together."

"It seems so. Are the Andioneti still with us?"

"Those that remain? They've been uninvited." he snarled. "Their sick can rot. Their crops can wilt. Their rainy season can drown them all for all I care."

"And Etara?"

"Isn't happy, but I'm still on my feet."

"Thank Geva for that."

He nodded a fraction, the closest to amicable that he'd been since thanking me for paving his way to getting Buria in his bed. I grimaced at the memory.

"We'll be skipping the next few inhabited stops. We need to get out in front of the rumors," he announced.

They weren't rumors. The news circulating ahead of us thanks to merchants and traders was mostly truths, but I wasn't going to argue semantics. I just wanted a shower and to go home to my wives.

Meera wasn't going to let me out of her sight for weeks once I admitted the degree to which I'd been injured. Lying wasn't an option. She could check the tank logs at any time.

My father dropped his arms to his sides and stood there, watching me. I tentatively stood, waiting for him to launch into a tirade about how I'd failed to protect Buria or myself or see the danger earlier. He inhaled deeply and let it out loudly. After all that, he offered me a tight nod and left.

If that was his version of thanks, I'd take it over the alternative.

The one good thing about the damned signing ceremony at the end of the week was that we'd be back in the Narvan where we knew where we stood. Where we'd be surrounded by hordes of security. Where, for a few hours, I could enjoy myself with my wives and know that we were safe no matter what new rumors or news about Tyrant Ta'set might be spreading throughout the known universe.

TWENTY-FOUR

Anastassia

Tabor draped the dress bag over the table in the suite I shared with Vayen on the Iber. I'd made sure the bedroom door was closed, but it still felt decidedly wrong to have him there. Vayen and Daniel had both decreed I should remain aboard to prepare while they, along with Buria, and Tabor, when he was done here, would be on Jal to finalize everything for the ceremony. Though I'd been proclaiming that I wanted nothing to do with the damned ceremony other than to show up and do my assigned part, having them all scurrying around while I sat here about to be pampered for the day grated on me. The whole damned day grated on me.

His hair had been recently trimmed, and his face nearly glowed with health thanks to whatever treatment he'd undergone. Even his eyebrows appeared to have been groomed. His clothes, as always, were perfectly tailored, and though they were not what he'd be wearing for the ceremony, they lent him a dignified style I quite liked.

"I will warn you, the last time I wore a dress, I looked like a fool and the night ended in a spectacular fight with Daniel's biological father."

Tabor chuckled. "I look forward to that tale sometime."

I eyed the dress bag with trepidation. "Are you sure this will fit?"

"Yes, it's an Okashki original."

"I have no idea what that means but it sounds expensive."

He dropped his hand from the zipper and faced me with an incredulous look. "Some days I forget we come from different worlds." He shook his head. "The chairs at my house that you like, the form fitting ones? They are derived from Okashki technology. Her pieces fit any wearer perfectly. She was a brilliant Jalvian designer. Artorians aren't the only ones who can create things." He sniffed indignantly.

"Most of her clothing line has been destroyed by those looking to deconstruct her tech for more widely marketable products, like the chairs. This is one of the few remaining original pieces. So yes, it's expensive. Priceless, actually."

He opened the bag to reveal brilliant, red-orange shimmering fabric covered in intricate golden beadwork. He worked the bag down, dislodging a full-length skirt that spilled onto the floor. The fabric seemed to disappear in sections of the sleeves but the beadwork remained, gold beads joined by tiny red ones. I reached out to feel how that was possible and encountered a sheer fabric so soft, I couldn't help but caress it.

"This belongs in your gallery."

"Agreed. The few other originals I've found are locked safely behind clearplaz for viewing only. I haven't figured out how to get my hands on them yet." He smirked.

"I can't wear this. What if I spill something on it?"

"I assure you, it will survive the day. And so will you."

Even with boost in my system and the bond I shared with Tabor wrapping me in calm, I wasn't nearly as sure about that as he was. I reached into my pocket and held out one of the vials. "If this dress is as custom conforming as you make it out to be, there won't be room to hide anything underneath. You'll hang onto this for me? In case I need it later?"

"Absolutely." He effortlessly made the vial disappear into his hand and then into a pocket.

Tabor handed the dress to me. The weight of it caught me off guard.

"The one complaint the elite had with Okashki's work was that it was heavy. I figure it's not any more than you're used to carrying with your armored arsenal. Your armor is rudimentarily based on the same intelligent weave technology, though obviously for a different purpose."

I held the dress in front of me, warming to the idea now that it held a comforting heft. It was far from the drab heirloom I'd expected.

He reached into the discarded bag and pulled out a pair of matching shoes with blessedly sturdy rather than spiky heels. I supposed anyone carrying around the weight of the dress would want stability rather than alluring style. The skirt would cover them anyway.

"Also Okashki. They'll fit," he said confidently.

The door chime sounded.

"Perfect timing. That would be your team."

"I have a team?"

Tabor grinned. "I did say I would take care of you today, didn't I?" He headed for the door. "As much as I love Anastassia the Advisor, today you'll be the wife of a Jalvian elite. You'll have to trust that I know what I'm doing." He returned with two Jalvian women and a man, all carrying a multitude of cases and eyeing me up like a lump of clay about to be thrown on a wheel.

In true elite form, he said, "Introductions aren't necessary. They're here to do their jobs. Please let them do what they've been paid for. Vayen has placed two guards outside your suite door so you'll be secure while we are all elsewhere. You can contact any of us if needed, and if you need a distraction, get some work done." He pointed to the datapad by my side. "Ikeri will be here later to help you into the dress. Shortly after the guests arrive, I will come to Jump you both to the ceremony so you can make your entrance." Tabor turned to speak to the team he'd brought for a moment.

I'd made plenty of entrances, but most of them involved the busting open of doors and firing weapons. The idea of this one, wearing this dress, of having to put on a performance for the exclusive audience Tabor and Vayen had curated, set my nerves on fire. Sneaking off into my closet to procure another drop of boost sounded like a good plan.

Except I'd already had two.

The Seeker part of my brain informed me that craving the drug was becoming a habitual reaction to stressful situations. I was going to need to address that after this day was over. My boost intake was screwing with my stomach, making me not hungry. Even when I did eat, nothing set well.

"Ikeri has been instructed on how to activate the dress and shoes and can contact me if she has any difficulty," Tabor said.

"Good luck wrangling everyone." He was going to need it.

I carefully draped the dress over the table, arranging the weight to keep it from falling off, and then closed the distance between us. The team stepped back and averted their attention to the cases they'd brought, arranging them throughout the room and setting up their stations. Tabor's hand rested on my arm, grounding me amid the invaders in my private space.

"Anastassia, you'll be fine. They'll take good care of you."

"I've never done any of this before," I whispered, knowing full well that when we were this close, he could feel every bit of my anxiety.

He licked his lips, and for a second, I thought he would kiss me, but his gaze darted to the room around us, to the hints of Vayen in the suite. Tabor remained as he was, hand on my arm, but nothing more. The air around us, however, filled with an invigorating charge that made me tingle inside and out. The intense and searing gleam in his eyes held an adoration that made me weak in the knees. And we were barely touching. That boded great promise for the consummation I'd promised him when this damned charade of a ceremony was done.

A flash of guilt broke the spell. I hadn't wanted anyone else, hadn't been with anyone else since Vayen had announced his first bond to me. I wasn't supposed to be doing this, entertaining the idea of actually being with Tabor with feelings involved. And the more I was around him, there were definitely feelings.

Everyone else seemed to be fine with the idea that I was taking a second husband. Even Vayen was resolved to it. He'd certainly not hesitated jumping into another bed when I'd put Buria in front of him.

My family kept saying they wanted me to be happy with Tabor. The crew, the entire damned Narvan, for that matter, expected me to behave as any normal consenting adult in a relationship would. The only one who seemed to be questioning the rightness of what I was doing was me.

Tonight, I would have to let that go.

Go with the flow. Thank the universe for boost.

I put on a confident smile for Tabor and all the effort he was making on my behalf. He squeezed my arm and then let go, nodding to a box he'd left on the table beside the dress.

"Mycel sent lunch for you. I figured the best chance of you eating was to offer something you'd actually want." He chuckled. "You haven't been eating much lately."

"Nerves," I said. "Too much on my mind."

"Understandable. After today, we can all move forward and find a new normal together, right?"

"Right." I hoped so. He sounded confident enough for both of us. Maybe he could drag me into normal with him.

"Good." Tabor leaned forward, clearly planning to kiss me this time before again catching himself. He spared the suite a quick look of annoyance before taking another step back. "My dearest and only, I shall see you in five hours. Until then, I must go wrangle our other couple and this entire ceremony into perfection. Enjoy your afternoon."

"You too."

For all his talk of wrangling over the past two weeks, he seemed to be having the time of his life. He'd even come to an accord with his two younger brothers. They were eagerly helping with the organizing, likely in the hopes of gaining his favor. His father and sister, not so much, but I was glad he'd found a measure of familial peace.

Tabor left, leaving me to face the team he'd assembled.

"You have your work cut out for you, I'm sure. Where do we start?"

After a massage that made even Seeker me envious of her skill, I'd undergone a thorough brow plucking, facial wrap, nail polishing, and hair washing. I'd heard rumors of women regularly undergoing these routines, but I'd never had the need for anything more than what I could do myself. I had to admit though, if I had an afternoon to waste, that was a pleasurable way to do it.

In between the treatments, I'd grazed my way through the delectable bites Mycel had sent, my stomach only slightly protesting.

While the two women packed up their supplies, the man approached the chair by the table where I was sitting in only my robe and underclothes, waiting for the final dressing. He tapped his chin, looking me over like a problem he'd been assigned to solve.

After a few commands in Jalvian that sent the women scurrying to relocate the dress on the back of the couch and the shoes on the floor beneath it, he stepped forward without any invitation and released my hair from the towel. He tapped his chin at that for a moment as well.

Meanwhile the women spread a cloth under the chair across from me and arrayed several cases on the table, opening them and facing them toward the other chair.

"Come." He gestured to the open chair. "Much work to do. Little time." He spoke in stiff Trade, as though he were more accustomed to only speaking Jalvian.

I took the other seat. The women cleared away the empty box Mycel had sent and resumed packing up their own supplies.

"You have something to do?" he asked, seeming to search for

something to offer me.

I got up and grabbed my datapad, silently thanking Tabor for the prompt at what Mr. Hair-and-Cosmetics would ask of me.

Settled back into the chair, I pulled up the current batch of reports from our new union members, composing a list of topics to discuss at our next meeting a week and half from now. After some trial and error, we'd arrived on three-week intervals as the most efficient option. Our delegates were required to be linked so they could Jump to the Iber, which currently housed our advisory sessions. Someday soon, we'd have to designate a neutral and secure meeting site on a world of our choosing. I'd suggested rebuilding one of the destroyed High Council bases, but Vayen had shut that idea down immediately. He was working on curating a list of options we could visit on one of our days off together.

With a skilled touch, the stylist managed to comb out my hair and was half way through trimming it before I realized what he was doing. Or maybe it was me needing the distraction of the reports so much that I'd lost myself for a little while.

"Is good hair. Just the ends," he assured me.

The snipping took on a rhythm that lulled my eyes into glazing over. The report blurred. I blinked rapidly, returning to alertness. I hadn't been sleeping well, too much having to remember our new schedule each day. Too much trying to stay busy and yet enjoy my time with Tabor, but not fixate on what Vayen might be doing with Buria. Then there was having to figure out things to do with Vayen on our days off. Neither of us was accustomed to sitting and doing nothing. Nothing being anything that wasn't working. It was going to take some time to figure out what we might enjoy together beyond sex. No matter how much Vayen was leaning on it as a coping technique, I had a feeling Buria had that method covered.

"Head forward."

The stylist released a sweet-scented cloud into my hair and worked his fingers through the damp strands. After drying it and spending several minutes wrapping strands around a heated rod, he stepped in front of me, hands empty, head cocked.

He nodded and stepped back around to envelope my head in another cloud. Clicking open another case, he spread an array of pins and clips on the table. In my peripheral vision, I caught a glimpse of a small fortune in red and yellow gems adorning the accessories.

Fingers worked through my hair with a gentle tug and then a pin vanished from the table. He repeated this several times until I gathered from the cold air on my neck, that he'd piled the curls on top of my head. The clips left the table. More tugging.

"Good," he announced. "Now, face."

I set my datapad down on my lap, guessing I'd have little chance to get anything further accomplished.

The women had long since finished their packing and were sitting on their cases near the door, chatting in hushed voices. They paid no attention to me. I was a job. I understood that completely and felt more at ease for it.

One case closed and was pushed aside, another was pulled closer. Then commenced what seemed like ten solid minutes of dabbing at my face. Through the few focused glimpses I got, the stylist wore a look of determination. My eyelashes fluttered as he pulled a black-laced brush through them. Another brush worked through my eyebrows. A flurry of brushes of various sizes swept over my cheeks, eyelids, forehead, nose and chin. Palettes of colors shuffled in and out of the case. A brush danced over my lips. It seemed like every pore of my face was covered in solid layers of cosmetics. Surely I must resemble Tabor's mother by now, a painted visage that couldn't disguise the ravages of experience and time.

As much as my mind was sure there must be a solid mask, constraint of movement, a lack of air, there was none of that, but I didn't dare touch my skin to see how it actually felt. The stylist stepped back and pondered his work, then swished his brushes a few more times over my cheeks and eyelids.

He grunted a semi-positive sounding noise and handed me a mirror. "Good?"

A stranger stared back at me. Her stunned face mirrored mine.

"What did you do?" I asked, wondering when he'd managed to stretch a complete prosthetic over my face.

"Is not good?" His forehead furrowed.

The door chimed. I checked my datapad for the time. It had to be Ikeri. I used my pad to open the door.

She took one step in and her mouth dropped open.

"Is too much?" The stylist nibbled his lower lip

"You look amazing. Dad is going to lose his mind," Ikeri gushed.

"Let's hope not. It would defeat the purpose of me going through all this." I stood, clutching my datapad like a security blanket, the one known texture in all of the uncertainty.

"Thank you. It's good," I said to the stylist, forming a smile with the full red lips that weren't mine.

He nodded and began packing his tools. I watched for a moment, searching for any easy explanation for the magic he'd performed, but all he had were the color palettes and brushes that I'd seen.

Ikeri clapped her hands, grinning from ear to ear. "Let me see it! Where is this dress Tabor has been going on about?"

I waved her over and joined her at the couch where the women had arranged the dress. Her head spun from the dress to me and back again.

"You get to wear this? Holy Geva. Buria is going to be pissed."

"Why? What's she wearing?"

"It won't matter. Dad will be drooling over you all night."

"Well, he can be pissed with Buria. It's Tabor's night, not his."

Ikeri let out a peel of hysterical laughter. "I'm on Dad wrath monitoring duty, got it."

"There shouldn't be any wrath. He's getting what he wanted. Come on, help me into this thing." I picked up the dress while she took the shoes. We headed off into the bedroom as soon as Tabor's transformation team streamed out the door.

I set the dress on the bed and peeled off the robe I'd been wearing since my earlier massage. My skin still felt soft and smooth from the oils she'd used. They'd left a faint scent, nothing overpowering but pleasing, flowery but not cloying.

Ikeri arranged the dress on the floor, allowing me to step into it. We pulled it up enough to carefully slide my arms into the sheer spiraled sleeves and then up over my shoulders. The weight settled into place, feeling natural to me. Ikeri fastened the mostly sheer back, encasing me in the roomy beaded art of the Desu family heirloom.

"Shoes," she prompted breathlessly.

I slid my feet into the shoes that were two sizes too big.

"Ready for the fitting?"

"I suppose?" I had no idea what to expect.

Her fingers pressed on something on my lower back, dancing there a moment and then she knelt down to tap the backs of the shoes.

"Stand still and breathe normally," she cautioned. "He said it would take a couple of minutes for the fibers to conform."

I did as instructed, silently marveling at the tightening creeping over my second skin. When the last of the shifting sensations faded, I took an experimental step, and not tripping over anything, another.

"It worked, I think."

When Ikeri didn't say anything, I turned slowly, allowing for the flowing skirt to move with me. She sat on the edge of the bed with tears in her eyes.

"What's wrong?"

"I never imagined getting to see you like this."

I settled next to her, smoothing the skirt over my lap and marveling at the perfect length of the long, pointed sleeves that covered most of the bony musculature on the backs of hands that shouldn't belong to a woman wearing this dress.

"To be fair, I never imagined looking like this, or having a reason to."

She wiped her eyes and smiled. "I'm glad you chose Tabor."

"Me too. Now go get dressed. He'll be here soon to get us."

Ikeri went back into the common room and then closed herself in the bathroom with the items she'd brought.

"Do you need any help?" I asked through the door.

"I've got it, thanks. Relax. I'll be out in a few minutes."

While she was occupied, I took the opportunity to visit my closet stash and refresh my boost intake. Though I'd be near Tabor most of the evening, there would be two hundred-some other guests to talk to and a jealous Vayen to deal with.

I tried sitting, but between the boost and my nerves, pacing became the better option. Not pacing, getting a feel for walking in the fancy-ass shoes, I told myself. The dress must have had sensors that synced with the shoes to find the perfect length. The skirt floated just a fraction above the floor in the front and drifted out behind me to puddle luxuriously two steps behind.

Ikeri emerged wearing a red dress with gold beading that fit her perfectly. Sleeveless, but with a tasteful neckline and floor-length like mine. She'd pulled her natural curls up into a loose replica of my stylist's creation and applied a few cosmetics of her own.

"You look lovely. Where did you get the dress?"

"Tabor." She grinned.

"No wonder you like him."

She rolled her eyes, "The dress had very little to do with that, Mom."

"Come here a minute." I went into the bathroom. She followed me in. Pulling one of the jeweled pins from the back of the curls on my head, I tucked it into the front of hers.

She grinned and hugged me. I wrapped my arms around my daughter, staring at the surreal sight in the mirror over her shoulder. Mother and daughter, dressed for a fancy gala, not a weapon or worry in sight. Who the hell were these people and why did the mother have my eyes?

Tabor's team had managed to erase twenty-five years from my face. The heavenly fabric masked the rest, smoothing the defined muscles beneath to a pleasingly curved womanly form. My hair looked like it had never seen a utilitarian braid, like it effortlessly curled into an angelic cloud every morning. None of it look starched or forced. Fucking magic for sure.

The door chimed again. It had to be Tabor. I took a deep breath.

"Stay here," Ikeri said, holding me back as she raced for the door to let Tabor in.

I emerged from the bathroom as he stepped into the room, catching him complimenting her on her dress. He smiled as his gaze settled on the pin in her hair. Then his eyes met mine.

"You were supposed to wait and make a big entrance," Ikeri scolded.

"I'm not a big entrance kind of person."

Tabor just stood there, staring.

"I'll, umm, go wait in the corridor." Ikeri stepped around Tabor and slipped out the door.

The calm of the bond, ignited by his presence, settled over me, soothing my stomach and the perpetual twinges in my arm and back, further easing my nerves. Since he seemed locked in place, I closed the distance between us until my hands rested on the shoulders of his long, dark grey suit coat. The heels of the Okashki shoes put me at eye level with him.

"Are you alive in there?"

He nodded slowly. "You're really going to sign a marriage contract with me. Indefinitely?"

"Those were the terms I specified, yes."

A grin spread across his face and lit his eyes until they gleamed. Excess liquid escaped down his cheek.

"Those better be happy tears."

"Very much so." He wiped them with the back of his hand.

"Is everyone ready?"

"They are, but for you? No one is going to be ready for this."

"Blame your team for going overboard. It wasn't my doing." But I was grinning from his rapt attention rather than annoyed.

However, the thought of facing a whole room of that made me go stiff. While I was plenty used to being the focus of a group, it was because of my position as Advisor or due to a threat or weapon in my hand, certainly not because of how I looked.

"I'll be right beside you," he said soothingly.

"Except when you're not."

"If we're separated, find me, take my arm, feel the calm of our bond. It doesn't matter who I'm talking to. This day isn't in your comfort zone. I get it. I'm here for you."

Despite being in the suite I shared with Vayen, I kissed Tabor's cheek. "Thank you."

Whatever the stylist had used was good stuff, because my lips didn't leave any color behind.

Tabor fairly glowed. I reminded myself that while I was in anxiety mode, he was having the best day ever. For all his hard work in putting this together, I'd do my best to not ruin it for him.

We retrieved Ikeri, and then Tabor Jumped us to the high-end hotel on Jal that he owned. We arrived at the designated jump point and were waved through by a team of twelve armed men and women all standing at different points within the room. Two more stood outside, facing in, door controls in their hands, ready to seal off the jump point should it become compromised. Buria and Vayen were taking security seriously.

There were several other sets of guards posted on the path to the lift and one in the lift. Six more stood outside it where we exited onto the top floor where the ordeal was to take place. Tabor gestured for Ikeri to go in but he remained in the foyer with me.

"Do you need a minute? Need a hit?" he asked.

I held out my hand. "Definitely."

TWENTY-FIVE

Daniel

Ikeri sprinted toward us as much as her dress would allow. She was grinning.

"Is Mom here yet?" Markus asked as soon as she was within hearing range.

"Oh yes. She's here. Just wait." Ikeri glanced from us to where our father stood with Buria at his side and to the closed doorway she'd come from. Swirling conversation filled the grand hall. Dignitaries from the Narvan worlds, Primes and Premiers and their spouses, milled amongst a vast assortment of faces that made up the majority of our union as well as other various guests Tabor and my father had invited. Everyone stood around the tall tables scattered throughout the room, tossing back the free drinks and nibbling on finger food from the outrageously decadent offerings on the large table in the middle.

Flowers in massive vases, full-sized shrubs and even all out potted trees draped with strings of tiny lights broke up the vast space, keeping the noise at a tolerable level. A pleasing array of instrumental music further dulled the din.

In keeping with the elite event, everyone had taken it upon themselves to show off their best dress and riches. There was enough sparkle in the room to finance our entire mission for at least a year if not two.

The three newsbots Tabor and my father had agreed to allow zoomed overhead, snapping still frames and broadcasting coverage within our undisclosed location.

My wives stood behind me, both having taken the opportunity to dress up and show off their expanding bellies. They were currently indulging in the delicious food Tabor had provided.

Markus wore his Jalvian dress uniform. I'd opted for keeping things simple in a pressed black shirt and pants with a light dress coat lined with a thin armored weave. My father had dressed similarly, other than wearing a white shirt which was a rare choice for him. It gave him a stately look, which seemed appropriate under the circumstances. Buria, beside him, wore a short red dress that clung to her body, leaving little to the imagination. Though she did have a very nice figure, I'd seen too much of it already.

"You look great," I said to Ikeri.

She rarely wore clothing that showed any skin or the shape of her body since her return to us. It was refreshing to see her dressed like a normal girl her age, like she might finally be ready to move past some of the trauma she'd endured.

"Thanks." She didn't look at me, her attention split between the doorway and our father, who was busy talking to Buria and Uncle Isnar.

Neko and Hedvika were working their way over. He kept getting stopped by various Narvan citizens. His frustrated voice hit my link. *"Keep an eye on your father. Tabor says they're here."*

"Why?"

"Just do it."

"I'll be right back," I said to my siblings and wives.

That was as far as I got before the doors opened and my mother walked in on Tabor's arm. At least, I assumed it was my mother. The woman beside Tabor vaguely resembled her, but was way younger, and smiling, and wearing a Geva-be-damned all-out gown. She could have been Ikeri's older sister. Holy Geva.

"Go. Go." Ikeri shoved me toward our father.

"What the hells am I supposed to do?"

"Is that Mom?" Markus whispered raggedly in the sudden hush of the room.

While the newsbots had a heyday, Tabor and my mother started the slow circuit of greeting guests. She didn't look our way at all. She might be wearing my father's bands on her neck and arm, but Tabor's jewels sparkled in her hair, making my father's gifts look drab and paltry in comparison. And Geva, that gown had to cost a fortune.

My wives joined the rush of renewed conversation, both rapidly gushing about the dress, her hair, and what someone had done to her face. "I want to know who she had. Find out. Please," Arden begged in my ear. "I need them, whoever it is."

She didn't. She was beautiful without any of that, but I'd quickly learned not to argue with a pregnant woman.

Since everyone thought I should, I headed for my father whose eyes seemed to be popping out of his head. He made to start for my mother. Buria caught his arm. He shook her off. Uncle Isnar, looking equally stunned, stepped in his way, putting one hand out in what appeared to be a feeble attempt to stop gravity. My father barreled past him.

He only came up short when I intercepted him. We were close to equally matched in size these days, though his augmented hand and mind could rip me apart if he was so inclined.

"Don't."

"What?" he said as if only just realizing he'd stopped moving and who I was.

"Don't fuck this up. The newsbots are watching the four of you closely. Go back to Buria and quit staring."

"Everyone is staring," he growled.

"And rightly so."

He glared at me. "She hasn't even looked over here."

"They'll get around to us eventually. They're doing what they're supposed to do. Exactly what Tabor warned us they would do. Calm the fuck down."

He snarled, "I can't."

I'd known his bond would cause discomfort in this situation, but he'd dealt with it all my waking life. Surely he could maintain control for one night.

Neko finally made it over to us. Hedvika remained at a safe distance, making a show of admiring a flower arrangement while Neko joined me in forming a wall.

"Hey, boss. You look good."

My father's glare slid from me to Neko.

"It looks like you need a distraction. How about I introduce you to Rok's new Prime?" Neko offered.

"Is it Tabor? I'd like to meet him right now."

"No. He declined."

"Fucking hells. Why?"

That announcement didn't surprise me as much as it did my father. What little I did know of Tabor lead me to believe he had his hands in a lot of dealings that would be greatly impeded by taking the public office of Rok's Prime.

"I don't know. I asked. He said no." Neko paused. "Actually, he didn't say anything. He just shook his head after ruining his brother and then walked away with Ana. They make quite a—"

I shot Neko a warning look.

"Right." He cleared his throat. "Anyway, Rok's new Prime. This way. Daniel, maybe you should meet him too."

I helped Neko herd my father away from the spectacle he'd been about to make. Buria gravitated to his side, further assisting our efforts. When Uncle Isnar joined in, I broke off, letting the three of them contain him.

Ikeri intercepted me before I could return to my wives. "How is he?"

"Just short of foaming at the mouth?"

She giggled and then turned to where our mother and Tabor were working their way closer. "She looks happy, doesn't she?"

"Looks, sure. But is she?"

"Yes, I think she really is." She stared wistfully at our mother. "Do you think I could look like that someday?"

Did she mean older and wearing a fancy dress or happy on the arm of a man? I went for a safe answer. "Sure."

"I hope so." She turned back to me. "How long until they do the signing?"

"You could get your own link and quit having to borrow mine," I teased.

"Yeah, maybe I should."

Her reply took me aback. She'd never voiced any desire to get one. I wasn't sure if her decision was in solidarity with my mother who no longer could host one, or because of something that been done to her when she'd been away from us.

"If you're serious, I'll take you anytime. Or Dad can. He'd be happy to, you know."

She nodded.

"About half an hour until the signing. Can you hang with Markus? My wives look hungry again."

"Sure." She headed for our brother.

Before I made it back to Meera and Arden, an unwelcome face came into focus near where my mother was heading. I wove through the crowd to the tall but hollow-looking Jalvian wearing a non-descript dark blue suit. He wore his hair slicked back from his face, lending him an even more gaunt appearance than my father's torture had left upon him. It wasn't unexpected that he was alone with ample space between him and any other conversation.

"Who invited you?"

"Your father," said the man whom I'd once called Uncle Jey. Before he'd betrayed our family. Before my father had ripped him apart and then slowly put him back together.

I'd half hoped it had been Tabor who had invited him so we'd have an excuse to explain the error and then toss Jey out. My father had a strange fellowship with him that I didn't fully understand. "A complicated history," my father had once called it.

If anyone would have an opinion on how well my parents were selling this second marriage to the general populace, it was this Jalvian who knew them both well, even if they now held him at a distance.

"What do you think of all this?" I asked.

"Still trying to wrap my head around it. Her I get, but him?" Jey shook his head. "If I wasn't standing here, I never would have believed it in a million years."

"He was the one who wanted a second marriage. Not her."

"That's what he said."

My father had talked to Jey about it? I wasn't aware they were on anything but business-speaking terms. He and I were alike in that one designation, at least I'd thought so. That my father may have confided anything to this traitor when he barely talked to me made me scowl

"She looks amazing. Like I remember her; well, not dressed up, but younger. When we all first worked together. Back when I hated every breath your father took." He chuckled. "At one time, I would have given anything to be in his place." He nodded to Tabor.

"What changed?"

"Your father got to her first. Or maybe she got to him." He shrugged. "Couldn't get between them after that. Didn't think anyone could." His gaze settled on Buria. He didn't look pleased.

"It wasn't like that," I said, feeling the sudden need to defend Buria in case Jey got it in his head to do something to defend my mother. He'd been her protector once.

"It's disconcerting seeing you looking like he used to," he said, looking down at me. "Like he did when I hated him."

"Stay away from my sister. Don't let her see that you're here. She's just finally getting herself together after the nightmare you caused."

Jey looked bored, like my warning was entirely lost on him. I could see how he and my father had butted heads for their first few years working together. I wanted to punch him too.

My mother's laugh made me freeze.

"How's he doing?" whispered Tabor who'd stopped beside me while my mother greeted Jey. "Your father?"

"Just short of exploding last I checked. You might want to get her over to him before he goes off."

Tabor nodded then took in my mother giving Jey a hug. While the sight surprised me—last I'd known, she wasn't speaking to him on any level—it was Tabor wearing the same snarl my father had worn when they'd walked in that put me on high alert.

"What the hells is going on with you?" I asked, not caring that I was snapping at him. Jey and my mother were too busy talking to notice.

His laser-like glare lit on me.

"I know that look, but you're Jalvian," I said.

There was no evidence of Tabor's usual cheerful demeanor. This was the man I'd met when he'd first come aboard the Iber, the one with the threatening edge. And now he seemed cornered, exposed, alternately grimacing and seething. He turned his back to the conversation between my mother and Jey and closed his eyes, his nostrils flaring with each breath. When he opened them again, his features eased, but he didn't turn around.

"You weren't supposed to see that," he said in a tone that made me wonder if we were elsewhere and I were someone other than the son of his new wife, if he would have attempted to silence me permanently.

"You're Jalvian," I repeated, glancing over my shoulder to check on my mother, only to find her smiling and Jey looking more at ease and lively than I'd ever remembered.

Tabor stared at me, lips pinched together.

"We're family now, I suppose. You might as well tell me what the fuck is going on."

"I'm not entirely Jalvian," he hissed.

"And in a matter of two weeks, you managed to not only get a marriage contract with my mother, but also bond with her? She's already got a bond mate," I hissed back.

"I'm well aware. So is she." He shook his head. "I didn't think it would be this bad. It wasn't, until her energy changed when she started talking to him." He jutted his chin toward Jey.

"If Jey is a problem, how do you plan to keep that quiet near my father?"

"I didn't think the bond would *be* a problem, not until just now. Geva, I haven't been near them together since this happened." Panic lit on his face.

"Does he know?"

"That your mother and I share a bond? No. That I'm part Artorian? That's in my record if anyone cares to dig. Neither of us knows how to tell him. Ideas?"

Why did everyone expect me to be my father's handler?

"I don't know, but I'm damned glad I don't have to deal with this bonding shit myself."

"None of it? Really? Have you tried?"

"Why would I want to? The two of you are losing your shit over each other. Or you will be soon enough."

He rested a hand on my shoulder, his confident manner slipping back into place. "The connection the bond offers is worth every second of aggravation. If I manage to make it through tonight, I'll explain what I did so you can try it. Mixed blood has to stick together."

Tabor's offer to explain anything about the bond was more than my father had ever given me. It was like my father had just expected me to know, to figure out if it was something I could do. If it was something I wanted to do, given that Arden was Artorian but Meera was not. Having concrete information would help in making that important decision.

"Good luck making it through the night, then."

Tabor exhaled loudly. "Here goes nothing." He turned to Jey and my mother with a smile on his face. "We need to head to the signing. We can resume our rounds after dinner."

She said farewell to Jey and resumed her place on Tabor's arm. Then they were off.

If he could manage himself that well despite his irritation with Jey, he had a chance at surviving my father. And if he made it through that, he would be a mentor I might want in my life. I silently wished him luck.

TWENTY-SIX

Buria

It might be our marriage day, but Vayen couldn't take his eyes off his first wife. I couldn't blame him entirely. She'd made quite the spectacle with her entrance. With her whole damned appearance.

This was supposed to be my day. Not hers.

It was like I'd turned invisible once she'd shown up. Even Elonka, who was in attendance with Gamnock and his other wives noticed the change. She had given me a consoling smile.

I wanted to pause the ceremony so I could pull Elonka aside and vent my frustrations to a sympathetic ear. However, I knew that wasn't an option. The sooner we got this over with, the sooner I could find a workable accord with Ana and spend a day a week working with Vayen, discovering how I could best fit into his mission. Hopefully, in some way that could benefit me if this didn't work out in long term. Maybe Daniel would have some ideas. He seemed agreeable to my offer of assistance.

Ikeri and Markus stood behind us, witnessing our signing. Daniel and his wives served Ana and Tabor. The wrinkled Jalvian recited the ceremony in his own language, which I only understood thanks to the translation function of my link. The Artorian woman beside him didn't appear to be very happy to be there, but she paused the Jalvian speaker every so often to offer her native language translation. Directly following her translation, a synth voice translated the passage into Trade and pumped it through the sound system throughout the room. Tabor had been explicit in wanting to honor both factions of the Narvan while also making sure as many attendees as possible understood what was being said.

He'd done an admirable job with the arrangements and facility.

I just wished he could have taken Ana elsewhere, maybe held their own ceremony so I could have mine. But that would have defeated the whole purpose, well, the political one. The one that Vayen had used to justify what he called "a selfish indulgence".

At first, I'd thought being an indulgence was fun, flattering even. But at times like this, when he was too wrapped up in Ana to remember I existed, even on my damned signing day, I wanted to scream. No matter how far I'd gone to cater to his every whim, she kept surfacing in his thoughts.

She made him miserable, wracked with guilt over me. Me, who she'd invited into his life. It wasn't fair.

The ceremony droned on, Jalvian, followed by Artorian, followed by Trade. By the second repetition of the next portion, I'd already tuned out again. Many of the attendees also had links and were probably as bored as I was with the endless translations. But some of them weren't linked, Tabor had argued. The media coverage could edit to what they needed for their audience. It made sense, but it took what seemed like forever.

And how dare Ana show up in that outrageous gown with gods-be-damned jewels in her for-once-not-braided hair? When Tabor said Ana would be wearing a dress, I'd expected the woman whose mainstay fashion statement was black and grey shapeless clothing covered by a well-worn armored coat, to look uncomfortable, out of sorts, awkward. I was the one with a body that made men speechless. The Tacesh Masters had made sure of that, and I'd put in a lot of effort to keep it that way.

Then she walked in, looking like she'd been born a Prime's wife. No, I considered, taking in the envious attention of the actual Prime's wives in attendance, she looked like The Advisor's wife. Like she was better than all of them. Like I, who was now also the Advisor's wife, was nothing.

"Are you ready?" Vayen asked.

I nodded, taking his hands and facing him, doing my best to block out the hundreds of eyes watching us and the bots flitting overhead, capturing us at every angle. At least facing me now, he had his back to Ana, who was about to embark on duplicate vows with Tabor. For these few moments, I had his attention.

The vows were repeated in all three languages after which we each, in turn, voiced our agreement loudly and clearly for all to hear.

Then it was time to sign. Two contracts were set on the table, each in print on thick white paper with bold black text. A Jalvian seal marked the top. An Artorian seal marked the bottom, just below the two lines where we were about to sign. I'd been practicing signing my name all week, getting the feel for a pen. Everything was done on datapads, on the network. This fallback to ancient print was something only Jalvians seemed to cling to for ceremonial occasions. I'd never had to physically sign my name to anything before, but Vayen hadn't blinked an eye when Tabor had told us what would be expected. The three of them probably did this all the time, being important, as they were.

I took the pen from the Artorian woman. Making every effort to relax my hand, to appear natural, I leaned over the table and skimmed the contract as Tabor suggested we do. Another effort to draw out the ceremony for the audience, I supposed. As if, having come this far, any of us would suddenly object to the terms.

Finding the contract in order, our two years before renewal specified in bold text, I signed my name and handed Vayen the pen. He smiled at me, a promise of delicious things later, and made his signature with an enviable flourish that left mine looking childish.

Ana and Tabor handed their pen back to the Jalvian officiant. Our contracts were held up for all to see, and probably more importantly, for the bots to capture. Gritting my teeth, I forced what I hoped looked like a smile as I noted that their signatures also flowed over the paper with a grace lacking in mine. It was then that my eyes fell upon the bold text in the middle that declared Ana had entered into a perpetual contract with Tabor.

Vayen's stiffening beside me hinted that he'd just noted that too. Had he never discussed terms with her?

We all turned to face the applauding crowd and then stepped off the platform into the well-wishing of Vayen's family and friends. Ana and Tabor were instantly enveloped in the tight cluster of Tabor's family and others eager to gain the favor of either Advisor.

Security lurked closely and openly while we were in the fray. I'd made sure of that. While I had no doubt that Vayen was armed, my dress and likely Ana's too, left little room for any protection of merit. Tabor might have been armed. I'd never asked him about that or his martial proficiency. My one job in all this was keeping everyone safe, and I'd taken as much precaution as I could without drastically inconveniencing our guests. My plan had passed Vayen's oversight with minimal correction. Security was the one thing in all this I felt confident about.

Not knowing most of the attendees, and having exhausted what little conversation I had to exchange with those that I did, I let Vayen have the attention. He was no doubt meticulously logging the favors and pledges offered in lieu of physical gifts. The invitation and security team had made it clear that gifts were strictly prohibited.

I stuck to Vayen's side, smiling and nodding, repeating my thanks in a cycle of five slight variations in an attempt to sound more personal. Another of Tabor's suggestions.

While we suffered through the barrage of compliments and promises, the staff efficiently swapped out the tall tables for larger dinner tables with chairs. The partially decimated buffet of pre-ceremony food was removed, the leftovers to be shared by the staff later, according to Tabor. By the time we'd worked our way to through to the back of the crowd, the transformation was complete.

Delicate, flowered centerpieces ringed with short candles adorned each table, circled with expensive-looking place settings. As much as Tabor's quick lesson in properly using such a setting had embarrassed me and annoyed Vayen, I was glad for it now. With so many people watching, I very much did not want any negative reason to draw attention to myself.

The lights dimmed. The crowd dispersed to the tables. We took our places at the now transformed table on the platform, set up similarly to those for our guests. Vayen's children along with Neko, his wife, and Karin's Premier took their places at a round table just below ours. Tabor helped Ana back onto the platform and into her seat in the middle. Vayen sat beside her, with me and Tabor at either end. I steeled my nerves for the most observed meal of my life.

Vayen leaned toward me, whispering, "Why would she do that? Perpetual?"

"I don't know."

She was his wife, mate, whatever they were calling each other these days. He could have easily asked her instead of me.

And started a fight, in front of everyone.

"It never occurred to me that she'd choose anything other than the minimum contact. If she didn't want this, why perpetual?"

"Maybe she doesn't mind it so much now."

If we could be so lucky. Should that be true, perhaps she would relax her hold on Vayen to spend more time with Tabor, thereby allowing Vayen more time with me. More likely, I considered, was that she'd done it to punish him for making them take seconds at all.

He turned to Ana, who was laughing at something Tabor said.

"Maybe," he conceded but he sounded even more put out than before.

Would I ever understand the hold they had over each other?

Our first course was served, disrupting further fuming on Vayen's part. He reached for the spoon on the right side of his plate. Ana's hand slipped over his.

I tried not to watch or listen, but they were only a few feet away. Tabor caught my gaze and shrugged before starting in on his steaming soup. I knew I was supposed to do the same. He'd suggested that I follow his lead if I found myself wondering what to do. Full of suggestions, that one.

Maybe he'd suggested perpetuity too, gaining Ta'set notoriety and favor for life.

Vayen and Ana talked quietly, her hand still on his, their meals untouched.

I mechanically lifted a spoonful of soup to my lips. It smelled wonderful and my tongue informed me that it tasted better than it smelled, but all my brain seemed to register was that he was telling her how beautiful she looked.

He'd said the same thing to me earlier in the evening. But somehow when he said it to her, it sounded like he sincerely meant it, meant it more than he had with me.

She took quick sip of the soup and then explained about the dress being an heirloom and the technology behind the weave of it, how it related to their armor. Tabor chimed in, offering further details on the Okashki line. I sipped my soup and tried to come up with something insightful with which to enter the conversation. Though I covertly searched the crowd for my one friend in attendance, for a glimpse of an understanding smile or nod, I couldn't spot Elonka amid the seated crowd of flashing jewels, bright smiles, and animated conversation.

By the time the next course came, I was still on the sideline of the discussion that now had drifted to speculation on whether the three Ocelon envoys might be won over. A translator unit had been installed at their table in the hopes it would help that cause.

"I've seen many of the other union representatives talking with them," Ana said. "Their scowls never seem to change though."

"Maybe the food will win them over," I suggested, popping the last of my allotted five bite-sized meat-filled pastries into my mouth. The buttery sauce lingering on the plate reflected the flickering candlelight.

So did the beadwork on Ana's dress. She seemed to sparkle while what I'd intended to be an alluring amount of exposed skin, mingled with the shadows.

Tabor smiled at me, but Vayen and Ana speculated onward as if I hadn't said a thing. At least she'd let go of his hand. Not that I would have dared take it with her right there. Even on our signing day, there were boundaries for seconds. In public, physical contact was for Ana and Vayen to take, allowing them to set the level of contact they as a couple were comfortable with. Which also meant, as long as I followed the rules, all blame for infractions of that comfort level sat squarely with Vayen, keeping me on the better side of Ana's temper.

The third and fourth courses passed in further conversation I didn't catch all of, thanks to Vayen facing Ana and Tabor most of the time. The free drinks were flowing again and the guests were taking advantage of them, their conversation rising to a boisterous level.

By the fifth course, Ana was on her second glass of wine while Tabor still nursed his first. Vayen signaled for a third glass of whatever he'd been pouring down his throat since the seared vegetables in a rich cream sauce that I hadn't been able to help but lick every hint of from my fork.

Vayen finally turned in my direction, raising his brows at the barely touched fruity concoction he'd ordered for me. "You don't like it?"

"It's fine," I said, hoping that didn't sound as snide as it did in my head.

Knowledge of the vast universe of alcoholic drinks had not been in my training, and the few selections the Masters had imbibed were not prevalent in the Narvan. On the occasions I did drink, I deferred to Vayen, who seemed intimately familiar with the contents of every bottle he got his hands on. I took a sip to appease him. It was too sweet to go with the food.

"I don't see that he got her anything, do you?" he asked, eyeing the ring on my finger with the giant, glimmering fire gem.

I did have to give him credit for the ring, it was far more ostentatious than the jewelry he'd used to mark his joining with Ana. But why did he have to keep asking me about her? Couldn't he ask what I thought about anything other than his damned first wife?

"Other than the priceless dress and the fortune in her hair? No."

He set his fork down to give me his full attention. I would have enjoyed that, except for the disapproval in his lips and eyes.

I must have spoken too loud or Ana had very good hearing because she answered before he could.

"They are family heirlooms, not mine to keep. As if I would wear this sort of thing any other day of my life." Her tone was surprisingly level and without any hint of malice.

"Now you're going to make me work hard to find more excuses to get you into dresses," Tabor said, his eyes dancing with merriment.

Ana snickered. "Good luck with that."

The next course came, saving me from further embarrassment. Vayen stared at his plate of red berries on yellow grains. From the slight tilt of his head, I guessed he was watching Ana and Tabor rather than the food growing cold.

It wasn't until our plates were whisked away, and a platter of desserts was placed before Ana and Vayen, that he seemed to rejoin us. Ana pointed out several of the selections, explaining what they were.

"You've tried them all?" he asked.

The jewels in her hair shimmered as she nodded. "I've sampled all of this. It was hard to pick from all of Mycel's creations. Tabor's cook," she explained. "Everything he makes is amazing."

"Tonight's menu was comprised of Anastassia's favorites," Tabor said.

Vayen downed what was left of his third drink and signaled for another.

At Tabor's urging, I sampled the desserts. Vayen sipped his fourth drink. His plate remained empty. His gaze flitted over the guests.

Below us, Daniel cast a worried look at his father. Meera said something to him, holding up four fingers. Daniel looked at me. Like I was supposed to keep his father from getting drunk? I'd picked up three solid things from Vayen: He'd try anything once, don't question his devotion to Ana, and what and how much he drank was not up for discussion.

Ana, however, was far more confident in handling the death-bringer. Her hand slipped around his where he held the already half-empty glass, subtly sliding his fingers away from it to intertwine in her own. With her other hand, she held up one of the bite-sized desserts in front of his mouth, leaving him no choice but to take her offering lest he arouse suspicion from the ever-watching newsbots and guests.

"Soak that up a little."

"We're having a talk later," he said to her loud enough for me to hear. The alcohol likely had something to do with his lack of volume control.

"I think Buria will require your attention later. Not me."

Her smile was not reflected in her tone.

She leaned around him to address me. "Do you dance?"

"Sorry, no."

Of all the things the Tacesh Masters had taught us, dancing, the tasteful social sort, was not one of them. They'd likely assumed our Masters wouldn't be taking us out in public for occasions such as momentous political marriage ceremonies.

"You were right," Ana said to Tabor. "I suppose that means me then."

"My feet are suitably warned."

She laughed, reaching for his hand, and then gracefully descended the platform. They walked to an open space on the floor near our corner. The music suddenly swelled, overtaking the conversational din, likely at some subtle cue from Tabor, or maybe he'd used his link to do it himself.

"I didn't know she knew how," Vayen's heavily strained voice informed me.

"Do you?" I asked, hoping to draw his attention back to me before he leapt over the table to rip Tabor apart.

"No. Never had the need."

Without Ana's watchful gaze and with everyone else's attention glued to the dancing couple below, I decided it would be better to ignore the rules in favor of avoiding a scene.

I wrapped my hand around his arm and stood, pulling him up with me. "How about we go do those social rounds Tabor suggested?"

It took me tugging on his arm to get him to face me.

"Why did she have to pick him?" he muttered.

"Would you rather she chose someone she didn't like? Don't you want her to be happy?"

When he finally averted his gaze from the elegantly dancing couple, he stormed down the three steps with me still attached to his arm. I didn't dare let go for fear he'd be more of a problem untethered.

The guests were finishing their meals and gathering around Ana and Tabor. As tables were deserted, the staff rushed in to cart them away. By the end of the second song, half of the tables had been removed and other couples flooded the now much larger dance floor. I finally spotted Elonka, but she was dancing with Gamnock. Not that I could run over and have a good, long chat with her. I sighed.

Vayen and I stood in the shadows, masked by shrubbery and flowers until his fists stopped clenching.

"Perhaps we should check on the Ocelon?"

"Did Tabor suggest that too?" he growled.

Guessing that was a rhetorical question, I kept my mouth shut and did my best to exude soothing energy. That was an Etara suggestion. I had no idea if that did anything, but I figured I should make an effort since it came from the woman who held Vayen's kill switch.

"Yes, fine. They can't put me in any worse of a mood." He did look at me then, actually look. Pulling me closer, he kissed my cheek. "Thanks for putting up with me."

While I had his attention and no one else's, I figured I might as well violate another rule and remind him who he was with. It wasn't her.

I kissed him, my hands slipping inside his coat and meeting with the weaponry I knew would be there as my fingers kneaded his back. His hands ran over my face and the back of my neck.

"How much longer does this fiasco go?" he asked in my ear.

I checked the time with my link. "At least an hour or two before we can slip away."

"We could leave now," he suggested, one hand working its way under my short skirt.

I swatted him away. "Plenty of time for that later. We have all night and tomorrow, right?"

"And a fresh vial of bang," he whispered.

I'd hoped he'd be over using that by now, but if anything, he used more of it. Not that I was complaining, exactly.

"Two hours and then you can tell me how you'd like to celebrate our signing," I said against his ear.

He nuzzled along my neck and then bit down just enough to send shivers through me. "I have some ideas."

"I'm sure you do." I put a little distance between us and straightened my dress. "The sooner we do our rounds, the sooner we can leave."

"Right." With a sudden determination, he took my hand and headed for the nearest bar station. "You want anything?"

I shook my head, thinking he didn't need anything either; he was just short of slurring as it was. Emboldened by his attention and Daniel's earlier warning glance, I said, "Maybe you shouldn't—"

His dark glare made it clear that the frivolity with me was only on the surface, a mere diversion from the gnashing of teeth consuming the rest of him. He couldn't stay this angry for the two years I'd signed on for, could he? Surely, he'd level out and this would be better.

With a fresh drink in his hand, we entered the social currents, stopping to chat with several guests. Though I did manage to get him over to Gamnock and his wives, our conversation was too brief to allow me any sense of respite. If Elonka sensed I wasn't happy, she didn't show it. All beaming smiles and giggles with her fellow wives, they sipped their drinks and offered their congratulations before we moved on. I supposed that meant I was doing a suitable job of appearing the proper part for the newsbots that were incessantly buzzing overhead.

If everyone had stuck to promises of business deals and showering Vayen with compliments to gain favor, we might have been fine, but at least one person in each cluster had to mention how beautiful Ana was in her dress, how happy we all looked, and how lucky Vayen was to have such an open-minded mate.

By the time we found ourselves in front of the perpetually scowling Ocelon envoys, Vayen was wound so tight I feared he might burst.

I'd only been to their world the disastrous once to meet them, so other than voicing my safe "thank you for joining us today" refrain, I stood silently by Vayen's side, wondering how I would contain him if necessary. I was about to contact Daniel for backup when Etara showed up next to me.

"Congratulations," she said absently, her gaze brushing over me to hone in on Vayen.

"I'm glad you're here." I hoped she understood my dual meaning.

Her nod indicated she had.

The Ocelon, two men and a woman, all with the thick, squat bodies born of their high gravity world, maintained a civil discourse with Vayen. Civil, but not showing any indication that our efforts to include them had gained us any favor. I was relieved. Maybe accepting that the deal he'd hoped to make with them wasn't going to happen would allow Vayen to relax or at least better focus on finding resolution for his feelings regarding Ana. Any of that sounded great to me.

"Has speaking to our other union representatives given you further insight into what we can offer your world?" Vayen asked.

"We do not need what you're offering. Many worlds don't," said the woman. "You insist we do. We don't."

One of the men nodded. "Good food, but take your threats elsewhere."

"We haven't threatened you." But it sounded like he was about to.

"Your warship orbited of our world," said the third Ocelon.

"We left." Vayen tossed back his drink and slammed the glass on the nearby table. Ice bounced out, skittering across the glossy black surface.

"Threat," repeated the third man.

"It's a threat if we stay. It's a threat if we leave. What's the difference?" He slurred the last few words.

Etara stepped in front of him, nodding to the Ocelon. "Thank you for coming. Enjoy the rest of your evening."

The tiny Seeker then grabbed giant Vayen by the elbow and physically dragged him back toward the platform table. Considering her size, perhaps not so much dragged, but pulled hard enough that he allowed her to lead him. There were two people Vayen didn't fuck with, Etara was one of them. She brought us over to the other one.

Ana was busy talking to Karin's Premier. Markus came to stand beside us. He nudged Vayen's arm and nodded toward the dance floor. There, at the back, in the shadows, Ikeri was matching steps with a young Artorian man.

"What's he doing here?" Vayen asked not at all quietly.

"She invited him," said Markus. "They've been talking."

"Talking."

Markus nodded. "That's what she said."

"It's good to see her having fun," I ventured.

"It is." All his anger fizzled, leaving him looking deflated.

Tabor approached cautiously. Markus gave him a nervous smile and then darted over to Daniel and his wives.

Tabor inserted himself between us. He leaned toward Vayen. "You should ask her to dance."

"Buria doesn't know how. Neither do I. Not exactly needed in my line of work."

"Anastassia."

"Like I said—"

"I'll feed you the steps. Just do it."

"Why?" Vayen snarled. "So you can laugh at me?"

"Because it would make her happy." Tabor sighed. "She's on

enough boost tonight to make anyone else float, but it's not enough."

Drugs were why Ana was so cheerful and smiling? The haunted woman who'd shown up on Brustus to bring me to Vayen was still in there.

"She said she would be here, that she would do her part." Vayen's voice sounded hollow.

"And she is."

"You fed her boost."

Tabor squared his shoulders and faced Vayen. "Admittedly, I did bring her a supply of it when we first met, but she's been the one taking it. When she's with you. Because of you. Is that clear enough? So go ask your mate to dance so she can maybe be genuinely happy for a few minutes tonight."

"She looked happy enough dancing with you."

"Boost works wonders. She wants only you, asshole. I'm just a consolation prize."

Vayen glanced over to Ana, then to me, to everyone around us.

"If that's true, how do you explain the perpetuity of your contract?"

"Pity? She got caught up in the moment when handing my family their asses."

"That, I can believe." Vayen drunkenly chuckled. "And you want her to dance with me?"

"No. I'd like you to burn in the ninth hell, but she would like to dance with you. So that's what we're going to do."

I had to appreciate how well Tabor could pull off delivering such ire while still sounding civil and appearing his charming self. I also couldn't help but admire how far he was willing to go to please Ana. Maybe he'd wear off on Vayen.

"Do you mind?" Vayen asked, surprising me with his courtesy.

"Of course not."

Maybe if I'd known the steps myself, I'd have been more put out, but I didn't, and I was relieved to be around people who knew how to talk him down from a critical level.

Vayen walked over, brazenly interrupting Ana's conversation with the Premier, and after a fraction of a nod with Tabor, asked her to dance.

As they took their places on the dance floor, the joy on her face outshone every smile she'd worn all night. That was what true happiness looked like.

Having seen it now, I knew it would never be mine.

TWENTY-SEVEN

Daniel

"Holy fucking hells, I've seen it all now. I can die." Neko said, his gaze locked over my shoulder.

Hedvika knocked him on the back of the head. "You cannot."

"What?" I spun around to discover my parents. Dancing. Together.

Arden let out a wistful sigh.

Meera shook her head. "That's trouble right there."

"What do you mean?" Hedvika asked.

"Those are the looks that lead to babies," Meera said.

Neko burst out laughing.

I slapped Meera's shoulder lightly. "Just no. No more of that talk about my parents."

"Have they ever done that before"? asked Markus.

"Dancing? Not that I know of." I turned to the still vacant chair where Ikeri had sat. "Has anyone seen Ikeri?"

"She's still busy." Neko nodded to where I now spotted my sister with her arms around a young Artorian from the science team. "Don't worry, big brother, I've been watching her the whole time. He's behaving."

"He better be." Yet, I was overjoyed to see her that close to anyone other than family. Maybe all this relationship drama with our parents had brought about a breakthrough for her.

Neko's eyes went wide. "Oh shit, that's how he's doing it."

"What are you talking about?"

"I thought it was jealous staring, but his finger is tapping in time. That's concentration." Neko smiled. "Tabor's feeding him the steps."

Tabor, who was bonded to my mother. He was helping my father?

They were working together? I found that impossible to believe. Now, Tabor convincing my father to dance with my mother and making a fool of him, that was entirely possible.

"Excuse me a moment." I marched over to where Buria stood next to Tabor.

"You better not be doing what I think you're doing," I said to Tabor.

He didn't turn to me. Sweat beaded on his forehead. "Shh. Busy."

Buria knocked her hip into me. "Leave him be. He's being sweet."

The thickness in her voice caught me off guard. She pondered the ring on her finger. "That is a gift better than any piece of jewelry."

"Dancing?"

She leaned closer. "Look at his hands."

One of my father's hands was doing nothing but holding my mother's and the other rested tastefully on the small of her back.

"No. Him." She nodded to Tabor.

He held his arms crossed in an effort to hide his fists. His glistening forehead was heavily lined and his lips pinched tight.

"Giving your mother the one thing she wanted today even though it's hurting him to do it."

That was what bonded mates were supposed to do. Not the hurting part, but knowing their mate and what brings them joy, doing whatever they can to make the relationship work. That aspect seemed to have been lost on my father.

Seeing my mother with my father, blissfully happy like this, wearing the dress he had provided, on his own signing day, had to be hard to swallow. And still, Tabor managed to keep his shit together. Clearly it was a strain, but he was doing an admirable job of covering it. Another area in which my father was sorely lacking.

I patted Tabor on the shoulder. "Thank you for this."

If this was what the bond really looked like between a couple, I was far more inclined to listen to what he had to say and maybe give it a try with my wives.

Tabor glanced at me for half a second and nodded. My father's footing faltered. He glared in our direction. My mother didn't seem to notice. Tabor returned to his task.

I let him be and scanned the remaining guests. The crowd had started to thin just before my parents created this new spectacle that everyone was now glued to with wistful smiles. The newsbots swirled overhead, eating up the footage.

Surely a couple who had just taken second partners and was still so in love must prove that a multiple marriage could work with an Artorian. The ceremony was a success.

As the music tapered off, my parents stepped apart, talking quietly and still smiling. I turned to Tabor to congratulate him on all his work that had made the evening a triumph.

A flash of motion caught my attention. The three Ocelon envoys stood at the edge of the crowd. One had a gun in his hand and it was aimed at my parents.

My breath caught in my throat. Buria shouted a warning. I reached into my coat for a weapon. Behind me, a chair scraped across the floor as someone shot to their feet, probably Neko or Meera. Divided between taking aim and silently shouting at Ikeri to find cover and for Meera to get Markus down, it took me seconds too long to fire.

Not impeded by any of those things, Tabor, who had been beside me, was instantly in front of my mother in the fastest non-jump point Jump I'd ever witnessed. The first shot hit him in the shoulder. His suit offered no protection. He staggered aside.

Screams filled the air. Guests scattered, racing out of the room. Security thundered toward us.

I fired, but there were too many people jostling me in their rush to flee. I hit the gunman, but not where I intended. He kept firing.

The second shot hit my mother in the chest. The third tore into her stomach. The front of her dress flushed deep red. Tabor, screaming for help, caught her before she fell to the floor. She hung limp in his arms.

Everything seemed to slow as the reality of what was happening hit me. My unarmored mother had been shot twice. My mother was dying. She might already be dead.

I tried to get a clear shot. Security shouted for everyone to get down. Panic filled the hall.

A fourth shot hit my father's coat to little effect. He stood there, watching my mother bleed, his lips drawn back into a horrific grimace.

No. No. This could not be happening.

How the fuck did the Ocelon get a weapon through security? They'd caught all of ours for Geva's sake. Granted, ours had been allowed, but I couldn't imagine that anyone in the security team was willing to suffer my father's wrath by letting anyone else enter armed.

Tabor shouted again. Neko was at his side an instant later, vanishing with my mother. He'd get her into the tank, but that would go faster with two people to get her out of that dress.

I opened my link to Meera. *"Get Ikeri to the tank. Tell her to help hold my mother until we can get her in. She'll know what I mean."*

The Ocelon with the gun dropped to his knees. Clasping his head, he let out an agonized scream. The other two fell beside him a second later, the three of them writhing on the floor.

"Etara! Contain him!" I yelled.

The only thing that could make this worse was my father decimating the entire Ocelon population while wrapped in his rage. If he had a mental hold on the three here, I had little doubt he could manage that feat even though we were far away from where that unsuspecting populace was going about their lives. He'd done it with the Arpex, though they'd shared a mental link and he'd needed help with that task. Since then, he'd spent years working solo with his death-bringer abilities. He was far more powerful now, as his tirade with the Andoneti had graphically illustrated.

We did not need more tales of Tyrant Ta'set running rampant throughout the known universe.

"I can't find Ikeri," Meera shrieked in my head. *"Arden is safe with Markus."*

My heart leapt into my throat. *"Ikeri? Where are you?"*

Tabor sank down onto the dance floor next to the thick smears of my mother's blood. Tears poured down his face as he reached for the woman who was no longer there.

Buria ran to the Ocelon, waving to the nearest security members to contain the fallen attackers. There was no need. They were already dead. I'd seen my father's handiwork enough times to know when his victims were past the point of no return.

"I'm on the ship. Jey grabbed me when the first shot hit Tabor," Ikeri finally answered.

Jey. My dislike for the man was only slightly tempered by the fact that Ikeri was safe and where I needed her.

"How's Mom?"

Ikeri's voice broke. *"I don't think she's going to make it. Dad should be here. Tabor too."*

Tabor didn't have tank access the last time I'd checked the profile list. But he was family now, or at least he was while my mother was still alive. If her life was measured in minutes, did I want him to have lifelong knowledge of my family's sanctuary?

"Daniel. Now!" Ikeri shouted.

My father staggered across the floor, hands gripping his temples. Etara trailed him, looking ill herself.

"Dad," I grabbed him, shaking his shoulders. "Get to the ship. Mom needs you."

Looking dazed and reeking of liquor, he nodded and vanished.

"Meera, get Arden and Markus to the ship."

"I've got this, go," Uncle Isnar gave me a shove toward Tabor. "Take him with you."

The tank room had never been so full.

Tabor looked around, dazed. "What is this place?"

"I'll explain later." I gave him a gentle push toward where my mother lay on the platform. Ikeri was pulling the last pins from my mother's hair. She dropped them on the floor. They landed with a hollow clang next to the blood-soaked dress.

My father was already at her side, ripping away her underclothes and shouting to Neko to start the cycle. Her chest was barely rising, her face slack.

"I can't hold her much longer," Ikeri cried. "Hurry."

Tabor grabbed my mother's hand, sobbing and saying something indistinguishable.

Ikeri's eyes went wide. "Keep doing that. Stay right there."

My father's gaze locked onto Tabor as if he'd just woken up. "What's he doing?"

"Helping," snapped Ikeri. "Neko, now."

My mother's body rose and then plunged into the tank gel until she was entirely submerged. As the bubbles settled, Tabor pressed his hands on the clearplaz and rested his forehead next to hers.

"That was too close," said Jey, who I now noted stood behind Neko.

I'd forgotten he was there. I didn't want him there. "You can leave."

My father's stern look of disapproval informed me that Jey's attendance wasn't my call.

"We're losing her," Neko's anguished cry brought us all to silence. Normally I avoided being in the room when anyone was naked, especially my mother, but now all I could do was stare at the tank with everyone else, willing her to live. Blood tinged the clear gel, still flowing from her wounds.

"Ikeri!" I silently pleaded for her to do more. To do something. Anything.

She shook her head. *"I'm not the one holding her here. He is."*

What the hells was I supposed to do with that? My father had been bonded to her all of my life, but he was just standing there looking as helpless as the rest of us.

I'd distracted Tabor before when he'd been coaching my father through the dance steps, but I needed to do something. Hoping I was helping rather than hindering, I stood behind him and rested my hand lightly on his bloody shoulder. Ikeri took the other one. Markus crept up beside me, and though he didn't touch Tabor, he was there lending his support.

How long we stayed there, I wasn't sure. I spent most of the time praying, eyes closed, trying not to see my mother's blood on the floor and in the tank. My father muttered quietly with Jey and Neko.

"She's improving slowly. The gel is struggling to combat both damage sites simultaneously," Meera assured me from her post beside Arden at the rear of the room.

"You both should go rest." I told her. *"Take the spare room. I might need your help later."*

"Are you sure?"

"Yes. Please rest."

Uncle Isnar arrived a short time later. "How is she?"

It worried me that no one declared that she'd make it. There were three people watching her stats on the tank terminal but all of them remained silent.

"I see," he said quietly. "If it's any consolation, Buria moved the bodies to the Iber's morgue for you to deal with as you see fit. We found a dead security guard in the bathroom. That's where they got the weapon and why it was such an effective one. The guests have all gone home. The hall staff has the cleanup well in hand. Buria has your marriage contracts. She said she'd put them in your suite."

"Thank you for taking care of all that," my father said, his voice sounding empty.

"Buria said to let her know if you wanted her to join you here. Figured there were a lot of people here already. Limited space and you were wrapped up in this." He nodded toward the tank.

"I'll talk to her."

Uncle Isnar took up the post Meera and Arden had vacated, leaving my father in the direct care of Jey and Neko.

It was half an hour later that my father uttered a, "Thank Geva," that somehow released all the emotion I'd been holding back. My hand started to tremble and my blood felt too cold in my veins. I let go of Tabor.

"Good news?" Ikeri's shaky voice asked.

"Nothing is bottoming out anymore," explained Neko. "She'll be in for about eight to ten hours yet. Lots of internal damage to repair beyond the obvious external wounds.

"She's never going in public without armor again," my father declared. "I don't care what the occasion is."

"Agreed," seconded the ghost of Tabor. "I think I need to sit down." His legs wavered beneath him.

I was going to grab him, but my father was suddenly there, throwing an arm around his rival and leading him to the chair by the terminal. Neko quickly vacated it.

"You good here, boss?" he asked uncertainly.

"Yes. Thank you for getting her here so quickly."

"Of course. Anytime. You know that." Neko stood beside Tabor as he sat in the chair with a sharp hiss. "I took care of editing out the aftermath of the attack from the feeds. Editing out the attack altogether would be ideal, but there were too many witnesses. Ana will need to be sure to follow protocols. The coverage was very...graphic."

My father nodded absently.

"The coverage was live. How did you edit it?" I asked.

Neko gave my father a sideways look. "Because one of us was cautious enough to require a time delay."

My father didn't seem to notice his comment, but I was thankful Neko hadn't fully given up his bodyguard duties.

"I'll make sure she understands that portraying an instant recovery is not an option," I offered.

"Good." Neko rested his hand on Tabor's back, looking at my father. "Can I leave him here with you? You know what I mean. Answer honestly, because if you hurt him, you and I are going to have a problem."

"Yes," my father said in his empty tone.

Neko turned to me. "If that changes, you let me know. Watch them."

I nodded, wishing I could sit down too, but I understood how my mother's two bonded mates, neither of whom wanted to leave her side, could easily erupt into something very ugly.

"I'll leave you to it then." Neko cast Jey a meaningful look.

"Yes. Now that Anastassia is back among us, I'll...leave." He shot the last word at me and then stepped into the void with Neko right behind him.

Markus chose that moment to storm over to my father, his normally pale face flushed and blue eyes narrowed. "You just stood there. Why didn't you help her? How could you do nothing?"

Leave it to the youngest of us to say what we were all thinking. For the attack to come from Markus, who had idolized my father from the day they'd met, was a testament to the depth of his obvious failings.

My father just stood there not making any effort to explain or defend himself. I didn't know how he could. Markus was right.

"To be fair," said Tabor, "he was very distracted and the attack was unexpected. I was showing him all the steps through the link so he could dance with your mother. It took a lot of concentration for both of us."

I was about to point out that the dance had been over and yet Tabor, who had only known our mother a couple of weeks, had the wherewithal to Jump instantly and shield her. While our father, who had been right there and wearing armor, was drunk and did fucking nothing, but the second I opened my mouth, Tabor shot me a warning glance.

"Oh," said Markus, his expression softening. "I didn't know you were both doing that. Sorry." He hugged my father. "I'm glad Mom is better now."

"Me too." My father hugged Markus for a long moment before facing Ikeri, though he kept his gaze lowered. "Why don't the two of you go rest. It's late. Take my room."

Ikeri gave him a hard stare, not as willing as Markus to excuse him, but after a moment, she did go, taking Markus with her.

"Could you grab a couple of chairs from the office?" he asked me.

I nodded, figuring I'd be within earshot for that quick excursion. Still, I hurried back with two chairs, placing them near where Tabor sat. He was looking decidedly white and weary.

My father had retrieved the large med kit from the wall rack by the tank and was cutting through Tabor's coat and shirt to expose his arm.

"If there's anyone else here that has even zero medical experience, I'd rather have them look at this," Tabor said, mustering a dull glare.

My father ignored him, and Tabor didn't appear to have it left in him to fight.

I moved my chair aside to give him room to work and sat. Once I was stationary, all hint of adrenaline left my body, leaving me nothing but exhausted. The hiss and hum of the air scrubbers and circulation system comforted me, a sound that reminded me of my childhood. We were safe here.

"You didn't have to do that. With Markus," said my father.

"He's already down one parent, by the grace of Geva only in the short-term. He needs you right now."

Was this what a real parent sounded like? Real, being the kind everyone else I'd ever met seemed to have. Not that I didn't love mine, but damn, they were difficult, unreliable, and just as likely to need me to keep them in line as the other way around.

"All right, I don't hate you. However, this is going to hurt." My father probed the edges of the messy wound that covered the majority of Tabor's bicep, removing fibers from his shredded clothing. The one plus of having an energy weapon wound was that there was no projectile to dig out.

Tabor sat through it all, wincing and hissing, but otherwise quiet and still. True to all the tales my father used to tell me of the original four of them having to hold each other over while one of them used the tank, he was an accomplished medic. He had Tabor sewn up as neatly as the gaping wound allowed and his arm slathered in healing gel far faster than I expected. Then again, maybe I'd nodded off while he'd been explaining about the tank and the ship that had once belonged to my mother's family. They seemed to be getting along well enough.

"Did you know about his bond?" My father asked, his tone at interrogation level.

Shit, I'd nodded off again. I wondered what I'd missed, but was relieved to find them both still sitting and doing nothing more harmful than glaring at each other. That was likely the future of any family gathering.

I rubbed my eyes and sat up straight in an attempt to remain awake. "Just spotted it tonight. Neither of you had been in the room with Mom together until then. You're like magnets, repelling each other."

Tabor's brows rose. "Accurate. Focusing on her instead of you helped keep the repelling under control."

My father scoffed. "And you figured this out, having one night of being in the room with a rival for her attention?"

"Two actually. The former advisor triggered it first."

"He's always been a problem for me too," my father admitted.

"She was glad to see him, which was likely boost induced, but the feelings coming from her were the same."

"You can feel what she's feeling?"

"Well, yes, and the frequency of the hum changes, like music, with her mood."

My father's mask slipped, revealing glistening eyes. His voice hitched. "And she can feel you this way too?"

Tabor looked worried. "Yes?"

Witnessing my father unravel was something I'd only seen once, back when he searching for Ikeri. Though I'd been younger and he'd shed more tears then, this was more unnerving. I leaned forward, jittery and exhausted but ready to intervene by physical force if necessary.

"And she consented to this bond after knowing you for only a few days," he whispered.

"Like I said, it wasn't intentional on my part. I hadn't had anyone to explore my Artorian side with before. No one I trusted, anyway. She did mention that she'd had a far different reaction with you."

My father pressed his palms against his eyes for a moment and drew a shaky breath. When he lowered his hands, his mask was back in place. "Far. Yes."

Tabor's gaze darted to me. Apparently finding support ready, he returned his attention to my father. He held up one unsteady hand. "We haven't... She wasn't ready. I don't want you to think that she jumped from your arms into mine. It's not like that at all."

"And even without that level of intimacy, you bonded with her and she accepted it."

"I'm sure you've seen my medical records. You know I can't..."

This was a conversation I could die without ever being a part of. And yet, on some level, I was glad to know that my mother's behavioral standards were higher than my father's. And to know that Tabor was willing to defend her honor to the man who'd run off to gleefully screw Buria within an hour of her being presented as an option.

"If you have enough Artorian in you to bond, I'm sure there are other methods you can employ."

Tabor nodded, thankfully without any clarification on whether that avenue had been explored or the depths thereof. Having shared that with Arden with Meera's consent, I wondered if that meant I also would be able bond if I decided to.

My father sat back and watched my mother floating in the tank, the gel again clear and her wounds less grievous than before. He slipped back into his empty voice. "I need to get some sleep. I suggest you two do the same. Wake me when her cycle is complete."

I watched him head for the open bedroom, only then noticing that he'd picked up the wrappers from the supplies he'd used and put the med kit away while I'd been asleep.

"Did he tell you about making a profile for the tank?" I asked, wondering how much I'd missed.

Tabor nodded. "Once I'm healed up."

"Did you get something for the pain?"

He opened his hand to reveal three pills. "He said it would make me sleepy. Do you think it's safe to take them now?"

"I think it's safe to say he's too exhausted to be a problem for you."

"I meant her. She'll be all right?"

"Yes. For Geva's sake, take those and get some sleep."

We were all used to the wonders of the healing tank. That he'd abstained from taking any relief for himself in case my mother might need him was, well, damned touching. My father could learn a thing or twenty from Tabor.

We both settled into our chairs, kicked back, and closed our eyes.

Now that the room was quiet and the lights had gone out after no activity, the sound of the gunfire echoed in my head as I drifted off. Every dream ended with my mother dancing in a blood-soaked dress while my father watched and slowly disintegrated into dust.

TWENTY-EIGHT

Anastassia

I woke in my room on the ship with Vayen sleeping in the chair next to my bed. The familiar sight calmed me, assuring me all was well and normal in light of the nightmares that had haunted the edges of my sleep. He still wore his clothes from the ceremony.

Snatches of what had brought me here filtered into my waking awareness, making me question if the nightmares were actually memories.

Vayen woke as soon as I sat up to reach for the bands that were always waiting for me on the table on the other side of the bed. They weren't there. I turned to him.

"What happened? Where are—"

"You don't have to wear them, not when you're with him. I wouldn't want to see him on you either."

Since when did he care about what was comfortable for Tabor? I'd worn the bands that signified our joining, both the neckband that had served to sell our ruse on Veria Minor and the armband that was his actual gift, for so long that the bands were part of me. Who I was. The idea of being without them for more than the few minutes it took me to wake up from tank time felt abhorrently wrong.

"Maybe I want to wear them."

He shook his head. "You're going to spend some time with Tabor. Quiet time. While we figure out what happened to you and how to fix it."

The haunted look on his face flooded me with concern. "Fix what? Vayen, what happened? We were dancing and then..." That's where the hazy nightmares started.

"The Ocelon attacked. Shot you. Twice."

I gasped. "The dress. Dammit. I told Tabor I'd manage to ruin it."

"The dress is your first concern?" He snapped. "Stassia, we nearly lost you. Thank Geva for Tabor or we would have."

Those weren't words I'd ever imagined coming out of Vayen's mouth. "What do you mean?"

"His bond with you. A real one. Not the shit kind I managed to fuck up." His gaze dropped to the floor. "You responded to it, even when you were unconscious. He kept you with us even while you were in the tank. While it was fighting to manage all the damage at once. Even Ikeri couldn't do that. We would have lost you."

There was so much there that I didn't know where to start. Vayen knew about the new bond? If he had hurt Tabor...

"Is Tabor all right?"

Vayen kept his gaze on the floor. "He got shot, but yes, he'll be fine. I stitched him up."

"You?"

"It was the least I could do." He glanced up for a moment. "Stassia, the kids like him. Actually like him, not just tolerate like they do with Buria. He figured out how to deal with the bond and me in the same room in one damned night. He walked me through dancing with you because he knew it would make you happy. He's..." Vayen let out a heavy sigh. "He's fucking perfect for you. I've never been."

I was torn between wanting to console him and being flooded with warmth, learning that Tabor had been accepted, that he'd gone so far as to stand back and let Vayen have a moment with me because I had wished it, even though I'd not given voice to the secret dream. He'd known. Tabor's bond was the real thing, the mutually open door Vayen and I had never had.

"That's not true," I said after a few seconds too long of silence.

"It is. We've made the best of it, on Veria Minor, Pentares, everywhere since. The best of who we are together. I do love you, Stassia, but no matter how much I mean that, I can never give you what have with him. That's what you deserve, what anyone deserves. Not this crutch we've both been leaning on for twenty-some years. Fuck, I can't even nail down how long we've been together." He raked a hand through his hair. "Does the time you were imprisoned count? My time? When we lived mostly apart? When we were barely speaking?"

I wanted to say that it all counted, but thanks to the damned Arpex, I was missing too many memories, likely integral conversations and arguments—parts of our lives together that he had full knowledge of.

If he didn't have a solid answer, maybe there wasn't one.

Maybe he wasn't wrong.

Not that I wanted to hear the answer, but I blurted the question out anyway. "Do you plan on forming a bond with Buria?"

"No." He focused on the end of the bed. "She's not... What I feel for Buria is different." He met my gaze for a second. "She's not first wife material. For me."

Not that I particularly liked Buria, but she deserved the truth of where she stood. "Does she know how you feel on that matter?"

"She knows I won't bond with her." His voice grew quiet, "I'm glad you get to experience a true joining, even if it's with him. Like I said, he's—"

"I've never asked you to be perfect, Vayen. No one is. We've been through so much together and even through the bad times, I've always loved you. I know you. You know me. We accept each other. Isn't that what the whole joined-contracted thing is?"

"I thought so." He shook his head. "But then I watched you with him and saw the blatant proof of what a real bond looks like. What it can do. We're a habit, Stassia. A two-person support group for the horribly maladjusted."

I was glad to be in bed, to not be on my feet, to have the comforting weight of blankets around me. "What are you saying?"

"That I'm ceding our days off together to him."

"The whole point of those days was that I wanted to spend time with you."

"Is that why you've been pouring boost down your throat when we're together? I dare bet every credit I have that you don't need drugs to tolerate him."

I didn't need a full bond to know that revelation had hurt him. He'd have recognized the drug in my system in the tank report and deduced the truth.

"It's not that I can't tolerate *you*. I can't tolerate that you're spending time with Buria. I also don't want to make you miserable for doing what is natural for you, what you need to do. It's not that I don't want to be with you. I want that too much. Boost makes reality easier to stomach so I can enjoy the time we have together."

"That's what I'm saying, Stassia. You shouldn't have to drug yourself to be around me. I understand why you're doing it, but you shouldn't have to be in a relationship where it is necessary."

"I never wanted to be. I was happy," I snapped at him. "You

wanted this. Now your answer is to punish me by taking away the one thing I did want with you?"

Vayen winced. "The priority right now is keeping you safe; you'll need to be in recovery for a while for the sake of the public anyway. You'll be staying solely at Tabor's estate until we can find out who poisoned you and how to deal with what's already been done."

Everything was moving way too damned fast upon just waking up. My emotions were running rampant, making my stomach cramp, my head pound, and the rest of me torn between needing a good cry or ripping Vayen's head off.

"Poisoned? What are you talking about?" Getting nearly shot to death wasn't enough?

"Get dressed. I'll show you."

"Show me now." I sat on the edge of the bed and wrapped the sheet around me, tucking it in securely over my chest. Not that it mattered. If I'd been in the tank, under dire circumstances, I assumed there'd been an audience for at least part of the time. The tank didn't allow for modesty in any manner.

That was not the way I'd wanted Tabor to see me naked for the first time for fuck's sake. The poor man had to be reeling as badly as I was. He'd had to deal with the shooting, and then facing Vayen with his bond exposed, and learning about our big secret: the regen tank.

At least I didn't have to figure out how to approach Vayen about getting Tabor cleared for tank jump point access. That was one little redeeming glimmer.

Vayen led me to the tank terminal, indicating I should sit down. I didn't disagree.

"If I was being poisoned, I'd think I'd know."

He leaned over me to tap on the terminal, bringing up the report from my tank time. "You did know. You just thought it was the stress of the ceremony and side effects of taking boost to deal with me. Tabor mentioned that you weren't sleeping well, that your stomach was constantly upset. He noticed. Stassia, I should have fucking noticed. I was too wrapped up in getting what I wanted to pay attention. I'm the one who's known you for-fucking-ever, who knows your normal. He's known you for a couple of weeks and he noticed." Vayen let out a frustrated growl.

He raked his hands through his hair again. It hung loose, disheveled, like he'd been doing that for hours. "I should have fucking known. Stassia, I should have looked into you like I do for every other fucking person Etara drags in front of me. But I didn't take two damned minutes for the one person who matters most. I would have seen the damage. It could have been reversed." His voice broke. "Now it's too late."

He pointed a shaking finger to the summary report where any physical changes from the last tank visit were logged. Since I'd taken a dip after fighting with the Jalvian semi-suitors, my heart, liver, kidneys, and stomach lining all showed significant damage. While I found that disturbing, my attention was locked onto the near flat-line stagger my stats had done for a solid hour after getting into the tank the night before. I should have been dead. I shivered. Pulling the sheet tighter didn't help calm the chills that raced through me.

His large, warm hands enveloped my shoulders. I leaned into him, seeking further heat or any additional sensory stimuli to prove that I was still among the living.

"From the type of damage, it has to be something you ingested, rather than absorbed through the skin or breathed in. Can you think of anything that tasted off? Anything you ate that was at all suspicious?"

The warmth of his hands suddenly didn't matter. Ice flooded through my veins. I knew exactly who had poisoned me.

Me.

"I'll probe every damned member of the Iber's crew until I find the culprit, I swear. This will not go unpunished."

"You don't have to look—"

Tabor burst out of the office doorway and into the tank room. "Anastassia, you're awake."

"Don't say another word. The truth will devastate him," Tabor decreed.

"I can't let the Iber's crew suffer. He'll kill someone. Someone entirely innocent."

Vayen squeezed my shoulders. "Stassia?"

Tabor shook his head subtly. *"The truth can wait for tomorrow. We nearly lost you. Give him a day to get his bearings."*

The truth wouldn't hurt any less after a day and people would suffer in the meantime. I reached out to Tabor, needing his support, the comfort of the bond we shared. Vayen moved around to my side where I could face him, making room for Tabor to stand next to me. I clung to Tabor's hand.

"There's no need to interrogate anyone." My voice wavered and then gave out, caught in the lump filling my throat.

I leaned further into Tabor, pressing my shoulder, my back against him, drinking in his quiet strength, letting it wash over me and through me. All the while, hating that I was doing this in front of Vayen, proving him right.

Vayen remained quiet. He crouched down, taking my other hand, ignoring Tabor. I didn't know how he was doing that, given his usual jealous snarl and gnashing routine. The fact that he was able to, that I could rely on them both just then, gave me the strength I needed.

"That night you told me that Buria sent you to talk to me, I'd thought you were done with her, that we could go back to being us. She was supposed to be here for a week so you could scratch the itch that came naturally to you. I could tolerate a momentary mistress, knowing we're different. I know I left the option open in my proposal, but I didn't think you'd take it. I never wanted you to take it. I thought my offer was giving you enough. That I was enough."

He seemed to be with me so far, gaze glued to my face. Breath shallow. Impassive mask firmly in place.

"You announced that you'd asked her to stay. I didn't hide how much that hurt me. I put it all out there and you ignored it. You fucking walked out the door like your damned bond to me meant nothing. You ignored what you did to me. Ignored it. You've never done that and that hurt far worse than any wound I've ever taken. I couldn't…"

The emotions that had been trapped beneath my anger and confusion earlier rose to the surface now, spilling out of my eyes like a fucking waterfall. Tabor held me tight on the inside, soothing, reminding me that he was there, that I wasn't alone like I'd been that night. If Vayen was projecting anything, Tabor's stronger bond trumped it.

They both waited patiently until I could form words again and had wiped my face on a corner of the sheet I wore.

"If our connection meant so little, was so weak, it was meaningless. I had no reason to be here, on your mission. Clearly what you have with Buria meant more to you, she could help to keep you calm. The kids have their own lives. Everything seemed so empty."

"But you had him," Vayen said thickly, glancing at Tabor.

"We'd just met that night. I didn't *have* anyone," I threw back at him. "It was Nacombic, if that helps." Knowing the name of the poison wouldn't matter, but he wanted answers. "I hadn't considered any long-term effects. The immediate result had been more pertinent at the time."

Vayen studied me, the muscles in his face working hard to crack through the mask he fiercely held onto. "But you didn't go through with it. He stopped you?"

It was distantly aggravating that he kept assuming Tabor had saved me. Then again, everything seemed distant, surreal. Sitting there at the tank terminal as I'd done hundreds of times before, many of those with Vayen present in one state of health or another, but now with Tabor too. With two men, whom I couldn't question, now seeing them here together, both loved me in their own way.

"You stopped me. Interrupted, I suppose." I explained my concern over what little remained of our bond causing him to possibly go on a rampage that would make Etara put him down for good.

"It was only one drop." Though, according to the report, poison was poison no matter the quantity.

Vayen closed his eyes and remained there, silent, his hand squeezing mine as if he were afraid I might try to get away. Like I had the strength for that at the moment. I waited for his outburst, holding my breath, but he did nothing more than let go and stand. His weight shifted to his right side as if his back was bothering him more than usual. He did not look at me, or Tabor for that matter.

"Take care of her," he said in a tone that might have been indifferent had I not known him better.

"Vayen."

He Jumped.

The problem was, even knowing him, I couldn't guess if he was going to go unleash himself on whomever crossed his path or drink himself into a stupor. Whichever it was, I hoped he went to the Iber to do it where he had people to watch over him.

Buria

I hadn't seen Vayen since he'd Jumped to the tank ship after Ana had been shot. He'd spared a moment for a quick link conversation to tell me that she was recovering slowly and to thank me for taking care of transporting and storing the Ocelon. That was all.

Sitting in my suite on the Iber, having long since changed out of my dress, I slept alone on the couch, waiting for him to arrive to celebrate our marriage contract. When I woke, he still hadn't shown up.

I knew how the tank worked. If she was recovering, anyone could move her to a bed after the cycle completed. There was no reason Vayen had to stay. While the injury had been grievous for sure, the tank would erase it just as it had my own. None of this was new to Vayen. He'd told me that they used the tank on a regular basis. Hell, Tabor was there according to the Premier. It was his time with her, he could watch her sleep while Vayen and I celebrated.

As much as I wanted to Jump to Brustus and unload everything in my head onto Elonka, I knew I couldn't. Public images had to be maintained and I was now on the managing side of that rather than the viewing.

I'd always told Elonka the truth, bared everything, and she'd been a true friend. That could no longer be the case. Now, the only ones I could turn to with my true problems and feelings were Daniel, Etara, Ana, and maybe Ikeri, though she mostly avoided me. Their youngest son, Markus, hadn't said a word in my direction. Tabor had too much to say, and I was already sick of all his oh-so-helpful advice. We might all be together in favor of the mission and keeping Vayen alive, but my little corner of that effort felt very lonely.

To stay busy, I replied to the few messages of congratulation from Cragtek friends. One of them asked after the Advisor's first wife, which made me wonder how much of the newsfeed had made it to the public and if Vayen had considered any of that when he'd gone off on the Ocelon.

Upon quick review of the end of the coverage, which was all over the public feeds, I found that Neko had already taken care of it. The coverage ended at the first two shots. Neko had issued a statement saying both Tabor and Anastassia had been wounded but would survive and that the perpetrators had been apprehended and swiftly dealt with.

Swiftly, indeed. But where was the man who had issued that deadly justice? I did my best to be patient, to leave him alone, filling my hours with a distracted effort at going over reports from Cragtek and monitoring my security crew.

After the whole day passed without a word, I opened my link to him.

"Where are you?"

"Alone. Be alone."

That didn't answer my question at all and even through the link, his words were slurred.

"Vayen, where are you? Are you safe?"

"Said, go away. Not old."

"What?" Not only was he drunk, he wasn't making sense.

"Stupid kids. Know who I am?"

Was he so drunk he didn't know if he was talking out loud or through his link? And was he, in fact, not alone? Good gods, if there really were kids harassing him, there were sure to be casualties, and in his condition, he might well be one of them.

I tried to get any sense of where he was through our linked connection but it was just slurred and disjointed conversation. He was a master at using his link, of covering his tracks, at keeping everything contained, apparently so innately that he could do it even when blind drunk.

Our connection snapped shut. Either he was distracted or he realized I was trying to get information from him. Dammit, how was I supposed to find him?

That he chose to spend our signing night watching Ana heal was irritating. That he'd moved on from that, not to me, not to the blissful couple of days I'd hoped we could spend together, but to get shit-faced alone, wounded me more than it should have. When we'd first met, he could do no wrong, but I'd come to know that he had issues. Serious ones. But still, I'd hoped.

Thank the gods I'd had the wisdom to only sign on for two years of this rather than a lifetime. As much fun as we had when we were together, and I couldn't deny that I did care about him, he was a volatile drunk. He claimed to drink to keep his abilities subdued, but he spent far too much time in that state to offset the rest of his downsides.

If Ana had thought I could cure him of that, she was wrong. She was probably the reason he drank so damned much.

The vision of the two of them dancing had firmly entrenched itself in my brain, playing over and over, taunting me with their happiness until I wanted to scream.

Two years. I'd honor my agreement with Ana to help keep him alive and do the bodyguard duty I was suited for. Hopefully with a good deal of benefits along the way, considering Vayen's connections, finances, and enthusiasm in the bedroom. After my contract was up, I could go back to Brustus or maybe somewhere better and bask in whatever fame and favor having been contracted to the Advisor of All gained me. As Elonka had said, I needed to watch out for myself.

Neko had done well for himself after doing his time with Ana and Vayen. There was no reason why I couldn't come out on top too.

Neko. Inspiration hit me. I sent him a request through my link. He accepted seconds later.

"Buria? What is it? Is it Ana? Is she all right?"

"Recovering and safe, yes. It's Vayen I'm worried about. He hasn't come back."

"He's venting. I gave him a few names to take care of. Low level stuff I trust him to do alone. He'll be fine."

"He's very drunk. And not here. It sounded like someone was harassing him."

"Shit. Hold on."

An image hit me a moment later. A beach, rocks. Boulders in grey sand. The sound of water lapping on the shore. A wavy pattern of sediments in the rocks came into sharp focus.

"How do you know where he is?"

"This isn't the first time he's wandered into trouble. Thankfully he's wearing his armor, and I know this location enough to have a jump point there. I have a tracker in his coat. Have for years, since he took it upon himself to liberate the lot of you, actually," he grumbled in my head. *"Either he knows about the tracker and hasn't*

removed it or never thought to check."

Vayen trusted Neko. He probably knew. I couldn't imagine him not being intimately familiar with every inch of weave in his armor.

"I'll meet you there. No offense, but I've had a lot more experience with belligerent Vayen," Neko said.

"I welcome the assistance."

I cut contact, quickly armed, and focused on the image Neko had flashed me, pulling the details together to form a jump point. When I stepped out of the Jump, Neko was already there.

Seven youths sporting an assortment of weapons ranging from long pipes to guns stood around a dark, armored mound on a rock. As we hurried closer, I could see blood on Vayen's face. On his hands. On the ground where the motley lot milled around him.

The three with guns all aimed them, not at Vayen, but at each other. The faces of the two I could see were strained, their hands shaking. The one with the pipe lifted it, readying a swing at Vayen's head while he faced the others.

"Stunner?" Neko suggested.

I grabbed mine and pulled the trigger. He did the same. All the youths fell to the sandy rocks. Vayen's head lifted a fraction, enough that I could clearly make out his disgruntled glare. He threw a bottle at Neko. It hit him in the shoulder.

Neko took the flying bottle in stride, ignoring it as he darted over to Vayen. I followed, taking up a post beside my newly contracted husband.

"Is that yours or theirs?" I asked, pointing to the blood on the ground around us.

Vayen shrugged, mostly ignoring us and eyeing the bottle he'd thrown as though he could will it back into his hands.

"They're going to start waking any minute. We should get him out of here," Neko said.

"Where? He can't go to the Iber like this. We're supposed to be celebrating our signing. People will talk. I'm sure you already used up enough favors to edit the full story of how the signing ceremony ended."

Neko frowned. "The Artorian estate then. Not that you should be there—for the same reason."

"I don't plan on parading around naked in the yard or anything."

Neko's distaste gave way to a tight smile. "All right then. Do you have a jump point there?"

"No."

He flashed me one and then vanished with Vayen in hand. It took me a moment to get the Jump set, at which point the armed youth were stirring.

"Where'd he go?" asked one of them.

"Be thankful he's gone." I left them to ponder how much more blood would have been on the rocks before the night was over.

Hedvika met me at the jump point, the foyer of the house. She wore a cautious smile. "Welcome."

I wasn't feeling all that welcome, but that was no fault of hers. Neko was right. I didn't belong here in the house Vayen shared with Ana, whether anyone else saw me there or not.

Hedvika led me down a tiled hallway lined with windows just above my head so I couldn't see out. Karin's light shown through the panes. Most of the house was dark but for dim lights along the floor that lit up as we walked toward them and faded behind us.

"They're in the kitchen. We'll get him cleaned up and then find him a bed so he can sleep this off."

"He doesn't keep a bedroom here?"

Now Hedvika scowled. "With Ana, yes."

"Got it." I resigned myself to not enjoying any sort of signing celebration with my new husband. Instead, I'd spend an awkward night listening to him drunk snore while Neko and Hedvika made sure I didn't stray into Ana's territory.

Neko leaned over where Vayen was seated, washing blood off his face while Vayen protested slurringly that he could do it himself.

"Sure, boss. I know, but I'm going to help anyway."

Vayen started to slowly slump toward the table. Neko pressed him back against the chair.

"Stay with me for a bit, all right? Let's see how much of this is yours and whether you need a dip in the tank or just a bed."

"Bed." Vayen pointed toward a dark hallway off the kitchen.

Neko noticed me and held out the cloth. "Can you take over here? I need to check the local network and see if there's any messy body count I need to cover up."

Vayen sputtered incoherently.

"Yes, I know you know how contracts work. Let Buria take care of you for a few minutes."

Neko sat across from Vayen, and from his vacant stare, I gathered he was deep in his link. I pulled the bowl of pink water closer and dipped Vayen's natural hand in it, scrubbing the blood from his nails and knuckles.

Knowing he killed people, that he talked about it like it was an ordinary part of everyone's job, and seeing the aftermath of him actually doing it were two very different things. This wasn't the mind stuff he did, that I knew killed people, a lot of them according to the reports from the Andioneti station and what I'd witnessed on Brustus. I'd seen it first-hand at the ceremony, but that wasn't at all like this. Bloody. Not in defense. He'd killed people for credits because he was mad. Venting, Neko had called it. What kind of person did that?

I fought to keep the bile from rising. "How many people did you kill today?"

Vayen stared at his fingers, the clean ones and the ones on the larger hand I'd yet to scrub. "Ocelon?"

"That was yesterday."

He shrugged. "Seven?"

It would have been a lot more if we hadn't interrupted his toying with those kids. Mulling over that small blessing, I emptied the bowl and filled it with clean water before starting in on his larger bio-engineered hand. That one was worse, knuckles swollen, blood dried halfway up his forearm. How did one get covered in that much blood? It seemed to me that logical assassins would fire a shot from a safe distance, collect the body and their payment. Apparently venting required more physical involvement.

"They deserved it," Neko informed me.

Did they? Did anyone? I didn't know if I could see his hands on me in the future and not see them like this.

When Vayen had freed the women of Tacesh, when he'd dealt with the Masters, had he been venting then too? Had that grand gesture been for me as he'd claimed or a way to blow off steam?

Were these also urges he dulled with alchohol, bang, and me? He'd alluded to something of the sort once, but seeing him now was more clarifcation than I cared to have.

I pushed Vayen's hair back and cleaned up the spots Neko had missed. Thanks to his altered skin, it appeared the majority of the blood had in fact belonged to his victims. He blinked up at me.

"Buria?"

He was just now noticing who I was? I resisted the urge to smack him but didn't bother to mask my annoyance. "It is my allotted time with you. Not that this is how I'd expected to spend it."

He looked at the bowl of red water and the cloth in my hands. Tears started to roll down his face.

My aggravation evaporated. I sat next to him and took his natural hand in mine. Neko stood. "There's a room down the hall for the two of you." He nodded toward the opposite hallway from where Vayen had indicated earlier, on the other side of the large living space, distantly visible from the table. The hallway was lit. I made out Hedvika standing near one of the doors.

"Thank you." I got up and tried to get Vayen to his feet.

He weighed about three of me and didn't budge. Neko took his other arm, and after a look at me to coordinate our efforts, we heaved together. Vayen shook us both off and buried his face in his hands.

I checked with Neko for the next course of action but he looked lost.

"Boss?" he said quietly, resting one hand on Vayen's broad, shaking back.

"Suicide. Anastassia," he said brokenly, his tongue thick with alcohol. "She tried. My fault."

Neko sat on the edge of the chair beside Vayen, keeping one hand on his back and the other on his arm. "The Ocelon shot her. That's not your fault. She wasn't trying anything."

I took his natural hand in mine, wondering how best to comfort my drunkenly distraught new husband.

Vayen shook his head wildly, sending his hair flying. "Before. Weeks ago. When I—" He drew a giant, gasping breath and pulled his hand away from me to cover his face again.

He didn't pull away from Neko.

His tears hadn't been for me. They were for her. Wherever the hell she was. Probably in a bed with Tabor celebrating their damned signing like I was supposed to be.

"Maybe I should go."

Neko shook his head, his gaze imploring me to stay.

"He's never been like this before. He shouldn't be alone."

"You're right here."

"You wanted to be his wife. This is the job," he snarled in my head.

"I wasn't aware a marriage contract counted as employment."

Neko's naked contempt left no doubt about his opinion of me. *"Then fucking leave."*

"I didn't ask for this. He wanted it," I shoved the words through

my link into Neko's, hoping he'd choke on them. My blow delivered, I spun around, intending to storm out of the room to find a quiet place to collect myself enough to be able to form a Jump back to Brustus. Instead, a pitiful whimper pierced my heart and made me turn back around.

"She's going to die."

"We all will, boss, but I'm pretty sure Ana is too contentious. She'll likely outlive us both."

Vayen's tears were back to flowing in full force. "Nacombic. Organ damage. Tank can't fix. My fault," he said between sputtering breaths.

"Sounds like her fault for fucking around with poison," Neko muttered with not nearly half the venom he'd thrown at me.

"Could have reversed it. Didn't take time to see. Diagnose. Could have saved her. Geva." He let out a strangled cry that devolved into body-wracking sobs.

His crying turned into coughs that quickly progressed to gagging. Neko got him up on his feet and dragged him over to the sink. I was glad I was across the room from the retching.

When he had nothing left to purge, Neko handed him a clean cloth and then a glass of water. "Why don't you go sleep the rest of that off. I'll see what I can find out about treatments for Nacombic poisoning. We'll fix this in the morning, all right?"

Vayen nodded slowly, his gaze locked on the floor and his broad shoulders slumped.

"You're still here?" Neko accused more than asked.

Not bothering to reply, I made my way to Vayen's side, and taking his arm, led him toward the room Hedvika had indicated. Once the door closed, I turned on the lights just long enough to get my bearings. Vayen was already undressed and working his way clumsily into bed by the time I turned the lights off and removed my outer clothes. I slid in beside him. He turned to face the wall and remained silent.

With pillows propped behind me, I sat next to the Advisor of All as he fell into an uneasy sleep. As I digested what he'd said, I wondered, would the death of his first wife make my life easier? After the grieving passed, his bond would dissolve. He would be free to be with me without the guilt. Gods, he might even stop drinking.

Managing the death-bringer would fall to me. No Ana meant no back up. If I failed and Etara activated his kill switch, where would that leave me, the widow of the Advisor of All? Certainly not on top of anything and probably the target of blame.

Would the union Vayen and Ana were setting up be enough to keep the systems at peace? Could Daniel step into Vayen's place with a firm enough hand, despite not having all of his father's abilities? There was so much at stake. Without Ana, the man next to me wasn't a two-year plan, he was a lifetime obligation. A high-pressure job with few benefits.

I sat in the dark, berating myself for all the choices that had brought me here. Had I been happier alone and free on Brustus, endlessly reliving our kiss and dreaming of being here beside him? I couldn't definitively say yes. With a heavy sigh, I slid down into the bed I'd made for myself.

Vayen tossed and turned until his arm wrapped around me, pulling me against him. As he settled into a calmer sleep, I couldn't help but wonder which of us he thought I was.

Me, I consoled myself. It had to be me.

THIRTY

Buria

When I woke in the strange bed, the only thing that was familiar was the man next to me. He was awake and staring at the ceiling.

"How are you feeling?" I asked, thinking that was a safe question to begin with.

"Like shit."

I swung my legs out of the bed and reached for his armor, knowing he had a tin of stims in a pocket somewhere. He'd used them before when he'd needed to sober up quickly or bypass a hangover.

"Leave it."

I bunched up the pillows behind me and sat back. Should I ask about Ana or what he'd said the night before? Maybe mention his body count? I twisted the corner of the sheet around two fingers and rubbed the satin edge with my thumb, hoping he'd speak first. But he didn't.

I went for a safe question. "What would you like to do today?"

Several minutes of silence stretched out before he finally spoke. "I'm sorry. None of this is going how I'd intended."

At least he was apologizing.

"Are you hungry?" I asked.

"No, but you probably are. Go get something from the kitchen. Hedvika keeps it well stocked."

I was starving and he didn't appear to be racing to get dressed or, for that matter, move anything other than his mouth. I figured I might as well grab a plate of something quick. After pulling on my clothes from the night before, I made my way to the kitchen. No one was around.

A search of several cupboards yielded a plate and then a cup that

I filled with water. The cold storage provided a generous assortment of cheese, fruit, and a portion of leftover meat. I filled the plate and hurried back to the bedroom. Vayen still hadn't moved.

Settling back into my spot, I held the plate out to him. He shook his head. It was unlike him to refuse food. I set the plate on the bed between us in case he changed his mind and then began to nibble on my meal.

"How did I get here?" he asked.

I took my time swallowing the bite of cheese. "I was worried after I talked to you. Neko knew where you were. He Jumped you and gave me the point."

"We shouldn't be here."

"I'm sure Ana would prefer you were here and safe rather than, well, where you had been."

His gaze shifted from the ceiling to the wall he'd faced the night before. Dammit, I shouldn't have mentioned her. But since I had, I figured I might as well jog his memory about what he'd said.

"She's all right? For now, after the poison, I mean? You mentioned that last night."

"Not really. No."

"Neko will find something to help," I said confidently. He seemed to have all the answers where Vayen and Ana were concerned.

"Maybe." He didn't sound at all hopeful. "At least she's with Tabor. He can help mask the discomfort. All I do is make it worse."

I forced a smile and rubbed his arm. "I doubt that, but enough of Ana today. We're supposed to be celebrating."

"Finish that." He nodded toward the plate. "I'm going to take a shower and find some clean clothes. Then we're leaving."

As long as we were leaving together, I was all for it. If there was any hope of celebration, both of us would be better off elsewhere.

A hotel room on Artor wasn't what I'd expected. I'd thought maybe he had a house somewhere, maybe a place the two of us could have together, like Ana and Tabor did. However, the hotel room was gorgeous, seemingly the best suite the place had to offer, given the quality of the furnishings and spacious three-room suite. The floor to ceiling windows offered a stunning view of the city.

He stood beside me, taking in the view with dull eyes. "I'm afraid I'm not very good company. You deserve better, especially today and after...everything."

"I'm sorry Ana was shot. I thought we had security more than covered. That never should have happened."

Vayen wrapped an arm around me, his large hand squeezing my shoulder gently. "That wasn't your fault. I thought security was more than adequate too." His gaze slipped from the view outside to the floor. His arm dropped to hang limply at his side. "She never should have been there. She never would have been wearing that dress, been unarmed, unarmored, if I hadn't driven her to this." He shook his head. "I just stood there. I froze. Buria, I fucking froze."

"You didn't freeze, you were drunk," I said as nicely as I could. Though I supposed his inebriated state was only slightly better than his inaction.

He winced. "I had one job all these years. One, and I failed on every fucking front. She's going to die and it's my fault."

"You'll figure something out. You've got Neko and the resources of entire planets full of doctors and scientists. Someone has to have a solution."

"You're right," Vayen said, sounding a fraction lighter. He cleared his throat and turned to face me, taking my hand. "This is supposed to be your day. What would you like to do? We could tour pretty much anything on Artor, or visit a beach? Do one of those couples spa things? I probably should know, or have at least made a semi-educated guess, but I'm sorry, I don't think very straight when I'm with you."

Despite everything else, I couldn't help but smile. He really was trying to do us right, better. Despite what he thought, it wasn't his fault Ana had been shot or that she'd taken such drastic measures on her own. I couldn't even fault him for freezing up. He'd been drunk and in shock. He might be her bodyguard at his core, but he was also her mate and they'd been having a moment that even I'd been choked up about.

I could be patient and tolerant as long as he was trying and preferably never covered in blood again like he had been the night before.

"Perhaps a walk on a beach later." As long as it wasn't the same one as where he'd nearly killed those kids. What I really wanted was to go back to those first few days we'd had together when I didn't have a care in the universe beyond what I wanted to try with him next. "For now, how about we just enjoy being together. Alone."

"That sounds perfect." He pulled a vial of bang from one of the many pockets in his coat and poured a third of it down his throat.

He'd never taken that much at once before. Was it possible to overdose on bang? Was that what he was trying to do, punish himself? Thank the gods I had Neko, the Premier, and even Daniel available at a moment's notice through my link if it came to that.

I reached out, intending to capture the vial and tuck it away somewhere that he couldn't take more, but he was too quick. He dropped it back into a pocket. I couldn't even tell which one.

"Buria, I'm sorry," he said, sounding like he truly meant it. "Bear with me. I promise I'll make this up to you."

Whether he was going to make up for losing our signing night to Ana, for his drunken killing spree, or what he was about to do now that his eyes had taken on the dilation of the massive dose of bang kicking in, I wasn't sure. Seconds later, his lips were crushing mine and his hands couldn't seem to get enough of me in them. I did my best not to see them and instead focused on the enjoyment of riding out however long it took for the dose to work its way out of his body. For now, he was mine.

THIRTY-ONE

Anastassia

I'd been at Tabor's house for only a few hours after Vayen had made his somber departure from the ship when Daniel interrupted my staring at nothing. I felt paralyzed, continuously replaying what had happened, from the dancing and getting shot to waking up from the tank and laying the truth on Vayen. Maybe Tabor had been right about giving Vayen a day or two before telling him how I'd come to be poisoned. But in my heart, I knew it would only have been delaying the inevitable.

"Mom, are you all right? Why aren't you back on the Iber?"

"I'm as well as I can be, I suppose. I know Tabor and I agreed to spend our days there in case you needed me, but your father decided it would be best if I stayed at Tabor's estate for a while."

Tabor sat beside me, shoulder against mine but giving me a semblance of space as if he knew I wasn't entirely there with him. Given the openness of our bond, he likely did know. I still wasn't used to that, the full understanding of one another.

"We want to see you, Ikeri, Markus and I. We need to," Daniel said plainly.

Unlike his father, Daniel had never been one to hide emotions from those close to him. I supposed that made him not like me either.

"I'll talk to Tabor."

"Tell him to take you to the Iber. If he won't, give me a point and I'll do it myself."

"Calm down a minute and let me talk to him."

I reached out to brush my fingers over the back of Tabor's hand, unsure if he was staring off like I'd been or deep in his link. "The kids would like to see me."

"That's to be expected." He glanced around the room where we sat comfortably isolated from his staff.

"You can take me back to the Iber to visit them. I don't expect you to share a jump point here."

"Don't be ridiculous. My family could visit anytime. Not that they likely will, but yours should be able to as well. It is your home now too, after all."

"Are you sure?" He didn't appear sure and the musical hum between us had taken on sharp notes.

"He's not coming, is he? Just the kids?"

"I will stipulate that, but I don't think he was part of the plan, no."

"Then yes, I'm sure." The hum resumed its calm musical tinkling. "There, I gave Daniel the jump point."

"Thank you." I tipped my head onto his shoulder, closing my eyes for just a moment while enjoying the soft warmth that emanated from the man I'd never known I needed. My mind wandered off into imaginings of meeting Tabor instead of Kess years earlier where I could have avoided my current situation altogether.

He shook me gently, waking me. "They'll be here any moment. Shall we go meet them in the gallery? Or you can rest here if you'd rather."

"I'll come." I shook sleep off and hopped off the couch. I'd barely gotten two steps when spots swam before my eyes. That had been happening more often. I'd thought it was due to my boost intake, but the tank had cleared that out of my system. That meant it was a new feature of my life due to the poison. Dammit. One night of weakness would haunt me to the end of my days.

Tabor wrapped one arm around my waist and set a more leisurely pace to the gallery. He sat on one of the benches, gently tugging me down beside him. I appreciated that he didn't tell me to rest or chide me for getting up too fast, he was just there guiding me calmly as though he were in no hurry and maybe wanted to sit rather than stand, though I was sure he could for hours without effort.

Everything seemed like an effort to me lately. As much as I'd hoped that was because of the looming ceremony or adjusting to the new schedule with our seconds, deep inside, I'd known it was due to what I'd done. Now there was no escaping the truth. And I'd have to tell the kids. How the hell was I supposed to do that?

Panic took hold. I couldn't hide this from them. They were sure to find out, especially Ikeri, who could see into my thoughts on a whim. But admitting my moment of despair, that I'd been willing to leave them, and the deep wound their father had inflicted was unbearable.

"I can't do this."

I found my way to my feet and stumbled out of the gallery. Everything a blur, I made my way back to the couch at the rear of the house where I worked my way into a corner, pulling my knees up against my chest. The aches Tabor's presence masked became more apparent now that he wasn't in the same room. My stomach roiled, both hungry and nauseous. The headache that I also could no longer attribute to my continual boost intake, returned.

It was well over half an hour later when tentative footsteps broke my stupor of misery.

Ikeri came to sit beside me. Markus settled on the other side of her. Daniel knelt on the floor in front of me, his arms wrapping around my shoulders, prying me out of the corner. He wasn't in armor today, just my son. I let him hold me until he'd taken his fill. Then it was Ikeri's turn. Markus, always hesitant with me, took my hand, gazing at me somberly as if willing me to see what he was too timid to say. I wasn't up to doing that, and I wouldn't have taken the chance of hurting him even if I were.

He leaned over and kissed my cheek. "I'm glad you're still here."

"Me too," I managed to whisper hoarsely.

I looked to Tabor, standing apart from us. *"You told them?"*

He nodded.

He'd shared my secret, but in this case, I was relieved.

I let him feel my gratitude. Maybe someday I'd feel comfortable speaking my feelings to him, but I was still adjusting to the unhindered emotions his bond allowed. Nothing felt stifled or filtered, and unlike Vayen's bond, I couldn't turn it off. Given the benefits, I didn't want to.

Tabor settled into a chair across from us, close enough to offer me relief without intruding on the kids. I gave him a burst of gratitude for that too. Leave it to the universe to hand me the perfect mate only after I'd poisoned myself. Fucking universe.

Ikeri smiled at me, likely picking up on my thoughts.

"He is perfect," she said, confirming my guess. *"Sorry, it was a loud thought."*

"Do you need anything?" she said out loud.

"Maybe some clothes. I don't know how long I'll be here. That depends on your father. How is he?"

Daniel and Ikeri shared a look.

"We haven't seen him," Ikeri said.

If he wasn't on the Iber, who knew what trouble he might be getting into given how out of sorts he'd been. "Buria or Etara, are either of them with him?"

Daniel shook his head. "They were both asking me where he was. I was hoping you knew."

Ikeri cast Tabor an apologetic nod before turning to me. "Could you use your bonded connection to talk to him, to make sure he's not..."

"On a killing spree?" I supplied. "I'm probably not the best choice of people to talk him down from whatever he's doing, given I'm the reason he's doing it."

"You could probe him with your bonded connection though, couldn't you? Without talking to him?" Daniel prodded.

I met Tabor's curious gaze. "Not when I'm here. Tabor's bond cancels his out. It's stronger."

A satisfied smile crept along Tabor's lips before dissolving back into his calm and collected expression. "That's unfortunate," he managed to say without any hint of the sarcasm that was very clear in my head.

He and Vayen may have reached an understanding while the tank had been saving me, but that didn't void their rivalry.

Daniel held up a hand, distracted for a moment. "Neko has him."

Relief settled on us all. Neko could manage the death-bringer. There would be no trail of bodies or avenging Etara to deal with. I was glad he'd turned to his steadfast shadow. Neko had been a good friend to both of us for a long while.

While I'd been thinking about Neko, Daniel, Ikeri, and Tabor were doing a lot of furtive glancing at one another. I gestured to Markus. "How about you and I go walk in the garden for a while so these three can have their conversation aloud."

"Mom," Daniel said softly.

"It's all right. You three have things to discuss. I get it. Brought this on myself, didn't I?" I patted his thick shoulder.

Markus followed me without a word or backward glance. When we reached the window-lined hall, he let out a quiet gasp.

"Impressive, isn't it?"

"I see why you don't mind spending time here."

"I don't," I said, meaning it wholeheartedly. "You'll need this." I handed him a breather mask from the box by the door as we went out.

After giving him a quick tour and explaining the effects of the stareopantika, we settled onto one of the benches near the fountain.

"Can I ask you something?" he ventured uncertainly.

I nodded. We didn't talk much beyond the obligatory parent topics, not nearly as much as I did with Daniel and Ikeri. When he was away, I knew he often had vid calls with Vayen and Daniel.

"I've been thinking about Jalvian customs and how they differ from Artorian or many others for that matter. Daniel's wives are happy. His marriage works. But what Dad wants, what you have now with the four of you, it doesn't. Not really, but from the outside, it looks like it does, for the public, I mean."

Inside the clear face mask, I could see how he worked his bottom lip between thoughts. Holding his head slightly cocked, he watched his fingers fiddling on his lap rather than looking at me. "I don't like Buria."

"Can't say as I'm a big admirer myself, though most of those reasons are not directly her fault, but your father does."

"But if he is truly bonded to you like Artorians are, he shouldn't like her either."

I appreciated that even my adopted kid seemed to be on my side. After a brief explanation of why Vayen's bond with me was never like other Artorians, Markus returned to his finger pondering for a moment.

"But Tabor is only part Artorian and he's able to bond to you and you to him. The right way."

Markus might not be blood, but he was at the center of this with the rest of us and working hard to process it all. I gave him my theory on the bond and the genetic manipulations that had been done to it when the Artorian people had fractured into two opposite tenets.

He nodded. "I like Tabor."

"Me too."

Markus peeked up to give me a quick smile. "Ikeri says Dad does too, but that it just makes him angrier instead of happy. He always seems to be angry lately."

"He's been having a hard time keeping himself in check with Etara's rules. I'd hoped Buria..." That was probably more information than he needed to hear.

"She was looking for him too. Daniel said she didn't sound very happy that he'd not come back to the Iber with us."

While I didn't enjoy getting shot or the fallout brought on by my visit to the tank, ruining Buria's signing night did offer a small consolation. If that made me petty, I was quite comfortable with that.

"I'm sorry he made you so sad," Markus said. "I know how hard it is to feel like you've lost your family, and he's been your family far longer than any of the rest of us."

I met the gaze of this young Jalvian boy who could have easily been Tabor's son, could have been my son with Tabor, and felt tears welling in my eyes. "I'm sorry that you understand how hard that is."

Crying in front of others was not something I did often, but there in the garden amid the sound of the fountain and the birds singing, behind the safety of the breather mask, I allowed myself a moment with Markus. He reached one arm out tentatively. I hugged him, all the while considering that he'd lost one family and now Vayen wasn't acting very fatherly and I'd almost checked out of his life for good.

I pulled away, clearing my throat. "Not that I can see the future, but you do know that if anything happens to me or Vayen, you will always have Daniel and Ikeri, right? And Tabor too. He did say that you're welcome here anytime. Between you and me, I'm pretty sure he's always wanted children, but he's not able to have them." I gently knocked my shoulder into his. "Bug him all you want. He's got a lot of childless time to make up for."

Markus grinned. "I'd like that."

"He would too." I winked. "Now, how about we go see if those three have come to a conclusion about what to do with me."

Markus nodded, following me back through the garden. Ikeri and Daniel met us in the windowed hall just as we were returning our breather masks. I folded my arms across my chest and waited for the proclamation I could see Daniel was ready to issue. I'd seen that expression plenty of times on his father.

"You'll stay here until Dad says otherwise to give him time to process...things. Ikeri will get you some clothes. I'll bring those and the dress from the ship so Tabor can see if it can be repaired."

"He thinks it can," added Ikeri.

Daniel shot her a look for interrupting him. "Meanwhile I'll talk with the doctors on the Iber. Tabor will check with his connections, and Ikeri will speak with Etara. I'm sure Dad is already harassing the Artorian University. Between all our resources, I'm sure someone can heal or reverse the damage that was done."

The damage I'd done. That everyone else was now scrambling to undo. Damage that had crushed Vayen. If the punishment for my actions was to spend a couple of days with Tabor, that was a sentence I'd gladly serve.

"I'll be here then. Let me know if or when anyone needs me elsewhere."

It seemed my children had expected resistance because my acquiescence seemed to throw them off. They lapsed into an awkward silence.

"Make sure you eat something, Mom," chided Ikeri. "The tank report showed that you've lost considerable weight since your last profile update."

"I will." Mycel would make sure of that, and again, I wasn't going to resist. I didn't need the tank to tell me that my pants were loose. I also didn't need my upset stomach to tell me why I hadn't been eating, but knowing everyone was now watching me, I'd do my best to keep my body strong so I could recover from what I'd done. I had a feeling that fully recovering from this was the only way Vayen would forgive me.

I'd been spending my days sitting in the garden, not feeling up to doing much of anything, but the weather was always perfect as long as I was aware of the water cycle. Tabor's family physician hadn't had anything to offer but a grimace upon examining me. The Iber's medical team had shaken their heads and done a lot of conferring. Beyond offering me pills to take the edge off the discomfort and nausea, they weren't currently able to do much more. Daniel had suggested multiple trips to the tank to keep the damage at a base level until we could find a cure. So far that and the pills were keeping me on my feet, but my spirits were hitting rock bottom. Two weeks had passed and Vayen had yet to speak a word to me. Not that I'd ventured to speak to him either, but my end of our connection was open. I'd already said everything I had to say.

Daniel had confirmed that Vayen was back on the Iber and going about his usual schedule, including his Buria time. That was all fine and well, except I wasn't included in that schedule.

I knew he was angry and hurt, but his bond, even weak as it was, had to be urging him to spend some silent time in my vicinity by now. If nothing else, I thought he'd be making an effort to help find a cure, but if he'd had a hand in anything I'd tried, no one had mentioned it.

Tabor was out on a business meeting. He'd been minimizing his time out of the house to a three-hour window where he could quickly do whatever required his in-person presence. Mostly he'd been sticking close to me, watching warily as I did my best to eat and sleep, neither of which was overly successful. His concern was constant in my head. Now, after two weeks, it bordered on suffocating. Worse, he could feel that too. Which led me to dealing with his anxiety over possibly losing me in the long term while waiting for me to verbally go off on him at any moment. I did a lot of breathing exercises in the garden.

Daniel's voice in my head offered a welcome disruption from my dismal thoughts. *"Mom, I hate to drag you into this, but we need you."*

To be needed for anything was a relief. My heart pounded, making my fingertips tingle.

"I can be in the gallery in five minutes. Tabor is out so you'll need to Jump me."

"Actually, Ikeri is going to do it. We figured this was a safe place for her to learn Jumping you."

Ikeri had gotten a link? And no one had thought to tell me until now? Why hadn't she said anything? My pounding heart sputtered and slowed. They needed me for Jump practice. That was all.

"Sure, yes. I'll be waiting."

I took off my mask as I went inside, storing it in the box and then turning to give the freshly tilled Stareopantika field one last glance. It seemed almost unsettling to have the empty expanse where so much life had been before last week's harvest. If I stared hard enough, I could almost make out the small spider-like bots that were working nutrients into the soil and depositing fresh seeds. Tabor assured me we'd have a new field full of life in six weeks.

I didn't hold out as favorable of a result for myself.

Ikeri arrived in the gallery with pink cheeks and her jaw clenched. Her narrowed gaze eased as she took me in.

"Problem with the Jump?" I asked, noting the freshly shaved patch of hair behind her ear.

"No. Dad."

Maybe they did actually need me for something after all. "Oh?"

"Buria can't handle him, and Etara is threatening to put him down. I know we're supposed to be letting you rest, but it was time to call in the big guns."

"I don't know how much gunning power I have at the moment. At least not with him. He's been ignoring me."

Her lips curved into a wicked smile. "Oh, you'll do just fine."

"I'm assuming you know how a double Jump works? You'll have to fill me in on how that came to be later." I pointed at her head where an implant now resided.

She nodded.

While she was busy taking me in, I used my bonded connection with Tabor to let him know where I was going. It took her a few minutes, but then we were at the jump point on the Iber.

Though it had only been two weeks, it seemed like I'd been away for months. I was out of sync with the crew and their current phase of the mission, no longer a part of it. It was as if I no longer entirely belonged here. Though I'd skimmed a few of the reports Daniel had sent me, I'd had a hard time focusing on any of it beyond knowing our work was continuing.

I followed Ikeri to Buria's suite. Within a few steps, I could make out the shouting inside. What surprised me was that Vayen wasn't fighting with Buria. Or, I revised after hearing her too, he was also in a screaming match with Daniel.

Ikeri palmed the door panel, allowing us front row access to the main event inside. Buria stood fuming on the far side of the kitchen. A shattered bottle lay at her feet along with a puddle of brown liquid. Dark splatters dotted her clothes and even her face. Daniel stood between her and Vayen, both off duty by their lack of armor or weapons. The two of them were shouting so loud it hurt my ears.

"Enough," I yelled. "Shut the hell up. Both of you."

Daniel shared a grateful look with Ikeri and then me before backing away from his father. He gestured for Buria to follow him. She gave Vayen a contemptuous glare as she walked by and out the door.

"Will you be all right if I leave the two of you alone?" Ikeri asked.

"I guess we'll find out. Go on." I nodded her toward the door.

The last place I wanted to be with Vayen after what had passed between us and his long absence was in the suite he shared with Buria, but it beat being alone and useless in the garden.

"What's this all about?" I pointed to the broken bottle on the floor.

"Nothing," he snapped. "You're supposed to be resting."

"I was. For two weeks. Were you ever planning to speak to me again?"

He looked away, his entire body tight and near vibrating, still wired for a fight.

I was not. Taking a chance, I closed the distance between us and wrapped my arms around his waist. A tremble passed through him. The reek of several layers of alcohol and sweat wafted my way.

"Anastassia," he murmured into my hair, his tone clearly disapproving but his hands ran up my back and settled on my shoulders.

My breath caught in my throat. He never used my full name when it was just the two of us. By choosing to stay among the living, had I ruined what had been between us, no matter how weak that had been?

I stayed as I was, prepared to ride out whatever storm he was about to unleash.

He pushed me back, holding me at arm's length, glaring at me intently.

"You were going to leave me," he accused.

"You left me first," I threw back at him.

Vayen took a heavy step toward me, his standard intimidation routine running on autopilot in his drunken state. His foot landed on a piece of the bottle and slid out from under him.

I reached out to steady him before his giant body went down in the slippery and jagged mess on the floor. His entire weight jerked hard on my shoulder as I caught him.

Despite how weak our bond was and his drunken state, my yelp caught his immediate attention. Once he'd gotten his feet solidly underneath him again, his hand ran over my shoulder, gently probing. When he found the spot, I gasped without intending to. I'd hoped to focus on what the hell had been going on here, but he had other ideas.

"You should have let me fall," he all but yelled.

I was about to agree with him when his drunken end of our connection revealed the many layers hidden behind his few words. So much anger. So much guilt. I saw through his eyes as I had lain bleeding on the floor while he couldn't move. While he didn't move. While Tabor, unarmored and new to us had Jumped in front of me to take the first shot and Vayen had done nothing. Nothing.

The mire of self-loathing came to an abrupt halt as he met my gaze and quickly tried to hide what he'd clearly not meant to share. "You should get to the tank," he said more calmly.

"Can't do that on my own."

"Right." He held out his hand.

The void deposited us in the tank room where he busied himself with loading my profile as I undressed. While I hadn't been aware of a damned thing the last time we'd been in the tank room together, his end of our connection revealed he was replaying that terror over and over as he watched me on the platform, sinking into the healing gel. I sent him what calm I could muster as the gel welcomed me into its liquid embrace.

When I came to in my bed, covered with a fresh sheet, my room was empty. However, voices down the hallway revealed that I wasn't alone. Pulling the sheet around me, I was relieved to find the pain in my shoulder was gone even though the rest of me felt as shitty as usual. My new normal.

There apparently hadn't been enough room, or maybe air, in the small office for Daniel, Tabor, and Vayen to have their loud and heated meeting. The three of them stood glaring at one another, Daniel's fists at his sides and Vayen with his arms crossed, both with their backs to me. As I entered the room, Tabor spotted me, and though his bond wrapped me in comforting warmth, his tidal wave of concern nearly knocked me off my feet.

Not knowing who's side I should attach myself to without further information, I asked with forced bravado, "What's this all about?"

Daniel and Vayen spun to face me. Feeling like I was suddenly on trial, I was tempted to retreat to my room until they'd reached a verdict. However, I'd had enough yelling for one day and if anyone was going to continue with that tone, it was me.

"Are the three of you done discussing my health without including me in the conversation?"

Tabor cracked a smile but Vayen and Daniel did not.

"Well, what is it that has you all so worked up?" I glared at Vayen. "Not that you've seen fit to care about me for the past couple of weeks."

Rather than look contrite or back down in any manner, Vayen drew himself up to his full hulking size and glared right back at me. "Your continued trips to the tank to treat the same exact issue have fucked up your profile even more than it was before. Now you're really screwed. Maybe you should just sit down and let us figure this out."

At least he seemed sober, and now that I looked closer, he'd showered and changed. Not that any of that made up for him being an ass.

"My continued trips? Four times since the signing ceremony. That's it. And it wasn't just my idea. Daniel suggested it and Tabor and I agreed. It was working."

"Was, yes. The first time. The tank has to account for natural changes. You keep treating the same injuries. It learns, Anastassia. Those injuries are now considered normal, part of your baseline, nothing to be repaired.

"So I have to let it progress for uneven amounts of time before doing another session in the tank? That would still work, right?"

He shook his head. "It's still the same general injury."

"There's nothing general about it," Tabor grumbled.

"No, there's not." Vayen took two steps toward me. "After all you've lived through, you choose poison? Good Geva, Anastassia, what the fuck were you thinking? How could you do that to the kids? To me?"

And just like the second before the first bullet had found a target, Tabor was in front of me. He shoved Vayen back. "You will not talk to her like that. In fact, you arrogant, self-centered, alcoholic..." He slipped into Jalvian as his tirade continued.

To my surprise, Vayen didn't fight back. Instead, he stood there, eyes wide and mouth gaping as Tabor had the spine to drive his palm into Vayen's substantial chest a second time.

Tabor took a breath and fell back into Trade, "You had her by your side for half your lifetime and you thought there wouldn't be repercussions when your attention wandered? That she doesn't have feelings about that? I assure you, she does. If you weren't such a fool, you'd know that yourself." Tabor pressed on, his silky voice made all the more condemning by his ability to maintain his composure despite the near electric spikes of energy snapping over our bonded connection. "I'd barely known her for a few hours, and thanks to you, I nearly lost her."

Vayen shook his head. "You wouldn't have ever had her if it wasn't for me."

Tabor didn't budge. "Neither of us will if you don't get your head out of a bottle and your ass. When you're ready to apologize to her and assist in finding a solution, she'll be at my estate."

The last thing I saw before Tabor whisked me into the void was Vayen's stunned face.

Tabor paced the length of the gallery, hands flexing and a hard static thrumming through our connection. "Sorry about that. He made me so damned angry."

I caught his arm as he passed by and pulled him close enough to kiss him. "Me too. Thank you."

He smiled against my cheek. The cracking static subsided.

"Seems you've gotten over the whole, 'he's the Advisor of All' awe."

Tabor let out a ragged bark of laughter. "Damn, I did actually push him, didn't I? Do you think he'll flay me alive the next time he sees me?"

"Like I'd allow that." I sent him a burst of assurance in case he doubted my sincerity. "You two I get, but why was Daniel in the middle of that conversation?"

"My fault. I asked him to join us when Vayen called me there and started going off about you using the tank on the scheduled intervals. As backup, you know? I figured he'd listen to his son more than me."

I shook my head. "Those two have been strained for a few years now. Too much alike, I think."

"I didn't mean to drive a wedge further between them."

A wedge. Like Buria, driven between me and Vayen. A chilling thought hit me. "Do you think when I got shot at the ceremony, when Vayen froze, that he was taking advantage of the situation? Intentionally not making any move to save me? If I'm out of the picture, he can have Buria or anyone else he wants."

Tabor took a step back, his gaze darting over me from head to toe as if taking inventory, all the while slowly shaking his head. "He couldn't have," he said adamantly.

"He easily could have. He hasn't been banging down the door to make sure I'm all right." Taking advantage of the Ocelon's attack would just as easily explain the anger and loathing he'd accidentally shared.

He'd never hesitated to protect me before. Even when we weren't on speaking terms.

The room began to blur and my body felt distant. The desolation that had erupted the night he'd chose to leave me hit me again.

Tabor wrapped his arms around me and held me tight as tears rolled down my face. This utter openness between us was so strange given how long I'd shared the truncated bond with Vayen. I dearly appreciated that Tabor was willing to offer comfort without saying a word, without professing that he'd never choose someone else, that he'd never falter in protecting me, and most of all, despite the fact that my distress was directly caused by his rival and without making any disparaging remarks.

"Come on," he said gently, nodding toward the stairs. At the top, he walked beside me, directing us toward my bedroom.

He often sat beside me on the bed when I wasn't feeling well. None of it felt strained or like he was hovering. I quite enjoyed his close presence, his quick smile, and his endearing offhand comments. Sometimes he read a book aloud, or drew out conversational bits of my life in exchange for his, sometimes he silently worked through his link while I used my datapad, but more often than not, he was simply present as if he didn't want to waste those moments. Having lived a work-focused life for so long, I couldn't help but love him for that.

The few times Vayen and I had taken our couple days away from the Iber, the conversation had felt forced. I knew he'd rather be working, that in the back of his mind, he was cataloging the hundreds of things he could have been doing rather than sitting on the couch beside me watching the local vids on Veria Minor, or going for a walk, or anything else we'd done. He was there because he felt guilty over Buria, not because he wanted to be beside me. And by the fact that he'd not bothered to visit or even contact me in two weeks, not because he needed to be near me. His bond to me was truly that weak.

It had been a while since Vayen looked at me the way Tabor was looking at me now where we stood outside my bedroom. He made no move to open the door.

Tabor licked his lips. The hum between us fluttered, the tone deepening. "I was thinking, if you're agreeable that is, that perhaps, in light of the tank not healing you, that you might be more comfortable resting within our bond."

He took one step toward his bedroom, tentatively guiding me along with him. "I prefer to sleep in my own bed, if you don't mind."

While I had entertained him a few times with the Artorian way of sex, he'd made no move to reciprocate or touch me that wasn't invited. And I hadn't done much inviting beyond kissing and keeping his hand-wandering confined to over my clothes. He'd been utterly patient, not pushing for more. Despite having not shared full intimacy between us, he'd illustrated his commitment by not only taking the first Ocelon shot, but by standing up to Vayen, knowing full well what the death-bringer could do to him with a few seconds of thought. He certainly deserved to be rewarded.

But I didn't want to use sex as a reward. Not with him.

I didn't need anything from Tabor that he wasn't already providing. Maybe for once in my life, I could have a relationship with a man just because I wanted to. Because I couldn't imagine not having him in my life even after so short of a time.

Because I loved him.

"I would like that."

"You would?" The hum between us grew deeper, wrapping around me from the inside, caressing, embracing.

I nodded, finding myself at a loss for words.

"To clarify, so I don't totally screw things up, I want you in my bed. Where you choose to sleep afterward is up to you," he said huskily.

A kiss seemed the best way to express my confirmation since words seemed to have left me. As our lips met, I reached into his mind and shared a few suggestions as to what I might like. He answered with the same eagerness he'd had in the garden the first time I'd shown him what Artorian sex was. His mental touch soft and agile as he danced his way through the pleasure points in my mind, exploring as his hands slipped under my shirt and his tongue dueled with mine.

We closed the distance between my bedroom and his with blinding speed. His all-encompassing attention erased all thought of anything or anyone else. From his confident mental touch, it was clear that he'd been taking notes on what I'd been doing in his head each time rather than just enjoying the moment. My mind and body ate up everything, reveling in the openness of fully shared intimacy.

When the back of my legs bumped against a soft, satiny surface, I gathered we'd arrived at his bed in the dark room. Everything came to a sudden halt, his hands froze, one on the nape of my neck, the other on my hip, holding me against him. He didn't so much as vacate my mind as hit pause, like fingers resting on terminal keys.

"Lights on or off?" he asked against my ear.

Though he was doing his best to keep his opinion to himself, as Ikeri would say: he was having very loud thoughts.

"On." I wanted a reminder of who I was with in case pleasure knocked me into autopilot.

He grinned, teeth rubbing against mine.

The lights came on, dimmed, but enough to see by so I didn't trip over anything as he tugged my shirt over my head. I took a step back to take my pants off while he unfastened his shirt and removed it. Figuring I might as well go all in, I slipped out of my underclothes and slid onto the bed. The bedcover was satiny bliss against my skin.

Tabor stood at the end of the bed, his gaze hungry, but still wearing his pants.

"Whatever makes you more comfortable," I said in response to the uncertainty flowing from his mind to mine.

"It's more that I don't want to make you uncomfortable. In my experience, women don't usually want to see...that."

"The contract is already signed," I said, shaking my head. "If you're getting me in all my mid-life glory, it's only fair that I get all of you."

He chuckled. "I'm definitely winning in this situation, but if you insist." Tabor removed his pants but hesitated at his underclothes.

I nodded.

He shrugged and slid them down his legs to step out of them. The surgeons had done a fine job. While I knew what should have been there, the expanse of shiny skin, thin and pulled too tight, made it appear that no phallus had ever been there. Like he'd been born androgynous. I might not have Buria's depth of knowledge on the subject, but I'd been with enough men of varied tastes to know more than the one erogenous zone most focused on.

"Not so bad then?" he asked softly.

"Nope." I patted the bed next to me.

He stretched out on the bedcover, but rather than reaching for me, opened the top drawer on the bedside table. "I did mention having other ways to please you, didn't I?"

I lifted my head to glimpse an assortment of intriguing toys. "You did advertise that, but we can get to those later. I have a feeling you'll do just fine on your own if you continue what you started."

He broke out the smile that made his eyes twinkle and my heart flutter. "Yeah?"

I nodded. His eager response on all fronts at once made me gasp and removed any doubt about the truth of my statement for both of us.

THIRTY-TWO

Daniel

My father stood there, staring at the spot where my mother had been before Tabor whisked her away.

"Dad?"

"Get out. Out!" he roared.

Every nerve in my body went on high alert. "What are you going to do? Dad, you can't go after him. You can't. Mom would never forgive you."

And after talking to Tabor these last couple of weeks and seeing how he cared for my mother, neither would I. She needed this. Him. Especially now that she was unwell.

"Go home to your fucking perfect wives." He shoved me backward so hard that I saw stars when my head hit the wall a second before the rest of me.

He let out a wordless roar. I hadn't seen him so furious since he'd annihilated the population of Brustus upon finding Ikeri. Meera wasn't here to drag me away to safety this time.

"Get out!" he screamed in my face, all the while driving me into the wall with his modified hand on my chest.

I scrambled to shove calm at him over our natural connection like Etara had told me to do if he flipped out. If anything, my efforts only seemed to infuriate him more. The pressure on my chest intensified until I couldn't catch another breath. I clawed at his hand, my efforts quickly turning to trying to break free rather than helping him.

"Dad," I gasped, beating on his arm with all of my fading might.

He eased up only enough to grab a fist full of my shirt to yank me a step forward and then slam me back into the wall again. "Leave," he ordered, driving the word into my brain with an agonizing twist that made my legs go out underneath me.

He let go as I dropped to the floor, my head swimming as I gasped for air. His command echoed in my brain until I could think of nothing else.

Though I knew I needed to stay, that I needed to try to talk him down, I couldn't fight his compulsion. I Jumped to my suite.

"Daniel?" Arden rushed to my side. "What's wrong? Are you hurt? Meera!" she yelled over her shoulder.

I'd made it as far as my knees before Meera took Arden's place in front of me. She ran her hands over my head, shoulders and chest before holding them out to help me up. "Who did this?"

"My father."

Arden stood at my side. Her hand slipped into mine, squeezing. "Where is he? Do we need to send for Etara?"

As much as I didn't want to say it, the pain in my head and chest and the rage that had emanated from him couldn't be denied. "Yes. I need to talk to her. And to sit down."

Meera nodded, gesturing Arden to the terminal and taking my arm to lead me to a chair. I dropped into it, resting my aching head against the padded back. The flash of agony he'd inflicted to drop me to the floor and the disorienting sensation of his driving command refused to abate. Saliva pooled into my mouth no matter how many times I tried to swallow the nausea down.

I pushed myself out of the chair with single-minded purpose and dashed to the bathroom. Meera was beside me in seconds, her hand smoothing my hair away from my face as I hovered over the toilet and purged the contents of my stomach. When there was nothing left, she handed me a cold, wet cloth.

"Etara will be here momentarily," Arden said from the doorway. "Did your father do that thing he does? To you?" She pointed to my head.

I got to my feet and nodded, not wanting to admit it in words. But I would have to when the death-bringer's warden arrived. Even knowing he'd held back, that he'd only inflicted a fraction of what he could do, I shuddered. He'd done that. To me.

"Daniel," Meera said softly, pulling me against her, wrapping her arms around me.

My chest ached and the back of my head throbbed, but I basked in her comfort. A peaceful sensation settled over me.

Arden joined us, her head on my shoulder.

The two of them guided me out of the bathroom and onto the couch. What the hells was I going to tell Etara?

Meera sat beside me. "Oh," she gasped, clutching her stomach.

"What is it?" My own misery vanished as concern for her took over.

She grinned. "The baby. It's kicking." She grabbed my hand and placed it on her stomach.

Sure enough, motion fluttered under my hand. Joy surged through me, through her. Meera, having no natural speech had never broadcasted feelings to me before. Oh Geva, did that mean my efforts at opening myself to a bond with her were working?

Meera's eyes went wide. "What's that sound?"

"I don't hear anything," said Arden.

A soft hum curled around me, sinking into my muscles, my very bones, dulling the aches my father had inflicted inside and out.

It was just like Tabor said it would be. This was what my mother had with Tabor that she'd not had with my father. No wonder he was so angry.

Meera shook my shoulder gently. "Do you hear it? I'm not crazy, am I?"

"The bond. It worked."

She leaned closer and kissed my cheek. "It's wonderful. I'm so glad you chose to try it."

"Me too."

I glanced over to Arden. "Come here." I held out my hand to her.

She reluctantly joined us on the couch, keeping her distance from me as much as the space allowed. "Etara will be here any moment, I can keep her occupied if you'd like to have some time together," she said.

"You and I will have this too. Give it some time. The process might be different between us because Meera isn't Artorian."

Arden nodded but maintained her distance. This was exactly what I didn't want to happen, setting them apart from another. The two of them were so close.

"Tabor said his was triggered by an intense emotional connection. Like when we both felt the baby just now. We just have to wait for our moment."

Or maybe I wasn't supposed to bond to more than one person, but Tabor thought it was possible. I wanted to believe him.

When the door pinged to announce Etara's arrival, Arden leapt off the couch to answer it. She slipped away into the bedroom once she let Etara in.

"I'll talk to her," Meera whispered. "I'm sure you're right."

I prayed I was, and then I asked Geva for the strength to get through the conversation with the keeper of my father's death key.

The petite Seeker entered, her robes swooshing with each step. Though she was smaller than Ikeri, little Etara managed to project a large aura of strength and calm.

"What's he done now?" she asked, looking me over as if she could see right through me. Like Ikeri, she probably could.

"You might as well just look. It will be easier to judge what must be done."

She held my gaze for a moment and then nodded. Just like when Ikeri sifted through my thoughts and memories, I didn't feel Etara at all. While I was used to my sister traipsing about, having Etara wandering in my brain was disconcerting.

"I knew I liked that man." She smiled but that quickly slipped away. "Your father attacked you?"

"He did." And even though I was pissed as all hells that he had, I felt guilty admitting it to her, knowing the price he might have to pay.

"Do you know where he is now?"

"Hopefully where I left him. I can check if you need me to."

She sucked in her lips for a moment. "Only if you promise to leave immediately if he's still in a rage. I don't want to see you hurt further."

I rubbed the tender spot on the back of my head to find a lump there. "Agreed."

"I could come with you," Meera offered.

No way in all hells was I putting her in my father's path any time soon.

"Or I'll just stay right here," she said quickly.

I'd have to remember that she could pick up on my emotions now that our bond was active. Silently apologizing, I gave her a quick kiss and Jumped back to the ship.

The tank room lights had gone into standby. They flooded the room with light seconds after my arrival. The rest of the ship was dark and silent. I sat down in the chair by the terminal, still unsteady on my feet, and considered where my father might have gone. A quick check with several contacts on the Iber confirmed that he wasn't in public view. Perhaps he was apologizing to Buria, wherever she'd gone.

I used my link to contact her. *"Is my father with you?"*

"He's not allowed to speak to me without a major apology."

"Got it. Thanks." I cut contact. Whatever had erupted between the two of them before she'd panicked and called me in to mediate must have been pretty bad.

I tried Neko but he didn't answer. Undoubtedly, Narvan business was more pressing at the moment.

Considering who else my father would have turned to for either venting opportunities or a sympathetic ear, I composed a very short list. He didn't have many friends.

Uncle Isnar answered immediately. *"We haven't spoken since the signing ceremony. Since he was too drunk to do a damned thing for your mother."*

"All right. Thanks." I cut contact.

He had been celebrating pretty heavily that night. Then again, he'd been drinking a lot for the past year or two. Even when he wasn't visibly doing so, I could smell it on him. He'd been sober when he'd confronted my mother earlier, I prayed he was still was. Geva, what chaos would he cause if he combined that level of rage with alcohol?

Skimming my link, I checked newsfeeds from the Narvan and the Rakon Nebula, his usual haunts, searching for any mention of crowds falling over dead or unexplained massacres. Thankfully, nothing stuck out. Then again, maybe he just hadn't gotten to it yet.

Talking to Jey was a last resort, but my list was that short.

"Didn't expect to hear from you," Jey said in a bored tone.

I didn't have time for our usual disdain-filled banter. *"My father isn't with you by any chance, is he?"*

"No. Should he be?"

"He's in a mood. The kind that will get him killed if I don't contain him."

That got Jey's attention. *"Shit. I haven't spoken to him since I reamed his ass for what happened to your mother. I'll keep an eye out and let you know if I hear anything."*

It seemed my father's current list of friends was zero to possibly one, depending on where Neko stood.

Having run out of other options, I resorted to the natural connection I shared with my mother. *"Does Dad happen to be groveling at your feet right now?"*

She was several minutes in answering. *"I'm guessing it will be days or even weeks before he's willing to speak to me again. Why?"*

I really didn't want to tell her, given the physical stress she was already under, but if anyone could intercede with Etara and possibly get my father's wrath under control, it was my mother.

"Mom, he went off on me after you left. With his Arpex abilities I mean. I tried to get him to calm down, but he was too far gone. He's not on the ship anymore or the Iber, no one knows where he is. I had to show Etara what he did, but now I don't know what to do."

In a matter of seconds, she went from my ailing mother to the woman who had fought six Jalvians for fun. *"He did what?"*

Even though her telepathy was weak, I had no problem picking up her fury.

"I checked with Uncle Isnar, Buria, and Jey. Apparently, he's on all of their shit lists and they haven't heard from him. Neko isn't answering."

"Dammit. Neko can track him. Unless your father has disabled his tracer. Give us a few minutes. We'll be right there."

With nothing more to do on my father's behalf, I returned to my suite where Etara was waiting.

Meera cast me a worried glance from the couch where she sat rubbing her stomach. "Any luck?"

"If you consider it lucky that he wasn't there to go after me again, then yes. As far as locating him, no."

"Giving him Buria was supposed to prevent this," Etara muttered.

That confirmed who had orchestrated this mess. "Maybe you should have instilled a compulsion to avoid alcohol instead of driving my parents apart."

Etara flinched. "I'm doing my best to keep him on a path that allows him to remain among us. Drinking has been dulling his urges. I'd hoped Buria would be a better solution."

Having encountered him sober and his urges undulled, I couldn't entirely fault her tactics. "My mother will be here any minute. She'll know what to do."

"Let's hope so or I won't have a choice in what I have to do." Etara joined her hands in front of her, the long sleeves of her robes flowing over them as she bowed her head.

Leaving her to her meditation, I pondered the closed bedroom door and my distraught second wife within. Why couldn't my bond kick in with both of them at the same time? That would have made things so much simpler. Guilt over inadvertently hurting Arden tempered my joy of the new connection with Meera.

Meera got up and came to stand next to me. "You need to focus on this. I'll smooth things over with Arden."

"Thank you."

I hugged my beautiful and compassionate first wife, reveling in the feel of her firm, round belly between us. Soon we'd have a child to add to the chaos of our lives. Arden's pregnancy wasn't far behind. If my bond with her didn't activate soon, hopefully the birth of our baby would help her feel included.

Just as Meera closed the bedroom door behind her, Tabor arrived with my mother. She must have given him a direct jump point.

"Sorry to invade. She insisted," Tabor said, nodding toward my mother.

My mother, looking far more herself than I'd seen in quite a while, with her hair braided and wearing her armored coat, detached herself from Tabor's arm and strode over to me.

"What exactly did he do? Show me," she demanded.

For the second time, I opened my mind and replayed the raw memory. When I finished, she was livid. My mother would have hugged me or at least offered a few comforting words, but that wasn't who she was just then.

She turned to Tabor. "Remain on the Iber with Etara. We'll be in contact if either of you are required." Then her attention was fully on me, her hand gripping my arm. "The Artorian estate. Now."

When we arrived in the foyer, yelling directed us toward the conference room. Neko, decidedly red with rage, was mid-chewing out two men I didn't know. They were neither definitively Artorian or Jalvian but had the typical hardened look of the pool of private enforcers he and my father employeed.

We ducked back out and waited for him to wrap up his chastisement. After he'd laid down a few threats that would have made my father proud, Neko sent the two men running out of the room and then out the front door.

The second time we entered the conference room, he sat at the table with his head in his hands. His eyes were closed.

"What?" he asked tersely.

"Your tracer on Vayen. We need a location. Now," my mother demanded.

Neko rubbed his face, sighed, and then stood. "Fucking hell. What's he done now?"

"He went semi-death-bringer on my son and I will not stand for it."

If she'd had the ability to shoot lasers out of her eyes, the room would have been annihilated. I didn't think I'd ever seen my mother so angry. And she'd never played the "my son" card before, at least not with me present.

"Is Etara close behind?" Neko asked.

"She's in the wings if necessity demands it."

"Let's hope necessity doesn't." He gave my mother a challenging stare. Neko may have been close to both of my parents but he was tight with my father. "I'll get you a location, but I'm coming with you."

"Fine."

Neko closed his eyes again, sinking deep into the network. Minutes slipped by until I thought my mother would implode The tension rolling off of her heightened my own, building into a tornado of anxiety over what would happen when we did find him.

"I have a location, but not a jump point."

"Where?" my mother demanded.

"Brustus," he said to me. "Let's go."

I Jumped my mother to the public jump point Gamnock had set up on Brustus. Buria had denied being with my father, but I wondered if she knew he was close by. And what the hells was he doing close by?"

"Were you aware that he had an apartment here?" Neko asked delicately.

"I'm not surprised, but no, I didn't know," my mother said.

"It's been in his name, well, one of them, for years. Maybe it was an emergency fallback plan."

"Or maybe Buria lied about their relationship," she muttered.

I didn't want to believe that. In fact, I didn't want to know anything further about my father unless it had to do with him groveling at my feet and profusely apologizing. I guessed my mother was hoping for the same thing. Knowing my father's moods, I doubted either of us were going to get what we wanted.

"For what it's worth, Ana, I'm fairly certain he was not involved with Buria until very recently."

"That's currently not worth much, but I'll take it under advisement."

He nodded and set off for one of the taller buildings near the spaceport. "This way."

As it turned out, my father was currently holed up in the prime top floor suite in Buria's building. At least he wasn't waist deep in a bloodbath or causing some inerasable public scene.

We entered the building and took the lift to the top floor. The suite door was locked, but Neko made quick work of it. We barged in, expecting the worst. At least I was. Neko seemed to be making far more noise than necessary, but maybe that was to alert my father to our presence so he didn't come out with guns blazing.

The lights were on their night setting, illuminating enough to reveal minimal furnishings. My mother wasn't having any skulking around. She found the light controls and activated them.

The few pieces of furniture in the common room and dining area appeared to be high-end which was not at all my father's style. They were likely leftover from whomever had lived here previously—some-one he'd probably killed in his extermination of the original Brustus residents. However, the scattering of food containers and empty bottles was evidence that he'd spent time there, though he apparently had not invested in any cleaning bots.

"Get out," said a raspy voice from the hallway off the common room. It reminded me of how he'd sounded when he'd come back to us on Pentares, when he'd been gravely wounded taking out the High Council.

My mother strode toward the voice with single-minded purpose. We hurried to keep up with her. The crack of her fist meeting his face indicated we weren't fast enough.

He grabbed her wrist but made no other move to retaliate. At least not visibly. My mother went stiff and uttered one word before collapsing onto the floor. "Etara."

Simultaneously contacting Tabor with a hastily assembled jump point and bolting to my mother's side brought me under my father's horrified gaze.

"No," he repeated non-stop as he dropped to his knees beside me, reaching for my limp mother whom I held.

Like all hells was I letting him touch her. "If Etara doesn't kill you, Tabor will."

He blinked rapidly, shaking his head. "I didn't mean to. I didn't."

"You sure meant it when you did the same to me. Get the fuck away from her."

Neko stood staring at my father as if he were a stranger. He replaced the stunner he'd held with a pulse pistol.

"Sorry, boss." He fired.

The tight, controlled beam blew my father back, his knees

speeding over the floor until his back hit a wall. Cracks spread out around him. His eyes rolled back and blood poured from his nose.

"He'll live," Neko assured me.

Voices behind me confirmed the arrival of Tabor and Etara.

"Not for long," I said.

As they approached cautiously, Neko placed himself between them and my father. "I'm not sure what he did to her exactly, but you'll want to get her to the tank," he said to Tabor.

"He did this?" Tabor looked from my unconscious mother to my father, his fingers twitching and his stance ready to attack. "Move."

"I can't do that." Neko held up a hand. "I know you're pissed. I get it. Really, I do. But I can't allow you to hurt him."

"I'm not going to hurt him. I'm going to kill him," Tabor yelled.

"If I don't do it first," said Etara, gazing down at my prone and bleeding father.

"Perhaps we all need some time to cool down." Neko dropped to a crouch, laid a hand on my father, and Jumped.

It was three days later that Neko contacted me to speak to my father. We'd just wrapped up a union introduction on a space station and my mind was filled with ideas of what to offer them and what they could provide for us in return. The station appeared to be well off and advantageously located to several surrounding worlds, one of which the homeworld of the majority of the station's occupants. Visiting the world was next on our agenda. Speaking to my father was not.

Seeing him so out of control that he'd taken down my mother, even though she'd attacked first, was the breaking point. Attacking me and then her, attacking family, that was a new low and I wasn't going to stand for it.

"Who will be there?" Mostly I wanted to know how much of an audience I'd have and who I could expect to hold me back.

"The three of us, you, me, and him," Neko said.

"He had better be talking to my mother."

"He will. Etara went first since she was on the biggest rampage."

"Don't bet on it."

"In terms of deadliness."

Neko had a point. As angry as I was, he was still my father and I didn't exactly want him dead. What I wanted was impossible. He'd been through too much, been altered too far. He wasn't the man he used to be, and that wasn't entirely his fault. However, he was still at the controls of the killing-machine that was his body. If his hold on those controls was slipping, I'd hand that necessary task to Etara. If his death ended up on my hands, it would be vicariously.

"Where?"

"I stashed him at Isnar's. In one of the cells. A few years ago, we installed a dampener that disrupts all link and telepathic functions. It seemed like the best place to keep him safe and contained."

Neko, now the current Advisor of the Narvan, had worked closely with Uncle Isnar, now Premier of Karin, when they'd been in service to my parents. I imagined that new cooperation led to things like private places to stash linked people to use and contain as they wished.

"I'll be there shortly." I cut contact. I could have Jumped immediately, but I needed to gather my wits first.

I considered contacting my mother but she needed to have her own conversation with him. If they stayed together after that, I'd be amazed. After all, she had Tabor and a real bond now, not to mention her health issues to deal with.

Meera and Arden were busy in the kitchen making what was probably some sweet treat. They'd both been craving those lately. While the two of them were back on good terms after the activation of my bond with Meera, Arden had been standoffish with me. I'd have to carve out some time for just the two of us very soon before things festered further.

Talking to my wives would relax me but I had no intention of going easy on my father. Maybe Uncle Isnar would have some advice. He'd had it out with my father a few times, including outright quitting. I didn't know of anyone else who had gotten away with that and lived, not anyone who had been in my father's personal service, anyway.

I let Meera and Arden know that I was going to visit my uncle, donned my armor, and Jumped to Karin.

His housekeeper, Merona, met me and directed me to his office. Neko and Uncle Isnar sat across from one another. Both of them were scowling, though their tone sounded amicable. Neko stood the moment he spotted me.

"Same ground rules for you as for Etara. You won't release him and you won't touch him in any manner. Clear enough?"

I was already contemplating loopholes, but I nodded.

"One of us will be in the room with you. Your choice."

There was no thought needed on that. I pointed to Uncle Isnar. If things did go badly, my uncle was far more likely to be on my side than my father's. He'd been my mother's friend first.

Neko gave Uncle Isnar a narrow-eyed stare as though he were drilling home a private agreement. Uncle Isnar nodded. He stood and silently led me to the lift to the underground level where I'd seen Buria contained years before when Ikeri had been kidnapped.

As the lift brought us down, Uncle Isnar cleared his throat. "For the record, the rule is that you can't kill him, not that you can't touch him. If it wasn't for the fact that there's a line to have at him, I'd have done a lot of fist-touching already."

I winked at him. "I knew I'd picked the right chaperone."

"Neko seems to think you might have inherited your father's temper. Hence his rule modification." He cracked a smile. "If it helps, that little Seeker had him on his knees. Interestingly enough, her abilities eluded my dampener."

That she'd done to him what he'd inflicted on us made me a little lighter. While I almost wished I had the ability to do that myself, I was glad there was one other person who could enact full justice on him in a way that might sink in. I was like my father in more ways than I wished already. Having the responsibility over controlling abilities like his, was one I didn't feel confident about being better at.

The lift stopped. The door opened to complete blackness. A soft light came on and quickly brightened, illuminating the four cells. I'd imagined him pacing, probably cursing, shaking a fist, or shouting threats. But he sat huddled on the cell floor, wearing what he'd had on in the tank room days ago, his shirt crusted with dried blood from his nose. He didn't appear to have any weapons on him and he hadn't been wearing his armor.

The cell offered a toilet and a small sink. A cup sat on the edge of the sink, the only visible throwable weapon. I felt secure with my chances against my mentally-bridled father with a cup.

As we approached, he didn't look up, he didn't move at all. At first I thought he was sleeping, but then I noted his subtle rocking.

Uncle Isnar leaned close but spoke through our natural connection. *"He started doing that last night. We'd planned to give him a few more days before allowing anyone else to see him after Etara's visit, but we're concerned that keeping him here much longer might be doing more harm than good."*

"Why? What's he doing?"

"I don't know how much you knew or remembered about when he was away from us, when we lived on Pentares?"

I thought back to those years of living among people who didn't look like me, who didn't understand me. When my only semblance of friends were Uncle Isnar and Neko, but they were also constantly on my ass to live up to their standards. I never could. Not there. Not when my father was missing and while watching my mother slowly lose hope that he would ever come back. Ikeri, who resembled my mother, who was only different on the inside, fit in with her people, but I'd hated it there.

When my father had returned, I'd thought we would leave, that we could return to the life we'd known on Veria Minor, but he'd changed. That's when everything had started to go wrong. Unchangeably wrong. He'd had constant nightmares, spoke to people who weren't there, whispered to himself when he thought we didn't notice. That's when I first remembered seeing him drinking, though it had only been a habit that my mother muttered under her breath about.

I looked to Uncle Isnar now, waiting for the clarification I could see was coming from the face I knew so well. Of the two of them, he'd been the one to do his best to fill the fatherly role during my father's absence. Neko had been the enforcer, the spy, the guard, and sometimes like an older brother who tolerated me with a sigh and covered for me with my mother or Uncle Isnar.

"They held him in a cell for years with a dampener just like this one. That's where this tech came from, by the way, the wreckage of one of the Council's strongholds. Your father didn't talk much about what happened while he'd been imprisoned, but it messed with his head. I had Etara come in this morning and do her calming thing on him but she agreed that we should get him out of here sooner rather than later."

If Etara said he needed to get out, I wasn't going to argue. She could see into his mind with a clarity none of us had.

"All right, so why are we doing this here?"

"We need to know if he can be trusted with family or if we need to call Etara back in to end this. Again, her suggestion."

"Got it."

He nodded. "I'll be over here by the controls. If this goes poorly, step back, and I'll reactivate the cell field."

Surprised he didn't just decree that I remain outside the cell footprint, I nodded. I supposed Uncle Isnar knew me well enough.

He left my side and returned to the wall by the lift to activate a control panel I could see blinking there. The field shimmering around my father crackled once and then dissipated.

My father shot to his feet, eyes wild for a moment before the caged animal look dissipated like the containment field. He stood there, working his jaw but saying nothing.

So much for groveling. Not that I could imagine my father doing any such thing with me or, for that matter, anyone but maybe my mother. Yet, I'd hoped for some form of contrition without having to try to drag it out of him. The fact that he remained silent, that he offered nothing beyond a challenging stare negated any sympathy I'd briefly harbored for his confinement.

"Well?" I asked.

"I…"

It was like watching the inner workings of a terminal lock up. He intermittently started to say something but then his lips pressed tight or his teeth ground together. His nostrils flared and his fists worked at his side. His head tilted, eyes squeezing shut and then opening to glare at me again.

"Nothing? Really?"

The deadly calm of my senses readying to deal with a threat settled over me. I took a step closer, my boots resting on the line that indicated the cell wall, daring him to do something.

"You… I told you to go."

"Like I could leave you alone after seeing how angry you were at Tabor and Mom? Not knowing what you were going to do next? I couldn't just leave. You were about to go off and then Etara would have to take you out."

"Maybe you should have let her," he snarled.

Without any conscious thought, I was suddenly right in front of him, shoving him with every ounce of force in my body. He staggered backward. I followed him, step for step as he watched me, gaze darting over my armor and my as-of-yet empty hands.

"If you ever hurt Mom again, Neko won't get a chance to save you. You won't be in any shape to put up a resistance when I call Etara in to finish the job."

His gaze wavered and then dropped.

I waited, pulse thundering in my ears, for some further level of acknowledgment, maybe a promise that he would never do that again, any hint of an apology. He gave me nothing.

Frustrated beyond words, I spun and exited the cell. The field activated as soon as I was over the line.

Striding toward Uncle Isnar, I locked away the memories of the man whom I'd proudly called my father, the one who'd rolled in the mud with me on Veria Minor, who had secretly taught me how to fight on Pentares, and guided me on his mission to unify as many people as possible, to make their lives better because all the shit he'd been through had taught him how to do that. That man was gone. This one might have looked like him, but he was a fucking disappointment. I wanted nothing further to do with him.

THIRTY-THREE

Anastassia

Neko tried again to convince Tabor to stay behind. "Ana should meet with him alone."

"No. Absolutely not," Tabor decreed.

Isnar sat at his desk watching Tabor with a quizzical smile. Neko did not appear amused in any manner. He stood beside Isnar, doing his best to drive his wishes into me with a baleful stare.

If I was going to attempt to speak to Vayen, having Tabor glaring over my shoulder wouldn't help anyone, a fact that Neko and Isnar had been dancing around for the past ten minutes.

I turned to my bristling second husband, pouring assurance through our connection. *"Neko will be with me. You trust him, don't you?"*

"Neko isn't the one I don't trust."

"I know. He's going to have to earn that back. From both of us."

"I don't like that this field prevents natural speech as well as link functions. I can't help you if I don't know what's going on."

I took his hand, breathing slowly in and out to calm both of us. *"Neko will be with me."*

He nodded slowly. *"Please woman, for the love of Geva, be careful."*

"I will. I promise." Leaving Tabor in Isnar's care, I stood and gestured for Neko to lead the way.

My first husband's keeper rested a hand on my shoulder and squeezed gently. "Thank you, Ana."

"How did the meeting with Daniel go?" I asked as we entered the lift, envisioning older Vayen facing his furious younger self, a man almost the same age as he'd been when he'd come to work for me.

"Isnar went down with him. From what I heard, I'd have to say, not well. No apologies were issued, shoving and threats ensued."

"Damn Vayen. What the hell is wrong with him?"

"The shoving and threats were Daniel."

"Oh."

Neko shook his head. "I think it's safe to say that they won't be on speaking terms any time soon."

My heart ached to hear that the once tight duo had been further torn apart. The news wasn't particularly surprising, given how stubborn they both could be, but sad, nevertheless.

"Where do you intend to release him, assuming he doesn't go off on me?"

Neko sighed. "Tabor doesn't want him anywhere near you. Politically, I'd prefer you and Vayen at least made an effort to be together in public. Tabor is your second and he shouldn't supplant your first. He can't, without undoing all the work you've done at championing this policy transition."

"I understand."

"We'll see if Isnar can make Tabor understand." Neko opened the lift door to the dark underground prison.

When the lights came on, Vayen was on the floor in the middle of his cell sitting cross-legged with his hands on his lap, facing us.

"I told him you'd be coming. For the record, he appears to be in a better state than when Daniel arrived earlier," Neko said quietly.

I wasn't sure how to take that given that nothing had been resolved when Daniel left, and yet, Vayen was better? Leaving Neko to deactivate the containment field, I cautiously approached Vayen's cell.

Vayen stood stiffly, rolling his neck and shoulders. He looked past me to Neko. "Can we have a few minutes?"

"Sorry, boss. Can't do that. Assurances have been made."

Vayen winced. "Anastassia, I wouldn't—"

"You *did* hurt me so don't even breathe those words."

He bowed his head. "I'm sorry. I am. I didn't mean to. I didn't want to."

I kept my feet safely on the outside of the cell line. If Neko needed to activate the field, I had no inclination to be stuck inside with a rampaging Vayen.

"Did you want to attack Daniel? He was only trying to protect you from yourself. You hurt him too. How are we supposed to trust you?"

"You shouldn't," he whispered.

"Don't pull that martyrish shit with me. Either you have control of your abilities or you don't."

He studied my face with forlorn eyes. "I'm trying."

"Not hard enough. I've put up with the rampant drinking. I've given you space, allowed your excuses. I've conceded with giving you everything you've wanted, even when it nearly killed me. There's nothing more I can give you. I'm empty. I'm out."

His voice wavered, "Anastassia, please."

"Go make your excuses to Buria. Unless you've lashed out at her too?"

He looked away. "She isn't speaking to me."

"Seems to be a common theme. You better thank your Geva that Neko hasn't joined those ranks yet or you'd have been dead days ago."

"I know." The quiver in his voice tugged at me. "Anastassia, please."

Even if I wanted to help or make him feel better, what the hell more could I do? He was the one out of control, and dammit, he'd used his mind shit on me. That was a line I'd never expected him to cross.

"What is it that you want from me?" I asked.

"Could you stay with me for a little while? Please?"

Tabor was waiting and likely fidgeting and driving Isnar nuts. Neko surely had better things to do.

I waved Neko over. He seemed hesitant to leave the control panel but after a moment of consideration, drew his pulse pistol and approached.

"What's the long-term plan?" I asked.

"If you're willing to release him, he can't stay here. He needs to be seen. The Iber, with you, would be ideal. The crew there reports throughout the Narvan and beyond. That should get the word out that all is well."

"All is far from well," I snapped.

"I'm aware. Publicly, I mean." He cast Vayen a sympathetic glance. "If you're not willing to stay with him on the Iber, maybe the Artorian estate? I could help monitor the situation."

The situation. That was what he was now, the man I'd loved.

I watched Vayen, trying to get a feel for what he might want, but other than looking decidedly pathetic, he was keeping his opinions to himself.

Tabor would surely vote for the Artorian estate where he trusted Neko to look out for me. But Neko was right, it had been weeks since I'd been on the Iber let alone seen anywhere with Vayen. Maybe having to maintain his public image would help keep him more in line than being able to lean on Neko, who was too tolerant of Vayen's vices.

Knowing there would be definite gnashing of teeth from Tabor no matter what I chose, and not entirely trusting Vayen myself, I decided giving into his request would be the best indicator of what our immediate future held.

"You have twenty minutes of my time."

Neko frowned. "Ana, Tabor isn't going to like the delay."

"I'm aware, but as you said, Tabor is my second. He's going to have to make peace with that for the sake of our public image."

Neko nodded tightly.

"Neko could go reassure him everything is fine," Vayen suggested.

"Nice try, boss." He backed away, taking up his position by the control panel.

I shook my head and faced Vayen. "Nothing is fine. You realize that, right?"

His head hung lower. "I know."

Silence stretched out between us as minutes slipped by with no move toward resolution.

Very slowly, he held out his hand to me. I eyed the line on the floor, knowing I was safe right where I was. If I took one step forward, I'd be taking a chance I didn't know if I was up to taking.

"Stassia, please."

Despite my intentions to be smart, to be safe, my heart flipped.

A bubble of anxiety built up in my stomach. My hands went cold. I wanted to trust him. I wanted him to be like he had been when we'd first started the Iber mission, when we'd been happy. But he wasn't and he had hurt me. Badly. Several times.

He took a hesitant step toward me. Then another.

I managed to keep my feet glued in place for a few seconds longer. One traitorous foot crossed the line.

That appeared to be all the incentive he needed. He wrapped his arms around me and hung on tightly. It was strange to not feel him in my head, to not have any indication of our bond, even weak as it was, but the dampening field blocked all of that.

"Whatever you need me to do, I'll do it," he whispered in my ear.

His open-ended offer revealed his desperation. "This is your last chance to give me an honest answer. What do you want from me, because I mean it, I don't have anything else to give you."

A tremor passed through him. "I need you beside me, to keep me whole. I thought other distractions would work, that Buria would take the edge off, but none of it is enough without you. You're my center, Stassia. Without you, I'm... Well, you saw what I am."

I let his rarely spoken honest and sincere words wrap around me for a moment. His familiar touch soothed some of the anxiety swirling inside me.

"How beside you do you need, because I will not give up Tabor."

"I wouldn't ask you to. You've got what I always wanted."

I eased my stance so that I could press my cheek against his. He made a soft approving sound.

"Your terms, whatever they might be, as long as I can be near you more often than not," he said.

Desperate, indeed.

"I'll agree to a trial period, but if you use that on any of us again, that's it."

He nodded. "Understood."

"I'll need to talk to Tabor, but then we'll give the Iber a try."

"Thank you, Stassia."

As much as I wanted to comfort him, he was the one who'd fucked up. He would have to give me a lot more than words before I could fully trust him again. I pulled out of his embrace and turned to Neko.

"Give me ten minutes to figure out an agreeable arrangement with Tabor and then bring Vayen up."

Neko snorted. "You're going to need longer than that, but sure. We need to have a talk down here anyway." All hint of humor vanished as he turned his attention back to Vayen.

As I rode the lift back to the main floor, I hoped their friendship withstood whatever was passing between them. Vayen would need all the help he could get if he wanted to remain among the living.

THIRTY-FOUR

Buria

When the knock sounded on my door, I expected a messenger from one of my security staff, Elonka popping by for a visit, or maybe a package delivery. I certainly did not expect the Advisor of All standing there, wringing his hands with his gaze bouncing from the floor to my face like a rubber ball—even if he was my contracted husband.

Torn between demanding that he leave and curiosity as to why he'd changed his mind, I fell back on my training and gestured him inside. He was the Advisor of All, after all.

He stood with his back against the door and licked his lips, his gaze finally settling on my face. "I may have said some things I didn't mean."

Glad the door was closed and that we were well out of earshot of anyone else, I ignored everything the Masters had taught me and allowed my anger out. "You sure sounded like you meant it when you said you never wanted to see me again. When you said you regretted signing a contract with me. That you regretted *everything* with me."

He worked a hand through his hair, raking it back from his face. "I was drunk."

"You're always drunk."

He winced. "Buria, I'm sorry."

"You threw the bottle at me. You hit me with the damned bottle, Vayen. What the hell?"

"I'm sorry. I don't remember doing that."

"That's why I called Daniel in. I didn't know what else you were going to do."

"I'm sorry. I'll try to be better."

"I don't believe you." I shook my head. "You've made no effort to make us appear legitimate, hiding us away in that suite on the Iber. You don't want any semblance of an actual life with me. You wanted me in your bed and that's it. And while that was fun. I'm over it. Either treat me like your wife or leave."

He blinked a few times and then cocked his head, studying me. A slow smile crept over his lips and lit his eyes. "All right. Pack your things. You're moving."

"Moving where? I don't get a say? I can't just leave. I have a job here and I'm not giving that up no matter how much you smile at me."

"The top floor. I claimed that apartment years ago so I could be near you when I wanted to be. Without being creepy. Unless you think that's creepy. I didn't mean it to be."

He'd done what? "You've stayed there? In this building?"

He nodded. "On occasion before and recently, when you are too angry to talk to me."

"Like now? How would you know? You haven't been talking to me either."

"Buria, we might not be bonded, but I can skim your thoughts. I mean, I don't do that often, but well, when words aren't an option between us..."

Skimming my thoughts? I drove my fists onto my hips. "You were really damned drunk that night. Did you actually remember what you yelled at me or did you skim that too?"

He glanced away.

"That's what I thought. You know what? I'm not moving any-where. Not until you prove you mean to do better. If that's too much work for you, then sleep upstairs and tell everyone you're with me so you can keep your precious political face clean."

Something dark and ugly flashed over his face and then vanished. His nostrils flared as he inhaled. "All right. How can I prove it to you?"

"When you're with me, no drinking and no bang. No other drugs. Either you want to be with me or you don't."

"I do," he said softly.

"Then prove that I can do for you what you need without the rest."

He nodded, licking his lips and starting toward me.

I held up my hands. "I don't mean right now. I'm still mad at you."

"I could maybe convince you to be less mad?"

"I mean it, Vayen. I'm not just here for sex."

He slowed his approach but came to stand before me. "Would you at least like to come see the apartment? Maybe doing some shopping to make it your place would help you be less mad?"

"You mean our place. We have a marriage contract."

"And it will be your apartment after those two years."

His declaration made my breath catch in my throat. How many of my thoughts had he skimmed? While I scrambled over the future plans I'd been pondering recently, praying there was nothing there that might set him off, I managed to say, "You can see the future now? How do you know we won't renew?"

Vayen smiled sadly. "You won't." He leaned down to kiss my forehead. "But that's all right. We'll enjoy now."

With a chill in my bones, I took his hand and went upstairs to see what my future looked like.

THIRTY-FIVE

Anastassia

Vayen's week-long probation on the Iber had gone well enough considering that Daniel made every effort not to be in the same room as his father. The few brief encounters that had been unavoidable had been cold and impersonal on both sides.

Now, four months later, while in the public eye, Vayen and I smiled at one another, I allowed his arm around me, and we shared amicable conversations. Within our suite, he slept on his side of the bed and kept to himself during waking hours, mostly working through his link near wherever I was sitting with my datapad or resting. The majority of our private conversations revolved around finding a solution to the effects of my Nacombic poisoning.

He might have been entirely hands-off on that quest for the first couple of weeks when I'd stayed with Tabor, but now he was obsessed. He'd taken me to the Artorian University for long days of observation and evaluation and then to a host of specialists on Artor, Karin, Jal, and even to Peter Strauss on the Verian Station. In the depths of his desperation for a cure, he'd Jumped me to Pentares to see if my kind had any solutions. The last months had been a whirlwind of Jumping, doctors, and medications and therapies that hadn't worked. All the while, the negative effects caused by a single drop of Nacombic continued their slow compounding damage on my internal organs.

The main takeaway everyone had concluded was that Nacombic provided three alternatives. An instant death, a fast death, and a long, painful death. I'd opted for the last one.

The Iber's medical team, composed of the brightest minds from the Narvan, had been the first to examine me with Daniel and Tabor in attendance. Now, I was back with Vayen beside me.

"You'd know more than me about what's going on in there," Etara said, holding her hands over my stomach while staring Vayen down. "I'm not sure what you think I can do."

From my position on the examination table in the clinic on the Iber, I tried not to pay attention to the medical staff lurking nearby, doing their best to be covert in their attempt to hear what was going on.

"The University doctors say they can slow the progress, but that's not stopping or reversing it. What do you see?" Vayen asked.

Etara dropped her pose of attempting to see anything. She rested her small hand on my arm.

"I see a man demanding to alter the natural order of the universe."

Wrath spiked in his gaze. The entire room filled with a malevolent cloud. The staff fled to the far side of the clinic, pressing themselves against the wall. A few ran out the door entirely.

"Vayen," I said as calmly as I could manage through his thick broadcast of panic-inducing terror. "You're doing it again."

"I know," he said darkly, his face impassive.

His broadcasting came to an abrupt end as he dropped to his knees, grasping his head. Yet, he still glared at Etara.

"Would you like me to continue?" she asked. "I think it's safe to assume that Ana would prefer you remain among the living while she's still one of them."

"I would," I affirmed.

Vayen's head bowed, but unlike the other recent times he'd briefly slipped into dark mode, he didn't apologize or attempt to make amends.

As he defiantly pulled himself to his feet, Etara cast me a worried glance. He'd been slipping more frequently in the past weeks and neither of us had him under much semblance of control.

Etara maintained occasional contact with Buria, checking in on Vayen's behavior. Whatever Buria was doing was working, he seemed to be maintaining more control when he was on Brustus. Or maybe it wasn't her at all, but being away from the stress of the Iber and our mission.

In my desperation to help Vayen, I'd given my blessing to him drinking again. That, along with being near me seemed to mostly keep his dark urges suitably dulled. Except, he didn't drink before we met with anyone about my declining health.

Etara quickly tucked her concern away, replacing it with a stern scowl. "For that less-than-grey outburst, you owe me a full day of diagnosis work when we meet our next prospective union members."

"You can shove your—"

I sat up as fast as I could, making me light-headed. Thankfully my voice remained firm, though spots danced before my eyes. "Vayen. Enough."

"It's not," he groused. "What good are any of them if they can't fix this?" He gestured forcefully at my torso.

No amount of even the death-bringer's threats had brought about a solution to what I'd done.

"It can't be fixed. I did this and now I have to live with it."

"You won't though. That's the problem."

I slid off the table, blinking the spots away. The moment my feet hit the floor, blackness rushed in. Too fast. Dammit, the doctors said I had to take my time getting up and down, but I didn't want to. I wanted to move as I always had.

Vayen caught me as I faltered, instantly my comforting mate rather than wrath monster. That alone was worth the cost of nearly fainting.

Cara, one of the Artorian doctors I'd been working with to prepare for the delivery of Daniel's hybrid children, approached us hesitantly. "We've gone over the care plan the University provided based on your most recent evaluation. There was a note I'm supposed to pass along." She eyed Vayen warily.

"Yes"? I prompted.

"I'm assuming this means something to you? Nan says, you're even now?"

"I suppose we are." I squeezed Vayen's hand, hoping to keep his attention on me so he didn't spook the staff again.

He pulled me closer, my back pressed against his broad chest. His arms closed around me, locking me against him.

"So what is this plan?" he asked, his tone verging on hostile.

Etara gave him a warning look. "Do you want to owe me two days?"

Cara glanced between the three of us as though she wished to be anywhere else before returning her attention to me. "The University will be sending a canister of specially programmed nanites. We're to run them through your system for six hours each week. We will do a thorough assessment before and after. They'll evaluate you once a month in-person and fine-tune the programming as necessary to minimize the progression of declining cell production. They've also supplied a diet plan and several new medications to try. I or doctor Viketi will administer those daily or provide appropriate dosages to a care provider of your choice if you will be elsewhere."

"But she can work like normal, right? Continue her usual activities?" Vayen asked.

Cara turned to Etara. What passed between the two of them, I couldn't see, but I guessed she was silently asking for help so as not to set Vayen off again.

I thought it best to save both of them from his wrath. I'd already had several vid conferences with the team Nan had assembled to oversee my care plan, though I hadn't yet broached those details with Vayen.

I leaned into him, hoping the peace he garnered from my proximity balanced what I was about to say. "I'm supposed to not push myself, take it easy, and only do light exercise. So, if by working you mean taking vid calls and sitting in on meetings, then yes, I can continue working. As to anything else, probably not."

And I wasn't about to push my luck either. As it already was, I was tired all the time, generally feeling like shit, and not sleeping well except when I was with Tabor. Being near him brought me back to near normal, but as soon as I returned to the Iber, or even if Tabor was in the next room when I was at his estate on Rok, the effects of the poison were back at the forefront.

I didn't think it was possible, but Vayen managed to hold me tighter yet delicately enough that it didn't hurt. His chin rested on the top of my head. Tucked against him, I felt safe, like he wouldn't allow anything to harm me further. A tenderness that brought tears to my eyes flowed through our bonded connection.

"When the nanites are ready, please let me know, I'll get them myself," he said quietly. Calmly.

"Yes, Advisor. If you'll both give me a moment, we're getting the first round of medication prepared. Once that is administered, you're free to go." Cara left us under Etara's care to gather what she needed.

While I had spent time in the clinic, consulting with the staff on occasion, that had been on my terms. That I was somehow no longer free to come and go chaffed me. But I'd brought this on myself. Slowing the progression sounded a hell of a lot better than looming death. Not that I feared my end, hell, I'd far outlived my own expectations, but now that I shared a bond with Tabor and seeing the outright fear in Vayen's eyes, I wasn't in a hurry to make my exit.

"Once they're done, we have the rest of the day. Where would you like to go?" Vayen said in my ear.

"Maybe home? We haven't seen Neko and Hedvika in a while."

Neko knew how to watch over Vayen and keep him contained when I wasn't up to it, and from what I'd read of the side effects of the medication they were going to shoot into me for the rest of my days, I wasn't going to be up to much.

"Sure. That sounds good." He kept me tightly in his arms.

As much as I enjoyed the days I spent with Vayen not working, I secretly yearned to be near Tabor for the relief he offered me. I did my best to hide that from Vayen, but when he'd suggested that I spend a couple more days a week at Tabor's estate, I didn't have it in me to argue, even if that meant he'd spend more time with Buria. But he hadn't. I loved him for that.

The crew didn't.

Etara, Daniel, and Ikeri kept me briefed on his behavior when neither Buria or I was around to distract him from everything he kept pent up inside. I'd asked Markus to visit, and he'd done so twice, also providing a distraction for Vayen, or perhaps, more of a reason to keep himself under control. Unfortunately, Markus was only there for a couple of days at a time. Ikeri helped calm Vayen as much as she could, but with Vayen devoted to my care and me not up to much work, she and Daniel were spearheading our mission. Our children were grown and busy.

While Vayen had managed to return to good terms with Jey and Isnar, neither of them was in a position to hold him accountable, and they no longer had the close camaraderie that Neko shared with Vayen. I was going to have to figure out how to stay conscious and coherent enough to be his center while also finding the relief I needed to keep my own temper in check. Being in constant pain made me edgy.

What I really wanted was to curl up on the couch next to Tabor and take a nap while he worked. But it wasn't one of Tabor's days and Vayen needed me. I sighed.

Cara returned with an assistant bearing a tray. "Would you please have a seat?" She gestured to the examination table.

Vayen reluctantly let me go. He stayed only two steps away, barely giving Cara and her assistant room to work.

The first injection didn't seem so bad, only a rush of heat down my neck that offered almost instantaneous relief to my perpetual aches and pains. I gave Vayen a reassuring smile.

Next came the ordeal of swallowing three large pills and two the size of a stim. The small ones were easy. The larger ones stuck in my throat, making me want to gag. I swallowed the rest of the water the assistant offered me to get them down.

Cara gave me a warning look before the next injection. I braced myself but still wasn't prepared for the burning sensation that raced through every vein and lingered there. A metallic taste filled my mouth. My face flushed.

"Stassia." Vayen's concern flooded my head.

I held up a shaking hand, unable to form words.

"That one should get easier once it builds up in your system," Cara said. "You may want to lie down for the last one."

"What is that? What are you giving her?" Vayen demanded.

"The treatment you demanded to prolong Anastassia's suffering," Etara answered without mercy. "Let the doctor do her job."

"That's not what I—"

I held out my hand to him, hoping he'd shut up and take it. The burning, though less intense, remained inside me, rubbing me raw.

His large hand enveloped mine, warm, comforting, safe.

"Here we go," Cara warned.

A tingle entered my body, spreading from my arm to my chest and then outward, until every inch of me filled with jittery energy, like getting a light shock everywhere all at once. Sweat poured from every pore. I couldn't keep my eyes open or seem to catch my breath.

"Breathe through it. It will fade," Cara assured me.

"Anastassia." Vayen squeezed my hand. "How often does she have to do these?" he asked Cara.

"Every day. Four of the pills twice a day. Two of them three times."

"All right," he said weakly.

Once Cara and Etara had backed away, Vayen pulled me close. "Let's get you into bed so you can be more comfortable."

I nodded and wasn't surprised that he Jumped us from the clinic straight to our bedroom at the Artorian estate. My hands felt semi-numb as I struggled through pulling my shirt over my head and fumbled with removing my shoes. My pants were becoming a frustrating challenge as the room wavered and blurred.

Tender hands helped me out of my pants and guided me into bed, pulling just the right combination of sheet and blanket over me how I liked it. Rather than retreating to his side of the bed or leaving the room to work, he stayed sitting on the edge of the bed beside me, stroking my hair.

"Are you all right here?"

I made an assenting noise, wanting to drift off and be oblivious for a while.

"I mean here with me. He can do more for you than I can."

I felt around for his other hand and squeezed it. "Here, with you is good."

"It's not," he choked out before leaning over to kiss my cheek, "but I love you for lying."

When I woke five hours later, I opened my eyes to an unfamiliar room, but a welcome face. "Tabor? Where am I?"

He shook his head and chuckled. "Do you truly have so many rooms in your grand Artorian estate, my dearest and only, that you don't even recognize this one?"

"What?" I sat up slowly, trying to shake the fog of medication-induced sleep from my brain.

"Vayen asked me to stay with you, to help ease the discomfort while the medication does whatever it's supposed to do." He waved a hand in the air.

"He did what? He invited you to the house?"

"Yes, he did," Tabor said softly, running a finger along my jawline. "I stand by my statement that he's an alcoholic asshole, but he does love you, and I think he's finally understanding the proper conduct of a bonded mate."

I didn't know what to say other than I was immensely thankful. With Tabor's bond cancelling out Vayen's, I couldn't convey those feelings directly to him. I'd have to use words later.

"How are you feeling?" Tabor asked.

"Better." I burrowed in closer to him and closed my eyes, enjoying the soft hummming comfort that our bond provided.

"Good. Vayen said he did a diagnosis on you when you first fell asleep. We should have him take another look and see if all that discomfort was worth it."

"You seriously want to have Vayen come into this bedroom right now and do his diagnosis thing on me? While you're here, in the house I share with him?"

Tabor shrugged. "He invited me. He offered the room. I could give a viscu's ass what he thinks about anything else, but your wellbeing is one thing we both agree on."

"All right. I guess?" The absurdity of it all made me giddy. Or maybe that was a side-effect of the treatment. "How about, for the sake of my sanity, I get dressed and we go out to a slightly more neutral space to speak to Mr. Death-bringer."

Tabor nodded and reached over to the bedside table to hand me my neatly folded clothes.

"You folded them?" I laughed as I dressed.

"He handed them to me that way. I thought you said he never folds anything."

"He doesn't." Warmth flooded through me.

We found Vayen and Neko deep in a discussion that ended the moment Neko caught sight of Tabor beside me. Panic flashed across his face. He shot to his feet.

"Sit," barked Vayen. "I invited him."

Neko sank back into his chair, staring at Vayen with wide eyes.

Having Vayen and Tabor in such close proximity confused my senses. There was an unfamiliar unity to it, like I was more whole, more complete. I had a sudden urge to cry that had nothing to do with being sad.

After working past the lump in my throat, I managed to say, "You wanted to take a second look?"

Vayen nodded. "How are you feeling?"

Like I needed to sit down. Between his open concern and Tabor's, and Neko visibly losing his mind over having his two favorite people in the same room on apparently amiable terms, there were altogether too many loud feelings going on.

Tabor pulled out a chair at the table for me without any urging on my part. I gratefully took it.

"I honestly don't know how I'm actually feeling. The bond masks a lot." I'd have to wait until Tabor's cloud of calm and comfort departed to get a true read on my status, but I very much didn't want him to leave just yet.

As Vayen leaned forward to rest his hand on my thigh, Tabor stepped back. Vayen shook his head, his voice slightly distant. "I want to see the difference. Touch her."

Tabor rested his hand on my shoulder. I slid one of mine over

Tabor's and the other over Vayen's. In that instant, all was well in the universe. Peace settled over me.

I became aware of Vayen in my mind, not like our bond, but in my thoughts, observing. He said Ikeri called it wisping, but he apparently wanted me to know he was there rather than only skulking about.

Vayen gasped, his fingers flexing on my leg. "It's like the calming balm and so much more. Amazing."

"Yes."

"Thank you for allowing me to see the bond," he said more to Tabor than to me.

"You're welcome," Tabor said in a tight but polite tone that made me proud of him. He'd grown remarkably since the first days we'd met, back when he was giddy to be around me and awed by Vayen. I sent him the sensation equivalent of a hug.

I felt Vayen departing my mind and going distant from his body as he did when diagnosing.

He was silent a long while, his hand still under mine. When he came back to himself, he nodded slowly. "I can see what the medicine is doing. Knowing that, I'll look again in a few days. I'll have a better idea if it's making progress in inhibiting the cell decay then." He kept his hand on me as he looked to Tabor. "I'd like to gauge the effect your active bond has on her health. Would you leave the room?"

Tabor squeezed my shoulder and then backed away. The moment he left the room, the air grew colder, silent, more stagnant. A queasiness lit in my stomach and the usual aches returned to the forefront of my awareness. If the treatment had made any significant difference, I couldn't feel it. Then again, they expected me to undergo this every day so I supposed that hadn't been any sort of a quick fix. In fact, it wasn't a fix at all, merely a slowing of the decay. Prolonging the inevitable, as Etara had harshly pointed out.

Vayen went distant again. Neko got up and headed in the direction Tabor had gone. When Vayen came back to himself, his somber expression filled me with dread.

"What? What did you see?"

"You should stay with him, not me," he said thickly. "My bond to you offers you nothing. His..." Vayen sat back and rubbed his hands over his face. "The difference in your physiology is remarkable when his bond is active."

"I'm not going to argue, but I don't want to leave you either."

Sorrow lined his face, highlighting wrinkles at the corners of his eyes I hadn't noticed until just then. I'd seen him exhausted before, but this was a different kind of weary.

"How are you doing?" I asked.

"Don't worry about me."

"But I do."

He smiled. "I'll talk to Tabor and see what we can work out. You need him. I need you." He chuckled. "We're a fine mess, aren't we?"

"We are."

For the first time in a long while, I had the urge to kiss him. I got up slowly, and then sat on his lap before he got the chance to stand. With Tabor out of the room, I could feel Vayen. A heavy sense of sorrow flowed between us.

I leaned in and kissed him, sinking my fingers into his thick hair. He was hesitant, but then he kissed me with the fervor that I fondly remembered. I was distantly aware of a set of footsteps approaching and then coming to a sudden halt before making a speedy retreat.

After a few minutes, I pulled back, resting my forehead against his. "You know, in a traditional Jalvian home, all the spouses live together. When you're both nearby like you were, when both bonds are active, I feel the best I can be."

"You can feel mine when he's right there?"

"Not like now, when we're alone, but yes." I took his natural hand and pressed it to my heart. "I do feel you and you do help."

His eyes took on a glassy sheen. "I'll think about it. I don't know as Buria would be on board with that. Or you, with her."

"You have a point. Sorry, I forgot about her for a moment. You were being all sorts of distracting."

He grinned, his old charming self for a second. "Any time you're up for a distraction, you let me know. That's your call, but I'm definitely up for it if and when you are."

"Noted."

"If that isn't going to be right now, I should go talk to Tabor before I push my luck and point out that our very soundproofed bedroom is right over there."

It lightened my heart to hear his playful tone, to know he hadn't lost it amid all we were dealing with. After a quick kiss to his cheek, I slid off his lap. "We wouldn't want you to press your luck and undo any of the very favorable progress you may have made with me."

He smiled solemnly. "We definitely wouldn't want to undo that."

"Go on then. I'm going to go find a more comfortable chair to curl up in while the two of you fight over me."

Vayen grinned, but shook his head. "I don't think I'd win but I'll attempt to play nice."

"Thank you." I sent him all the gratitude and warmth I could muster and then went to the common room to sink into a plush chair.

Away from both of my mates, the side-effects of the medication were greatly amplified. Chilled, I reached for the thin blue blanket Hedvika kept on the back of the seat beside the one I'd chosen and covered myself. My head began to throb. The metallic taste returned to my dry throat. Vayen might not think his bond offered me any comfort, but it did. It was a shame that he couldn't diagnose me from a distance so he could see the difference he made.

As time crawled by, I considered summoning one of them, or maybe both so I could find a little relief. I was in a silent debate over which one I was craving more when Hedvika appeared.

"Neko is monitoring the negotiations so you don't need to worry about them. Can I get you anything?"

I'd been told not to touch stims under any circumstances and I didn't dare take anything else on top of what Cara had given me. "Water, a heavier blanket, and a cold cloth?"

Hedvika smiled. "Right away."

I woke to her settling a thick blanket over me. A glass of water sat on the table beside me, and seeing me awake, she handed me the cloth. I took a long drink of water and then folded the cloth and draped it over my forehead.

"Thank you."

Settling back against the chair, I again closed my eyes. Not that I necessarily wanted to sleep more, but sleep did offer a welcome oblivion to the unpleasant reality of my body.

"Stassia." I woke to Vayen gently shaking my shoulder. Tabor stood behind him.

I yawned and rubbed my dry eyes. "You're both still alive? You have a plan then?"

"Yes. We'll deal with that later." Vayen peeled the blankets off me and handed me a long grey sweater that had hung in my closet for years. It had been a gift from a client on Veria Minor, made from fibers she'd woven herself.

"You might want that instead of the blanket. We need to go."

I sat forward to work my arms into the sweater. "Go where?"

Tabor grinned. "The Iber. We're about to be grandparents."

Daniel

Meera crushed my fingers as another contraction hit. The medical staff bustled around us, readying the room for the birth of my first child. Arden held Meera's other hand, her own stomach heavy with my second child.

"You're never touching me again," Meera decreed just as my mother walked into the room, followed by Tabor and my father.

My mother nodded to the doctor and strode over to observe Meera's readings on the vid beside the bed. "Don't even bother with threats like that," she said lightly. "After a few weeks, you'll be right back in his bed. These Ta'set men are magical like that. Making you forget all kinds of things with one of their smiles."

My father grinned, watching her every move. Tabor hung back by the doorway of the now very cramped room. He smiled at me and watched us all with misty eyes.

That my mother might have been willing to overlook what my father done to her and to me because of a fucking smile made me want to punch something. I very much wanted to demand that he leave the room but I didn't want to upset my mother, who, though she was here as she'd said she would be, had an almost transparent quality about her. She'd mentioned that she was starting a new round of treatment today. It appeared to be taking a lot out of her.

Meera groaned. Once her jaw unclenched, she glared at me. "It's going to take a lot more than a damned smile."

As much as I wanted to calm her, the sharp spikes of pain rippling over our bonded connection and the ear-piercing static each contraction brought prevented me doing anything helpful.

"Where the hells is Ikeri? She's supposed to be here," I yelled at no one in particular.

It was three contractions later before my Seeker sister finally showed up. She offered me an apologetic nod and hurried to take her place behind Meera where she pressed herself against the wall to stay out of the way. A sudden cloud of calm fell upon me and I assumed Meera too because her grip on my hand eased. The next contraction passed with only loud breathing and no groaning. The static dropped back into a semblance of our usual melody.

"Thank you."

Ikeri gave me a mental hug.

An alarm went off on the monitor. Medical staff poured through the doorway, bringing more equipment with them. Habit drove me to lock gazes with the man I used to rely on for safety.

"She'll be all right. Your mother will make sure of it," my father assured me as one of the staff asked him and Tabor to step outside so they had room to work.

In an instant, I forgot about him and lost two and a half hours to panic, despite Ikeri's calming efforts. I was entirely wrapped up in my bonded connection with Meera, offering reassurance that I desperately needed to believe myself. My mother and the clinic staff worked to keep Meera conscious so she could deliver the baby naturally like she wanted to. Her eyes had just rolled back for the second time when the doctor announced that we had a daughter.

The room seemed to go silent though I could see the staff injecting Meera with something. My mother manually monitored Meera's pulse. She spoke quietly to one of the nurses, who nodded. Two others were off in the corner where they'd taken our daughter. Arden grabbed my hand. That felt distant too, like this was maybe a dream.

"Daniel, can you feel Meera? Listen to your mother."

The fear in her voice snapped me back into the flurry of activity. The cacophony rushed over me. I blinked rapidly.

Feel Meera. I followed our bonded connection and locking onto her, held her tightly in my mind.

"I can feel her."

My mother nodded. "Keep her with you. We've almost got the bleeding stopped. I had the same thing with Ikeri." She glanced over to where my sister stood, her face ashen.

Ikeri may have witnessed many things in our time on the Iber, but this was her first birthing. The process did not appear to sit well with her. For that matter, it wasn't sitting all that well with me either.

Remembering how Tabor had kept my mother with us when she'd been fighting for her life in the tank, I did my best to emulate him. Focusing everything on talking softly to Meera, being as calm as I could so she wouldn't panic in her mind, I blocked out the activity in the room. It wasn't until I felt movement in the warm hand I held that I dared divide my attention between her and everyone else.

There were fewer people in the room now. My mother, with dark circles under her eyes, sat on a stool beside Meera, watching the monitoring vid. Ikeri and Arden stood in the corner where they'd taken my daughter. A wrapped bundle lay in Arden's arms. She smiled down on it while Ikeri pulled back a corner of the blanket to run her fingers over the baby inside.

A nurse darted in, whispered with my mother, and then left.

Meera's eyes fluttered open. "Where is she? Is she all right?"

Arden hurried over and placed the wrapped bundle beside Meera. She smiled at me, her now empty hands going to her own stomach. "Someone seems to be eager to meet his sister."

Meera grinned, peeling back the blanket just far enough to see the dark wisps of hair on our daughter's head. She ran her finger over our baby's cheeks and then her little nose. "She's just perfect."

"Just like her mother," I said.

Meera beamed up at me.

"What's her name?" asked my mother.

"Mika," I announced.

"I've had the name picked out since I was a little girl," Meera said.

"I like it." My mother rubbed her eyes and stifled a yawn. "Would you mind if I borrowed little Mika for a moment? Now that all is well, I'm sure her grandfathers would like an update and to meet her. Then we'll leave you be."

As strong as I knew my mother to be, she'd been exhausted when she'd arrived hours ago. She looked like she was having a hard time keeping herself on her feet, let alone holding a newborn.

"I'll come with you."

I held out my arms to Meera, who placed my daughter in my hands for the first time. Mika was so much lighter than I expected.

I had a daughter.

When I tore my gaze from the sleeping face in my arms, my mother was smiling at me. She nodded toward the door and opened it. Tabor and my father sat a seat apart in the row of chairs in the hallway. While both of them had appeared to be busy on their links, they simultaneously leapt to their feet upon spotting us.

My father glanced at my mother.

"Meera is fine," she said.

His gaze remained locked on her.

"I'll be fine too."

He gave her a dubious nod but turned his attention to me while Tabor attached himself to my mother. The strain on her face eased as she leaned into him. He wrapped an arm around her even though my father was right there. I expected some snarling or a cutting remark, but my father's attention was locked solely on me. His sharp and abrasive demeanor melted away as I handed Mika to him.

He held my daughter delicately in the large hands I'd seen covered in blood, pounding on people, slamming into me. He ran a giant finger lightly along her cheek. Her eyes opened and she let out a cry that made me want to grab her back and return her to Meera where she belonged, rather than in the hands of my death-bringer father. But he held Mika to his chest and spoke softly to her. She quieted.

Vague memories reminded me that my father had mostly been the one to raise us when we'd lived on Veria Minor. Despite all that had changed in him since, it seemed he'd retained his knack for childcare.

Tabor and my mother were engaged in a hushed conversation, their attention focused on each other. I didn't know what to expect from my father as we hadn't exchanged a friendly word in a long while. I was still waiting for his apology for slamming me around and using his Arpex shit on me, but I took a deep breath and attempted to extend a truce for the day.

"Her name is Mika."

"Mika," he repeated, rubbing her tiny fingers that were wrapped around his thumb.

When he finally tore his gaze from my daughter to look up at me, our natural connection exploded into life. A rush of love and pride brought an instant lump to my throat. In that moment all that had been standing between us fell away. He tenderly placed Mika back in my arms.

He stepped back, his face returning to its stony exterior. His emotional exchange switched off. Despite what he'd shared with me, we were right back to where we'd started. I didn't want to be back there. I wanted my father.

"Dad, what did I—"

He spun on his heel and left.

The conversation beside me came to an abrupt halt. "Where did he go?" my mother asked.

"Hells if I know."

"He seemed…" My mother shook her head. "I'll talk to him."

"Don't waste your energy." I did my best to cover my disappointment and handed Mika over to her second grandfather.

Tabor held her uncertainly. He glanced at my mother.

She nodded. "You're doing fine."

"I've never held a baby before. Never thought I'd get to. Thank you for this." He grinned at me, melting away some of my paternal resentment. "If you need anything, you'll let me know?"

My mother rolled her eyes. "You just admitted you don't know anything about babies and you're throwing out a blanket offer like that? Next thing you know he'll take you up on it and you'll have sleepless nights with a wailing infant on your hands."

"That would be perfectly fine by me. I'll figure it out."

"I suppose I could offer some tips." My mother winked.

Their lighthearted banter made me laugh. "In a few weeks I may take you up on that, but I'll need mother here for Arden's turn."

"Anytime." Tabor handed Mika back to me and wrapped his arms around my mother instead. "This was supposed to be his time, but since he's being an ass, I vote you stay with me."

She kissed his cheek but slipped out of his arms. "Be that as it may, if it's his time, I should deal with his assiness before we have another situation on our hands. One of you will share whatever arrangement you hammered out with me at some point?"

"I'll transfer the schedule to your datapad."

My mother nodded and then gave me a quick side hug. "Congratulations. Welcome to the pure exhaustion of parenthood."

"Thank you for being here. For helping."

"Of course. I'll try to rest up before the next one."

Apart from Tabor, she again took on a brittle transparency. She offered me a smile that failed to animate her face and then headed off in the direction my father had gone.

Tabor also watched her leave. When she was out of sight, he turned to me. "I did mean that, you know. Anytime."

"I know. Thank you."

He nodded and then Jumped.

I might not have the father I wanted, but it seemed Geva had offered me a second one, and for that, I thanked her.

Buria

THIRTY-SEVEN

Vayen stood in the kitchen, absently stirring something in a pan on the cooktop. It seemed like absently covered everything he did lately. However, that was an improvement over throwing things, screaming at me, and drowning himself in alcohol and bang.

I watched him over the datapad in my hands from where I sat on the very comfortable couch I'd picked out for the sitting room just off the dining room and in view of the kitchen to the left. He hadn't been joking about letting me buy whatever I wanted for our apartment. The credit chip he'd given me seemed to be bottomless. He'd never questioned the cost of anything or my choices, just kept refilling the balance on the chip and went about his day. Mostly I did my shopping on days he was with Ana. Doing it in front of him felt blatantly spiteful.

Showing off my purchases was one of the safe things I could talk about with Elonka. She was in awe of my recent spending and had helped me pick out a few things, giggling manically over the prices. Gamnock was lucky that he put his first wife in charge of household finances. Elonka had expensive tastes.

Vayen finally snapped out of whatever had him occupied and bustled around the kitchen. A few minutes later he set two steaming plates on the table.

"I hope you're hungry," he called out, peering around and then spotting me on the couch.

I switched the datapad off and set it down to join him at the table. The nest of noodles covered in a creamy white sauce and topped with slices of seared prantha made my mouth water. He might be distracted, but he could definitely cook.

"What were you all wrapped up in?" I asked, waving at his head as I picked up my fork with my other hand.

"Fucking Ocelon. I regret ever approaching that damned planet." He sighed. "They've managed to pull together their own union of dissenters."

Still dealing with my own slippery bunch of youthful dissention here on Brustus, I understood his frustration. "How much of an issue are they?"

"They've managed to send out messengers to spread negativity against us to nearly every world and station we've tried to incorporate. They're not making our mission easy. Not that it ever was. There are enough rumors following me around without their help."

Rumors. He still hadn't accepted that most of those were truths. I kept that observation to myself and inhaled the aromatic steam floating up from my plate. My mouth watered.

"There's some wine in the cold storage if you want. I put some in the sauce."

Was this a test or even worse, was he asking me to test him? I didn't keep any alcohol in the apartment, not only because I didn't drink much, but because I didn't want to tempt him to drink at all. That he'd brought a bottle and was offering it to me was new.

I put on a smile and decided to see where this was going to go. "Why not."

He got up and went to the kitchen, returning shortly with a single glass of pale amber wine. Condensation beaded on the glass. He placed it beside my plate and returned to his seat. Though he picked up his fork, he didn't do anything with it.

My stomach rumbled. He could stare off into nothing if he wanted, I was hungry. I took a bite and then couldn't stop.

"You like it?"

I nodded, too busy chewing.

"Tabor's cook gave me the recipe for the sauce. Mycel, you remember him from the signing ceremony?"

"I remember his food."

Vayen chuckled. "He's been helping me figure out what to feed Anastassia when she's with me that follows her restricted diet. Even with his help, she isn't eating as much as she should."

As if realizing he was veering off into Ana conversation over our dinner, he shoved a bite in his mouth and chewed slowly. At least he was making an effort at conversation.

"Meera and Mika are doing well?"

He nodded, smiling. "Quite. I saw them yesterday."

"Oh? And Arden with the new baby too?" I asked, carefully leaving out any mention of his son. That particular topic seemed to lead to an instant rotten mood.

Vayen smiled. "Dreydon? He's a kicking and punching little ball of energy. He's either sleeping or flailing every limb. No in between."

I'd yet to meet the grandchildren in person, but Vayen had proudly shown me still frames. Young children weren't really my thing anyway and our time together was limited. I preferred to spend that publicly when possible, in the hopes of both helping his cause and being acknowledged as his second wife.

"If he's that active at three months, just think of what a handful he'll be at three years."

His smile faded. He nodded somberly.

Not sure where I'd gone wrong with that comment, I tried the wine and scrambled for something else to say that might keep him in a positive mood.

I held up the glass and then took another sip. "This is very good."

"I thought you might like that one. Not too sweet. Not to dry."

"You tried it?"

"Dinner at Tabor's," he said quietly.

As far as I knew, he was on speaking terms with Ana's second but that was it. "You had dinner with them? At his house?"

He eyed my wineglass and licked his lips. "Yes. The nanite flushes are working to slow the declining operation of Anastassia's organs, but the treatments to allow her to host the Nanites take a lot out of her. It goes better for her if we're both there."

"You and Tabor. Together?"

He nodded.

She'd been undergoing the Nanite treatments for months. This was the first I'd heard of him and Tabor supporting Ana together. And being at Tabor's home in a capacity other than just dropping her off. Staying there, eating with them. Just how *there* was he exactly?

I drank half my wine, the question dangling on my tongue. Maybe it would be better received if I made a preemptive peace offering. "You could have a glass, if you want."

He shook his head. "The agreement was none."

"I know, but I'm willing to—"

"Don't be willing. I need you to hold me to this dry time. Anastassia conceded a few weeks in. Without anyone to check me, it will be too easy to fall back into it."

"All right." I did have to give him credit for that, but the damned question demanded to be asked. Was I the odd spouse out? "Are the three of you...sleeping together?'"

He froze, his fork halfway in his mouth. He set the bite down uneaten. "Not in the way you're implying, no." He took a deep drink of his water, clearly wishing it was something stronger and sat back in his chair. "Like I said, she's better when we're both there. Mostly it's him, helping her. I've seen undeniable evidence of that, but she's adamant that I help too. We've set up a shared bedroom at his place and at the Artorian estate. Mostly she's with one or the other of us, but when she's having a bad day, we're both there if we can be."

Tabor had been given his own room at the Artorian estate? I drained the rest of my wine, fuming over the recollection of my reception there. Not that I had any inclination to share a bed with Tabor and Ana, but that Vayen did, even if it had nothing to do with sex, made my jaw clench.

"Do you want more?" he asked calmly.

"Yes. I'll get it." I went into the kitchen, poured a third of the remaining contents, drank them in full Vayen fashion, and then emptied the bottle into the glass and returned to the table.

He'd finished half of his meal by the time I sat down. Since I didn't drink often, the two quickly imbibed glasses were making me feel hazy.

He ate in silence for a while, watching me warily. "Can I tell you something? I guess, more to the point, can I tell you something and be assured that you will keep it to yourself?"

That got my curiosity going. I set down my fork and eyed my wine glass. I took a drink of water instead. "All right?"

"Anastassia and I aren't... We haven't been together intimately since the night I went off on everyone. She hasn't entirely forgiven me yet. Maybe she never will."

The wine I'd slammed took the hard edges off of everything in the room, including him. And his announcement. No wonder he didn't care about the credits I was spending. I laughed. "So the only time you're currently getting any sex is with me?"

He nodded slowly, scowling at my glass.

Finally, I had something from him that she didn't. "If you're going to finish eating, you should do that. We have business to attend to."

"Do we?"

"If you're all mine, we definitely do."

He eyed his plate and mine. "We could heat this up later."

"Good plan." I held out my hand, admiring the soft lines of my arm and his face as he came closer. "I may need a little guidance."

"I think I can manage that."

He lifted me onto my feet and then into his arms to whisk me into the bedroom where he settled onto the tall, thick mattress and luxurious layers of silken sheets and soft blankets that I'd bought with his credits.

If Ana didn't want him, I'd take everything he had to give.

"You could stay more often," I suggested.

In the weeks since his announcement that Ana had cut him off, spending time in bed with me seemed to be all he wanted to do. He might not be drinking when he was with me, or using bang, but he had another addiction: sex.

"Can't get enough of me?" He chuckled, falling back onto the bed beside me.

"It's been a while, maybe we could go out to dinner or some of the public stuff that you said we need to do so we can be seen. If you were here more, we'd have time for that."

"I don't really care what people see." He ran his hands over my hip and along my ribs, inching upward to cup a breast.

I caught his hand in mine. "Wasn't that the whole point of the signing ceremony? Of officially having seconds?"

It wasn't that I didn't enjoy his attention, but he was falling back into keeping me shut away behind closed doors for one purpose only.

He pulled my hand away and stroked my stomach, slowly sweeping downward. "The policy talks have come a long way in six months. I'm not worried about it."

He nibbled on my neck. Normally that would have made me squirm but I was fed up.

"I'm not your bed slave, dammit. I'm supposed to be your wife. I'd like to go out and be seen as such."

"Is that how you think I'm treating you?" He sat up and starting yanking clothes onto his body. "I owe Etara some diagnosis work. If you want to be seen with me doing that, you're welcome to join me."

So he'd been pushing his limits with Etara again. Only being on the Iber one day a week offered the benefit of not being dragged into family drama or getting roped into Vayen containment agreements with the little Seeker. It also meant I was out of touch with what trouble he got into when I wasn't there.

I sighed. "That's not what I had in mind."

No one on any of the small colonies or sparsely populated stations where Etara employed Vayen's talents would care if I was by his side or not. They wouldn't know who I was. None of that would get our names into the newsfeeds in a popular light.

"If that isn't good enough for you, maybe something more opportune will come up next week." He fastened his shirt and pants and slipped his feet into his boots.

"Goodbye, Buria." He Jumped.

I used my link to check the time. We'd still had half a day left. I sighed and fell back on the bed. He was just angry that I'd called him out on violating our agreement. He'd be back next week and hopefully be in a better mood. And if I was lucky, he'd have had time to think about what I'd said and maybe do something about it.

THIRTY-EIGHT

Daniel

"How was my father when you visited him?" I asked Arden who was propped up on a stack of pillows on one side of me nursing Dreydon. Meera was out in the common room walking with Mika, trying to get her back to sleep. When my mother had welcomed me to the exhaustion of parenthood, I hadn't thought she was being so literal.

"You're supposed to be sleeping," Arden chided.

"Yes, well, you're waving breasts about and it's a bit distracting."

She giggled. "You wouldn't know what was out if you had your eyes closed.

"I'd imagine it."

She poked me in the shoulder. "If you're intent on getting in a bad mood..." She sighed. "Your father, I don't know. It's hard to tell. He's different with the babies around. Kinder. Maybe you could come with us next time and speak to him yourself."

"I've tried to talk to him. Actually, talk, I mean. He doesn't want to. I don't know why, but he won't. I don't know what I did. How the hells am I supposed to fix whatever pissed him off that badly if he won't even tell me what he's pissed about?"

She leaned over to kiss my forehead. "I don't think you did any-thing. I think he's just that angry in general. Your mother, her health, he's taking that hard and very personally."

"As he should. It's his fucking fault."

Arden pursed her lips, likely censoring what she really wanted to say. She wasn't one to speak her mind without editing it first. I supposed that was her upbringing in a prominent diplomatic family.

"She made her own choices. He didn't poison her. She did."

"He wasn't there at all. That was the problem."

Arden wasn't wrong exactly, but it wasn't her mother that was growing weaker by the day.

"I need to go for a walk," I announced.

"Now?" She glanced at the time projection on the wall.

"I need to clear my head," I said more calmly.

She gestured her free hand toward the door. "Be quiet out there. I haven't heard Meera or Mika in a while. Mika might finally be falling asleep."

"I will." I gave her a quick kiss and slipped off the other side of the bed. I felt for my clothes, slipped them on quietly, and went out into the common room.

Meera was asleep on the couch with Mika tucked against her chest like she'd sat down for a moment and collapsed there. The soft music of our bond hummed to life. I smiled at them both in the dim nighttime lighting.

Mika's first tooth seemed to be causing all levels of hell for our sleep cycle. I covered Meera with a blanket up to where Mika lay. The music faded as I tiptoed out of the suite.

With nowhere in particular to go, I wandered the corridors, greeting crewmembers and feeling my mood lighten with their idle banter.

My communication pin pinged. "Commander, you may want to head to the loading bay. There's a possible code black situation."

Fucking hells, did my father never sleep either? I Jumped to the closest point I had to the loading bay, having seeded personal jump points throughout the ship for just such emergencies. By the time I arrived, there was no possible about it, my father had an unfortunate crewmember up in the air by her neck while another beat on him with an arm-long length of conduit. Whatever words he was attempting to spew at them were incoherent.

"Ikeri, are you up?"

She answered groggily. *"I am now. Dad again?"*

"Yes. Loading bay." I flashed her a jump point.

"Be right there."

One benefit of my sister finally having her own link was that I now had a reliable and speedy partner for containing the disaster that was our father.

I considered, not for the first time, just letting Etara flip his kill switch. Guilt, as it always did, followed that thought like a slap across the face. He was my father. I shouldn't wish him dead. Besides, his death would crush what little life my mother had left.

Ikeri arrived seconds later. She excelled at using flashed jump points, probably from all her experience holding memories during transfers. "I'll get him."

My heart thundered in my chest as my diminutive little sister marched right up to my ranting father and demanded that he put the woman down. He dropped her, which wasn't exactly what we were going for, but it did the job. The two crewmembers scrambled toward the exit.

"Hold up. I need to talk to you before you go anywhere," I said as they hurried by.

They drew to a halt at the entryway. Hoping they'd stay there and logging their faces into memory in case they didn't, I ran to intercede before my father got it in his fucked-up head to do to Ikeri what he'd done to me and my mother.

"Don't you dare," Ikeri yelled at him. "What is wrong with you?" Tears welled in her eyes.

There seemed to be only one thing in his, blind rage. That darkness haunted me every time I looked in the mirror and saw those same eyes staring back at me.

"Get back," I gave her a push, not wanting to hurt her but not trusting my father to feel the same way.

He swung at me, his cold touch tickling its way into my mind. I knew what it felt like now, what to watch for, and I wasn't about to let him use it on me again. Regretting nothing, I dodged his swing, drew a pulse pistol, and fired.

He went down, blood pouring from his nose, but he was still conscious. I didn't dare pulse him again, not at such close range and without his armor. Endorphins already racing through my body, I stood ready for a fight.

I glanced at Ikeri, who had wrapped her arms around herself. Tears ran down her face. "He was in my head. I felt it. Him."

The only thing saving my father from a beating and Etara's end was that fact that Ikeri was still on her feet and speaking. He might have been in her head, but he hadn't attacked. But fucking hells, Ikeri of all people did not need to feel that level of malice. Not from anyone, especially our father.

She sniffed and tried to speak again. "I don't think he even knows where he is. It's like he's on autopilot." She shook her head, long curls bouncing over her shoulders. "I don't want to get Etara. Please don't say we have to."

"We have to do something." I stormed over to my father, getting right in his face, my hands free and ready if further action was required.

"Is that what you want? Someone else to put you out of your fucking misery? Well, you can just fucking live with it."

He knelt there, staring at me, rage boiling behind his eyes. His face twisted into a grim mask. Was he daring me to hit him? Daring me to get Etara? Ikeri claimed he wasn't fully aware, but I saw the light there. I'd seen him in action enough to know that he was just as present as any other time he'd unleashed his abilities on unfortunate souls.

"You can fight me all you want, but you do not touch my mother and you don't fucking dare touch Ikeri." I did punch him then, even knowing it was what he wanted. We were in agreement on that one thing. He went down cold.

"Can you contain this? Offer them the usual. I'm going to give Dad a vacation at Uncle Isnar's resort."

Ikeri nodded, but didn't move. I reminded myself that my sister was a healer not a fighter. She didn't have my mother's steel spine and she wasn't usually involved in any initial contact. She didn't witness when our offers were ill received or our father lost his temper over threats, not caring whether they were empty or not.

After making sure he wasn't moving, but was still breathing, I hugged Ikeri. She shook from head to toe.

"I'll have Neko talk to him. That put him on good behavior for a few months last time."

"He needs Mom. She's been at Tabor's for three days. He's always worse when she's not around."

I didn't have the heart to tell Ikeri that Mom was worse too, and that's why she was staying at Tabor's longer than usual. He kept me updated on her condition daily. Ikeri could wait for that news until tomorrow when she was calmer.

"I'll talk to her. Go have some tea and rest. We have negotiations tomorrow and I need your help. We certainly won't have his." I nodded to our father.

"All right." She wiped her face on her sleeve and took a shuddering breath. Once she had herself composed, she headed for the liability risks waiting near the entryway. If anyone could talk them into accepting our payoff for silence, it was Ikeri. She might be a Seeker, but she was also a Ta'set. She didn't shy away from using her abilities to get what she wanted.

❧

"It would probably be best if you didn't go down there," Neko informed me. He'd just come up from having a talk with my father in Uncle Isnar's underground prison.

It seemed that giving my father half a day to come to his senses on his own wasn't adequate.

"Not brimming with apologies?" I scoffed. "Not surprising. I'm assuming you wrung some sort of 'don't fucking do that again' agreement out of him?"

Neko gave me an odd look. "Something like that, yeah."

"What?"

"You sounded just like him there for a minute." He shook his head. "It's like nature decided to have a do-over."

I shrugged. "Strong family genetics."

"If that's the case, may I suggest that you don't take up drinking to cope with your problems?"

A bitter snort escaped me. "I've seen how effective that is."

Neko nodded. "I'd also suggest leaving him there for another four to six hours until he's fully sober and maybe have Isnar do the releasing. Lay low for a day or twelve, if you follow me."

"Got it."

He started toward Uncle Isnar's office but then turned back. "Thanks for stopping him before he went over the edge. We're not ready to lose him yet."

Yet. Did Neko know something I didn't or did he just fear the same thing as the rest of us, that my father would indeed dive over the edge of crazy one of these days and cause some epic disaster where Etara was forced to switch him off for good?

I left Neko and Uncle Isnar to be my father's jailers and Jumped to Tabor's house on Rok.

As I walked out of the gallery and past the atrium corridor, I caught sight of Tabor and my mother out in the garden. The fields beyond were currently fallow and neither of them were wearing breather masks. Assuming it was safe without any of his potent medicinal crops in bloom, I went out to join them.

They were both doing rudimentary Seeker forms in the grass. I couldn't help but note how stiff my mother's motions had become. I approached slowly, giving them plenty of time to notice me.

Tabor helped her to her feet and they came to meet me. My mother's face scrunched up. "Isn't it your sleep cycle?"

"A crisis required averting."

"And now you're here." She sighed. "Where is he?"

"A cell at Uncle Isnar's."

Her footing faltered. Tabor was there right beside her, catching her and covering her fumble as if it hadn't happened.

"He should visited me here. He knows he can. That he's supposed to if he feels he needs it," she said more to herself than either of us.

"He does know," Tabor assured her. "But he doesn't always think straight when the urges take hold. You said so yourself."

The desperation on her face broke my heart. I didn't dare tell her that he'd nearly gone off on Ikeri for fear the knowledge would suck the remaining life out of her.

"Mom, can you talk to him? Like you did before? Maybe he could stay at Neko's with you for a little while? Ikeri and I can handle the Iber and the damned Ocelon-led shit for now."

"Did he hurt anyone?"

"One of the crew, but not permanently. Ikeri is taking care of it. Though if this keeps up, idiots are going to start poking him to see if they can get a payoff too."

"You make them sign the confidentiality agreement, right?"

"Of course, but someone is going to drop a hint eventually. There've been too many incidents. The odds are not in our favor."

"I know." She looked wearier by the minute.

"I'm sorry to put this on you. You're supposed to be resting."

"That's all I do. Rest." She grimaced. "Truth be told, it doesn't help. I'm just bored and more focused on every discomfort. And I'm driving Tabor nuts."

He grinned, elbowing her lightly. "You are not."

"Don't listen to him," she said to me as she winked at Tabor. "He won't admit it."

Even though she was visibly miserable, she had the energy to tease him and he kept right up with her, the two of them jokingly bickered all the way back to the house. It was a drastic departure from the actual bickering she and my father had done all my life. I let their lightheartedness distract me from the looming task of dealing with my father for a few minutes.

When we stepped inside the house, they both became serious.

"Do you want me to come with you?" Tabor asked my mother.

"Yes, but I might be able to reach him better if I'm alone."

"If you're in more pain, you mean." Tabor scowled. "Woman, don't be that evil. He doesn't deserve that."

I thought he did. It surprised me that Tabor seemed more sympathetic to my father than we were.

"Fine, load me up with pain killers then, and let me get this situation dealt with so I can get back to all that important resting."

When Tabor left to get her medication, I asked, "Can the bond really do that? Take the place of pain killers?"

"It's quite miraculous. Don't discount what you have with your wives."

"Only Meera. I tried with Arden. It didn't work."

"She's full Artorian." My mother visibly pondered that until Tabor returned. She pulled up her sleeve and stood patiently while Tabor injected her medication with practiced skill.

When he was finished. She pulled her sleeve back down. "I'll let you know how it goes," she said to Tabor. "Get some work done while you don't have to babysit me."

He shook his head. "Maybe I like babysitting you. It's good practice for the actual babies." He winked at me.

"Get me out of here," my mother said, half-laughing and holding out her hand to me.

I took it and stepped into the void. We arrived in Uncle Isnar's foyer moments later. I greeted Merona, letting her know we were there to see my father.

"I'll let the Premier know. He did want to speak with both of you. When you're finished below, of course." She bowed and left us.

We headed for the lift. "You know I'm going down there with you, right? I'll hang back but..."

She nodded. "Maybe wait in the lift out of sight? Keep the door open."

"Sure." I was relieved that she hadn't fought me on that.

"I was thinking... Your father couldn't get the bond to work with Sonia either. They were both full Artorians."

"Who?"

"The woman he'd planned to join with before I ruined his life. There are enough records and vague recollections that I was able to put her part in our past back together myself."

I chuckled. "Mom, you didn't ruin his life."

She didn't share my humor, instead she looked more somber than before. "No? Look where we are. What we're dealing with. If I had left him to his life on Artor, he'd be whole and happy. He'd be himself. Fully, not these brief glimpses we're left with."

Arden's words on accountability ran through my head. When it came to my father, I agreed with them. "He made his own choices, Mom. What he is now isn't on you."

"It is. The root of it, anyway. I was the one who had the University fuse the damned Arpex larvae to him. He wouldn't be the death-bringer if I hadn't done that."

"No. He'd be dead. None of us wanted that."

She gave me a pained smile. "No, we did not." Then she shook her head slowly. "Anyway, my point is that maybe it's a faulty genetic thing. Chesser did bond to me, though I didn't understand what that was at the time. I believe it was truncated like Vayen's because it wasn't mutual like I have now."

This was all new to me but I couldn't see how it helped other than to say I was possibly defective in the full Artorian department.

We got in the lift. Our voices went flat in the confined space.

"Ask Arden to try to initiate it," she suggested.

"What? I don't think that's how it works, Mom."

"Just because men are told they're supposed to be the ones to initiate a bond, doesn't mean women can't, just that it's not how things are traditionally done. We're knocking traditions left and right. Why not try one more?"

"I suppose it can't hurt."

"Exactly." She gave me a motherly smile of approval.

The lift came to a stop.

She squared her thinner-than-they-used-to-be shoulders. "Yes, I'll be careful. Stay in here unless you hear me say otherwise."

I nodded, wishing she could stay in mom mode and didn't have to be quite so commanding. But she had been used to being in charge long before I'd emerged from a stasis tube and her life had turned upside down.

I leaned against the wall as far as I dared, but only a corner of his cell was visible. I wanted to scream when she deactivated the containment field, but announcing my presence would surely set him off. If he wasn't in a rage already.

THIRTY-NINE

Anastassia

I approached Vayen slowly. He had his back to me, but from his stiff stance, I gathered he knew I was there.

"Here we are again."

"I can't keep doing this, Stassia."

"No, you can't." As angry as I was with him, I could hear his ragged breathing and see him trembling. My gut told me he was in control of his abilities but the rest of him was a wreck. I entered his cell and wrapped my arms around him.

He fell apart on my shoulder, great wracking sobs that pierced my heart. To see him so low brought tears to my own eyes. I held him until he was done.

"You should have come to me," I said. "I can't help you if you don't let me know you need help."

"I was going to, but then it was too late."

"What about Buria, doesn't being with her help? Weren't you supposed to be with her?"

He shook his head and uttered a frustrated groan. "She's pissed at me again. I haven't gone there in a couple weeks."

"Avoiding her isn't going to solve anything."

"I don't think talking will either. We want different things."

Sensing we needed to have a discussion that was more of a Seeker session, I tugged him toward the narrow cot and sat beside him, keeping one of his hands in mine so I could track his pulse and tension level.

"What does she want?"

He sighed deeply. "Are we really doing this? You're going to give me relationship advice on my second wife?"

"Whatever is going on is affecting you, so yes, I am." And at this rate, she wasn't going to be his second wife for long.

"She wants social recognition, to be in the newsfeeds. Hells, I don't blame her, she deserves something out of this, but she doesn't seem to realize how being publicly tied to me will rarely be in her favor. Tyrant Ta'set and all." He huffed and shook his head. "I'm trying to be seen positively with her in public, but working beside me on the mission or being seen with me at Cragtek isn't what she was hoping for." He raked his hands through his hair. "Frankly, I'm not what she hoped for. I've tried to be better, to not make the same mistakes, but Geva, I don't think I have it in me to do this right."

"You could release her, void the contract. There are no children involved." As far as I knew she wasn't able, but that didn't mean he couldn't find some other way around that obstacle. He'd shared the memories of how many alternate suggestions he'd made before I'd caved to conceiving Ikeri. "There isn't a child, right?"

"No."

I let out a sigh of relief. "Then yes, if you both agree, you can cancel the contract. Assuming you don't want to manufacture some reason to push through a contractual void on your own."

"That would ruin the status I was hoping to give her."

"I assumed as much."

"So would voiding the contract early," he pointed out.

"Then you need to talk to her, find some compromise. Explain what you're trying to give her. Unlike you, she can't read minds."

He smiled weakly. "Yeah, all right."

I turned to face him, silently begging him to look at me, to see me and fully understand what I was trying to say. "Now, as to your first wife problem, I can't do this again." I waved at the cell around us. "I physically can't. Mentally can't. When I told you I was empty before? When I had nothing left to give you? I have less than that now. The nanite treatments are becoming less effective."

He gripped my hand with vice-like force. "Already? They said they would alter them as needed, that they could tweak the treatments."

"They have. Several times." I rested my other hand on the one clutching mine. "I'm doing the best I can to fight this, but it's taking everything I've got. Having to come down here, to be in this field," I shuddered, my mouth getting drier by the second. "It brings back everything from when the Council made me help them develop this damned thing. I can hear it. I feel it."

His pulse thundered beneath my fingers. Mine wasn't much better and I was getting lightheaded on top of it. "Here's the thing, I'll keep doing it, because I'm not letting you go. But if you want to help me, do what you have to do to keep us both from having to be down here."

"I will. Stassia, I promise I will." He pulled me into his arms and held me tightly.

I smoothed the hair back from his face and kissed him. He didn't push for more. "We're going to the Artorian estate. I need quiet and a bed. These pain killers and the field are making me nauseous. I need one or both of you with me."

"Whatever you need," he said solemnly.

"I've told you what I need. I need you to hear it."

He nodded. "I do."

"Neko will be watching you. Leave the Iber business to Daniel and Ikeri. They'll let us know if they need help or have questions."

"I will."

He was being too agreeable to be believable. "Don't just say it, mean it."

"I do mean it, dammit."

"If you need to drink—and believe me, I get it, I wish I could find a little relief in that too—stay at the estate, or in our suite. Stay out of the public eye, all right?"

"Yeah."

"All right, I have to go speak to your host and then, when you're free to go, you will Jump me to a bed and sit next to me in it while I attempt to be unconscious until my insides cease trying to rip their way out."

"Stassia, is it that bad?"

"Take a look for yourself when I'm asleep. I really just want to sleep. Very much. Please."

"Yes, all right," he said, his voice wavering.

I held his face in my hands, unable to look away from the sorrow. Knowing I'd crushed his hope that I'd be able to maintain my health indefinitely, that by some miracle I'd be all right, made me feel every bit as evil as Tabor had called me.

"I'm sorry." Exhaustion and all the raw emotion made it impossible to maintain my authoritative role. I crumbled, devolving into just as much of a wreck as he had been.

He scooped me up and ran to the lift. He came to a dead stop when he met Daniel there.

"I need to get her out of here. Now," he commanded.

Daniel shook his head. "I'll take her."

Vayen shouldered his way into the lift with me in his arms. "Either make this damned thing work or get the fuck out of my way."

The tension level around me made the air sing, and that made my ears hurt and my head pound. I could feel the air, I observed distantly. It felt like tiny cuts against my skin, burning.

"No, Stassia, stay with me." He shook me. "Up. Now. Get her out of this fucking field."

The door closed and the lift began to move. Vayen said something that sounded like begging, but I couldn't make out the words. I tried to make my mouth work, to tell him I wouldn't leave him, but everything was so distant, like I was standing outside myself. It was far more comfortable there except I could hear Daniel's panicked voice join Vayen's.

Gripping tightly to my body with invisible fingers, I fought to push my way back inside, even if it meant returning to the driving pain. The sounds and lights around me were suddenly sharp, as if someone had turned the volume all the way up. I gasped, filling my lungs with air that burned and cut, but assured me I was still alive because of it.

The sensation of a Jump promised relief, a bed, and Tabor's warm and peaceful hum along with Vayen's silent comfort. I gave myself over to that promise and let everything else slowly fade away.

When I came back to my body, it felt thick, the wrong shape. The room smelled like disinfectant and there were no other bodies on the bed beside me.

And then there were.

Tabor's soft hands ran over my cheeks. "Woman, you scared the hells out of me. Don't ever do that again."

Vayen's large calloused hand gripped my arm tightly. "Agreed."

"Water," I managed to say through my parched throat and dried-up tongue.

Knowing they were both there brought me comfort but everything else still felt very wrong.

One of them sat me up while the other brought a cup of water to my lips and tipped a meager trickle down my throat. I found my own hands and took over, draining the contents.

"More."

"You'll have to wait until the doctors clear you for more," Tabor said gently. "They had to go in and remove the worst of the damage to your organs. That should give you some relief, but also means we have to be much more careful with you," he aimed the last bit at Vayen.

That couldn't be right. "They said they didn't want to do that. That it was a last resort."

"It was," Vayen said with a tremble in his voice.

"We thought we'd lost you. The University doctors didn't hold out much hope, though they did their best through the flurry of profane threats being thrown at them," Tabor groused the last bit over me at Vayen.

"Let him be." I coughed my way past the dry spot in my throat, hazily recalling holding on to my body and shoving my way back inside it. "I told you both that I wasn't leaving you."

Vayen nodded, watching me with glistening dark eyes.

Slowly settling back into consciousness, I studied one of my hands. The skin was stretched tight, fingers thick. Everything felt swollen.

"A side effect of the medication they had to give you to prevent infection after the invasive surgery. The swelling should go down in a few days. It's already better than yesterday," Vayen said.

"Yes, yesterday, my dearest and only," Tabor said boldly in front of Vayen. "So you are going to stay in bed and rest. As much as you hate resting, that's what you're going to do. And you will let the doctors and surgeons do their job without making angry faces at them or telling them what they're doing wrong. You will concentrate on recovering and trust that the rest of us have everything else under control."

"As long as you're both right here where I don't have to worry about you."

Vayen nodded, his grip on my arm easing.

"Like I would be anywhere else." Tabor smiled. The hum around me amplified, filled with soft tinkling and raindrops. I eased back into the pillows, closing my eyes, content in the comfort of the bonds we shared.

FORTY

Daniel

I settled onto the couch in the suite my parents shared on the Iber, having set Mika on a blanket on the floor, and handed Dreydon to my mother to hold. The urge to keep my hands ready to take over at a moment's notice was nearly impossible to control. I pressed my palms onto my lap. My mother did her best to cover the tremble in her hands but the nerve damage was becoming more prevalent. Soon there would be no hiding it.

She arranged Dreydon on her lap where her legs could do the supporting instead of her hands. "He's... I don't know, he made some excuse as he always does. He's not here, so you can relax."

The only communication I'd had with my father since I'd watched my mother stop breathing in his arms at Uncle Isnar's four months ago had been impersonal messages traded by link. It was Tabor who provided daily updates on my mother's health to Markus, Ikeri, and me.

It wasn't the threat of my possibly lurking father that kept me from relaxing.

"Shouldn't he be here with you? You said the bond helped keep the pain manageable."

"Don't worry about me," she chided, tickling Dreydon's feet.

He giggled, kicking, his arms pumping for more.

I did worry. So did a good portion of the crew. When my father wandered about on his own, he tended to be abrasive, and as more than one person had coined it: snarly.

Everyone had noted by now that when my mother was by his side, he was tamed. Solo, he was to be avoided at all costs.

Rumors followed both of them. Ikeri was doing her best to

manage those, shaping the narrative for everyone reporting back to the Narvan. The second marriages of The Advisors couldn't be seen to be deviating from the Jalvian norm. We needed to keep them in line with what people were expecting from a standard multiple union. Where Jalvian families generally lived together with their multiple spouses, there were enough outliers who maintained amicable separate family arrangements that what my parents had first set out to do was seen as normal. But things had changed.

My father and Tabor were known to spend inordinate amounts of time with my mother. Together. It felt like everyone was salivating for a juicy tidbit to slip, some proof that there was more going on behind closed doors.

My arrangement with Meera and Arden was exactly what the rumor mills wanted to titter about with my parents. I might have ignited the multiple marriage revolution, but no one gave a shit about me beyond that. I wasn't the almighty Advisor of All.

Now that Arden and I had established the traditional version of the Artorian bond thanks to my mother's suggestion, I was doing everything I could to educate the Narvan's public on the different types of bonds and their benefits. Foremost in that effort, to combat those rumors, I was making it abundantly clear that bonds could be used to support a wounded or ill mate.

I'd been working with Buria to help promote a more positive public image for my father outside of the Iber. If none of the diagnosing volunteer work he did made it into the newsfeeds, the fact that he was spending time out and about with his second wife did. That Buria wasn't part of any secret foursome bedroom activities was generally accepted knowledge since she was only spotted occasionaly on the Iber for her one day a week and never on Rok. Tabor and my mother never visited Brustus.

Whether my father and Buria were actually getting along or not was hard to tell. I rarely saw him with her outside of their public engagements. However, he could be contacted at a private, secure terminal on Brustus two nights a week. The crew had tested this several times as incidents had arisen. From the fact that they could have contacted me, but found legitimate reasons to need his input, I was inclined to think they were being asked to verify where he was by their sponsors in case any other rumor fodder might be waiting to be exposed.

Thankfully, he'd been, for the most part, keeping his abilities to himself. Yet, it sure seemed to me that Etara was more on edge than ever, always hovering nearby when he was on the Iber away from my mother. I hoped she was shadowing him now while I was here.

Ikeri did what she could to offer my mother comfort with her Seeker gifts, but I didn't have any of those. I had my children. Ikeri assured me that they offered just as much comfort as she did. That idea seemed foreign. I'd never pictured my mother as the doting grandmotherly sort, but here she was, smiling and laughing over my son.

She and Tabor spent several afternoons a week with their grandchildren, giving Meera and Arden breaks. Tabor was even more enamored with them than my mother was. The way my father and Tabor had arranged their schedules, making sure at least one of them was available for my mother, there was always one baby visit a week that fell on my father's watch—always one day that he made himself scarce for a few hours.

Arden and Meera had made arrangements with my father without my involvement, allowing him time with the babies. Time I didn't have to see him and he didn't have to see me. They claimed he was different with Mika and Dreydon. They weren't concerned that he'd harm the children, accidentally or not. Having seen him lose himself in his abilities too many times, I didn't have their faith, but I did have to trust my wives. Or so they kept telling me.

"You don't have to stay with me. I know you have plenty to do. They're not that mobile yet. I can keep up with them," my mother said, leaning down to exchange Dreydon for Mika.

Leaving them in her care with Tabor around was more like leaving them with Tabor with my mother to assist. Putting that obligation on her alone, in her condition, wasn't something I was comfortable with.

"I have time, Mom."

I made the time, not knowing how much she had left.

My once vibrant mother had faded. The grey in her hair grew more prevalent every week and though she wore the same clothes she always had, there was less of her beneath them. The sleeveless shirt she wore now confirmed that the muscles she'd diligently maintained all my life were melting away.

"I wish I had been ready for you when you were a baby," she said, not looking at me, keeping her attention safely on Mika, who was snuggling sleepily against her grandmother.

"I'm sure you did fine. I lived, didn't I?"

She smirked, shaking her head. "I was an awful mother. The fact that you made it past a year old was completely due to your father. I have enough of my own memories to know that." She glanced up at me and then her gaze darted away. "Arden and Meera are a thousand times better at motherhood than I was."

I reached across the couch to give her a gentle poke in the shoulder. "You're still my mother. You've gotten better at it."

She nodded, glancing at me again with a tremulous smile.

My mother didn't do emotional very often, but more often of late, she slipped into moments of openness. She did her best to cover those too. They clearly made her uncomfortable, but I wished she'd say more, share more, let me in closer.

She'd always maintained a distance around herself, a barrier. Tabor was the only one fully immune to it.

"Do you think you'll have more?" she asked.

She absently arranged the curls that had started to form in Mika's dark hair as it grew longer. They reminded me of Ikeri's.

"Mom, we're barely sleeping as it is."

Her soft laugh caught me by surprise. "According to your father's memories, I said the same thing when he wanted Ikeri." She settled back into the couch now that Mika had closed her eyes, resting peacefully in her arms. "He would have loved to have had more kids."

The thought of having more siblings, of what our life would be like with a bigger family, and now dealing with my father teetering on the edge of blackness, and my mother's health failing, boggled my mind. "I can't even imagine."

"Neither can I, but he would have loved it. Things might have been different if I'd been more compatible with bearing Artorian babies. He might never have pursued the Narvan again if he'd had a house full of little Ta'sets to occupy him."

My childhood memories were foggy, but I had enough clarity to feel justified in saying, "You'd have gone insane."

She eased her head onto the back of the couch and smiled softly as she closed her eyes. "You're right. But it might have been worth it."

When she didn't open them again, I started to worry. "Mom?"

She didn't respond.

"Mom?"

Still nothing.

I scooted closer, sliding one hand under Mika and the other

over my mother's wrist. Her pulse thrummed evenly, albeit slowly. Relieved, I carefully lifted Mika from my mother's slack arms. As much as I didn't want to talk to him, it wasn't usual for my mother to fall asleep during my visit, especially not deep asleep in an instant.

"Something's not right with Mom."

My father appeared inside the front door two breaths later. Skirting Dreydon on the floor, he ignored me and rushed to my mother.

He ran his hands over her bare arms. "Stassia, wake up."

I couldn't remember ever hearing my father call her that until that day in the lift at Uncle Isnar's. Not that it surprised me that they shared private endearments, but it did that he'd been worried enough to slip them out in front of me, twice. The last time, she'd stopped breathing.

My heart leapt into my throat. I clutched my obliviously sleeping daughter to my chest and got out of his way.

"She was just sitting here talking and then her head dropped back and she went to sleep. She is just asleep, right?"

"Dammit, I told you the injection was a bad idea," he muttered as he shook her gently. "Stassia, come on, wake up."

Her head lolled from side to side, arms jangling limply as he jostled her. She didn't wake.

"I'm going to look inside. Stay here in case I need you."

With my free hand, I moved Dreydon out of my father's shadow as he knelt beside my mother and dropped into his diagnosis trance.

When he came back to himself, my mother still hadn't stirred. Dreydon was rolling around and going to get stepped on. I grabbed him too and wished, for the fifth time that day, that he was as sedate as his sister.

"What did you see? What can I do?" I asked, knowing I couldn't do a damned thing with both kids in my arms.

To my surprise, he held out his hands and took Dreydon from me. "I sent for Cara, she leads your mother's care team."

I knew that, thanks to Tabor, but I kept any snarky replies to myself in favor of riding out his civil tone for as long as it lasted.

He hoisted Dreydon up to hang almost half over his shoulder and patted his back. Dreydon settled down and made quiet contended noises. My amazement must have shown.

"You were the same way," he said quietly.

"Should we call Ikeri in? Should I have Arden take the kids?"

"We'll wait to see what Cara says." He sat next to my mother, staring at her as if he could will her to wake up while pounding out a rhythmic beat on Dreydon's back.

The beat jogged a distant memory. I stood there, listening, trying to pinpoint what was tickling my mind. The memory burst into clarity.

"That's a song. You used to sing it to me."

He nodded, smiling faintly.

I tried to remember the words, but all I kept coming up with was the sound of his voice in a vague melody. Just as I was about to dare to ask him to sing it, Cara pinged the door.

My father used his link to let her in. She strode over with a medical case in her hand, ignoring both of us with sleeping babies and focusing solely on her patient.

"What happened?"

I explained how she'd just dropped off and that we were unable to wake her.

"What is she on?"

"Her usual dose of pain medication," my father said. "She seemed extra tired today. I told her it was a bad idea, that she should see you before taking it, but you know her. She insisted she was fine."

Cara nodded. "I assume you took a look?"

Looking deflated, my father nodded. "The lines are growing thinner."

"But no new damage?"

"Not that I can see."

"That's good." She opened her case and ran a scanner over my mother's head and torso. "Nothing appears overly out of order. The medication just hit her harder than it has been. We'll have to either adjust the dose, though that would mean not as much pain coverage, or find something different that her weakened system can tolerate so she can remain awake." She returned the scanner to her case. "We both know she's not happy with sleeping as much as she does."

"Not happy." My father snorted. "You don't hear the half of it."

He'd gone from patting to rubbing a slow circle over Dreydon's back. I tucked my father's secrets away for future use.

"She'll be all right?" I asked.

"I don't like how low her blood pressure is, but I think so, yes. Normally, I'd suggest a stimulant to bring her back around so that we could verify that her blood pressure will increase, but her system doesn't tolerate those favorably. She should remain under observation."

"I'll stay with her," my father said.

"Let me know if anything changes." Cara nodded to us both and headed for the door to let herself out.

"I can stay, if you were in the middle of anything," I offered.

"I wasn't," he said, his voice taking on a more familiar edge.

"Then why weren't you here? She doesn't need a full dose if you're with her."

His hand stilled on Dreydon's back and his eyes narrowed. Dammit, I wasn't trying to piss him off.

"What I mean is, you don't have to leave every time I'm here."

"I..."

If he'd been going to end that with 'don't', we both knew it for the lie that it was. In an effort to preserve what little peace we had between us, I decided on a retreat.

"I'll leave you to it then. You'll let us know if anything changes?" I held out my hand for Dreydon.

He pondered the baby on his shoulder for a moment and then had the nerve to get all snarly looking about handing me my son so that I could leave him alone like he clearly wanted me to.

With both of my children in hand, I left with the same haste Cara had.

FORTY-ONE

Buria

I checked the time again. The crowd was starting to get restless. If Vayen stood me up, I wasn't sure how to handle it. Addressing the Artorian audience about the benefits of bonding outside their kind was not a topic I had actual knowledge of. Even early on, when Vayen had been so enamored with the idea of us, he'd made it clear he wouldn't bond with me.

However, the general public didn't know that. Daniel, who was the one guiding the public narrative behind the scenes, had been adamant about us maintaining a vaguery regarding the details of our relationship. It grated on me to go along with it, knowing that every time Vayen addressed the issue, he was speaking of his bond to Ana.

Maybe I should have pushed for him to try it with me at the start. A bond might have helped keep the passion and moments of emotional openness we'd had at first as opposed to the neutral politically-centered partnership we had now.

Elonka had told me to watch out for myself, always gushing how she had found fulfilment in being part of Gamnock's business. I'd managed the same with Vayen, but it wasn't exactly the fulfillment I'd been hoping for. Maybe I'd been deluding myself, but I'd hoped we would have found something real together by now, that there might be a glimmer of hope that either of us would want to renew our marriage contract. In public, when we did these appearances, he put on a believable show, enough that even I bought it at first, but I'd come to understand that his affection was just another mood swing.

The rally organizer gave me another look. I shook my head. He scowled and signaled for another of his young Artorian speakers to come up to testify how her bond with her new non-Artorian mate had impacted her life.

Vayen was the figurehead of this movement, far outshining Daniel who had lit the initial torch. If he didn't show, the cause would take a heavy hit.

Chancing that I'd set him off, I contacted him through my link. *"Are you coming?"*

"Dammit, Buria, I'm busy. Anastassia had another episode. I can't leave her right now."

I did my best to tone down my frustration. *"Sorry to hear that. You should have let me know. I would have cancelled your appearance before the rally started."*

"Fucking political shit. Daniel should be the one up there talking about how bonds are the answer to true fucking happiness, not me."

"I'll talk to him about it for future appearances. Should I cancel your schedule for the rest of the day then?"

"Yes." He cut contact, leaving me standing there on the stage with the crowd expectantly watching me while half-heartedly listening to the young woman speak.

If anyone had told me two years ago that I'd have been employing my hospitality training for the Advisor of All, I'd have thought it a cruel joke. It still sort of was.

I'd had a few opportunities to act as his bodyguard, the one thing I was truly qualified for. He'd liked the bed slave training the most, but we'd moved past that now. Administration was my fallback plan. I supposed my years of brutal training under the Masters had ended up serving me well.

After all, here I stood in a stage with thousands watching me, wearing fine custom-made clothes as befitting a wife of the Advisor of All. I was as far from a slave on Tacesh as I could get, and yet, a bitter taste lingered in my mouth. Being the wife of the Advisor of All wasn't as grand as anyone thought it was. It was an extravagant apartment, jealous looks everywhere I went, and a heart filled with disappointment.

When the young woman finished, I signaled the organizer. Her face fell as I came forward on my own.

"I regret to inform you that the Advisor cannot be here with us. As many of you know, his first wife is ill. She has suffered a setback this morning and requires the comfort of the bond you have all been talking about here today. We thank you for your understanding during these troubling times."

As I started to back away, someone shouted out, "How has the bond benefitted you?"

It didn't. I wasn't supposed to be the mouthpiece of any of this. These appearances were supposed to help Vayen's people, help him maintain positive public relations. The only part of this I wanted any more was the recognition as his wife so that when I no longer was, I could ride that out with benefits. Our contract didn't have that much longer to go.

"How has the role of second wife impacted your life?" asked another.

The crowd hurled a rush of questions at me, all of them yelling over one another. The mass surged forward, knocking several people to the ground in their rush to be heard.

"Calm! Be calm!" shouted the organizer as she waved her hands, signaling for the security team.

I spotted uniforms fighting their way through the tightened crowd, heading for those who had been knocked to the ground.

A woman surfaced in the crushing mass near the stage, looking dazed, her head bloodied. I ran forward to pull her up out of the throng. My hand had just met hers when the first impact knocked me backward. A second one hit my chest, driving the air from my lungs. A deep burning sensation rocketed through me. My clothes contained a light armored weave but it wasn't as effective as a full armored coat. My public image was supposed to be one of confidence in a better future, not fear of attack. Vayen didn't wear his armor during our public appearances, though he had his altered skin as back up. I did not.

I touched my hand to my chest. Rather than the cool cloth I'd hoped to feel, my hand met with heat and wet. Screams and shouting surrounded me, drowning out all thought. When I gathered my wits enough to shakily look down. I could see where the second energy burst had obliterated the weave and tore into my chest, leaving a gaping wound behind. The tank might help if I could get there, but I wouldn't be able to get into it myself. As blackness edged my vision, I realized I didn't even have the wherewithal to form a Jump to the tank room.

At least Vayen hadn't been here. He likely would have gone death-bringer on them all. I sent a silent thanks to Ana for saving lives by keeping him occupied elsewhere.

All of us, saving lives.

Big hands grabbed me. Familiar hands. I blinked, trying to focus on the blurry man. The disorienting sensation of a Jump came next. Then bright lights. The gel in the tank sparkled with the promise of healing.

"Buria, hang on."

He tugged my clothes off, leaving me distantly cold. It was getting harder to breathe, the effort more momentous than it seemed like it should be. I tried to speak but nothing came out.

"I'll do what I can to contain this. Did you see who shot you?"

I blinked again. His face was wrong, too young, unscarred.

"Daniel?"

"Yeah. Nevermind, we'll talk after."

Then he was gone from my side and the ceiling came closer. Just as it started to fall away, the gel enveloped me. I gasped at the unsettling sensation of drowning and reflexively fought the rush of fluid invading my mouth. A sudden heaviness slowed everything. The bright room outside the clearplaz tube blurred and then I couldn't keep my eyes open any longer.

I woke in a narrow bed with Daniel sitting beside me, a distant look on his face that indicated he was probably busy on his link. Making more noise than probably necessary, I sat up, making a point to keep the sheet tucked around me. Not that he hadn't already seen me naked. Twice now. But being his father's wife, it felt very awkward.

He blinked a few times and turned to me. "Feeling all right?"

I nodded, pulling the sheet back to allow myself a peek at my healed chest which looked as if nothing had happened. Though I'd been in the tank once before, it's miraculous capabilities still amazed me.

"Is your father here?"

Daniel shook his head. "He's with my mother and Tabor."

"But he knows I got shot, right? He'll be here when he can?"

He pulled the ring Vayen had given me from a pocket and handed it over. "There's nothing for him to do here. You can use the shower across the hall. I'll see if I can find you some of my mother's clothes to get home in. What you were wearing is in the trash."

"Nothing for him to do? I was shot!"

Daniel stood and took a step back. "I know. I was monitoring the rally. I don't send you places without keeping an eye on the results."

"He didn't send you?"

Daniel, having adopted his father's impassive face, gave me nothing.

"He doesn't even know, does he?"

"Probably not. He's been with my mother since late last night when she had a seizure." At least he had the grace to look apologetic.

Surely, having rescued his father's second wife, Daniel would have used that to gain favor with his irritable father. "You haven't told him?"

"Hells no. He'd ask how I knew you'd been injured and then he'd find out I had a hand in placing the two of you there to begin with. He'd figure out a way to make this all my fault." He shook his head and held up his hands. "I'm arranging these appearances as a favor to you and to Neko. Middle man. That's it."

"Vayen doesn't monitor feeds? Keep an eye on where we're supposed to be and what happens before and after like you do?"

"Buria, this is Narvan business. Whatever he attends is because you or Neko ask him to. The Narvan is Neko's realm now, not my father's." He took one more step back, leaning against the doorframe. "While you were out, I analyzed the newsfeeds. Your shooter and two accomplices were identified and have been detained by enforcers. Baring my father's intrusion, Neko will make sure they publicly pay for attacking the Advisor's wife."

"Thank you."

He nodded. "On one hand, you did get shot and it would have been fatal if not for the tank, but on the other, getting shot while attempting to aid that woman has gained you a lot of good press and sympathy. So, there's that?"

"Better than nothing. How do I play this with the tank?"

"The tank is secret and will remain so. You were wounded. I brought you to our private clinic where you were treated by the best doctors our credits can buy. You'll spend some time out of the public eye recovering. Cancel and refuse any other appearances for a while. Beyond the fake recovery, there's no need to place yourself at risk of a more successful attack. I'm guessing the only reason they dared act this time was because my father wasn't there."

That he wasn't. He wasn't here either.

I sat up farther, swinging my legs over the side of the bed. Familiar looking clothes sat folded in the open shelves on the wall beside me. This was Vayen's room.

His son watched me warily. He'd approached me a year ago with this middle man deal between me and Neko, who talked to me directly as little as possible.

Whatever Vayen saw in his son to garner such disdain, I didn't understand. While Daniel and I were at least on business terms, the rest of Vayen's children were standoffish with me. I wasn't their mother.

"What do I tell him when he finds out so that you don't get an earful about this?" I asked.

Daniel sighed. "Whatever you need to. He already hates me. Can't get any worse, I guess."

"Hate is a pretty strong word."

"It's an accurate word." He pointed out the door and to the right. "My mother's room is next door. Grab whatever you need, but maybe don't let him catch you in it. He's particular about her stuff."

"Thank you."

He nodded and Jumped. After a quick shower and Jumping home in borrowed clothes, I stood in the middle of the bedroom, staring at all I'd bought. Vayen had given me everything credits could by, but when it came down to it, that wasn't enough. Not enough to make a marriage contract worth renewing, not even with the very real possibility of becoming his only wife in the near future. I'd done the job, as Neko had once called it. Vayen had given me my freedom years ago. I didn't need him to offer it again. This time, I was taking it on my own.

Vayen arrived in our apartment the day after I'd been shot and healed, no thanks to him. He absently said hello and sat down at the terminal, his fingers flying over the keys. Having had plenty of time to stew, I strode right over and planted myself beside him.

"Perhaps you'd like to ask how the rally went?"

He didn't look away from the vid. "I'm sure it went fine."

"Fine?" I slammed my hand down on the terminal, mashing his fingers into the keys and not caring one bit. "I got shot right after making excuses for your lack of attendance. If it wasn't for your son, I wouldn't be standing here right now. And did you even give a moment's thought to me or the event where you were supposed to be? No. There was a riot when the shots started and three people were killed."

He leapt out of the chair. "I was busy taking care of Anastassia.

That isn't an excuse, that's a damn good reason to not spend time at some fucking rally where people are going to think what they want and do what they want no matter what Tyrant Ta'set says.

"Anastassia doesn't have much time left, and anyone who thinks I shouldn't be spending all the time with her that I can, can just fuck the hells off."

"So, your second wife nearly dying is not a priority. That doesn't even get a mention. Not a spare thought. Got it." I pointed to the front door he rarely used. "How about you go spend all the time with Anastassia that she has left and don't bother coming back here again."

He stood there seething. An itch worked its way up my spine and into my brain, reminding me that antagonizing the death-bringer was not a wise course of action. But dammit, I was allowed to be angry. Wasn't I?

"Why did you call Daniel instead of me if you needed to get to the tank?"

"I didn't. I wasn't in a state to contact anyone." I scrambled for a way to keep Daniel out of trouble, but Vayen was staring me down with a violent storm brewing on his face and that itch made me suspect he was already skimming my thoughts. "Daniel has been setting up the appearances for us, working with Neko to gain us public favor and to help guide the multiple marriage debate in a more positive direction."

He pointed a finger at me. "You said you were setting those up."

"Yes, well, I had some ideas but not the contacts to make them happen. Daniel does. I knew you wouldn't go along with any of it if I told you he was involved."

"And he allowed a riot? He allowed you to get shot?" Vayen said, verging on shouting.

"He didn't allow anything. He wasn't there in person. You were supposed to be."

Vayen's jaw clenched, muscles rippling in his neck. After a moment he let out a frustrated growl. "Do you know who shot you? I'll take care of them."

"Daniel already did. Neko wants it handled with a public sentencing."

He threw up his hands. "So what do you want from me?"

That he didn't know crushed any remaining feelings I had for him. "Nothing. Like I said, just go."

"Buria," he said plaintively. "I don't want it to end like this."

"It's not your choice. It's mine. Get whatever you're taking and get out."

"But we've got four months of our contract left. People will talk."

"Don't like what they might have to say? Move your precious terminal down to my old apartment and spend your days there."

His gaze darted around the spacious apartment.

"You want all of this back? Keep it," I yelled.

His anger fizzled, leaving him looking exhausted. "No. I intended for this to be yours. You've earned it for putting up with me."

"I wasn't looking for a reward."

"I know. I'll come by tomorrow when you're at work to get my things. I can't think straight right now. I haven't slept in two days." He held out his arms. "Can I at least hug you before I go?"

I was kicking him out of the apartment he owned, filled with everything he'd paid for, yelling at him, and he wanted to hug me? "Are you serious?"

He started to nod.

"No, you can't fucking hug me. You can't be bothered to care that I almost died yesterday! You don't get anything from me. Get out!"

He bowed his head, closed his eyes, and Jumped.

Relief washed over me. Giddy laughter burst from my lips. A torrent of tears followed immediately after. I crumbled to the expensive, thickly piled pale green rug and rocked until the tears stopped flowing.

I didn't need him and he certainly didn't need me.

Almost two years beside the Advisor of All had given me all I needed to move forward on my own. I pulled myself up and stood, wiping my face dry.

If I had my way, I wouldn't need anyone ever again.

FORTY-TWO

Anastassia

When Tabor Jumped me to the suite I shared with Vayen on the Iber, I'd expected to be alone for a couple of hours. Vayen wasn't due back from Buria's until evening. However, he sat on the couch, a near empty bottle in hand. His head leaned against the back as if his neck had gone on strike.

He mumbled something incoherent in my direction.

"Perhaps I should stay?" Tabor suggested. *"You're still recovering. You shouldn't be alone."*

"I'm not. I've got this. Go to your meeting. I'll check in with you in a few hours. We can go from there."

"You're sure? I am glad he's here to help you, but in that state, is he really all that helpful?"

"I'm sure."

I forced a confident smile onto my face. A year ago, I would have meant it. Now, I was doing my best to drag myself through the day let alone support anyone else. But Tabor had been devoting nearly every moment of his time to caring for me, and he did have important businesses to run. Those operations supported Neko and the people of the Narvan.

As much as my own comfort had become a priority, given my condition, I did still care what happened to the people I'd spent so long guiding. I wanted to see, or at least hear and read about their successes. It brought me a measure of solace to know they were in good hands.

Tabor cast Vayen one last worried glance and then Jumped.

The moment he left, the music and comfort that I relied on to maintain my façade vanished. If he ever knew how much I needed what he and his bond provided, he'd never leave my side. I made my way on trembling legs to his drunken substitute.

Where Tabor's bond filled the room when we were near one another, Vayen's had shrunk to a close proximity bubble, as if it were slowly collapsing in on itself. When I made it to the couch and eased myself down beside him, a light blanket of peace took the edge off. I pulled out my data pad and forced my stiff fingers to semi-productivity.

"What're you working on?" Vayen slurred beside me.

"Nothing important. Following up on a few messages from that station we toured a few months ago. The one that was having issues with farming production?"

He patted my thigh and nodded.

Since he was attempting to be present despite his state, and the meaning of words in the messages were getting lost to the brain fog brought on by the pills I'd swallowed before Jumping, I admitted defeat and set the datapad down. I hadn't had a productive day since... I couldn't remember when. My usefulness had become a sporadic productive hour at most. It was fucking depressing.

I felt his gaze on me and met it. "Buria?"

He nodded, finishing off the contents of the bottle and setting it on the floor beside his boots. "May I hug you?"

"Of course." I shifted toward him so I could lean my head on his shoulder. My forehead pressed against the heat of his neck, I wrapped my arms around him. "You don't have to ask."

The heavy weight of his arms settled around me. He let out a long sigh as if all the liquor-scented air was slowly exiting his body. "You're not exactly mine anymore. Asking seemed best."

He had a point but it seemed cruel to confirm it. "You're mine, and I say always."

"Thank you," he said raggedly, sitting back but keeping one arm around me.

"Do you want to talk about it? Buria, I mean?"

He shook his head. "Moving out tomorrow."

"Your choice or hers?"

"All her. I can't blame her for it. She's right."

My miserable mate was all mine again. Except, I could never be all his in return. I rested my head on his shoulder, enjoying the heat of his neck against my forehead.

"Feeling all right? Need Cara?" he asked.

"No. She cleared me this morning. The new meds are working."

"That's good. Sorry, I'm bad company today." he said.

"I'm not the greatest myself. Would you settle for being bad company together?"

He chuckled weakly.

If my drunken mate was all mine again and neither of us was up for doing a damned thing… A spark I'd thought gone rekindled to life. I didn't trust my body to be up for his Vayen-sized appetite, but my mind wasn't opposed to the idea.

I pulled away just enough that I could look him in the eyes. "Maybe our two-person support group for the maladjusted could deviate from its usual meeting format tonight?"

"I don't think we—"

I slipped into his mind along the slender tendrils of our bonded connection and rubbed up against places I hadn't been in a long while. Neither had anyone else.

His sharp intake of breath confirmed that I hadn't forgotten what exactly he liked. His response was hesitant at first, gently feeling his way around as if he expected to find Tabor lurking or maybe for me to collapse.

I considered how far I wanted this to go, what boundaries I was comfortable with given I'd been solely intimate with Tabor since Vayen had gone off on me and Daniel. I'd had no inclination to until now. But now he was in my mind and all drunk and pliable. And mine. I kissed him hard and deep with more zeal than I knew I still possessed.

He needed no further urging. His hands hungrily wandered my body while he did fantastic things in my head. I spent a grand total of five seconds comparing his methods with Tabor's before getting lost in the sensations and giving myself over to the contentment of all he was offering.

For a short while I left the misery of my body behind and forgot everything I could no longer do. I was fully me again and everything was how it should be. And then the crash of light came and euphoria took me away from even that, letting me simply be. I floated there for a blissful moment.

Then it faded and I landed back in the weary husk of my body with my heart wildly pounding in my throat. I fought for my next breath with black spots dancing before my eyes.

"Stassia?" Vayen's worried voice broke through my daze.

"I'm fine," I lied, somehow finding the energy to kiss him to sell my deceit. "Maybe we could find our way to the bed? I might need to rest and you, my dear drunken mate, should sleep that off."

He gave me one of his rare smiles that melted my heart. "I can't promise that I won't pick up where I left off when I wake up, but yes, that sounds like a good plan."

"Promise you'll stay beside me and not get into trouble?"

"I might get into trouble beside you if you keep looking at me like that."

I'd missed his attempts at being charming and at humor in general, but I couldn't stifle my yawn. "I don't think I can handle any more of your trouble today, even the good kind."

He nodded solemnly. "Pills kicking in?"

I nodded and checked the time. "Injection in eight hours."

"I've got Cara lined up."

Tabor did them himself, but Vayen had stopped when my doses had gotten higher, when the effects had become more visible.

"I can't. Not when I see what they do to you. I've hurt you enough."

"They keep me alive."

So did Vayen. It would be easy to give in any morning. Any night, for that matter, to just step back and let nature take its course, but he needed me, and I also wasn't ready to leave Tabor yet. We'd had so little time together in the grand scope of things.

"Thank Geva for that, but still. I can't," he said.

"It's all right." I grabbed my datapad and considered if getting up was worth the effort or if maybe I should just take a nap right there.

Vayen slipped one arm under me and scooped me up with him as he stood. At one time that would have been an admirable task, but I'd lost a third of my body weight since the night I'd landed a drop of Nacombic on my tongue.

He kicked the bottle over with his first step and stumbled on the second, but managed to get his feet under him after that. With an extra sway to his steps, he got us both to the bedroom without incident.

Though it was barely early evening and I hadn't eaten much at midday, I wasn't hungry now either. I undressed and huddled under the blankets while Vayen stumbled off to the bathroom. It seemed I was always cold these days.

After a quick note on my datapad to let Tabor know I was fine, I switched it off and closed my eyes, not even caring that the light was still on. I was just drifting off when Vayen lumbered back in and shifted the entire mattress as he got into bed beside me.

"No company tonight?" he asked from his side of the bed.

I'd been spending so many nights with either just Tabor or Vayen on one side, and Tabor sleeping on the other, that sharing a bed with Vayen alone felt odd. Like I'd forgotten how to do it. When it was the three of us, both of my mates slept as far from each other as they could get without falling off the bed, leaving me to float alone in the middle. Neither dared claim me. It was comfortable in terms of having both bonds around me and provided maximum relief so I could get a decent night's rest. It was also lonely.

"Just you and me."

I gathered my nerve and slid closer until my back rested against his chest.

"Thank Geva." He draped an arm over me and pulled me tight against him.

The heat from his body was heavenly. I sighed with relief.

Even though his breath stank of liquor, and he started drunk snoring in no time flat, I smiled to myself. In his arms was where I belonged.

With Buria off Vayen duty, I found myself spending more nights alone with him. More accurately, I gently told Tabor I was giving him a little more time off a week so he could keep his businesses afloat. That way I didn't feel quite as guilty for monopolizing his time when I was with him. It also gave me some time alone with my death-bringer mate who wasn't taking the abrupt departure from his second wife well.

On one hand, Vayen hadn't had any major incidents lately. On the other, he had a drink in his hand pretty much anytime he wasn't sleeping or passed out. He barely left our suite and when he did, rumors followed him back to me through the kids and messages from the crew. He might not be entirely drunk when he was out and about, but he was usually halfway there and anyone could smell it on him. He didn't join any of the landing parties, limiting his mission involvement to brief meetings in his office, or reviewing and responding to messages and reports from our suite. All in all, it was a workable stalemate to managing both of our situations.

Ikeri sat beside me on the floor, running through the Seeker forms in, what had to be for her, a painfully slow progression. My muscles had given up their grace and flexibility in favor of sharp twinges and stiffness.

"Daniel is going to be here any minute with Mika and Dreydon. Are you sure you don't want to meet with him elsewhere?" She cast a worried look at the bedroom door.

"Your father is asleep."

"The kids are loud, Mom. What if they wake him up?"

"He'll behave."

She gave me a skeptical look.

"We'll deal with that if he wakes up. Tabor is tied up in meetings all day, and I don't want to be far from your father."

"But you said his bond doesn't even help if he's not right next to you."

"It doesn't. I don't want to be far because he needs me close."

"Oh." She switched to the next position while keeping an eye on me. "How is Tabor taking you spending more time with Dad again?"

My daughter had a tendency to turn every conversation into a Seeker session. The inner workings of my relationship with my mates wasn't daughter territory. "How are things going with that Artorian boy from engineering?"

She scowled at me. "He's fine, Mom."

"How fine?"

She groaned.

I started to move to the next form but my knee locked up, sending me off balance. Ikeri caught me, keeping me upright.

"That's it. I'm done for the day," I decreed.

"Mom, we're not finished. Cara said stretches are good for you. They keep your joints loose."

"Do they look loose to you?" I dropped into a chair and sighed with relief.

"Fine," she stood upright and then reached down to touch her palms flat to the floor.

"Show off."

Ikeri cringed. "I wasn't."

"I was teasing."

She smiled uncertainly. "Let me help you with your hair? Brushing doesn't hurt, does it?"

"Not since I switched meds. That one made my scalp feel like raw nerve endings.

Ikeri dodged into the bathroom and came out with my brush.

She'd helped me braid my hair a few times before. Without Tabor nearby, it bothered my shoulders too much to get my arms up that high and behind me. I preferred when Vayen helped with my hair. He did magical things to my scalp with his fingers, but Ikeri did a suitable job with the basic task.

She brushed lightly, taking too much time between swipes to hide what she was doing. I'd had enough of everyone attempting to be delicate with me.

"I know it's thinning. No need to be sneaky about it."

"Why is it falling out?" she asked quietly.

"Too much strain on my body. Hair is superfluous when it comes to preserving resources for basic functions."

"Sorry, Mom, it's just..." She dropped the brush on her lap as she sat in the chair beside me, the handful of hair concealed in her closed fist. Ikeri stared at the floor, tears swimming in her eyes.

I sent her what little peace I could muster over our natural connection. There wasn't anything to be done about it. Every week, when Cara did my thorough examination, she went on about how wonderfully I was doing given what I was dealing with. I'd thought she was just attempting to maintain my positivity. However, the University doctors who did monthly checks, said the same thing. Maybe they were all laying on the encouraging bedside manner to keep Vayen at bay.

"I should be the one calming you," she said, sniffing.

"Yes, well, you're my daughter. Humor me."

She wiped her eyes and smiled.

While she was being acceptant of my motherliness, I decided to delve a little deeper. "So, this boy in engineering. Is that serious?"

"It's too early to tell. Maybe."

"Would you like it to be?"

She smiled brighter. "Maybe."

"Is he anything like your father?" I asked, not sure if I was going to be relieved one way or the other.

"Artorian, yes, but the only abilities he has are solving problems in the Iber's systems."

"And his family?"

"Not on board. I did see a still frame." She shrugged. "Dad knows I've been seeing him, so I'm sure he must be cleared on a thousand levels by now or he'd have vanished mysteriously from the crew."

I wished Vayen was conscious for this conversation, to see our daughter smiling about a boy, to hear her talking like nothing had happened to put a several-year-long hold on this part of her life.

"I'm glad you're happy," I said after I got past the lump in my throat.

"He would love to meet you. In person, I mean. If you're up for it sometime."

"Cara says I'm supposed to be limiting my interactions with people outside family. Compromised immune system."

"Right." She sighed.

"He could meet your father though."

"He already has and lived to talk about it." She smirked. "By which I mean like it was an amazing grade on a test that he'd spent months studying for."

I laughed. "Have you been seeing him that long?"

Ikeri smiled slyly. "Maybe."

"Just don't end up bonded to him without a joining offer firmly in place? Please?"

"Deal."

The door chimed. Ikeri got up to let Daniel in. To my surprise, he had Arden with him as well as his children whom I had expected. I hadn't been making excuses with Ikeri, I really was doing my best to limit visitors. While Arden was family, neither of Daniel's wives were on my immediate list. We talked via vid call once a week. I thought that was more than enough, considering my circumstances.

"Oh good, you're here too," Daniel said, grinning at Ikeri.

Mika trundled her way toward me. Dreydon followed behind her. He let out a gleeful scream, holding his arms wide to be picked up. Ikeri intercepted him.

Arden stuck to Daniel's side, grinning every bit as wide. I sighed inwardly, already guessing what they were about to announce.

Mika stood beside my chair, attempting to climb onto my lap. I pulled her up.

The bedroom door slid open a few inches, as though the hungover man inside was questioning what in all the hells had made enough noise to wake him from the drunken dead. His gaze met mine. I shook my head.

"Arden is pregnant. We're going to have another one," Daniel announced proudly.

"Congratulations," I said while noting Vayen's glower dissolving into sagging shoulders and a bowed head. The bedroom door closed.

If Ikeri noticed her father's brief appearance, she didn't mention it. Her attention seemed consumed with Dreydon in her arms. I ate up the sight of my daughter holding a child, knowing I wasn't going to be around long enough to see her with her own. Assuming she chose to have any, but from the tenderness on her face with her nephew in her arms, I had a feeling she would.

Maybe with the boy from engineering, maybe with someone else. I'd probably never know that part of her equation either. I busied myself with arranging Mika's curls to hide any indication of my maudlin thoughts from my observant children.

Arden, Daniel, and Ikeri launched into an animated conversation that required minimal input from me. Despite the grandchild in my arms, I felt like I was no longer fully there. Hugging Mika, I hoped they would continue on like this, as a family, when I was truly gone.

I'd felt moderately energetic at Tabor's estate, getting a little work done on my datapad while he sat nearby holding vid meetings at his desk terminal. But then it was time for him to deliver me to the Iber for Vayen's few days of solo babysitting-me duty.

As much as I hadn't been looking forward to being away from Tabor's pain-shielding bond, I'd been eager to get back to Vayen's side. He'd been spending more nights than not with us at Tabor's estate lately. Since he didn't relish sleeping in the same bed as Tabor and me, no matter that no one was touching and that they slept on opposite sides, I had to assume that he was having a difficult time managing his dark side. It was that or that he missed me that badly, but from his semi-conscious state when he'd arrived each time, I had a feeling it wasn't about me specifically, but for support.

I settled onto the couch in the Iber suite doing my best to keep my movements sure and my hands steady under Tabor's observant gaze.

"Are the new injections helping with the tremors?" he asked, referring to the medication change I'd started the day before.

It seemed like Nan was always sending something new for Cara to try. Not that I minded them trying to find solutions, but the constantly changing combinations of medication made it difficult to ascertain which one was causing trouble when my body decided to rebel. Today was a rebelling day. I did my best to hide that from him too.

"Yes." I waved him off. "I'll be fine. Go on and good luck with the negotiations."

"Gamnock won't know what hit him." Tabor grinned.

I didn't have the heart to point out that his recent booming business successes likely had a lot more to do with his connection to me than his haggling skills. Not that his skills in that area were lacking any more than they were in any other area. The one thing I didn't hide from my second husband was my adoration for him. After a lifetime of hardship, he deserved every second of that that I had left to offer.

His grin grew even wider. He rushed over to land a kiss on my cheek. "You'll let me know if you need anything?"

"Yes. Now off with you." I playfully pushed him away.

The suite door opened and Vayen strode in. Tabor straightened, nodding his greeting to my first husband. "Her medication is on the table."

There was a second nod but no more words. Whatever passed between them was through mind speech or link. I had no idea how connected they were in that manner. It felt awkward to ask.

Tabor gave me one last look and then Jumped.

The couch sagged as Vayen sat beside me, his hands in his lap. I didn't smell any liquor on him but I didn't know if that boded well or not.

"The Ocelon rebellion has grown to the point we can't ignore it any longer."

"I wasn't aware we were ignoring it. Daniel said—"

"Figure of speech." He sighed. "Those obstinate bastards are poised to attack several of our unified worlds."

"I assume we're not going to allow them to do that."

He nodded. "It's the how I need to ask you about."

"Etara would probably be the wiser choice to consult with."

The pleading in his eyes shut me up. I nodded.

"I can stop them without any harm coming to our people. I can save everyone who has joined our union."

"How many are you considering killing?"

"Enough to make them not attack again."

"All right, so what's the question?" I asked.

"They're already calling me a tyrant and a monster. Wouldn't my action against them just prove their point?"

"Yes, but those that you protect, if they call you their savior, does that balance it out? Which side's opinion matters more?"

"Yours."

If he needed someone to take the blame for his decision, I figured it might as well be me. He wouldn't have had the Arpex ability if I hadn't let Nan fuse him with them to begin with. Not letting him die had been my choice, and now he was struggling to live with it.

"Be the savior, strike down the opposition."

His voice shook, "And Etara?"

"I'll talk to her."

He nodded, sliding closer until his shoulder bumped against mine. Recently he'd grown more hesitant to touch me, as though he'd ceaded that aspect to Tabor. Though we'd been making public rounds together on the Iber when I was up for it, in private, he'd relegated himself to my first husband in title only.

As to his second wife, Vayen's contract to Buria had expired. Though they'd been separated for months before the contract ended, the rumors had been minimal then. When it had become clear there would be no renewal, they'd exploded. Speculation rippled over the seedier newsfeeds.

I had reached out to Buria after it was clear she and Vayen were over both as a courtesy regarding our arrangement, and to make sure she understood about keeping her mouth shut. Though she had been hounded for interviews since the expiration, she'd done as I'd asked. She may have wounded Vayen badly, but our conversation had revealed the wounding was mutal.

I didn't fault her for using her fame to start her own security business. Many high-end Narvan clients were already clamoring for her services. Daniel remained in fairly close contact with her, keeping me apprised of her dealings and likely using her to his advantage in true Ta'set form.

I relaxed against Vayen. My death-bringer mate hadn't been an easy man to love these past few years. No one understood his flaws as well as I did. Being one of his flaws, I had an advantage in that arena.

The vague relief of his bond took the edge off the worst of the rebelling in my body's internal war between life and death. Life was under heavy fire today.

I reached out and found his hand, entwining my fingers with his. We sat there for a few moments, me doing my best to ease his weary conscience through our bonded connection and him so still he might have been frozen. I couldn't handle being on high alert in my condition. I needed him to step down from whatever ledge he was on today.

"If I asked you to make those spicy noodles but then could only eat a few bites, would you hold it against me?"

He squeezed my hand. "As long as you eat even a few bites, I will make you anything you want."

Clearly eager for something to do, he got up and went into the little kitchen. Within minutes, he had water in a pot and everything he needed sitting on the counter. He began methodically chopping peppers. I watched him work, catching his subtle glances in my direction and returning his smiles. He had more than enough on his mind without having to worry about me.

Everyone had a lot going on, but still, I kept the internal war raging. I wasn't ready to leave them yet. Vayen and Tabor needed me for their own reasons. I wouldn't let them down as long as I had fight left in me.

Without Vayen's bond active beside me, my joints stiffened, every muscle ached, and my head began to throb. By the time he announced the meal was ready, a sharp stabbing pain had developed in my gut. I forced a smile, but though I did my damnedest to stand and go to the table, I couldn't get off the couch.

"Stassia?"

The concern in his voice cut me. He had the lives of so many hanging over him. He didn't need mine added to the number. I tried again, driving my fists into the cushion to propel myself forward enough to shift my weight toward my feet.

"I just need a minute," I declared, knowing he could see my arms shaking and the sweat I could feel on my forehead. Why was doing even the simplest things so damned hard?

He set the steaming plates down and came over. The moment his bond enveloped me, an involuntary sigh of relief escaped my mouth.

"Come on, eat your few bites and then you're staying glued to my side for the rest of the day." He half-carried, half-guided me over to the table and helped me into the chair. Rather than sit across from me as he usually did, he slid his chair around to the side of the table and sat, his knee nudging against mine.

He ate quickly and with a single-minded purpose that made me wonder when he'd last taken the time to eat rather than drink a meal. Only wearing clothes and not masked with layers of weapons and armor, it was plain to see that he'd been losing weight too. My once muscle-bulked mate now resembled the memories he'd shared of when he'd first arrived on Pentares, wiry and gaunt. Like Jey since Vayen had put him back together: hollow.

I chewed slowly, savoring the flavor of the simple meal, all the while knowing that it wouldn't set well but comforted by the familiarity of it nevertheless. He'd managed to put the perfect sized portion on my plate, exactly six bites. We finished at the same time.

He nodded toward my half-filled cup of water. "Drink it. Cara said the fluids help with the muscle cramps."

I dutifully drained the water.

"Are you up for a walk?" he asked.

I managed to stand on my own, but held the edge of the table, wondering if I dared let go. Could I fake my way through a walk with his long legs and fevered pace? Being seen together would help his image and Cara would be happy to know I was getting the exercise she kept nagging me about. I tried for a confident smile and hoped it didn't come off as the wince it really was.

"As long as you're beside me."

Vayen nodded solemnly.

The stabbing jolts in my gut begged to point out that if he had stayed beside me in the first place, we wouldn't be dealing with the effects of me poisoning myself, but the relief of his bond won. I waited by the table while he darted over to slip on his armor. Then he helped me into mine. Since the Ocelon had shot me, Vayen made sure I didn't go anywhere in public without my coat. A year ago, I wouldn't have noticed the added weight, but now it felt like another whole person sitting on my shoulders.

I took his arm. Vayen didn't say anything when I leaned on him more than I wanted to admit I needed to. He let me set the pace, which was agonizingly slow for him as we headed down the corridor toward the lift. The lift door closed as he input the floor for the command center.

Just as I was about to mention that it was Daniel's shift in command and that perhaps we should go be seen elsewhere, Vayen cleared his throat and turned to me all earnest and concerned.

"Would it be easier for you to not be on the Iber? I mean, would it be more manageable to be around Tabor? He helps far more than I do. It's not that I begrudge you spending more time with him, but it won't do either of us any favors to have him next to you every second in public here."

The simple and clear answer was yes, that would be better for me to remain with Tabor, but our lives weren't simple. "It wouldn't do you any favors to have me permanently at Tabor's estate."

"Stassia, this isn't about just me. I don't like seeing you in more pain than you need to be just because he's not here." He raked a hand through his loose and longer-than-usual hair. "Not that you need to be in pain. Fuck. You know what I mean, right?"

"I do. But honestly, Tabor has business he can't take care of when he's babysitting me. So you get a turn."

He shook his head. "You can't tell me Tabor wouldn't find a way to do whatever the fuck he needed to do while you were attached to his side. It's only because you're telling him to bring you to me that he's doing it. I don't care what he tells you, he definitely doesn't want to leave you here."

My heart began to pound harder. I didn't need the two of them getting into a possessive bond battle over me. "Did he say something to you? I told him—"

"Stassia, he doesn't have to say a word. And to be clear, he doesn't. It's on his face every time he leaves."

"Oh."

The lift door opened, exposing us to the bustling activity and attentive glances of crewmembers who were busy outside of the primary command center. I put on a smile, took a deep breath, and stepped out of the lift, begging my steps to be sure and my tremors to be masked by Vayen's hand that was suddenly over mine. While I concentrated on remaining standing and trying to ignore the sharp jolts in my stomach, Vayen nodded to those that required acknowledging and gently pulled me along with him to talk to those who warranted a short conversation. Too distracted by my own body, I couldn't follow much of what was being said. I let Vayen handle it. Once the initial hubbub subsided, we headed inside.

I took the brief break in our social duties as an opportunity to propose a solution. "Would you be opposed to me doing daytime social duty with you, even if we did it more often, but then me spending behind-closed-door time on the Iber with Tabor in his suite here so I can be close to all of you? I know you hate the bed sharing arrangement, but that is an option if you need it. I don't like the thought of you spending all your nights alone."

Though he'd brought the topic up, his face fell now. A wave of trepidation rushed through our connection as though I'd confirmed his worst fear. "I don't—"

Sirens went off in the corridor. The Iber rocked, knocking me off balance. Vayen grabbed me, holding me upright. Lights dimmed and then flickered before resuming their usual cheery glow.

"Go." I pushed myself away from him, nodding toward the door at the end of the corridor. "I'll get there on my own."

Vayen went spine straight a second and then turned to me. "Fucking Ocelon opposition." He gave me a quick once over and then ran for the door.

The moment he was gone, I sagged against the wall. That also served to get me out of the way for three officers who rushed by in Vayen's wake.

So much for the Ocelon going after our unified worlds. Or maybe they were and had enough excess resources to send ships to attack the Iber itself. Having one well-known flagship of our mission did have its drawbacks.

The Iber took another hit. Shouting erupted in the command center. I clung to the wall, not wanting to land on my ass amongst the supplementary operations posts.

Daniel's faithful assistant Frad dashed out the door and toward me. "I'm supposed to escort you inside," he announced warily, as if waiting for me to bite his head off.

"Thank you."

I took his arm and tried to confidently fake my way through the thirty-seven steps it took to get into the command center. Thankfully Frad took my leaning on him in stride.

He seemed torn as to where exactly to deliver me so I tapped his arm and released myself into the orbit of my wrathful-looking mate who was staring at the damage report. I caught bits of the information that flowed past him on the vid, but Vayen's head blocked most of the view.

Daniel was busy shouting out orders, clearly and confidently as though he'd been born to this. The crew followed without question. I was quite proud of my son just then, seeing him in action that didn't require the same personal level of violence his father preferred.

I pulled out the smaller and lighter datapad I kept in my pocket these days and requested Etara's presence in the command center. If Vayen went off, I needed someone besides me to be able to rein him in.

Daniel had things well enough in order. No one needed me, hell, most of the crew had never needed me. I was just a celebrity, a figurehead in Vayen's shadow these past few years.

Vayen didn't interfere with Daniel's command, but I got the sense that he was gritting his teeth to keep it that way. Not that I saw anything wrong with what our son was doing. It was likely more that Vayen himself wasn't the one giving those orders.

The Iber was giving a good fight, but we were outnumbered. Daniel issued the order to call for assistance from the nearest members of our advisory union.

"We promised to protect them," Vayen said loudly. "Not that they'd have to protect us."

Daniel glanced over as if just then noticing our presence. He gave Vayen a deadpan stare. "If you'd like to remove the need for that assistance, have at it. But only if you can keep yourself under control."

Etara burst into the room as if she expected a disaster already in progress. She came to a halt beside me. Vayen glared in my direction.

"Just a precaution," I said calmly before proceeding to bring Etara up to date on the situation and our proposed solution.

The little Seeker closed her eyes and sucked on her lips. Her hands clenched at the ends of the long, flared sleeves of her robes. After a moment, she opened her eyes and let out a sigh.

The Iber rocked again. I grabbed Vayen to steady myself.

Etara shook her head. "While I see the wisdom of your solution, I don't like it. I'd rather you hold out until the union back up arrives."

"Then you don't see the wisdom at all," Vayen said.

Another shot hit the Iber. The little Seeker cast a worried glance at the walls.

She held up a hand. "I'm weighing your wisdom with mine. Can I trust you to maintain control?"

His dark glare and tight jaw made me think the answer was a definite no, but he mumbled an affirmative sound. Was she really going to buy that?

Etara looked to me. Like I was going to confirm that he was capable of control? He wasn't, and we both knew it.

"Perhaps if the target was more confined than the entire opposing force?" I suggested. "Making an example of a few to impress the threat on the many?"

In the past, Etara had agreed to those terms, phrased many different ways.

"I would condone that," she announced. "Can you select the threads of only those directly attacking us? Not every soul on those ships?"

"That's too specific," he grumbled. "It doesn't work like that."

"A minimum number then," Etara suggested.

"Define minimum." He scowled as the Iber was hit again. "And define it quickly."

Etara took a quick look at the ships surrounding us. "Two hundred lives."

Vayen shrugged. "Done." He closed his eyes and tipped his head back. One hand shot out to pull me closer until my back was pressed against the front of his armor. His other hand rested on my shoulder.

I felt him distantly in my head, as if he were far away, but desperately trying to pull himself closer, to hold on to me more than physically. Reaching out with what little telepathy I had left, I held on to him through to our bonded connection as hard as I could, putting all my energy into being the anchor he needed.

The smaller ships around us went quiet. Two of the larger ones stopped firing while three others continued. Daniel focused his attacks on those.

Four ships arrived together, identifying themselves as our reinforcements. Daniel greeted them and sent them after our remaining targets. The two ships that had stopped firing were now making a retreat.

"Let them go," I suggested. "Someone needs to spread the word of what happened here."

Daniel nodded to me but avoided looking at Vayen. The crew did not, their excitement at witnessing the death-bringer in action filled the room. The flurry of reports and orders resumed, but the mood had shifted toward victory. I let it wash over me as exhaustion sunk in, the heavy-in-the-bones kind that made my eyes beg to close regardless of where we were or what we were in the middle of. I forced them to stay open, but that effort wouldn't hold up for long.

Vayen came back to himself. "I can't do that again," he whispered to Etara. "Don't let me do it again."

She nodded solemnly.

"Are you back? All the way?" I asked, sagging against him and not bothering to hide it.

"Thanks to you, yes," he said in my ear.

"Could we go home now? I don't think I can walk."

"Yes. I'll get Tabor here for you." He sounded as weary as I felt.

"No." I squeezed the arm he had around me. "Just you, one last time."

The next thing I knew we were in our suite and I was on his lap. His forehead pressed against mine. I held onto him as he wept.

❧

When I finally pried myself out of bed around midday, I found Tabor sitting on the couch with Vayen. They were talking quietly.

"Could you give us a minute?" Vayen asked Tabor upon noticing me.

"Certainly." Tabor bowed the slightest bit and walked out of our suite.

"What's this all about?" I asked, not really wanting to know, but my pounding heart demanded answers.

"Your pills first," he said, pointing to the table where he had set out my assortment of morning meds. "Toast?" he asked as if nothing was going on.

Being that my stomach rebelled even more than usual if I didn't eat something with my morning regimen, I nodded. He set a plate with my thick buttered slab of toasted bread and a glass of water in front of me at the table and took his seat.

"I moved your clothes to Tabor's suite. Let me know whatever else you want there. I didn't know what all you wanted. Or needed. Or..." his voice hitched.

The toast, even slathered in butter went dry in my mouth. "We don't have to do this as an all-or-nothing move."

"I know."

But apparently, we were.

He sat there quietly, looking utterly miserable while I ate my toast and swallowed my pills. When I finished, he nodded and stood. I made no move to join him. He pulled me to my feet and held me there for a long while.

"I get it now. How you felt that night," he said into my thin and brittle hair. "I'm so sorry that I fucked this up. All of it."

"I feel pretty confident in saying that we both made shitty decisions that night. You were not alone in fucking things up."

"Yes, well, I had everything and now I have nothing."

"I'm still—"

He shook his head and took a deep breath. "Stassia, I release you from—"

I clamped my hand over his mouth and backed up a step so he had to look me in the eye. "Don't you dare. I will not be released! From anything. I was yours first and I'm staying that way."

When I pulled my hand away, the slightest smile quirked his lips.

"You still have me and you always will. I mean it. Always." I drilled that into his head as hard as I could. "I'll be standing right there waiting in your ninth hell whenever you get there. You hear me?"

He wiped at his glistening eyes and nodded. "What about him?"

"Tabor is way too much of a saint to have to spend eternity with the likes of us."

Vayen chuckled softly. "He is."

"You'll come to see me every day? And maybe at night sometimes? You'll make me get out of bed and go for a walk so we can have some time alone together?"

"I promise."

"I love you," I said, both out loud and in his head in the hopes that he'd remember it when he was sitting here alone, drinking until he felt nothing else.

"I know." He'd never been one to give much voice to feelings but he filled my head with love, with memories of us together, until I was overwhelmed by it all. "I love you too," he said as he Jumped me to Tabor's suite and deposited me into the care of my second husband.

Vayen left without a word. The finality of what he'd shared, what had passed between us took my breath away and left me feeling cold and detached from my body.

"Anastassia?" Tabor tentatively reached out to me.

His concern threatened to smother everything Vayen had shared with me. I wasn't even remotely ready to be done feeling any of that yet. I wanted to crawl inside myself and hold onto it as hard as Vayen had held onto me when he'd taken his allowed two hundred lives.

"I'm sorry. I need to..."

Tabor stood aside and let me stumble into the dark bedroom. As soon as the door closed, sealing me away from everyone, I crawled into bed and gave into the pain in my heart and mind just as much as my body.

FORTY-THREE

Anastassia

Tabor shook my shoulder gently. "You have visitors."

My heart leapt at the thought that Vayen might be there. Though he'd followed through on his promise to see me nearly every day for the first few weeks I'd been in Tabor's suite, days had begun to lapse between our visits. Our walks had become shorter and then stopped altogether as my strength waned. Despite my offer, Vayen hadn't spent a single night with us.

In the months since I'd moved into Tabor's suite, Vayen appeared a little emptier every time I saw him. His visits had gone from half a day to hours and more recently not even that. It had been six days since he'd last stopped by. I missed him dearly.

"The kids are here," Tabor said softly as if he sensed my hope and was trying to let me down easy.

I sat up slowly. "Help me get dressed?"

Tabor nodded, already handing me a pullover shirt. The pants were more trouble for me. He helped slip them over my legs and tugged them up my hips to fasten them.

"Shoes?" he asked.

"I'm not planning to venture beyond a chair, so not today." Or very likely, any other day and he knew that, but he still asked.

He slipped thick socks over my perpetually chilled feet and helped me off the bed. The nerve damage had progressed to a point where I had a hard time standing let alone walking. I hated the helplessness of it all. Cara had provided an automated chair for me so that I could get around the Iber if I wanted to. I didn't want to be seen in the damned chair unless Vayen was with me. And he wasn't here.

The comfort and calm of the bond I shared with Tabor dulled the sting, but I wasn't in the mood to be mollified. Tabor had been beside me night and day for months. While I loved the man dearly, I craved time alone. Time alone meant either being heavily drugged or suffering the unshielded agony that my body had become.

Tabor eyed the mobility chair, keeping one arm around me and one hand firmly under my elbow. "Walking or sitting?"

"You know I hate that thing. I'll walk."

Patient to a fault, he moved inch by inch with each forced step I took. Upon appearing in the common room, Ikeri leapt from her seat and rushed to my other side. Another layer of ease settled over me as she exerted her Seeker abilities.

"I'm sure you have more deserving clients to expend your energy on."

"Shut up," she muttered, sounding like her father.

Daniel stood, shifting from foot to foot as though he wanted to do something but didn't know what. He was a handsome young man, just like his father had been. Markus sat on a chair beside Daniel, watching me with a sorrow-filled gaze. When he'd visited months before, I'd still been walking beside Vayen. I'd been able to laugh, to smile without forcing it.

My hands began to tremble. I clenched them into stiff fists to attempt to keep the shaking under control. The tremors were always worse when I got distracted by emotions. That had been happening far too often lately.

Tabor and Ikeri got me over to the chair where Ikeri had been sitting. As comfortable as the couch was, I had a hard time getting out of it even with help. That was a struggle I didn't need my children to witness.

"Before I sit, come here." I caught Ikeri in a hug before she went to the couch.

Tabor took a step back but remained within touching range in case I needed steadying.

In plain clothes today, my daughter wrapped her thin arms around me. Far wirier than I'd ever been and shorter, she felt delicate, but I knew she had her own kind of strength. "Who's the lucky boy this week?" I asked.

She snorted. "You make it sound like I'm working my way through the crew."

"There's nothing wrong with reviewing your options as long as you're being responsible about it."

"Kursen is an intern with the Jalvian botanists that came aboard last month. And like I keep saying, it's not serious."

"It's never serious until it suddenly is."

"That's very true," Tabor said, winking.

Ikeri laughed and took a seat on the couch.

I held my hand out to Markus. Our skinny, little Jalvian boy was no longer skinny or little. Though on the slighter side of a typical Jalvian build, he was gaining muscles as well as inches. He stood taller than me, his long arms wrapped carefully around my shoulders.

"I'm not going to break," I said quietly.

"I've missed you," he whispered back.

"I've missed you too. I'm glad you came. Have you seen your father?"

"Not yet. I'm waiting for Ikeri to give me the all-clear. They said he's been in a mood."

"Sounds about right. Do make sure you visit him before you have to go back though. It would make him happy to see you. Even if he doesn't act that way."

"He's not like that with me." He subtly nodded toward Daniel.

"Good."

Markus gave me a quick peck on the cheek before returning to his seat.

"Your turn," I said, waving Daniel over.

My son hugged me not as if I would break, but as if I would vanish if he didn't hold on tight enough. He hugged like his father.

"Mom, are you all right?" he asked in my ear.

I nodded, throat thick and unable to speak.

"I'll drag his drunk ass over here if it will make you happy," Tabor said, knowing as he always did, what was upsetting me.

"Please? When the kids leave?"

"You're serious?" he asked.

"You weren't?"

Tabor smiled in my head. *"I'll be right back. He'll need fair warning to sober up."* He Jumped, leaving me in Daniel's care for a few moments.

The promise of seeing Vayen soon, no matter what condition he might be in, lifted my spirits.

"How are Arden and Meera? The kids?"

"Everyone is fine, Mom. Growing bigger, all of them. Well, except for Meera. Thankfully. I don't think I could handle another double shot of infants."

"I'm happy for you."

"Where'd he go?" Daniel nodded to where Tabor had stood.

"Errand. He'll be right back. Help me sit?"

Daniel held my arms as I eased into the chair. Once I was safely in place, he returned to his seat.

"No further news from the Ocelon opposition?" I asked.

"Thankfully no. Dad seems to have quelled their desire for rebellion. At least for now."

"Make sure you keep it that way. Have nearby worlds patrol for signs of another uprising. You have records of which other societies joined them?"

He nodded. "Dad provided a list of the minds he touched, where they came from. I circulated the list to the union at the last meeting."

"You attended the meeting? Where was your father?"

Daniel avoided my gaze. "He wasn't up to it."

I'd never wanted to put union duty on Daniel, to drag him into that aspect of our lives. He was capable, but so young, and dammit, he didn't need more obligations to take him away from his family.

"I know." He held up a hand. "I'm not advising anything. Just consulting as needed. When the two of you are busy. When I'm asked. I promise."

Apparently, I wasn't doing a very good job of keeping my feelings off my face. I nodded to put him at ease.

"The new facility is very nice. Camendis was a good choice. Very hidden, yet a beautiful world to view behind the safety of thick plaz."

I hadn't seen anything other than the plans. While Vayen had included me in choosing the location, I'd never set foot there and I likely never would. He was the Advisor of All. I let him advise.

As long as I kept talking, I didn't focus on the mounting pain that was building in Tabor's absence.

"How is your father?" I asked, hoping to get a feel for what I'd be facing shortly.

"You haven't seen him?" Ikeri asked.

"Not for almost a week. Why?"

Daniel shook his head. "Neither have I. As far as I know, no one has. I assumed he was holed up here with you."

Tabor was probably right in his assumption of Vayen's condition.

"What does the rumor mill have to say these days?"

Markus turned to Ikeri and then to Daniel, even more interested than I was. I had a feeling General Tellison kept him busy and often ensconced in his crew with the intent of shielding Markus from Ta'set drama.

"That your health is declining," Ikeri said carefully.

Daniel rolled his eyes at his sister. "There is conflicting speculation. Dad is spending all of his time with you. He's a washed-up drunk. That he's meditating."

"That he's communing with Geva, praying for a miracle," Ikeri interjected.

Daniel scoffed. "That he's unable to climb out of a bottle long enough to take care of you, so you left him for Tabor."

I cringed.

Daniel continued, "I've switched your...his suite steward three times, but they all talk about how many bottles they bring to the room and how many empties they take away. If he would get his own damned liquor it would help, but he's in no shape to do that. Frankly, I think he's given up on his public image entirely."

"I didn't leave him," I declared.

Ikeri nodded. "We know."

"I suppose it was a bit optimistic of me to think that no one would notice I was no longer living with your father."

"That hasn't been confirmed one way or the other. It's just speculation," Ikeri said.

"Just as dangerous." The pain was getting hard to ignore and making it even harder to concentrate.

I broke down and reached out to Tabor over our bonded connection. *"I need you."*

"He's passed out. I can't wake him, but I did prop him up so he at least won't choke on his own vomit if it comes to that. Should I have Cara look in on him? She'd keep quiet."

"Since I can't check on him, yes, please. And thank you."

"Anything for you, dearest and only."

I seriously did not deserve that man. When he returned to my side a minute later, I hit him with as much gratefulness as I could muster in my condition.

The soft vibrating hum of our bond swirled around me. I sighed as the stiffness in my body eased. Tabor stood behind me, his hands on my shoulders, thumbs subtly working at knotted muscles. I wanted very much to drop my head back against him and close my eyes. But the kids were here and I didn't know when I'd see them all together again, or for that matter, if I ever would.

Tabor cleared his throat. "I'm not trying to rush you off, but your mother has about fifteen minutes before she's due for her pills, something to eat, and a nap."

"We could get you something from the dining hall," offered Markus. "Whatever you want."

"Her diet is very restricted," Tabor said gently.

It struck me that Tabor would have made a wonderful father if his mother hadn't maimed him. The thought made me melancholy. Or maybe it was knowing I wouldn't see Vayen anytime soon. Or knowing that he was losing himself in liquor to curb his darkness. I watched my children watching me, all of them with varying proficiency at covering their trepidation over seeing me as I was.

I managed a half-smile. "Food doesn't sit well with me anymore. The doctors have me on a liquid diet. But that was very nice of you to offer. I wish I could take you up on it."

Markus smiled weakly.

While I had his attention, I distracted myself from the lurking depression by asking how his training was going. Markus grew animated as he spent the next ten minutes speeding through everything he'd done in the past few months.

"I'll make sure I visit more often," he said, glancing at Tabor over my head and then getting up to give me a quick hug.

"Maybe hold off until tonight before checking in on your father. He had a rough day," Tabor suggested.

Daniel gave the two of us a suspicious glance.

"I did say that I didn't leave him, didn't I?" I snapped.

Tabor's fingers pressed into my shoulders.

"Sorry. I think I need my pills and that nap."

"And something to eat," Tabor said.

I very much wanted to stand and hug my children as a whole person, but I wasn't feeling very whole and standing was too much to ask of my tingling legs and numb toes. When Cara had said my circulation was joining the declining body functions, I thought she was being premature, but it turned out my personal doctor did know what she was talking about.

"You'll bring the babies next time?" I asked Daniel.

"Sure, Mom. If you're up for it."

I wanted to be, even more so for Tabor, who adored having

grandchildren. He deserved something uplifting out of the depressing mess I'd made of our perpetual marriage contract.

Ikeri gave me a long look and then a kiss on the cheek before joining Markus at the door.

Daniel knelt and pressed his hands over mine on my lap. "You'll let me know if you need anything? Either of you?"

He looked so much like his father whom I so badly missed, who was lying in a drunken stupor in our room down the corridor, alone. Daniel's face began to blur.

"We will," Tabor said quickly. "Stay right here," he said to me as he followed Daniel over to the door where Ikeri and Markus stood. He spoke to them quietly and briefly. When they left, he came back to my side.

"Full disclosure, I may have slapped your highly inebriated first husband around a little in my attempts to wake him."

"He won't remember."

The tone of the bond's hum changed, taking on sharp notes.

"It's how he doesn't remember to visit you that I don't understand. Anastassia, what kind of husband does that when his wife is so ill?" Anger crackled in the undercurrents of his calm and collected tone.

"The kind who feels guilty about causing his wife's dire illness."

"As if his behavior makes up for that in any way? Fucking unacceptable!"

I didn't want to hear any more. I couldn't. Anger fueled my muscles enough to get me out of the chair and most of the way to the bedroom without his assistance.

Tabor caught up to me without any effort. "Anastassia, you need to eat and to have your pills."

"The pills, the fucking nutrition drinks, the damned doctors, they can all fuck off!" I started for the bedroom again, holding the wall with one hand to pull myself along. "I'd like to be alone for a while."

"I don't think that's wise."

I didn't fucking care, but he wasn't the one I was mad at. That was everyone and everything else. "Then can you at least let me pretend that I'm alone for a while?"

He stood three steps away, arms across his chest. "If you'll eat and take your pills."

"Fine, but bring them in here." My legs started to cramp up and I almost tripped over my numb foot.

"I could bring you to the garden if you'd like."

"Do not be nice and make peace offerings right now! I'm angry and I want to be angry." Tears ran down my face. Whether they were from anger, frustration, or general embarrassment from knowing how stupid that sounded, I didn't care.

"I definitely should have hit him harder while I had the chance," Tabor said not quite under his breath.

He stood back and let me struggle onto the bed on my own before dashing out and returning with my pills and a bottle of the thick, milky fluid that was now my sole source of nutrition. Once I'd consumed his bargaining chips, I slid down on the pillows and under the covers. He settled into the chair beside the bed, not touching me in any manner. I turned my back to him and cried for the soft snores, familiar heartbeat, and heavy arm over my waist that I missed so terribly that it rivaled the pain still racking my body.

It was several days later as I half-woke from a drugged stupor that I heard the voice I'd been missing. I couldn't force my eyes open but at least I could hear Vayen. The drugs held my pain at bay, which was a blessing almost worth not being able to see him. It sounded like Tabor had intercepted Vayen at the doorway to the bedroom.

"About fucking time you showed up." Tabor's voice held a hard edge.

"I thought it would be easier for her not to see me. Not like I've been."

The bond's hum grew sharper as did Tabor's tone. "No one gives a fuck about how your drunk ass has been. This little time we have left should be about her."

"How little?" Vayen asked somberly.

"You'd know if you were ever fucking here."

I tried again to force my eyes open, to access our bonded connections to let them know I could hear them, but everything was weighted and distant. Tabor didn't often get angry, but he was now and I wasn't able to protect him if Vayen flipped into dark mode. Straining against the sluggishness got me nowhere but frustrated.

"After everything that woman has encountered in her life, only one thing in this entire damned universe broke her. You."

"I—"

"There are no acceptable excuses, you arrogant—" Tabor slipped into a furious flurry of Jalvian before switching back into Trade. "By some miracle of Geva, she's forgiven you, and then you desert her at the end? She fucking needs you!"

"She has you. And thank Geva for that. You've given her everything I can't."

Tabor let out a rueful laugh. "I won't argue that point." He slipped into Jalvian again.

"You know I understand all of that, right?" Vayen's voice had taken on a brittle edge.

"I would certainly hope so, oh mighty Advisor of All. But she doesn't speak much Jalvian, and no link, so no translator. She gets upset when I speak my opinions of you, and on the off chance she's able to hear us, I don't wish to cause her further distress."

"Then you might want to keep your voice down and watch your damned tone," Vayen growled.

"Do you want to rip my mind apart for speaking the truth? Go right ahead."

I wanted to sit up, to yell at them both to stop before Tabor got hurt, but I remained trapped in my sleepy, sluggish shell.

Vayen let out a long sigh. "Like I'd take out the one person keeping her alive?"

"How about helping with that, dammit? She needs the comfort of your bond too."

"You can't honestly say that you want me here with her."

There was a sharp grunt. I imagined Tabor had worked himself up to poke or push Vayen. I waited anxiously to see how Vayen would retaliate, but it was Tabor who spoke.

"Because of you, I'm losing her and there's not a damned thing I can do about it. After all those years alone, I thought I was finally getting everything I'd ever dared dream of. In perpetuity. That's what she'd offered me. That's what you took from me."

Still, I waited for a punch or groan that might indicate Vayen's response, but there was only uncomfortable silence.

"Exactly. So why would you want me here?"

"Because she's miserable without you. You may be the reason she's slipping away from us far before her time, but as you pointed out once before, you're also the only reason why I'm with her at all."

Tabor exhaled loudly. When he spoke again, he'd returned to his controlled demeanor. "What relief I offer her isn't enough anymore. The drugs are getting stronger and her lucid moments shorter. Don't be the monster they say you are. Be here when she's awake. Hells, be here when she's sleeping. For the love of Geva, help me keep her comfortable as long as we can."

Footsteps drew closer. The familiar weight I'd been longing for settled onto the bedside next to me. His rough hand brushed over my cheek and then rested on my arm, radiating heat. The relief I expected to feel from his bond was less than before. Maybe the drugs were dulling the effect, but my gut told me that just as I was fading, so was our weakened connection.

"We can put a camera in so you can monitor when she's awake if you'd like," Tabor said quietly as though they hadn't both been going at each other in the doorway loud enough to wake anyone in the suite.

"Yeah?"

"And if you need to continue drowning in a bottle, perhaps do that here? It would save me ducking out to check on you for her." Tabor's footsteps placed him on the opposite side of the bed. "I might also be inclined to join you. Sitting here while she has last meetings with friends and contacts, not exactly saying goodbye, but knowing that's what it is, isn't easy."

"You check on me?"

"I do."

Vayen's fingers rubbed slow circles over my arm in heated spirals. The musical hum of the bond I shared with Tabor resumed its peaceful tinkle. With both of them there, an ease no medication could match settled over me.

After a few minutes of silence, Vayen asked, "Do you happen to have anything strong on hand?"

Tabor left, but returned before the ease lapsed. A bottle clinked on the lip of a glass and then another. A lighter weight settled onto the other side of the bed. Safe in the knowledge that my mates were with me and getting along as well as they could be, I relaxed, no longer fighting the lulling, sleepy effects of the drugs.

The familiar scent of liquor brought me back to drinking with Merkief, Jey, and Vayen after completing Kryon contracts.

I could hear the three of them gruffly grousing, slinging a tenuous mix of teasing and insults. Eventually, Merkief grew tired of moderating the eternal feud between Jey and Vayen and went to bed. His audience having left, Jey emptied his glass and stumbled to his room. Alone, Vayen's gaze met mine.

As usual, in trying to hold my own against those three, I'd had at least one drink too many. I did my best to hide my wavering steps as I got up and put my glass on the counter. Vayen's hand caught my arm as I stumbled over my own feet.

"Come on. I'll help you to your room."

If it had been anyone else, I would have yanked my arm away, delivered a scathing retort, and made my way on my own, but his hand was warm and steady and I was so tired. I nodded.

When we got to my room, he lingered in the doorway.

"You going to be all right?" he asked.

I took stock of my aching body, the alcohol blurring the memories of the contract but knowing it must have been brutal to make me feel so rough.

"No. I don't think so." I shivered though the room was the same temperature I always kept it. "It's so cold in here."

Vayen approached my bed hesitantly and then leaned down to cover me with blankets. No matter how many he piled on me, the chill remained. I reached out to him.

"Would you stay here with me?"

Vayen's lips curled into a smile that melted the ice in my bones. He slipped under the blankets and wrapped his arms around me. "Always."

FORTY-FOUR

Daniel

I'd said goodbye to my mother three days ago but I wasn't ready for her to leave. She'd been more talkative then, more aware. Awake.

They had her on a heavy stream of pain meds now, making her sleep more often than not. At least when she was sleeping, when the dose was high enough, the pain that drew her face tight and clipped her words was invisible.

The medical staff had departed an hour ago, declaring nothing more could be done and that her time was near. They'd left her in Etara's care, who now stood in the corner of the room near the head of the bed, surveying all of us.

I would have preferred my mother's room on the ship, a private place for her to pass, but she'd chosen the bedroom in Tabor's suite on the Iber. "A place none of you will ever have to go again," she'd said.

I supposed there was some wisdom in that, and it was a larger space than her room on the ship, considering everyone in attendance. Neko, Hedvika, Uncle Isnar, and Jey lingered just outside the bedroom doorway. Neko and Uncle Isnar were talking quietly, but due to the utter silence around my mother, they seemed loud. I tried to block them out, to pay attention to Markus who was glued to my side at the foot of the bed. Arden and Meera stood just behind me, their calm presence keeping me on my feet when I wanted nothing more than to sit beside my mother one last time.

Her bed was already occupied.

My father sat on her right with Etara lurking behind him. He gripped my mother's hand as though he could hold her among the living a little longer. Ikeri stood behind Tabor, her hands clasped in front of her and head bowed. I imagined she was doing whatever soothing Seeker magic she could for our mother. Tabor sat on my mother's left, in the same place he'd been for weeks now except when my mother would send him out to have a few brief private minutes with any of us. If anyone was keeping her among the living, we all knew it was him. He held her other hand in his lap, his thumb absently circling her knuckles. His eyes were closed, making me wonder if he was concentrating on whatever whispers remained of their bonded connection. Maybe he was telling her we were all there.

That we were ready.

I wasn't.

That she could go.

I didn't want her to.

Meera's hand slipped into mine. Arden whispered calming words in my head. As much as I loved them, none of it helped. My mother was dying.

The room was still, the air barely enough for all of us. When my mother drew her last breath and none other followed, we instantly knew her absence.

With the exception of Markus and Meera, we all felt what little had remained of our telepathic connection to her seal off as though it had never been.

My mother was gone.

The faintest whimper came from my father. Though I had on rare occasions to glimpsed the emotions he kept locked beneath his steely countenance, I didn't recognize the quivering man whose face defined devastation. Perhaps this was the man only my mother knew, the heart of who he was that he kept hidden from the rest of us.

As though we had all ceased to exist, he slid closer to the frail shell that had been my mother, pulling her into his arms. With a quaking breath, Tabor released her hand, allowing my father to take full possession. Tears streamed down Tabor's face as he slid off the bedside to stand beside Ikeri. He wrapped his arms around my sister, whom I only now realized was weeping just as much as he was.

My own tears did not come.

A slight jostle behind me signaled the rest of them squeezing into the room. I glanced over my shoulder to see Jey's anguished face.

Uncle Isnar stood beside him, pressed against the wall, trying to be unobtrusive while he fell apart. It was seeing the naked grief of my mother's oldest friend who had been a steady force throughout my life, a trusted confidant and surrogate father, that made my throat constrict. The room took on a wavering glimmer as tears welled in my eyes.

My father turned to say something to Etara.

"Are you sure?" she asked, not looking at him, but at the rest of us.

He turned back to my mother, running his hand along her face, through her hair, tipping her head to rest on his shoulder.

"Yes," he said just loud enough for me to hear. "Beyond this lies only blackness. Please, Etara."

Even though my mother had warned me this might happen, I'd hadn't thought he'd do it. But she did know him better than all of us. Probably more than all of us combined. My father wasn't an easy man to know.

"Do you need a minute?" she asked hesitantly, as though we might change his mind.

"No. Now." His jaw clenched. "I can't hold it back any longer. Etara. Please. Now."

Etara rested a hand on the top of his head, her eyes filled with sorrow. My father's body jerked, the muscles in his neck and face pulling taut. He held tight to my mother's body and made no further sound. After a moment, his muscles eased. He sank into the pillows, head lolling back until his cheek came to rest against my mother's hair.

"No," Neko whispered. "You can't."

But he already had. My parents would greet Geva together.

For a second, I saw them arm in arm and was glad that neither of them would be alone. I was thankful that my father's death-bringer abilities had left the universe. I was relieved that the years of my mother's pain had come to an end.

Then tears flooded down my face and all I knew was sorrow.

I woke in my bed with Arden beside me. I had no recollection of returning to our suite. There were sounds in the kitchen and the scent of something cooking that any other day I might have jumped out of bed to taste, but today, I wasn't hungry. Instead, I stared at the ceiling, picturing my parents in a bed like this one, their bodies growing cold and stiff. I'd have to compose a speech for both of them now. I'd expected my father to do that duty for my mother. Then there was the ceremony. My mother had left instructions. Again, I'd expected my father to handle that. Or Tabor.

At least I still had Tabor. Thank Geva for that.

Tasks began to pile up in my brain until the list of things that now fell to me in my father's absence became an overwhelming barrage. There was so much I needed to do, yet I felt paralyzed as if grief had chained me to the bed.

Arden stirred beside me. Her eyes opened and she smiled. Two rambunctious toddlers leapt onto the bed without warning.

"Daddy!" they shouted in unison, climbing over me and Arden to snuggle between us, planting an elbow in my chest and a foot in my stomach.

I wondered if Ikeri and I had ever done this with our parents. It hit me that I'd never be able to ask. All the things I'd never be able to ask. They were both gone.

I'd seen enough dead people in my twenty-two years that I didn't expect that death would faze me anymore, but dammit, it did.

At least I had my own family. Markus and Ikeri didn't. Fuck. I needed to get up. I had things to do.

I moved to the edge of the bed and sat up. Mika climbed onto my back. Dreydon grabbed my arm. "Stay," they implored.

"Daddy is hungry," Arden said, pulling the kids off me and tickling them until they were giggling hysterically.

My father had used to do that to me. It was my earliest memory of him, his hair short and wearing Verian clothing. I wiped at the tears running down my cheeks.

"Come on. Let's let Daddy get dressed." Arden pulled her robe over her bulging stomach and herded the kids out of the bedroom.

Geva, we'd have another little Ta'set running around in a few weeks. My mother wouldn't be here to coach the birthing team whether they wanted it or not, to offer her semi-Seeker support to Arden, to hold her third grandchild. I grabbed my pillow and cried into it, muffling the mewling noises until I thought I had myself under control. No one came to check on me even though it had been well over half an hour since Arden had left the room.

I found myself sitting at the table, my plate half empty, a fork in my hand, though I only vaguely remembered getting dressed and leaving the bedroom.

Meera kissed the top of my head and finished clearing the rest of the table. She set the dishes on the counter for the cleaning bot and then came to sit beside me. Dreydon climbed onto her lap. She reached around him to rest her hand on mine. Comfort and a soft melody surrounded me.

"Tabor has asked to see you," she said after a few minutes. "When you're ready, he said."

I couldn't imagine that Tabor was ready either, but we both knew what needed to happen. My mother had planned it all so we wouldn't have to. In charge right up to the end.

"I'll be back soon."

I stood, and surveying my family, couldn't help but smile just a little. The bond surrounding me tinkled and blanketed the cold of my loss with a comforting balm. I took a moment to hug each of them before setting out into the Iber's sterile corridor to make my way back to Tabor's suite.

My mother was right. I didn't want to go there ever again.

I palmed the panel, knowing that she wasn't going to be the one to answer the door, having prepared myself for this in the weeks before when she couldn't leave her bed, but still wishing with all my heart to see her face when the door opened.

Tabor stood just inside. He wore clean clothes, evident by his always pressed, and well-fitted attire. I couldn't recall a time when I'd not seen him entirely put together. Today was no different. His hair was neatly pushed back from his face, as if not a strand ever dared be out of place. He wore the same somber smile he'd given me for the past few weeks. He'd just lost his wife whom he'd been bonded to just as my father had been and yet nothing seemed to have changed for him.

Was the manic explosion of grief I'd expected from my father hiding behind Tabor's calm exterior?

"Tabor, are you all right?"

"Not in the least." He blinked slowly. "But there are tasks to be done, and I shall stay on my feet until they are finished. Then I might break."

"You don't have to break alone. You know that, right?"

His chin dipped a fraction. "Thank you for that, but I've been alone most of my life. I'm just thankful to have had a short reprieve."

Tabor might not have been the father who raised me or taught me how to use my link, who had taken me with him on the years-long search for Ikeri that led me to the man I'd become, but he was the father I still had. He'd patiently shown me how to use my bond with Meera and Arden, supported my decisions, cared for my mother, and doted on my kids even more than my own parents had. As my mother had once said, 'He's the man I never knew I needed'.

"That reprieve is not over," I declared.

His eyes glistened. *"It's very quiet in here,"* he said brokenly through the natural connection we'd only used a couple of times.

I hugged him, and somehow that felt more natural than the few times I'd hugged my father as an adult. Tabor was less daunting, having softer edges to his own kind of fierceness. We stood there a moment, sharing our grief until I thought I might fall apart again. I wondered how long I'd be teetering on that edge.

Would it ever go away?

Tabor dropped his arms and stepped back, clearing his throat. When he spoke out loud his voice was just as confident as always. "Your parents wished to be ashed in the Jalvian way. No memory sticks, but to be scattered."

"That was my mother's choice, but my father would want to be buried with his family."

Tabor shook his head. "He wanted ashes too. We talked quite a lot these last weeks. Finally." He smiled sadly. "He suspected the bond break would be too much, that he would snap. He didn't want your mother to know, he was afraid it would make her linger longer, and she was in so much pain."

"He didn't say anything to me." But my mother had.

"He... We'll get to that shortly. First, we need to get their bodies to the crematorium. They specified the facility in what used to be Cragtek. Your father set up a new business there with people he trusted. Etara has prepared their bodies."

I followed him into the bedroom and was surprised to see Ikeri and Markus there. It didn't look like either of them had slept and both of them were wearing the same clothes they'd worn yesterday.

My parents wore simple Verian attire, all weapons and adornments stripped away. They looked as they had in my childhood except my mother was much thinner and my father's hair was long. They were both greyer.

"Would you like a moment alone with them before we go?" Tabor asked.

I shook my head. I'd said farewell to my mother when she was alive. If left alone with my father, I feared I'd beat him into a second death for leaving everything in my hands without warning.

"Do you remember the jump point?" Tabor asked.

I nodded. "It was one of the first ones he made me learn."

Ikeri and Markus stood aside while Tabor picked up what was left of my mother. I gathered my father's gaunt, but still substantial body into my arms. We Jumped to the former Cragtek facility, and after seeing their bodies into the crematorium ourselves, Jumped back to Tabor's suite.

Ikeri sat on the couch, curled up on one end, her feet tucked under her. Markus sat beside her, staring at the table in front of him where I noticed my mother's joining bands sat beside several other items.

Tabor gestured to the couch. I sat on the other end. Any other day I would have felt cramped, but today, I was glad for the snug fit beside Markus and Ikeri.

"Your parents asked me, separately I must add, to oversee their affairs. I apologize if this is uncomfortable for you. I asked them both to choose someone more fitting, who has been closer to you and more involved with your lives, such as Neko or Isnar." He sighed. "Your mother and father, again, separately, were adamant that this duty fall to me."

It amused me in a twisted way that both of my parents felt the need to keep Tabor occupied, knowing he'd be a mess after my mother's passing. While Neko or Uncle Isnar would have been fitting executors, they had their own obligations my parents had already foisted upon them years before. Tabor was, as of yet, unencumbered.

He drew a deep breath and exhaled slowly. "All right then, first of all: your mother. Ikeri, she wished you to have the arm band, her joining gift from your father. Daniel, you are to hold the neckband in keeping for Mika. It is a replica of the joining gift your biological father gave to your mother. The original one was stolen," he added.

Ikeri reached for the arm band my mother had worn as long as I could remember. She held it in her lap, her fingers tracing the etched surface.

"Markus, I'm afraid you're stuck with me. Your father asked me to become your guardian until you come of age. I'll leave it to you as to what that entails beyond the standard legal obligations. I'm well aware that you've lost two sets of parents already. I can't imagine what I could do to make up for any of that but you are welcome in my home at any time."

Markus nodded, his gaze locked on the table.

"The knife," Tabor pointed to a blade with a hilt etched in a similar pattern to the neck and armband, "is for you, Daniel. It was your mother's, from her first days on Artor. It's the one weapon of hers that your father smuggled with them when they left the Narvan and went into hiding on Veria Minor. Though she didn't say so, I suspect it was a gift from your biological father as the pattern matches the neckband."

I'd known she'd carried it only because it was often on her person when I had to disarm her to get her into the tank. I'd never seen her actually use it, but I had little doubt that she had. Thankfully, she'd left most of that part of her life behind when they'd vanished from the Narvan the first time. My father's abundant body count since more than made up for her restraint after my arrival in their lives.

I reached out and took the knife and neckband, placing them carefully in my lap. The cold metal was a poor substitute for my mother.

Tabor eyed the table and its remaining contents. "Before we proceed, I would share with you a few things your parents likely neglected to say. Over the past few weeks, I talked with them both quite extensively."

"Did he—" Markus asked.

"No," Tabor said. "He did not specifically share with me that he had planned to leave you yesterday, but he knew it would be soon. The darkness in him was growing too much to contain no matter how much he drank. He suspected your mother's death would drive him over the edge and wanted to be prepared."

"He could have prepared by telling us," Ikeri snipped.

"I suggested that too," Tabor said. "He didn't want to burden any of you on top of your mother's impending passing. His words. To be honest, I think we can all agree that he wasn't good at sharing things."

"Like feelings," said Ikeri, sounding no less peeved.

"Or his mate," I said before I could stop myself.

Markus snapped to me with an appalled face.

Tabor chuckled. "True. Yet, we did have an understanding, and in the end, I think we might have even been on friendly terms. As much as your father had friendly terms."

Even Markus cracked a smile at that.

"What I wanted to share with you is that they both had regrets. I hope that knowing those may help you move past resentments you may be harboring."

"I think Mother's Seeker training wore off on you," Ikeri remarked.

Tabor smiled. "I'd like to think so." He picked up the six memory chips sitting on the table, swirling them around in the palm of his hand with his fingers. "Markus, your father regretted allowing you to give up your family name. While he did definitely want you to be part of his family, he pushed for you to be a Ta'set for political gain. If you wish to retake your family name and rebuild their legacy, he has given me the means to do that. That offer stands as long as I am alive to fulfill it."

Markus glanced at me and then Ikeri. He started to shake his head but then stopped and let out a ragged sigh. "I'll think about it."

"Ikeri, your father regretted to his last day what he did to push you away the day you became a Seeker. At the time, he felt it was necessary for you to know the truth for your own safety. The irony of his error and what happened to you because of it haunted him as badly as the weight of all he'd become. He hoped, not for your forgiveness, but that once he was gone you might find enough peace to not let the weight of what transpired hold you back any longer."

Tears ran down Ikeri's cheeks as she nodded.

"You," Tabor turned to me and smiled, "have become everything he wished he had been, the very best of his hopes and dreams. Though he did regret all the darkness he brought into your life from such an early age, it did shape you into who you are today. He was immensely proud of you. Regrettably, rather than making sure you knew that and celebrating your accomplishments, he allowed jealousy to drive you apart. For that he was deeply sorry."

A massive cache of confusion and anger cracked open. All the years of terse conversations and hard looks between us could have been avoided if my father hadn't been such a self-centered ass. If he had just said those words to me even once, I might have seen him differently, might have remained close to him and learned so much more. The loss of the years his pettiness had taken from me hurt almost more than having watched him die the day before.

And he was sorry? Now? Fists formed on my lap.

Markus touched my shoulder. "Focus on the first part. Let the anger go."

I'd be angry if I fucking wanted to. Damned Markus, my father was always openly proud of him and everything he did. He had attended Seeker training for far less time than we had and yet he thought he could use those lessons on me?

A heavy cloud of calm pushed down on me, easing my muscles

and extinguishing the fire Tabor had inadvertently lit. That was how Seeker shit was done.

I glared at Ikeri. She offered me an apologetic smile before signaling that I should return my attention to Tabor.

He cleared his throat. "Your mother had her regrets as well, but she conveyed them in the messages she prepared for each of you. Full disclosure, I was there when she recorded these. She wanted to be fully aware, which meant dialing back her medication, and so, she needed me beside her. If any of you wish to talk about what she said, I am at your disposal at any time."

Tabor handed each of us two memory chips. "The second one is from your father. When he divulged that he would be leaving soon, I told him what your mother was doing for you. She composed hers over several weeks. He handed his to me yesterday. I don't know what is on them but I do hope they offer you some comfort."

I dropped the chips into my shirt pocket, the barely discernable weight instantly became an itch I couldn't wait to scratch. I wanted nothing more than to run to grab the nearest datapad and listen to my parents' voices.

But we weren't finished yet.

A stack of paper remained on the table. Tabor slid it over to sit in front of him and settled back into his chair. "That leads us to the distribution of assets."

It hadn't occurred to me that there were any assets to distribute. All my life it felt like we'd been moving from one location to another, that as soon as something felt like ours, we were on to the next place or back in hiding somewhere. To overhear any conversation involving credits, one was led to believe every single one was tied up in financing something important for a cause, a project, government requests, fleet upgrades, keeping the Narvan running smoothly and every other obligation my father's mission had tied us to.

"One thing that both of your parents agreed upon is that the Iber's unification mission ended with them. The advisory union they brought together can now fulfill the purpose for which it was created. The time of Advisors of All is over."

Tabor chuckled ruefully. "However, your parents have left you options. Your mother had her wishes, and as I said, she suspected, but was not certain, of your father's intentions. He also had his wishes. Where they overlapped, I will see those things through. The rest is up to you." He held up the first paper. "This is the deed for the house on Veria Minor. Ikeri, your parents have left it to you. Your mother hoped that one day you would take her place there as a Seeker to the Verian people. She informed me that Minor is more tolerant than Prime and that you would be welcomed there."

"And my father?" she asked.

"Wanted you to be happy. Wherever and with whomever you eventually decided on. He did mention hoping you would take some time for yourself away from the Iber and Seeker obligations. That maybe in doing so, you'd find the peace you deserve."

Ikeri wiped at her eyes and sniffed before rising to take the deed from Tabor. Once she returned to the couch, he picked up the next sheet.

"The house on Frique is to go to Daniel. They realized it was small and your family is likely to grow larger than it can sustain, but it was your mother's first home of her own and she wished it could benefit the next generation. Her ship below and its contents will fall under your keeping. As to the tank, they asked that access for all current users be maintained, including Jey. They were both quite firm on that particular point."

"Fine." Knowing the tank would remain available for my family was a relief.

Tabor stretched forward to hand me the deed that bore my mother's handwriting.

"Markus, your parents did not wish to burden you with belongings you may not want. You're young and your future path is still quite open." He picked up the next sheet. "When Vayen took you into his family, he put the credits from your birth family into safe keeping for you. As it turns out, he had an enviable knack for investing and your family was wealthy even before he worked his magic. Until you turn twenty, this has all been put into a fund from which you can draw as you desire, within reason." He passed the sheet to Markus.

Markus scanned the page before turning to the three of us, one at a time as if looking for help. "This can't be right."

"I assure you, it is. I said the same thing. Vayen went over the numbers with me twice. As I said, enviable."

"What am I supposed to do with all of that?"

"Speaking from experience, live comfortably and enjoy yourself. Put the rest away for your future generations. I assume one day you'll have a little dynasty of your own, no matter which family name they bear."

Markus carefully folded the paper and gave me and Ikeri an apologetic smile.

"Oh, don't feel bad for them." Tabor shook his head. "They just have a little more of a headache to deal with." He picked up the next sheet. "The matter of the estate on Artor is where your father and I disagreed. I hope you'll honor his wishes. He wished it to go to Neko and Hedvika."

The estate was huge, and would make a perfect home for my family, including any children yet to come. The Friquen house was too small. Neko didn't have any kids. It was just the two of them in that giant place. I pictured my family at the estate, my kids running through the halls and up the stairs. My wives and I in the giant master bedroom I'd only glimpsed. The room my parents had used. The sound-proofed room.

"No, I'm good with that," I announced quickly.

"Me too," said Ikeri. "Father and I fought too much there. It belongs to the Advisor of the Narvan."

I couldn't disagree with her, and I wasn't the Advisor of anything.

If the mission was going to be over, what was I supposed to do? I'd never considered other options beyond assisting with whatever my parents were doing. Did I even have other options? My skillset was well-suited to this mission, but what the hells else did it apply to?

Tabor looked relieved. He set that page aside and picked up the next one. "Ikeri, you've established yourself as a Seeker. Markus, you've got a solid hold on an excellent career ahead of you. Daniel, however, is a bit of an oddity in that you possess a multitude of skills but little formal training." He handed the page to me.

I turned it over to find it was a letter with a Jalvian seal at the top. While I skimmed the words, Tabor clarified the contents for Markus and Ikeri.

"His honorary rank as Commander has been made official. Meaning you can advance through the traditional means, if you choose to further pursue a military career." He sat back in his chair and winked at me. "I'm told that though the mission to bring new worlds and colonies into the union has concluded, the military, medical, and technological support your father promised the current members will keep the Iber busy for the foreseeable future. Someone will need to lead that particular endeavor."

My skin tingled and my heart raced.

"One of the last things I witnessed your father doing was to put a motion to the union to fill that position. His nominee was unanimously approved. That position is yours with the Narvan's support if you want it."

"Yes!" I tried not to jump off the couch or shout, but considering that everyone started laughing, I may have failed at both.

I'd lived on the Iber longer than at the estate on Artor and it was the only home my children knew. Frique would make a good vacation home when we needed a break, and hell, an addition to the house with a new cooling system would make it comfortable. Not that I had a credit to my name. I'd never had to worry about finances before. I supposed an actual military position did offer pay, so an addition shouldn't be out of the realm of possibility.

"And that brings us to the last of this pile." Tabor hefted the considerable stack of pages into his hands. "This list of your father's investments and what he'd been funding was up to date as of last week. I say your father's, but the list includes your mother's credits too. He took over everything she had months ago, when she was no longer able to deal with those obligations."

"You should have a portion of that," Ikeri said.

Tabor shook his head. "Thank you, but I have my own funds. I never needed your mother's credits. They belong to the two of you as long as you can keep track of them and maintain what funding of your father's you decide to honor. That's where the headaches come in. How Vayen kept this all straight, I'll never comprehend."

He stood and handed the stack to me. There were two sections, divided off from one another. I handed the smaller of the two to Ikeri, letting her have the surprise of our financial windfall while I thumbed through the pages to learn our raft of obligations. The number on the last page was staggering.

"How are we supposed to maintain this?"

Tabor pointed to Ikeri's stack. "That's what you're funding."

I braced myself and held out my hand. Ikeri passed the pages back to me, looking worried. The number at the end was barely a tenth of the total I'd first seen.

I read the number again, counting all the zeros. Was there even a word for that large of a sum? "But that means..."

"That you could buy everything on Artor, Jal, and probably another world of your choice. Again, an enviable knack for investing." He raised a hand. "Do keep in mind, that just because that total is at the end, does not mean those funds are immediately available."

I stared at Ikeri, dumbfounded. All of our lives it seemed like my parents whispered about having to come up with credits to fund this or that, like the entire system was holding together by a prayer. Yet, they were sitting on this fortune.

"Read a few pages and tell me what you see," Tabor instructed.

I skimmed the first four pages. Common businesses of every variety, social services, tech developers, drug companies, and weapons manufacturers filled the list. I noted they were organized not by city or even world or system, but by date. The first handful were all on Artor and from the date, must have been when my father first signed on with my mother as her bodyguard. From there they branched out through the Narvan and as the pages turned, to the Verian Cluster. There was a long gap in the dates and then investments on Pentares. A section of sparse additions to the list that coincided with our return to the Narvan and then an explosion of entries on all the worlds to which we'd traveled on our search for Ikeri. The last fifteen pages were investments in businesses on the union worlds.

"Most of these credits are tied up." I stared at the number on the last page. "If we want credits, we have to sell something."

"Not exactly. Those accounts are earning interest. You can both live very comfortably off that without making a dent. However, if you do wish to sell anything, for instance, if you wish to take on funding a large endeavor, your father has advised that you take into consideration which worlds you're pulling funds from, and how much and how often so that you don't throw economies into turmoil."

We could throw an entire economy into turmoil. I threw my head back and laughed at the absurdity of what our parents had left us.

Ikeri gave me a questioning glance. I handed her the last page. She gasped.

"And that brings us to the final order of business. Your mother did not turn all her credits over to your father. She made one last investment of her own and she entrusted the funds for upkeep to me. I shall endeavor to learn from your father so that her project never need worry. It was meant to be a surprise for him, for all of you, a place to be at peace once your mother was gone."

Tabor again stood. "Leave your things here. We'll be back shortly."

He flashed me a jump point and I assumed Ikeri too as she looked at me and shrugged. We both Jumped to find Tabor already there with Markus. He must have known the point well.

We followed him out of an alcove painted with a swirling pattern that I realized was the same as my mother's joining bands. A clearplaz ceiling let in the evening light. From the Karin's familiar visage rising in the sky, I realized we were on Artor. Potted plants that reminded me of the ballroom where my parents had married their seconds, were scattered in the wide and long room. We seemed to be alone there.

"What is this place?" Markus asked.

"A healing center. She didn't want her name on it in any way so that it couldn't be defaced or boycotted by those who didn't approve of the Ta'set name now or in the future. I'm sure you know not everyone is a fan of your parents."

I nodded, as did Markus and Ikeri.

Tabor waved his hand over a sensor panel. Soft light filled the space.

"She specified all the details, though it was up to me to see them through in person, mostly by vid calls because she needed me near her in the last couple of weeks." He ran his fingers over the walls and leaves of the plants as we walked, making me wonder if that was his way of touching her too.

He opened a door and activated the light inside. Another long room with smaller rooms along one wall and benches along the other. "Next week there will be acolyte Seekers here, both any Verians that wish to experience another culture and Artorians with healing skills. Etara has been asked to oversee them. Housing will be provided across the street in the first additional building of what she hoped to be an expanding complex as land becomes available."

Ikeri grinned. "Maybe I could stay here with Etara?"

"If you'd like." He smiled at her. "I may have saved a room for you in anticipation of your request, despite your mother thinking you'd prefer the quiet of Veria Minor instead."

Ikeri wrapped her arms around him. I wasn't the only one who appreciated my mother's grounded and thoughtful second husband. Tabor lit up with her attention, his somber countenance lifting for a moment.

"Before I get to the big surprise, let me show you one big secret your mother kept from your father."

A burst of curiosity almost made me forget why this building was here. We crowded around Tabor as he led us out of the Seeker room, back into the main room and then through another door into darkness. He took my arm and pulled me further inside. I reached for Ikeri who caught Markus behind her. I wished I had my father's artificial eye so I could get a glimpse before everyone else.

When the lights came on, my jaw dropped. Ten regen tanks, each in its own small room with a curtained entry pulled aside, lined the long space.

"What the hells is this?" I stammered.

"Once she was gone, your mother figured it was time to give the advantage of working regen tanks to the public. She turned over everything she knew about the tanks, along with still frames and gel samples she had me take, to the Artorian University five months ago. They engineered them from there and will be distributing them to public health centers throughout the Narvan and to those who can afford them. For profit, benefitting the University. That should help reduce your funding obligations to them as well," he noted. "These ten tanks are to remain free for any Narvan citizen to use as long as they have a profile in the system. Everyone is to have access to creating a profile."

"Ten tanks will hardly be enough," Ikeri said.

"It's a start," Tabor said heavily. "As more property and funds become available, we can expand."

"We will," Ikeri said firmly.

Tabor nodded and then pointed to the nearest tank. "The University developers incorporated the terminal right into the tank face so there's no need for additional equipment." He gestured to a lift door. "There's a profile scanning room and multiple recovery and holding rooms upstairs. The staff will use your mother's guidelines for triage and priority cases."

"And this isn't the big surprise?" Markus asked.

Tabor gestured for us to follow him out of the room. We went back to the main space with the plants, where I noticed additional doors.

"What are those rooms?"

"Offices for counselors and therapists. There is also a small med clinic for non-emergency care upstairs." He pointed to a stairway near a glass door where we seemed to be headed. The first stars twinkled overhead through the transparent ceiling.

"Since her return to the Narvan, after your time on Veria Minor, your mother has been buying up property in this area. I'm not sure that this center was her intent all along. Sometimes your mother's mind was a mystery."

"Most of the time," I said, thinking of how often we'd wondered what she was doing and how often she'd stumped my father who knew her better than anyone else.

"This area was meant to be for your father, but I'm guessing you'll appreciate it too." Tabor opened the door, waving his hand over another sensor as he did so. Lighting came on outside, illuminating pathways lined with bushes and flowers. It reminded me of Seeker Tomias's garden. We'd often played there when Ikeri and I had lived on Veria Prime while my parents fought with each other and reclaimed the Narvan from the Arpex. As we walked the central pathway, the garden opened up to a circular walk. In the middle was a tree I'd nearly forgotten but instantly recognized. It now stood three times as tall as me, its high branches outstretched as wide as it was tall. Several benches sat in its shadow.

"What is it?" asked Markus, noticing me and Ikeri smiling at the tree.

"A gift Dad gave Mom when she made him do the full courtship ritual of gifting before they joined. Neko still tells the story of how allergic he was to it and how Mom laughed but loved the tree. She took it with her to Pentares, made Uncle Isnar and Neko water it the whole trip there even though they were afraid they'd break out in hives too. They didn't," I explained.

"I thought she'd planted this when we got back to the Narvan," Ikeri said.

"She did. She had it dug up and brought here a year ago. If the crew didn't make sure that tree survived the transplant, she threatened to kill them." Tabor laughed.

"She probably would have, even then," I said, chuckling.

Tabor grinned. "She did love to lay down a good threat. Thankfully the tree made it and is flourishing. The grounds crew survived."

"He would have loved this," Ikeri said softly.

I nodded.

"You don't even know the surprise yet." Tabor gestured to the four corners of the garden. "At one time a house stood here. A family lived in it and they were happy. The mother had a small garden over there." He pointed to a rectangle of native Artorian vegetables, some of which looked ripe and ready. "Two brothers played in the backyard." He pointed to a grassy square lined with flowers. "And a woman met a young man that would become her mate many years later right by that table." He pointed to an outdoor table with benches beside it.

Tears welled in Tabor's eyes. "I wish he was here. She worked so hard to surprise him." He looked up to the stars and Karin shining brightly, drawing a shaky breath before continuing. "The Council your parents used to work for demolished your father's family home to prove their hold on him. It was all he had left of the family he'd lost and he was devastated by it. This garden sits on the lot where his home once stood."

I didn't think a place that had been so long gone could affect me so badly. I quickly made it over to one of the benches before my vision dissolved into a wash of tears.

If anything might have brought my father enough comfort to keep the darkness at bay, this might have been it. Or it might have crushed him completely. That she would go so far as to do all of this for him despite all he'd put her through with the Buria fiasco, made me outright weep. That he hadn't made it here to appreciate her gift made the tears come even harder until I didn't think I could breathe.

Ikeri sat beside me, her thin arm around my shaking shoulders. She was crying too. I clung to her, this one person in the universe who fully understood the tragedy of it all.

When I finally wiped my face on my sleeve and made an attempt to brush Ikeri's blotchy cheeks dry with my hands, I caught Tabor holding Markus. The two of them appeared decidedly Jalvian, as though they belonged to one another naturally. Geva did truly work in mysterious ways.

Tabor, noticing me watching them, slowly made his way closer, keeping one arm around Markus. "Your mother asked for no visible memorial, nothing to mark her resting place. She did not want any reason for people to desecrate this place, yet she wished for half of her ashes to be spread here once your father had passed, hers to be mixed with his. I thought we might spread them under the tree."

Ikeri clutched my hand, tears again streaming down her cheeks. I forced a "Yes." through the slurry of plascrete that seemed to fill my throat.

Markus nodded.

"And the other half of her ashes?" Ikeri asked, her voice barely above a whisper.

"To rest with me, in my garden on Rok," he said uncertainly as though he were waiting for us to argue with him.

Ikeri pulled me along as she made a beeline for Tabor. It was there under the moonlight, in the garden he'd created for my mother to give to my father, that Tabor broke.

I wanted to bring him elsewhere, somewhere for him, somewhere that he might find comfort, but I'd only Jumped him once before and my mind was a jumble of emotions, making my concentration absolute shit. Instead, I settled for joining Markus and Ikeri in holding Tabor in the garden my mother had created for my father as his body quivered and heartbreaking keening noises leaked from his lips.

In the end, I was the only thing holding him up. He stood against me, sobbing even though his tears had run dry.

"Can you Jump him to my suite on the Iber?" Ikeri asked. "I'll watch over him tonight. He shouldn't be alone."

I nodded. "Can you get Markus?" Ikeri rarely did double Jumps, but at least he was familiar

"Yes."

I pulled Tabor into the void. We emerged in Ikeri's plant-filled suite.

Markus waited for us in the common room while we got Tabor settled onto Ikeri's bed where she sat beside him and lit a candle.

"Calming balm?" I asked.

"Worth a try. He's been holding the broken bond at bay longer than I thought possible. I'll do what I can to ease him and then get some sleep. I could use a little ease myself," she admitted.

I hugged my petite sister and kissed her forehead.

"Could you get Mom's band for me? I want to hold it," she asked in a timid voice that belonged to the little girl I used to play with on Veria Minor and during our first years on Pentares.

"Of course. I'll be right back."

I gathered Markus and we went back to Tabor's suite to collect everything he'd given us along with a change of clothes for him. I hoped he'd be up to going with us to spread the ashes. Which, it occurred to me, would be ready by now. I decided to get them myself so he wouldn't have to. He'd done his part. It was my turn now.

"You're staying at my place today," I informed Markus. "Let Meera and Arden spoil you. They need a distraction and the kids need to see their favorite uncle."

He nodded. "I'd like that."

"Good. Go on then, I'll be there shortly."

I watched him head off before returning to give Ikeri her deed, the memory chips, and the arm band. With a driving need, I left her to her task and all but ran back to my suite.

FORTY-FIVE

Daniel

Markus sat on the couch, his chips clutched in his hand and the folded page containing his finances sticking out of his shirt pocket. Dreydon sat beside him, chatting non-stop as if nothing was wrong. Arden had assured me that she and Meera had sat the kids down and told them that they wouldn't be going to visit their grandparents to play anymore, that they were gone, but after a few tears and a quiet twenty minutes, the two of them had sprung back to their usual selves.

It wouldn't be that simple for the rest of us.

Meera spotted me first, catching me in a side hug with a sleepy Mika in her other arm. "Nap time. Thankfully."

I gave my daughter a quick kiss and watched them head off into the kids' room. Arden emerged from the tiny room I used as an office with a datapad in her hand. She handed it to Markus and then caught sight of me.

"You can go in there," I said, waving him toward the office. "I'm sure you'd like some privacy for that. Meet you back out here after?"

Markus nodded, extracting himself from Dreydon. When he'd closed the door, Arden came over to hug me, her chin resting on my shoulder as the warmth and hum of our bond soothed the worst of the raw wounds gaping inside me.

"I need to watch these. Can you give me some quiet time to do that?" I asked, holding up the chips.

"From your parents?"

"Yeah."

She nodded, but pointed to the pile of paper and the neckband. "And all that?"

"I'll explain it later with both of you, but for now, know that we're staying with the Iber, and we have a fortune, and a vacation home in the woods."

Arden squeezed me. "I'd rather have them."

"Me too." I kissed her cheek and made my way through the minefield of toys to the bedroom.

Sitting on the bed with the datapad in one hand and the two chips in the other, I debated which one to insert first. My mother's passing was no surprise, and though I dearly wanted to hear her voice and see her animated face, I needed to know what the fuck my father had to say for himself for his sudden exit from my life. I shoved his chip into the data pad and sat back on the pillows.

His face came alive on the pad, looking grim and gaunt as he had for the past few months.

"Doing this for Markus was easy. Ikeri, not as much. But you..." He sighed.

Ice clinked just off the camera view. Of course he was drinking. It seemed like that was all he'd done for years. I wondered if he'd been sober when he asked Etara to flip his kill switch.

"*Vearta.* That was the word I used for your mother when you were a baby, when we were struggling to live together on Veria Minor. Geva, the fights we had. I'm not sure which of us wanted to strangle the other more. And yet, under all of it, we loved each other."

He took a sip from his nearly empty glass and stared off for a moment. "I'm sure you think I'm *vearta.* You're right. I've been impossible. Nothing pleases me." My father stared hard into the camera, his gaze boring into me. "That is not your fault and I shouldn't have put it on you. But I did."

He looked away and then down. The familiar sound of pouring and then his glass was full as he again brought it to his lips.

"Chesser had it too, this darkness in him. And he leaned on this too." He raised the glass again. "It wasn't bad when I was your age. Geva, when I was your age." He smiled sadly. "I had a safe job, a little house, and a woman I'd planned to join with. I was probably a bit *vearta* then too but I was still good. I had no inkling of how much darkness there was in the universe, how much I was capable of holding inside me."

He drained half the glass and set it down heavily on a hard surface. "Then your mother came back into my life and tempted me with promises of fortunes and influence, with a position I'd never thought possible. It was all downhill from there. I was racing downhill, I mean, full-bore and arms wide open. I thought I could handle it, what I was becoming. I did for a while, sort of. Though if you talk to Jey, and I hope you will someday because Geva, the stories he can tell you, well, he'd tell you I wasn't handling shit. But then your mother and I and you and then Ikeri, we had those years on Veria Minor. Those were good years, Daniel, they were. I miss how we used to be, you and me."

He stared off again, giving me time to take him in, to see how weary he really was, the lines on his face, the haunted look in his eyes, how much more grey had spread through his hair, overtaking the black. He'd always been my father, the one I'd loved as a kid, and then struggled to please, to be worthy of. That was how I'd seen him, a nebulous, more vibrant version who had come to despise me, who only spoke to me about work, who had time and tenderness for my children but not for me. This man on the datapad looked like Jey, worn and ruined.

How had I not seen that?

"I remember watching you sleep in my arms, wondering what you'd be like when you grew up. I'd pictured you working with me at Dugans. You loved that place, and you knew every damned thing about those movers." He chuckled. "What I'm trying to say is that I always wanted you to work with me, beside me. I just never meant it to be while I was indulging my darker side. I didn't want you to embrace that too, to have it take hold of you.

"But it didn't. Despite me dragging you back to the Narvan, and all the shit that happened to you and your sister, everything you learned about me and your mother, that you saw us do, and then came to do yourself, you stayed you. You kept the balance I never could."

He poured the contents of the glass down his throat. "And instead of being happy for you, it really fucking pissed me off."

He leaned forward. The recording stopped.

I fisted the blanket beside me, breathing fast and hard. How the hells could he leave me with that? I grabbed the datapad, intending to rip the chip out and throw it across the room but his voice stopped me. I returned the pad to my lap.

"I'm sorry about that. And everything else. I was going to erase it and start over, but I'm running out of time."

A more sober version of my father sat before the camera now. He wore the clothes he'd on when he'd died beside my mother.

My father watched me in silence. Emotions ran across his face faster than I could identify them.

"I hope you see where I went wrong with your mother, with you, the mission we set out on together, and avoid all of that. You've become... Ah fuck, you know I'm not good with this shit, but Tabor said I should do this for you, and hells, if you're seeing this, I'm gone. I suppose it shouldn't matter if I come off as the fucking mess I am."

He sighed long and loud before drawing himself up to face me again. "I never meant to push you away, but with your every success and accomplishment, I could only see how much I'd fucked up, made the wrong choices, focused on the wrong things.

"You are everything I wanted to be, everything I'd dreamed I could have been when I first took that job as your mother's bodyguard. I wish I could have told you how proud I was, how much I admired your restraint, the way you bring people together that doesn't require threats or leverage or bribes. You're not perfect, no one is, I know that, but you're good and that's something I never was."

Hearing the words from him, watching him say them, meant so much more than when Tabor had reiterated them. They didn't erase the years of tension that had festered between us, but there was a newfound acceptance where only the grinding of teeth had been.

"It physically hurt to see your life unfold, when every day further illustrated how far off the mark mine had ended up. Yes, that was selfish of me. I've struggled with selfishness as long as I've worked for your mother. Clearly, that is a struggle that will go unwon. I doubt I could make things between us any worse than they are, so I hope you'll stick with me."

This was the version of my father that had awkwardly hugged teenaged me on rare occasion, that had slipped in sparse words of praise, that being so hard-won, filled me with a glowing sense of accomplishment. I missed that man.

My father mustered a half-hearted smile that quickly fell apart. "The blackness, that's where I think I left off. Etara knows how hard I fought to hold my urges back, and believe me, I had plenty of experience with my darker side long before the Arpex alterations, but the more I used my abilities, the easier they came to me, not just with the Arpex, but anyone. The temptation was always there, to twist even the slightest bit to get what I wanted, to slip into a mind and see, to take. To take by any means, not just the mind-twisting, but to get my hands dirty. I missed that too, the rush of it. Some days, unbearably so.

"Drinking dulled the urges, but being drunk all day every day wasn't an option. Being near your mother or Ikeri helped, but when that wasn't enough, I was sure a distraction would help. I thought Buria was the answer, but that only fucked things up more, and then we nearly lost your mother. Even though we got her back, she and I were never the same. Her bond with Tabor was so much stronger, and fuck, they were happy. I couldn't blame her for that, not when it was my fault that she'd found him."

He stared off over my shoulder again. "She doesn't have long." He glanced up at the corner of the datapad and then back at me. "I have a feed of her room in here so I can keep an eye on her. Tabor has been giving me hourly updates. Truthfully, he's been doing a hell of a lot more than that. It's probably weird of me to say, but I hope you will all keep him in your lives. He would have made a far better father for the three of you than I ever did."

That was unexpected, and yet having his permission made me feel less guilty about wanting to keep Tabor in a fatherly role. Tabor may have said the two of them had an understanding, that they'd talked, but to hear it from my father lent a comforting credence to everything Tabor had shared with us.

My father's countenance turned grim. "As of nine days ago, what little remained of the bond I shared with your mother vanished. Thank Geva I happened to be in the room with Tabor and your mother when it happened because he caught me. Literally held me down and talked me into sharing his side of the bond he has with your mother. He's been keeping a constant open connection with me for nine fucking days and helping handle the pain for your mother. I have no idea how he's doing it."

I had no idea Tabor had been helping my father that way. I'd kept a connection open with Markus on occasion when he was little, when he was scared to be alone at night without my father. I knew how draining that was. Granted, Tabor and my father both had a natural Artorian connection, which had to ease the process, but nine days straight? And while using his bond to comfort my mother and care for her in the rare moments when she was awake? The man deserved a medal.

"Tabor told me that you have this kind of bond with Meera and Arden too. I'm glad. The natural kind, before the genetic alterations is better, I think, especially since it's not limited to only Artorians. Make sure you point that out to the movement against genetic manipulation, but clear it with Neko first."

He shook his head. "Sorry, there's so much I want to say but I can barely concentrate. I can feel her slipping away through Tabor. Once his connection with her snaps, there will be nothing holding me back. I've asked Etara to be there to do what must be done. Don't hold that against her."

Considering the alternative of my father taking everyone out with him, and having witnessed her compassion and efficiency, I harbored no ill will toward Etara. She'd been beyond tolerant of my father's behavior. It was a testament to her patience or perhaps a fondness for my father and his mission that she'd allowed him to live as long as he had.

"I've given Tabor a list of our assets. He's agreed to help the three of you get through this. If he does half as good of a job with you as he's done helping me keep my shit together and taking care of your mother, you're in excellent hands."

We were. I only hoped I could reciprocate the same level of assistance because the man was going to need it for a while.

"I'm sorry to leave you with neither of us, but it feels like we've been holding you back long enough, and for me, staying would have disastrous consequences. Not that I've been of much use lately." He sighed.

"You've stepped in with the union for us. I never asked you do that. I didn't want any obligations of the scope your mother and I took on to land on your shoulders. What you've been doing, consulting, acting as an agent for them, that's one thing, as long as it leaves time for you to spend with your family."

He stared at me though the pad, drilling his will into me. "For the love of Geva, the time of Advisors of All is over. It's not that I don't think you could step into the role. It's that I know damned well that you could. I'm asking...no, dammit, I'm begging you not to. Let the tyrant die. Bring some honor back to the Ta'set name if nothing else. You can do that where I couldn't. I've given you all the tools. I know you're ready to move out from under my shadow."

I didn't fucking feel ready, but I supposed I'd gotten a further start in life with parents beside me than he or my mother had. Was anyone really ready?

"Watch over Ikeri and Markus and your children. I'm sorry I won't be here for the next one. I hope you'll tell them about us, that they'll know more than whatever public opinion might be in the future, though if you choose to leave it at that, I understand. I haven't exactly earned any favors from you."

That, he surely hadn't.

"Arden assures me that she and Meera will take care of you. We had a talk when she last brought the kids to visit. She's a perceptive one, don't hold her deductive skills against her either. I made her promise not to say anything.

"Take care of Meera and Arden and be good to them. As if you could be anything else. You ended up with the best parts of both of us, for which I'm deeply thankful."

He glanced up at the feed of my mother's room again. Tears welled in his eyes. "Tabor says today. She's going to die today."

He rubbed his hands over his face, scrubbing hard, and then yanked them back through the long grey strands. Drowning in bottles had not been kind to him.

"We had a deal, your mother and I. At least I thought it was a deal." He chuckled ruefully. "She would always tell me that no one could kill me but her. I figured I could get into all kinds of dangerous shit, and she wouldn't get pissed as long as I didn't die. As it turns out, we both just sucked at words. What she actually meant every damned time was that she loved me. I didn't realize the truth of it for years. Today she's going to get her wish."

Tears shimmered in his eyes. "I guess this is the part where I tell you that I love you and that I hope you'll forgive me someday for what I'm about to do. I do, you know. I always have. I'm sorry."

The screen went black.

I thought I was out of tears, but I was wrong.

From the hushed female voices outside the bedroom, I gathered Markus was still occupied and the kids were sleeping. Not knowing when I'd get the chance, I swapped the chips, slipping my father's onto the bedside table.

I wiped my wet face on the sheet and sat back on the bed with the datapad in my hands. The sight of my mother's face made my heart jump. Not only her face but that it was so much more animated than it had been in the past weeks. She was a far cry from the woman who'd fought six Jalvians three years before, but there was still light in her eyes and color on her face. She sat on the couch in Tabor's suite, likely curled up in the corner of it since I could see the edge of a blanket on her lap. Ikeri often sat like that too.

"Hi." She grinned at me. "This feels silly, but I suppose I'll get used to it. There are some things I wanted to tell you, all of you. I'll make separate recordings so you'll each have one. I won't be there to see your children grow up, or for Ikeri and Markus to hopefully have some of their own. I wanted to leave something behind so you could share it with them. Some parts will likely be just for you, but well, you can decide which parts those are."

I noted that she'd neatly indexed the entire chip. Of course she had. I laughed to myself. There were hours of recordings. I forwarded to the last entry. She'd marked it as private.

She was so thin. The tendons stood out on her neck and deep lines etched her face. Her skin had taken on a brittle appearance. She wasn't smiling now.

"They tell me that I'll be on heavier meds starting tomorrow, that I'll be sleeping more often. I hate to say that I'm looking forward to that, but I am. This hurts. Everything hurts and I'm so tired.

"I'm sorry that I can't stay longer, that I brought this on myself. Had I known what was going to happen days or weeks later, I wouldn't have been so hopeless that night, but I couldn't see the future." She reached out of the frame toward where I guessed Tabor had been sitting.

"I'm sorry that I have to leave so soon. Everyone that dies, dies too soon, Daniel. Remember that. Enjoy them while they're there."

She eased back against the pillows. Tabor's hand intruded on the frame, holding the pillows in place for her until she settled in.

"I'm going to say goodbye to you today so we'll do this in person. But, well, I wanted to finish this collection for you and it felt wrong to leave it open. Unfinished. I don't like to leave things unfinished."

My mother winced. Tabor said something I couldn't make out and she nodded. He was back in a moment with an injector that he held to her neck. Her face eased.

"That's better. I should hurry this along. I'll probably be sleeping until you get here." She turned aside. "Can you give me a few minutes?"

"Are you sure?" Tabor asked.

"Five. This should hold me over that long."

He looked doubtful in the corner of the frame but he got up and then I heard a door close.

"Tabor has been working so hard to do everything he can for me. Daniel, if you can do one thing for me when I'm gone, make sure he's all right? Etara and Ikeri can help your father, but Tabor will be alone. I can't bear the thought of him going back to his house with his only company being his cook and the security team he doesn't want to see."

"I will," I said to the datapad.

Pain twisted the muscles in her face. "I forget how much of this he takes until he's not here. I love your father, Daniel, but this, with Tabor, is so much more. If I could take just one thing back in all my life, it would be that night with the poison.

She shook her head slowly, speaking between moments of clenching her teeth. "I will hang on as long as I can, to spare both of them as long as I am able, but in all honesty, I don't have much more in me. I'm so sorry that I have to go. I love all of you. I know I don't say that often, but I hope you remember that I do." Her grimace transformed into a pained smile. "That I did love you? What is the proper tense for oneself on their deathbed?"

The smile dissolved into a groan that brought Tabor running back to her side. The transformation as her body eased in his presence was amazing to behold. I knew he'd been helping her bear the pain of her body dying from the inside, but I'd had no idea that it had been to that extent.

"Anastassia, that's enough. He'll be here in a few hours. Rest now."

She nodded, giving the datapad one last forlorn look. "Take care of yourself, Daniel."

The recording ended and went back to the menu before starting to autoplay the first entry again. The vast difference in her appearance made my heart ache. That she'd kept going days after that last recording for Tabor and my father's sake was a true testament to how much she'd loved them both. I hoped I had the strength to do the same when it was my turn to fade away.

Tabor, Ikeri, Markus, and I gathered in the garden at the healing center that was not in my family's name but designed and entirely funded by my mother. She'd always preferred working behind the scenes. Credit for her deeds, other than the contractual sort, had never been her priority.

The sky was a gloomy grey, much like the balance my father had struggled to maintain with Etara. It seemed a fitting way to include him too.

I'd spent the morning composing a public statement regarding the deaths of my parents. Their deaths were real and witnessed this time, there was no chance they'd turn back up in a few years to save the Narvan from a future threat.

As per her instructions, I'd divided my mother's ashes before mixing half of them with my father's. I handed the plaz cylinder containing the remaining ashes to Tabor. He held them to his chest and didn't say a word. He hadn't spoken since his arrival half an hour ago. Ikeri stuck close to his side but he didn't seem to notice. The normally composed and put-together Tabor appeared disheveled and lost.

One by one my mother's guest list arrived in the alcove that served as the jump point for the healing center. Markus led them into the garden. With the addition of my children and one more guest, the same audience who had been in the room when my parents died gathered around us. I signaled that we should begin.

I'd half expected, more than half, really, that my mother would have written her own speech, but she hadn't. She'd probably expected my father to have something prepared. Tabor certainly wasn't up to the task.

Neko stood on Tabor's other side with Hedvika next to him, casting worried glances at his friend.

"It was worth it," Tabor declared out of the blue, maybe in response to a question Neko had asked over his link. "Every moment."

"I'm glad they are together," Jey said.

Uncle Isnar nodded, his gaze locked on the plaz container in my hands.

Etara stood quietly aside, her hands clasped together, staring at the grass.

Buria stood behind everyone, quiet, and not making eye contact. When she'd told me that my mother had recently contacted her, had congratulated her on her thriving business and thanked her for maintaining her silence, I felt justified in inviting her to the memorial. She may have only technically been family for two years, but even after, whenever we spoke, she asked after my parents. Her time with us might have been tumultuous but she'd handed it with integrity. She deserved some closure too.

My father's armor sat folded next to my mother's on one of the benches under the tree that had been his gift to her. Meera, with Mika on her lap, and Arden with Dreydon, sat on another bench. Arden had said she could stand like everyone else, but she hadn't been feeling well that morning and my second son was only weeks away. When I'd announced over breakfast that I wanted to name him after my father, she'd smiled and admitted she wanted the same thing.

"I told him I wanted to when I talked to him that last time. When he made me promise not to say anything," she said.

"It's all right. I couldn't have stopped him."

She nodded. "He cried. Daniel, I'd never seen him cry."

I was glad she'd told him. It gave me a little comfort.

Standing aside so they could all see the tree and the benches, I raised the container.

"My mother had specific wishes for all of this, but since this isn't solely her ceremony, I thought we might deviate a bit." I nodded to Markus.

He reached under one of the bushes where I'd hidden the supplies. He brought out two bottles.

"In true Artorian form, we'd each have one, but in consideration of my mother's constant ragging on my father for his drinking habits, I thought moderation might be more appropriate."

Uncle Isnar cracked a smile.

Neko snickered. "I can't think of a more fitting tribute than that." He held out his hand and Markus passed him one of the bottles. He read the label. "Oh, wow, I see you picked your father's favorite. He had a skill for working around your mother's watchful eye. One glass gradually became a bigger glass until it fit half the damned bottle or," he hefted the bottle for all to see, "liquor strong enough anyone without his fortitude only needed one glass to get drunk off their ass."

He opened the bottle and drank before passing it to Hedvika.

"I can't say that he was a kind man, but he was fair and honest in his own way. And she," Hedvika smiled, "she put up with him because she loved him, but she also gave him all of his hells on occasion." She drank and passed the bottle to Jey.

"I drank to them once before, thinking they were gone forever, and even knowing that they truly are this time, it seems no more real. Despite them courting death on a regular basis, it sure seemed like they should live forever. I wanted them to." He drank and passed the bottle to Uncle Isnar.

"Until we meet again, old friends." He drank several swallows before passing the bottle to Etara.

She studied the bottle in her hands, still avoiding anyone's gaze.

"I only drank once before and only because he made me. When we made this deal that brought us here today. I didn't want us to be here today," she said brokenly.

Etara took a surprisingly long pull from the potent bottle. She swallowed with a grimace and looked longingly at the bottle before passing it on to Buria.

Buria stared at the armor under the tree. "He said she was his weakness, but he was wrong. He was hers, though she had more strength than I could ever hope to possess."

That she chose to speak of my mother rather than focus on my father reassured me that she deserved to be here with us. She drank, and after turning the bottle over to Markus, stepped back.

He brought it over to Arden. She rested it atop her rotund belly. Dreydon, for once, sat still and quiet beside his mother.

"I'm afraid I will have to forgo the honorary drinking. Anastassia would haunt me forever if my lips touched that bottle while carrying her grandchild. That said, I didn't know them as most of you did. To me, they were doting grandparents for our children. They were busy and often distracted, but in the conversations we did have, it was clear they were enormously proud of all of you and what you've done to help further their dreams for the Narvan and beyond."

She smiled and brushed her hands over the bottle before holding it out to Meera.

My first wife blushed, her gaze locking onto me. "I wasn't prepared for alcohol to be involved or I would have said something earlier. I'm afraid Anastassia would frown upon me too."

"What?" I stared at my trim and fit wife, seeking confirmation before I got too excited.

"Yes, we're going to have another baby. That vacation home in the woods is going to feel very small." She smiled widely, casting the tree and empty armor on the next bench an apologetic glance.

Despite acting as host for the memorial to my parents, I grinned and ran over to hug her. Mika clapped her hands and grinned.

I took the bottle and stepped back. "I'm sure they'll understand, but just in case, I'll have a drink for both of you."

When I finished, I handed the bottle to Markus.

He looked at it uncertainly and then to me. I nodded. He was old enough to have surely sampled a few drinks by now.

"I don't remember my first parents. He gave me a new family, even though it was in a shambles at the time. She accepted me without question, allowed me to constantly invade their bed and eat up his spare moments with patience I rarely saw her allow anyone else. They may be gone now, but I'm not alone like I was last time and for that, I'm very thankful."

He tipped the bottle up enough to take a meager sip and immediately coughed and sputtered. He held the bottle out blindly as his eyes watered. Apparently, he'd never sneaked a few sips from my father's bottles like I had at his age.

Ikeri took the bottle and patted Markus on the back until he'd recovered. "My parents. Where to even begin? Sometimes it felt like we were the parents and they were the unruly children. They had their moments of being role models, but more often, they were cautionary tales. They loved us no matter what we did, even though we didn't always think so at the time. They were our parents and I loved them. They will be dearly missed."

She drank, and after a forced swallow that made her shudder and wince, passed the bottle to Tabor. He stood there, gaze unfocused, bottle in one hand and my mother's remaining ashes in the other. We all waited, only Jey shuffling his feet on the gravel pathway, likely seeking a position to ease an ache just as my father often had. They'd both endured injuries the tank hadn't had the opportunity to heal. Maybe, someday, I'd ask him about some of them.

"I..." Tabor shook his head and licked his lips. "I understand now why she did it. The place where she was is a vacuum, threatening to suck me in. You are here with me, but she was alone that night. She thought she was alone, even if she truly wasn't. Don't be angry with her for what she did, for the life she ended too soon and in such long-lasting agony—as though Geva was granting retribution to everyone who had ever wished her harm. That's what she said one day toward the end."

Tabor pondered the bottle, swirling the contents in a slow circle. "And he, once his bond had vanished, when he was eking out each last day on what I could feed him of mine..." He smiled sadly. "It was like the two of them were having a competition as to which one could hold on longer, both fighting to keep the other going, neither wanting the battle to end even though it would offer them both peace. In losing, they both won."

He drank, draining the bottle in a fashion befitting my father. No one made a move to stop him.

Markus opened the second bottle and passed it to me.

"I'm sure they've already found something to argue about."

Jey and Neko chuckled quietly.

"Thanks to the path they forged and all they've left us, we will never have to walk in their boots. They gave everything so we don't have to."

I raised the bottle and swallowed a hearty glug before handing it back to Markus. Before we got any further with the second bottle, I took the ashes over to the tree. Tipping the container, I let the gentle breeze of my father's homeworld deposit what remained of my parents into the garden my mother had designed. When the container was empty, a white haze covered the base of the tree and the ground cover around it. The rain the clouds overhead promised would carry them into the soil where they would become one with the world they both loved.

Having done the hardest part and with the strong liquor loosening our tongues, we passed the second bottle, sharing memories until it again ended up in my hands.

I took in the people who had been important to my parents, my sister and brother, my wives and children, my remaining father-figure, and those my parents called friends. These were the faces that had shaped their lives and would guide ours into the future. I raised the bottle to them and then the armor that sat under the tree.

"Though my parents both expected to be wallowing in the ninth hell, I prefer to think they're dancing together in Geva's hall to their own steps, in their own way, as they've always done."

I took a long drink from the bottle, savoring the burning in my throat and the subsequent unfurling heat inside me. After setting the now empty bottle aside, I took a deep breath and recited the memoriam that would be released to the public as soon as the ceremony concluded.

To some, Vayen Ta'set was a monster, a tyrant, a wrathful bringer of death. To others, he was a benevolent savior and protector. He was all of those and more: once a brother, twice a husband, a father of three, and a loyal friend to an exclusive few.

Beside him, Anastassia Kazan Ta'set was a force few wished to reckon with. Alone, she was even more terrifying.

She was many things in life: a soldier, healer, assassin, peacemaker, wife of two and mother of three. She was happiest when getting her hands dirty, sometimes with actual dirt.

She orchestrated peace where there had long been war. He brought those war-torn worlds together. Together they spread peace and unity to many other worlds beyond the system they called home.

Most will never know the enormity of the challenges they faced, separately, together, and sometimes with one another. Despite it all, they fought for every shared moment up until their last breaths, providing an admirable example for the rest of us.

Though each of them carried their own degrees of darkness, they brought an insurmountable light to the known universe that should never be forgotten.

About the Author

Jean Davis writes an array of speculative fiction and plays with chickens. When not ruining fictional lives from the comfort of her writing chair, she can be found devouring books and sushi, weeding her flower garden, or picking up hundreds of sticks while attempting to avoid the abundant snake population that also shares her yard. She lives in West Michigan with her musical husband, an attention-craving terrier, and a small flock of chickens and ducks.

Find links to all of her books, updates on new projects, and sign up for her mailing list at www.jeandavisauthor.com. You'll also find her on Facebook and Instagram at JeanDavisAuthor, and on Goodreads and Amazon.

If you enjoyed this book, please consider leaving a review. They are much appreciated. Thank you!